Undressed by the Rebel

ALISON ROBERTS

...(UK) Limited's policy is to use papers that are natural, renewable
...recyclable products and made from wood grown in sustainable forests.
...and manufacturing processes conform to the legal environmental
...regulations of the country of origin.

Printed and bound in Spain
by ... Barcelona

D0553350

Published in Great Britain 2015
by Mills & Boon, an imprint of Harlequin (UK) Limited,
Eton House, 18-24 Paradise Road, Richmond, Surrey, TW9 1SR

UNDRESSED BY THE REBEL © 2015 Harlequin Books S.A.

The Honourable Maverick, *The Unsung Hero* and *The Tortured Rebel* were first published in Great Britain by Harlequin (UK) Limited.

The Honourable Maverick © 2011 Alison Roberts
The Unsung Hero © 2011 Alison Roberts
The Tortured Rebel © 2011 Alison Roberts

ISBN: 978-0-263-25231-6
eBook ISBN: 978-1-474-00410-7

05-0915

Harlequin (UK) Limited's policy is to use papers that are natural, renewable and recyclable products and made from wood grown in sustainable forests. The logging and manufacturing processes conform to the legal environmental regulations of the country of origin.

Printed and bound in Spain
by CPI, Barcelona

Alison Roberts lives in Christchurch, New Zealand. She began her working career as a primary school teacher, but now juggles available working hours between writing and active duty as an ambulance officer. Throwing in a large dose of parenting, housework, gardening and pet-minding keeps life busy, and teenage daughter Becky is responsible for an increasing number of days spent on equestrian pursuits. Finding time for everything can be a challenge, but the rewards make the effort more than worthwhile.

THE HONOURABLE
MAVERICK

BY
ALISON ROBERTS

CHAPTER ONE

THE three men stood in close proximity.

Tall. Dark. Silent.

Clad in uniform black leather, motorbike helmets dangled from one hand. They each held an icy, uncapped bottle of lager in the other hand.

Moving as one, they raised the bottles and touched them together, the dull clink of glass a sombre note.

Speaking as one, their voices were equally sombre.

'To Matt,' was all they said.

They drank. A long swallow of amber liquid. Long and slow enough for each of them to reflect on the member of their group no longer with them. Cherished memories strengthened by this annual ritual but there was an added poignancy this year.

A whole decade had passed.

Two decades since the small band of gifted but under-challenged boys boarding at Greystones Grammar school had been labelled as 'bad'.

The label had stuck even as the four of them had blitzed their way to achieving the top four places in the graduation year of their medical schooling.

But now there were only three 'bad boys' and the

link between them had been tempered by the fires of hell.

Minimally depleted bottles were lowered but the silence continued. A tribute as reverent as could be offered to anything that earned the respect of these men.

The sharp knock at the door was inexcusably intrusive and more than one of the men muttered a low oath. They ignored the interruption but it came again, more urgently this time, and it was accompanied by a voice.

A female voice. A frightened one.

'Sarah? Are you home? Oh, God…you *have* to be home. Open the door… *Please…*'

The men looked at each other. One shook his head in disbelief. One gave a resigned nod. The third—Max—moved to open the door.

Please, please…please…

Ellie squeezed her eyes tightly closed to hold back tears as she prayed silently, raising her hand to knock for the third time. What in God's name was she going to do if Sarah *wasn't* home?

It was enough to make her want to hammer on the door with both fists. Her arm moved with the weight of desperation only to find an empty space. Too late, Ellie realised the door was moving. Swinging open. It was all too easy to lose her balance these days and she found herself stumbling forward.

Staring at a black T-shirt under an unzipped, black leather biker's jacket. An image flashed into her head. She'd passed a row of huge, powerful motorbikes parked outside this apartment block and she hadn't thought anything of it.

Oh…God! She'd come to the wrong door and here she was, falling into a bikers' den. A gang headquarters, maybe. A methamphetamine lab, even. Huge, powerful male hands were gripping her upper arms right now. Pulling her upright. Pulling her deeper into this dangerous den. Her heart skipped a beat and then gave a painful thump.

'Let me go,' she growled. 'Get your hands *off* me.'

'No worries.' The sexy rumble from somewhere well above her head sounded…what…tired? *Amused?* 'I'd just prefer you didn't land flat on your face on my floor.'

It was a surprisingly polite thing for a gang member to say. Ellie could do polite, too.

'I've made a mistake.' She had to step forward again to get her balance. It helped to drop the small bag she'd been carrying to plant both her hands on the chest in front of her and push. Good grief, it felt like a brick wall. Ellie risked an upward glance, to find the owner of the chest looking down at her. Dark hair. Dark eyes that held a somewhat surprised expression. No tattoos, though. No obvious piercings. And didn't he look a bit too *clean* to be part of a bikie gang?

She swung her head sideways and emitted a small squeak of dismay. There were two more of them. Staring at her. No, one was glaring. They were clad from head to toe in black leather. Jackets that were padded at the shoulders and elbows and tight pants that also had protective padding. Heavy boots. The gleam of zips and buckles might as well have been chains and knuckle-dusters. They were holding beer bottles. She had interrupted something and they weren't happy. There didn't seem to be quite enough air in this small room because there were three very large and potentially very dangerous men using it all up.

Ellie straightened to her full height, which was unfortunately only five feet three inches.

'I'm so sorry,' she said, as briskly as she could manage. 'I've come to the wrong door. I'm looking for Sarah Prescott. I'll…I'll be going now.'

She turned back to the door only to find the first man blocking her escape route simply by standing there and filling the space. Ellie swallowed. Hard.

'Look, I'm really sorry to have disturbed you.' She inched sideways. Maybe she could squeeze past and get to the door. She might have to leave her bag behind but that didn't matter.

The man didn't appear to move but somehow the door was swinging shut behind him.

'I…have to go,' Ellie informed him. Dammit, she could hear the fear in the way her voice wobbled.

'To find Sarah?'

'Yes.'

'Is it urgent?'

'Oh…*yes*.' Ellie had no trouble making this assertion. She even nodded her head vigorously for emphasis.

'Why?'

Ellie's jaw dropped. As if she'd start telling a complete stranger about any of this. If she had the time, which she didn't, why did he want to know anyway?

Lost for words, she stared up at this man.

'It's OK,' he said quietly. 'You're safe here.'

How did he know that those were the words she needed to hear more than anything? How did *she* know with such conviction that she could believe him?

For another heartbeat Ellie simply kept staring.

And then she burst into tears.

The heavy, straight fringe of deep chestnut hair made her face seem fragile as Max stared down at it. He saw this woman's fear and he saw the effect his words of reassurance had.

She let go.

She didn't even know him but she trusted that she was safe. Now he could feel the weight of responsibility pressing down on him. What had he been thinking?

And then those huge, hazel eyes filled with tears and he groaned inwardly. This was the last straw.

No. As he put his arms around this small, unwanted visitor and felt the firm bulge of her abdomen, which had been disguised by her baggy sweater, his heart sank even further.

Somehow, in the space of just a heartbeat or two, he'd offered protection to a woman who looked as though she was running from something. Or someone.

A very pregnant woman.

'Max…' The word was a warning. 'What are you doing, man? She's come to the wrong apartment, that's all.'

'No.' Max held onto the body shaking with silent sobs and did his best to guide her towards the sofa. 'Sarah Prescott was the previous tenant here. She took off to the States last week.'

'*What?*' Max felt a determined push against his chest that felt familiar. '*No.*'

Tears were scrubbed from her face and she gave a rather unladylike sniff. 'She's going on Friday. Tomorrow. That's why I'm here. I'm going to go with her.'

'She did go on Friday. Last Friday.' Max sighed and let his gaze drop to the oversized sweater. 'You really think they would have let you on an international flight? When are you due?'

Her mouth dropped open and he could see the wheels turning in her head. She realised he'd felt the shape of her body when he'd taken hold of her. A flush of colour stained pale cheeks but she said nothing.

Resentment at the intrusion into a private moment was long gone. Max could sense the spark of curiosity from the others now, albeit reluctantly, particularly on Jet's part. But this was a damsel in distress. She needed help.

'Come and sit down,' Max suggested. 'What's your name?'

'Ellie,' she said, but didn't move any closer to the sofa. 'Ellie Peters.'

'I'm Max. That's Rick, who's putting his helmet on the table over there, and this is Jet.'

That surprised her.

'His real name is James,' Max added. 'But he's always had a thing for flying and his hair's really black, see?'

Ellie gave a slow nod as she flicked a cautious gaze towards the other men.

Rick was near the window now. 'His hair's only that colour 'cause he dyes it,' he said casually.

Jet's snort told Rick he would pay for that comment later but Ellie's lips twitched. Good. She was starting to relax. Maybe they could find out why it was she needed to find her absent friend so urgently, offer some advice to solve the problem and send her on her way. The others had to head away themselves very soon and they didn't get together often enough to make sharing the last of this time a welcome prospect. No wonder Jet was looking so impatient.

'Can I get you a drink?' Max offered Ellie. His gaze dropped automatically to the bulge of her sweater. So obvious now he'd felt it. Curiously, he could still feel it. As part of that body shaking with sobs she'd tried so hard to stifle. A shape that seemed to be imprinted on his own body. She was eyeing the beer bottles on the table. 'I mean…water or something?'

'Hate to break up the party,' Rick drawled, 'but there's a guy on the street out here who seems rather interested in this apartment.'

Ellie's indrawn breath was a gasp. She slid sideways, making sure she wasn't in view. Closer to the wall now, she kept moving and peeped around the edge of the window frame.

'Oh…*no*…' The word was a groan. 'It's Marcus. I thought I'd lost him at the airport.'

'And who is Marcus?' Max stepped swiftly to look out of the window but the street below was deserted apart from a taxi and its driver.

'He's…um… He was my…' Ellie seemed to be finding it difficult to find the description she wanted. 'I was in a relationship with him. Briefly. It's been…hard to get away.'

The underlying message was unmistakable. Max tried to curb the slash of anger. 'He's *stalking* you?'

'Ah…kind of, I guess.'

'Where have you come from?'

'Today? Wellington. I think he must have hired a private investigator who picked up on my air-ticket purchase. He must have flown down from Auckland to be at the airport by the time I arrived.'

'Auckland…of course…' Rick snapped his fingers. 'Thought the little weasel looked vaguely familiar.'

Everybody's head swung in Rick's direction. Max and Ellie spoke together.

'You *know* him?'

'Marcus Jones. Orthopaedic surgeon, yes?'

'Y-yes,' Ellie stammered, looking bewildered.

Rick addressed the others. 'Had a little run-in with him when I was working in Auckland Central a few years back.' The huff of expelled breath was not complimentary. 'Guy with a nasty spinal tumour. I was keen to try a new approach. Risky but perfectly doable. Would have left him neurologically intact.'

The nod from Max and Jet accepted that Rick's judgement would have been correct.

'The weasel is persuasive. He talked the patient and his family into going with the standard protocol. Poor guy ended up quadriplegic and on a home ventilator. Probably dead by now.'

Max caught Jet's raised eyebrow and nodded. 'He follows the rules.'

'Hell, he thinks he can *make* the rules,' Rick said.

'Does he, now?' Max injected enough of an ominous tone into his query to earn approving glances from the other men. A glance at Ellie's wide eyes revealed that she had no clue what the unspoken conversation going on here was about but it certainly wasn't making her feel any more secure.

Should he take the time to tell her that one of the things that welded the three of them together was the shared conviction that sometimes some of the rules had to be broken? That they were all people who had no hesitation in doing exactly that if they considered it to be necessary?

He didn't have the time. The rap on his door was far more demanding than Ellie's knock had been.

'Open the door.' The owner of the voice was used to being in control. 'I know you're in there, Eleanor.'

Jet went to open the door.

'*No*,' Ellie breathed. 'Please...'

Max and Rick moved to stand on either side of Ellie.

Max tilted his head. 'He doesn't sound like he's going to go away without a little encouragement. You're safe here, remember?'

'Mmm.' The sound was hesitant but hopeful. It tugged at something deep inside Max.

'You'd like him to go away, wouldn't you?'

'Yes.'

'For good?'

'Oh...*yes*.'

Jet flung the door open.

'About time.' The small man in a pinstriped suit stepped into the apartment. 'Come on, Eleanor. I've got a taxi waiting for us.'

Ellie said nothing. Max could see the way her lips

trembled even though she had them pressed tightly together.

The newcomer took another step further inside and it was then that he seemed to notice Ellie's companions. He looked over his shoulder at Jet, who had closed the door and was leaning against it, his arms folded and a menacing look on his face. Max almost grinned. No one could do menacing quite as well as Jet.

Rick earned a look then. And finally Max. Good thing they were all still in their leathers, having only just finished their annual road trip, which was part of their tribute to Matt. Even better that they were all at least six inches taller, considerably heavier and quite a lot younger than the dapper surgeon.

Marcus Jones cleared his throat. 'Who are these people, Eleanor?'

Ellie remained silent. She looked remarkably like a small, wild animal caught in the glare of oncoming headlights, Max decided before flicking his gaze back to the most recent arrival.

He watched the way Marcus swallowed, revealing his discomfort. This man was a bully, he realised. The thought that he'd had the opportunity to bully the woman standing beside him was more than enough to fuel his simmering anger.

The surgeon spread his hands in a contrived gesture of appeal and directed his words to the men in the room. 'Look, I don't know what she's told you but this is nothing more than a minor misunderstanding. Eleanor's my fiancée. She's pregnant with my child and I've come to take her home.'

Max felt Ellie sway slightly beside him. He put his

arm around her shoulders and she leaned into him. He glanced down and met her eyes. He saw a silent plea for protection that no red-blooded man could have resisted. Especially an angry one.

'Funny,' he heard himself say mildly, 'Ellie told me the baby is mine, and you know what?' He speared the stranger with his gaze. 'I believe her.'

The silence was stunned and no wonder. Max was more than a little stunned himself by what he'd just said.

The baby is mine?

They were words he'd never expected to utter in his life and they were having a rather odd effect. Creating a weird tingle of something that felt curiously...pleasant. Good, even. They made him feel taller. More powerful.

Rick made a sound that could have been strangled laughter but was effectively disguised as a cough. Unseen by Marcus, Jet shook his head in disbelief and didn't bother to hide his smirk.

Max drew himself up to his full six feet three inches and didn't break his stare by so much as a blink.

'Eleanor...' Marcus narrowed his eyes. 'Are you going to *say* something or just stand there like some kind of stuffed toy?'

Jet opened the door. 'The lady doesn't want to talk to you,' he said politely. 'Why don't you play nice and get lost?'

'Don't tell me what to do,' Marcus snapped. 'I happen to be the top surgeon in the orthopaedic department of Auckland Central Hospital. I don't care what kind of gang you belong to. Get in my way and you'll regret it.'

'What are you going to do to us?' Rick said softly. 'Botch some surgery perhaps and leave us to suffer on a ventilator for the rest of our lives?'

'*What* did you say?' The stare Rick received now was intense enough to send a prickle down Max's spine. This man was dangerous. He tightened his hold on Ellie. 'Good God…I don't believe it. You're that upstart neurology registrar who thought he knew more than I did.'

'It was a few years ago,' Rick reminded him. 'I'm actually a neurosurgical consultant these days.'

'And I'm an emergency medicine consultant,' Max informed him. 'Your status isn't helping you much here, mate.'

'I'm on an ED locum run while I'm in town,' Jet murmured. 'But I'm usually a medic with the SAS. Your threats don't hold much water, either.'

Max heard Ellie's sharp intake of breath. Had she really thought they were gang members, too? She'd still trusted him, though, hadn't she?

He liked that.

Whatever was going through her head, she seemed to be feeling braver.

'Go away, Marcus,' she said. 'I told you a very long time ago that I never wanted to see you again.'

Marcus Jones was looking less and less sure of himself. He shifted his feet and glanced over his shoulder at the open door behind him.

'She's with me now,' Max added for good measure.

'My woman. My baby.' He smiled grimly. 'Now get the hell out of here and don't come back. *Ever.*'

They all watched from the window as Marcus Jones scrambled into the waiting taxi and left.

Rick chuckled. 'Nice one, Max.'

Jet shook his head yet again. 'Yeah…you certainly pulled a good rabbit out of the hat. Gotta love you and leave you, though, man. It's getting late.'

'Sure is.' Rick was reaching for his helmet. 'Gotta go, too, mate. We'll catch up soon.'

'But…' The ground was shifting under Max's feet. His mates were about to desert him and Ellie was still here. What the hell was he supposed to do now?

His friends knew perfectly well they were dropping him in it. They were enjoying it, for God's sake. Grinning broadly, even.

Max walked to the door with them, doing his best to think of some way he could beg them to stay without becoming the brunt of their mirth for years to come. They were having none of it. Rick thumped him on the arm.

'You'll think of something,' he said. 'Hey…your woman, remember? *Your* baby.'

He could hear the echo of their laughter even well after the door closed behind them.

CHAPTER TWO

THE throaty roar of powerful bikes faded but Ellie could still feel the reverberations.

Or was she still shaking from the face-to-face encounter with Marcus Jones?

Unbidden, her legs took her to one of the chairs around a table and she sank down onto it. Her worst fear had been realised. Marcus had found her. He knew she was pregnant and sounded absolutely confident that the baby was his.

But she had won. Not completely, of course. Her legs were probably still shaky because she knew he wouldn't give up this easily but she had won this round thanks to a most unlikely team of dark, leather-clad angels. They were, without doubt, the most impressive array of masculinity she'd ever been this close to and they had stood up for her.

Protected her.

Sent Marcus Jones scurrying away with his tail between his legs.

He wouldn't like that.

The tiny smile Ellie had been quite unaware of, as she had thought of her guardian angels in action, faded abruptly.

'You OK?' A chair scraped on the tiled area of the floor as Max took a seat at the other end of the table. He pushed a black, full-faced helmet to one side, where it clunked against the trio of beer bottles.

'I'm fine.' The sound had caught Ellie's attention. 'I'm sorry I interrupted your party.'

The corner of Max's mouth lifted. 'Hey, if it had been a party there'd be a damn sight more than three lager bottles left over and they'd be empty, what's more.' He rubbed at his face. 'No…this was…a toast, that's all. A token one at that thanks to the guys having to work tonight. It's a bit of an annual ritual, I guess.' His voice softened into a sadness that tugged at Ellie's heart. 'An anniversary.'

She had been watching his face as he spoke. Such serious lines… His eyes were dark brown—a match for wavy hair that looked like it had been squashed under that helmet for some time. The odd, wayward end of a curl was valiantly poking out here and there, giving him a rather charmingly dishevelled look that was enhanced by the faint shadowing of his jaw.

She watched his fingers as he rubbed the uncompromising line of that jaw. Funny, but she could almost feel the catch of stubble on her own fingers. Just a little rough. As though he usually shaved at least once a day but hadn't bothered on this particular occasion.

He had shadows under his eyes too and lines that looked emotional rather than age related. He couldn't be much older than her. No more than his mid-thirties. The echo of his tone lingered.

'Not a happy anniversary?' The query was tentative. It was none of her business, after all, but she owed this man something. Rather a lot, actually, and if he wanted to talk about whatever was on his mind, the least she could do was take the time to listen.

He was watching *her* now. Warily. Then his gaze slid sideways and he sighed.

'There used to be four of us,' he said simply. 'See?'

He was indicating a silver framed photograph that had pride of place on the bookshelf beneath the window. Four young men, probably in their early twenties, were lined up in front of four gleaming motorbikes. They all wore leathers and held a helmet under one arm and they were all grinning. The picture was resonant with the thrill of being alive and young and with the promise the future held. Ellie recognised Max and Rick and the one with the odd name—Jet. The fourth man was shorter than the others and had wildly curly hair. He looked younger. As though he was out with his big brothers.

'Matthew died ten years ago today.'

'Oh…' Ellie stole this opportunity to let her gaze rest on his face again. The bond between the three men when they'd decided to protect her had been unmistakable. He was capable of caring very deeply for others, this man. He still cared about a member of their group who had been dead for ten years. He was also capable of very deep loyalty.

Heavens, he'd been prepared to protect her—a complete stranger. No wonder her instincts had told her so convincingly that he could be trusted.

'I'm sorry,' she said softly.

Max looked up. 'Fate has the oddest little twists sometimes,' he said with an attempt at a smile that came out with an endearing crookedness. 'Matt died because there were people who were protocol police. A bit like your friend, Mr Jones.'

'He's *not* my friend,' Ellie whispered fiercely, but Max didn't seem to hear her. He had closed his eyes. He had the most astonishingly long, dark eyelashes.

'There were rules in place and they had to be followed.' He opened his eyes again but he was seeing a very different place from where he was sitting with Ellie on this quiet Sunday afternoon. 'Their egos wouldn't allow them to even consider they might be wrong. We were fresh out of medical school and what consultant would bend rules just because we had a hunch? Or let us juggle rosters so we could keep an eye on Matt? Even he said he was fine. It was just a headache. He'd sleep it off.'

Max paused to drag in a slow breath but Ellie stayed silent. She was happy to listen even though she knew this story wasn't going to have a happy ending.

'Didn't help that we were legends for the way we partied but by the time we came off duty, Matt was in a coma from a ruptured aneurysm. They kept him on life support only long enough for his family to think about organ donation.'

Max was eyeing the bottles again as though he wanted a slug of something. 'They didn't want us around,' he continued tonelessly. 'And why would they? Any hint of trouble Matt had been in for the past ten years had been associated with us. His sister, Rebecca, was convinced we could have saved him if we'd tried a bit harder. It was the worst time ever. Finally, we got our bikes and took to the road for a good, hard blast.

We came back to learn that they'd turned off the machines and Matt was gone.

'Anyway,' He shook his head, letting the memories go. 'We figured that Matt had been pillion that day. Riding out in style. So we do it every year. Go for a blast on the open road and then finish off with a nice, cold beer.'

'And I interrupted you.' Ellie's tone was full of remorse but Max smiled.

'But don't you see? We got the chance to play the heavies with one of them. Egotistical rule followers. The kind we didn't know how to deal with way back then. Take my word for it, it was a bonus.'

Max's smile was doing something very odd to Ellie.

This was the first time she had seen both sides of his mouth curl evenly. There was warmth there, unsullied by anything sad or grim. A warmth she could feel curling inside her, melting that hard knot of tension that was starting to make her back ache intolerably.

The adrenaline overload of the last thirty minutes or so was draining away to leave her utterly exhausted but that was OK because there was energy to be found in that smile, too. It really was quite extraordinary. It was just a shame she was too tired to smile back.

'So, that's my story.' Max raised an eyebrow as his face settled back into rather more intent lines. 'What's yours, Ellie Peters?'

He knew her full name was Eleanor now but he was still calling her Ellie. She liked that. Did she want to tell him her story?

Oh…yes.

Would he think less of her when he heard it?

Quite likely.

Ellie didn't want Max to think less of her so she didn't say anything.

Max waited patiently as the seconds ticked past but he didn't take his gaze off her face. Ellie shifted uncomfortably, the ache in her back getting worse. Her stomach felt odd, too. As if it was trying to decide whether there was enough in it to be worth ejecting. Fortunately, there probably wasn't. She couldn't actually remember the last time she'd had something to eat. Last night?

'Was he right?' Max asked evenly. 'Is the baby his?'

Ellie recognised the new sensation as disappointment. She had no choice other than to let Max think less of her. She owed him honesty, if nothing else.

'Yes.'

A whisper. A tiny word but, man, it hurt. If only it *didn't* have to be the truth. Ellie's eyes prickled with unshed tears but Max didn't seem to react at all.

'How did you meet him?'

'I…I was his theatre nurse. In Auckland. He didn't even know my name for the longest time but then he suddenly noticed me and he started being nicer to me in Theatre. Nicer to everybody, actually.'

An eyebrow as dark as those enviable eyelashes quirked. 'He wasn't usually nice, then? No, don't tell me, let me guess.' The padded elbows of the leather jacket were resting on the table and Max steepled his fingers as he spoke. 'Bit of a temper?' His thumbs and forefingers touched each other. 'Instruments getting hurled around when he wasn't happy?' Ellie watched his middle and ring fingers make contact. 'People getting verbally beaten up on occasion?'

Ellie's gaze flicked up from watching his fingers. 'How do you know?'

The steeple was gone, fingers curling into fists. 'I know the type. Go on, what happened after this miraculous personality transplant?'

'He…um…asked me out.'

'And you fell into his arms?' The words were just a little too bland and Ellie cringed.

'No,' she said hurriedly. 'I wasn't interested but…' She sighed. 'Marcus was very persistent and…and he can be quite charming, believe it or not.'

'Oh, I believe it,' Max said grimly. 'Control freaks are notoriously capable of charming the birds out of the trees if that's what it takes to get what they want.'

Ellie took a deep breath. She wanted to get this confession over and done with. 'I went out with him,' she said in a rush. 'But only twice.'

Max leaned back in his chair. The look on his face said it all and why should she be surprised? Two dates and she got knocked up? But then he frowned.

'He's not a man who likes to take no for an answer, is he?'

Ellie bit her lip. She really didn't want to talk about this. To anyone. She didn't even want to have to *think* about it again.

Maybe something of the shame, and fear, of that night was in her face. Max certainly saw enough to make him curse. Softly but, oh, so vehemently.

'The *bastard*. Dammit, I wish we hadn't let him go unscathed. If we'd had *any* idea…'

Ellie's head shake was determined. 'No. It would only have made things worse. He'd win in the end. *Somehow*. He always does.'

'Not this time.'

Good heavens, he made it sound like a promise but, sadly, it wasn't one that Ellie could afford to accept. Not for herself or the baby. Or for Max and his friends. They all had careers within the medical world. Damage could be done on all sorts of levels.

'I'm going to get well away,' she assured Max. 'Out of the country. I'll change my name and start again somewhere he'll never find us.'

'Uh-uh.' The negative sound had a ring of finality.

'What?'

'You can't let him win.'

'I can't fight. I tried. I even threatened him if he wouldn't leave me alone and guess what? I lost my job. He managed to make me look totally incompetent in Theatre and laid an official complaint. Nobody would listen to my side and I got shifted sideways to work in a geriatric ward and even that wasn't enough for him.'

Max said nothing but he was listening hard.

'He was always there. Ready to make things better if I co-operated. There were apologies and promises and threats. Flowers and phone calls and endless text messages that all looked completely innocent on their own. He'd be waiting for me when I finished a shift sometimes and I'd never know whether he'd choose 6 a.m. or midnight. My flatmate, Sarah, got freaked out so I left town. I got a job in Wellington. Sarah left a few weeks later. Said she was still freaked because Marcus kept turning up, wanting to know where I was, and she couldn't cope, not when she had Josh to think about.'

Max nodded. 'I met Josh. Nice kid.'

'Did you know he's Sarah's nephew, not her son?'

'She did tell me. Her sister died in some kind of accident a couple of years ago?'

'That's right. Sarah was the only family member who could take him. He's only nine so I didn't blame her for being so worried. She blamed me, though, for the hassles Marcus caused. So much that she didn't talk to me for months.'

'Why didn't you go to the police?'

'Who would have listened to some nurse badmouthing a well-respected consultant surgeon? I'd already had a taste of his influence on people when I tried to defend my job in Theatre. I had a grudge. I had no evidence of anything other than romantic gestures and texts from a man most people considered charming.'

'Did you know you were pregnant when you left?'

Ellie shook her head. 'It didn't even occur to me because I was taking a low-dose pill to control painful periods and it worked so well I often didn't get them at all. It was months before I twigged and by then it was way too late to do anything about it…even if I…' She trailed off with a sigh.

This was getting worse by the minute. He'd think she was weak in having gone out with Marcus in the first place. Stupid not to consider the possibility of pregnancy. Even more stupid not to go to the police and maybe he had a thing against terminations for any cause and she would have considered it very seriously, God help her, because…

'Not the kind of man you would have picked to be the father of your baby?' There was a wealth of understanding in Max's voice and Ellie's breath came out in a whoosh of relief.

'No.'

'Could be worse,' Max said thoughtfully. 'The guy's not *that* bad looking.'

Ellie's jaw sagged.

'And he's obviously got well above average intelligence.'

Was he trying to make a *joke* out of this? *Unbelievable*. Maybe her judgment of his character had been woefully misguided.

'Bit on the short side,' Max continued. His gaze rested on Ellie. 'And you're hardly a giant but…' He nodded. 'Maybe it'll be a girl. Petite and pretty, just like her mum.'

He was smiling at her again. 'Hey, if you'd gone to a sperm bank he would have looked pretty good on paper, wouldn't he? I'll bet his undesirable attributes are all due to nurture, not nature.'

The sharp flash of dismay—anger, even—that he could be belittling the nightmare she'd been living with for so many months gave way to something very different. Something rather wonderful. Something that made it OK that she loved this baby she was carrying. She didn't have to feel ashamed. Or guilty. Or terrified of what the future might hold for her child.

He'd not only made her feel safe, this man. He'd given her…hope.

Ellie's smile wobbled. 'Thank you.'

'No worries.' Max looked away. Was he embarrassed by the gratitude he might be seeing? 'So, do you know if it's a girl?'

'No.'

'You weren't tempted to ask the ultrasound technician?'

'I haven't had a scan.'

Too late, Ellie realised what she'd let slip as Max blinked at her. 'Excuse me?'

'I haven't had a scan,' she repeated. Did he not understand? 'If I'd gone to an antenatal clinic my name would have been recorded. I knew Marcus was trying to find me and I couldn't take that risk.'

'But didn't the hospital in Wellington get your details when you got a new job there?'

'I didn't get a job in a hospital. I went into the private sector. I had a job as a carer for a tetraplegic guy. I kept it up until very recently when the lifting got too much and then I finally managed to contact Sarah and she said she was going to the States and it seemed like the perfect solution so I sorted my passport and—'

'Whoa!' Max held up a hand. 'Rewind. Are you saying you've had *no* antenatal care? Not even a scan?'

'I'm twenty-eight,' Ellie said defensively. 'Young and healthy. I've had no problems. I've taken my own blood pressure at regular intervals and I even had the opportunity to test my own urine for protein and so on because the man I was caring for had dipsticks provided. I've taken all the recommended vitamin supplements and been careful with my diet. I had all the information I needed in my textbooks and I'm a nurse, for heaven's sake. I can take care of myself. I would have got help if there'd been any indication it was needed. I'm not stupid.'

The way his eyebrows lifted suggested that Max was reserving judgement on that score. 'How many weeks are you?'

'Thirty-six weeks and two days.'

'What position is the baby in?'

'I…' That was something Ellie had done her best to ascertain but would have to admit she hadn't succeeded in finding out. A small bottom and a head were hard to distinguish by palpation.

'You don't know, do you?'

Ellie had to look away. She pressed her lips together and encouraged the small flare of resentment she could feel forming.

'Where were you planning to give birth given your aversion to registering as a patient in a hospital?'

'I can go to a hospital. Somewhere else. Under a different name.'

'And if you happen to succeed in lying about your due date and actually get onto an international flight, how's that going to work if you go into labour at thirty thousand feet? Hours away from the nearest airport?'

He was angry. With *her*.

And it was unbearable.

He'd made her feel safe and then he'd given her hope and now he was taking those precious moments back. Ellie had never felt this miserable in her entire life.

So utterly *alone*.

* * *

Max was appalled.

He'd protected Ellie and now that he knew what he'd been protecting her *from*, he could only be grateful that fate had put him in the right place at the right time.

And now she was going to endanger both herself and her unborn baby with this insane plan to throw herself into a lifetime of hiding and deceit.

He couldn't see her face at the moment because she had dipped her head under the weight of his harsh tone. He could see the copper gleam of that thick mane of hair, however. And the tip of a small, upturned nose. What had he said about the baby? That it might be a girl—petite and pretty like its mother? He'd meant it, but he could have said more.

He could have suggested it might have that gorgeous colouring of her hair and eyes that would demand the attention of anybody. He might not be able to see her arms hidden beneath the wide sleeves of that sweater but he could guarantee the bone structure was as fine as her face and hands.

What he could see was the way they were wrapped around her lower body right now. Fiercely protective. And he could see the slump of her shoulders as though she thought the entire world was against her.

Hadn't she been through enough without him getting on her case as well?

'Sorry,' he said sincerely. 'I don't want to make this any worse for you. I'd like to help, if I can.'

She looked up and caught his gaze and Max couldn't look away. He'd remembered the attractive colour of her eyes but he must have forgotten their impact. He could *feel* that gaze. Like a physical touch. A handhold, maybe. One that asked for comfort. Or strength. He could give her that much, couldn't he?

'You wouldn't have a forwarding address for Sarah, would you?'

'No.' Max frowned. 'You do know why she decided to take off for the States in such a hurry, don't you?'

'Not really. She didn't say much in her email. I got the impression she was making a new start. Wanting a new life?'

'No. That wasn't the reason.'

Ellie looked horrified. 'She was trying to get further away from *me*?'

'No. Did she not tell you about Josh? About him being diagnosed with leukaemia six months ago?'

'Oh, my God!' Ellie breathed. 'No. I knew she was worried about him when I left. She thought he was being affected by the stressful situation. It was one of the reasons I left Auckland.'

'He didn't get diagnosed until they came down here. He got a lot sicker fast and she decided she had to try and find his father so that the possibility of a bone-marrow transplant would be there. She finally managed to track down the man on his birth certificate and found out he's a doctor working in California. She decided the best way to deal with it was to take Josh to meet him. Too easy to just say no with an email or phone call. She's planning to stay long enough to have the transplant done in the States if it's possible.'

'She might need help looking after him. I could do that. Poor Sarah. She needs a friend if nothing else.'

Her determination might be admirable but the wobble in Ellie's voice showed that she knew as well as he did that she was heading down a dead-end street with that plan.

'You can't go to the States right now, Ellie,' he said gently. 'Give it up.'

'Australia, then. That's only a few hours away.'

'Do you have any friends or relatives over there?'

'I know someone in Darwin.'

'That's nearly as far as the States. What about this side of Australia? Sydney or Melbourne or Brisbane?'

Ellie sighed. 'No.'

'How will you manage on your own?'

'I can get a job. I'm good at what I do.'

'I'm sure you are.' Max repressed a sigh. 'But do you think you'd get a position as a theatre nurse without having to produce a documented record of your qualifications? Without them wanting to know where you were last employed? Without talking to people there?'

Ellie looked away again. 'Yeah...I know.' Defeat darkened her words. 'I keep thinking and thinking about it and it's going round and round in my head and I just keep hoping I'll think of something that might work. Some way out.'

She gave him a quick glance and he could see that her eyes shimmered with tears. 'And I can't. I just have to take one day at a time and think about what I need to do *today*. For the next few hours, even.'

'What you need to do today is to make sure that everything's OK with you and your baby.'

Her nod was resigned. 'I'll go and see a doctor tomorrow, I promise. I'll find a midwife.'

'And you'll have the baby in a hospital?'

She shook her head. 'I *can't*. What if Marcus found out? What if he got the chance to do a DNA test or something and got evidence that it *is* his baby? He'd take it away from me.'

Ellie was gripping the table now. She pushed herself to her feet. 'I'm *not* going to let that happen. Not to me and especially not to this baby. *My* baby.' She turned away with the obvious intention of leaving.

'Hey…my baby, too…kind of.' Max was on his feet. He had to stop her going. If she left, he'd have no way of helping her and he'd taken on a responsibility back then when he'd claimed paternity. OK, it had been pretence and he could give it up now but oddly it seemed to be getting stronger.

Ellie got halfway across the room as she made a direct line for her small overnight bag that still sat near the door. But then she stopped abruptly. She put her arms around herself again and then, to Max's horror, she doubled over with an agonised cry of pain. It was then that he saw the dark stain on the legs of her jeans.

Had her waters broken?

He was by her side in an instant. Holding her. Helping her to lie down, right where she was. He was touching her and when he took his hand away, he saw the unmistakable smears of blood on his fingers.

'Don't move, Ellie,' he said. 'It's going to be all right. I'm just going to call for an ambulance.'

CHAPTER THREE

THE wail of the ambulance siren still echoed in his head as Max followed the stretcher carrying Ellie into the emergency department of Dunedin's Queen Mary hospital.

The sound had been the consistent background to a blur of activity that he had orchestrated from the moment Ellie had collapsed on his floor. He had been the one to place the large-bore IV cannula to allow vital fluids to be administered to counteract the blood loss. He had inserted a second line when it had become apparent that her blood pressure was already alarmingly low and her level of consciousness was rapidly dropping. It was Max who kept an eye on the ECG monitor to see what effect the blood loss might have on her heart rhythm and increased the level of oxygen being given as the reading of circulating levels slowly deteriorated.

This was far worse than any complication he might have imagined her encountering on an international flight. She would have been in trouble if this had happened only hours ago on a short domestic hop. Or out on the street before she had knocked so unexpectedly on his door.

She was in trouble anyway.

So was the baby.

Not that he could afford to worry about the infant just yet. He knew that the mother's condition was the priority. He had dealt with such cases in his department more than once. Ruptured ectopic pregnancies. Uterine ruptures. Trauma. But this wasn't some unknown woman who'd been rushed into his department by an ambulance with its siren wailing urgently.

This was Ellie and he'd promised her she was safe now.

'Antepartum haemorrhage,' he told the startled-looking triage nurse as the stretcher burst through the electronic doors into a brightly lit department.

'Max! What on earth are you doing here?'

He ignored more than one head turning in his direction. Maybe this wasn't the way he usually arrived at work and he rarely turned up wearing his bike-riding leathers but it was no excuse for unprofessional behaviour from his colleagues.

'Is Trauma One free?'

'Yes. We got the radio message. Someone from O and G is on the way down.' The nurse followed the rapidly moving stretcher. So did the receptionist, who was clutching a clipboard.

'We haven't got a name,' the clerk said anxiously.

'Ellie,' Max snapped. They were through another set of double doors now, in the best-equipped area in the department to deal with a critical case. The paramedics stopped the stretcher right beside the bed with its clean, white sheet. Staff were waiting, having been primed to expect them, and they were wearing their aprons and gloves, ready to begin a resuscitation protocol. They all knew their first tasks. The portable monitoring equipment from the ambulance would have to be switched over to the built-in equivalents. A junior nurse held a pair of shears, ready to cut away Ellie's clothing. A trolley was positioned near the head of the bed, an airway roll already opened in case intubation was necessary.

It was no surprise to see who was ready to control both the airway of this patient and the running of this emergency scenario. Jet was wearing theatre scrubs now and had a stethoscope slung around his neck. There was nothing unprofessional about his immediate reaction to seeing who had come in with this patient. He didn't even blink.

'On my count,' he said smoothly. 'One, two... three.'

There was a pool of blood on the stretcher as they lifted Ellie across to the bed. She groaned and her eyes flickered open.

'It's OK,' Max said, leaning closer. 'We're in the hospital now, Ellie. Jet's here and he's going to look after you. We're all going to look after you.'

Her eyes drifted shut again.

'GCS is dropping.' Max tried to sound clinical. Detached. It didn't work.

Jet was holding Ellie's head, making sure her airway was open. He was watching the rapid rise and fall of her chest and his gaze went to the monitor as the oxygen saturation probe on her finger began relaying the information he wanted.

He frowned and flicked the briefest glance at Max. 'What the hell happened?' he murmured.

'Massive haemorrhage. Seemed to come from no-where as soon as she stood up. Severe abdominal pain as well.'

The clerk was still in the room, hovering behind the nursing staff who were changing ECG leads, hanging the bags of fluid and getting a blood-pressure cuff secured.

'What's Ellie's last name?' she asked. 'How old is she?'

A registrar had his hands on her swollen abdomen. 'It's rigid,' he announced. 'Is she in labour? What's the gestation?'

'Thirty-six weeks and two days,' Max said.

Ellie was almost naked now. Totally vulnerable. Exposed to an expanding team of medical personnel. Someone from the obstetric department had arrived, closely followed by a technician pushing a portable ul-trasound machine. Jet was holding a mask over Ellie's face and frowning as he watched the numbers changing on the overhead monitor.

'Ellie…' He had his mouth right beside his ear and was speaking loudly. 'Can you hear me? Open your eyes.'

She wouldn't want to, Max thought. This would have to be absolutely terrifying.

'Are there any relatives who could give me her de-tails?' the clerk persisted. 'Did her husband come in with her? Or…her partner?' The woman knew she was failing in her task but she made yet another effort. 'The father of the baby?'

That flicked a switch in Max's head and its effect was magnified by how vulnerable Ellie was. How much trouble she was in right now. He had tried to protect her and somehow he had stepped into a new nightmare and was still by her side. Was she aware of what was happening? Still terrified? Did she know he was here?

She had been so determined to stay away from hospitals to protect her child. Maybe the best thing he could do for her at this moment was to respect that determination and carry on with what had already worked once.

'Yes,' he said clearly. 'I'm the father.'

Somebody dropped something metallic on the far side of the room and the sound rang out in the suddenly still moment following his statement. Jet uttered a low profanity but his gaze was still fixed on the monitor and the sound could well have been taken to be concern at a new development in Ellie's condition. Max was close enough to speak to his friend without being overheard by anyone else.

'I'll explain later,' he murmured. 'Just back me up.'

The clerk was happy, scribbling on the sheet of paper attached to the clipboard. 'Surname?' she chirped briskly.

Oh, Lord. If she got registered under her real name, they have to deal with Marcus Jones turning up and he'd have plenty of time to get here. Even if things went better than any of them could expect in this room, there was no way Ellie would be getting discharged in a hurry.

There was no time to think. In for a penny, in for a pound.

'McAdam,' he said wearily. 'We're married.'

The nurse, who was sticking on the leads required for a twelve-lead ECG, looked up, open-mouthed, and others exchanged astonished glances but the clerk knew she was on a roll.

'How old is your wife?'

'Twenty-eight.'

'Date of birth?'

As if *he'd* know. This had gone far enough. Far too far, judging by the look Jet slanted his way.

'Leave it,' Max growled. 'We can sort the paperwork later.'

'But we need—'

'Get out,' Jet snapped. 'We're busy.' He looked up, avoiding Max but catching most others in the room as he issued his orders.

'I'm going to intubate,' he warned. 'Oxygen saturation levels have fallen far enough. We need a central venous line in. And an arterial line.'

'I'll do that,' Max offered.

Jet gave his head a negative jerk. 'On your wife? I don't think so.' He nodded at his registrars, giving them the signal to get started. 'Get some bloods off as well. We need to know her blood group. Stat.'

'I'd like a rhesus factor and antibodies, too.' The obstetric consultant was watching the technician begin the ultrasound examination. 'Looks like we've got a central placenta praevia here and she's in labour. Fully dilated.'

Less than an hour later, in the middle of the life-and-death battle to save Ellie Peters, she gave birth to a tiny baby girl.

There was a paediatric team amongst the crowd in Trauma One now. And a consultant from the intensive care unit, who was a specialist in dealing with haemorrhagic shock resulting from such massive blood loss. Ellie was being cared for. The baby was being carefully assessed.

Having been forced onto the sidelines due to his own admission of involvement, there seemed to be nothing for Max to do other than watch. He was torn between watching the monitors to evaluate the success of the treatment Ellie was receiving and staring at the scrap of humanity the paediatric consultant was bent over.

'She's small but doing OK,' she pronounced eventually. 'I'm happy with her breathing but the heart rate's a bit on the slow side. Did I hear someone say the father is here?'

Ellie was deeply unconscious. The obstetrician was happy that the bleeding had ceased now that delivery was complete but the control of the blood loss might have come too late. The mother of this tiny baby was now on a ventilator to manage what looked like adult respiratory distress from fluid loss. Jet and the ICU consultant were worried about her kidneys. Her production of urine had virtually ceased and her most recent blood test showed deterioration in renal function.

Max had done what he'd thought was the right thing in continuing the pretence that he was the baby's father and he couldn't back out now. Jet wouldn't say anything because he'd asked him to back him up and the brotherhood that they made up, along with Rick, was glued together with a loyalty that would never be broken. There were plenty of other people ready to say something, however. To point him out and draw him into the case that this department would be talking about for a very long time.

'You're the father?' The paediatrician didn't know him so there was no undertone of astonishment. 'Good. Come with us. We're going to take your daughter upstairs and she'll need you.'

Max took a step towards the group looking after the baby. And then another. And then he stopped.

'I can't...' He looked over his shoulder at Ellie. And then back to the baby, now dried and wrapped in soft, warm towels. What the hell had he got himself into here?

Jet's voice was calm. 'Nothing you can do for Ellie at the moment, mate,' he said. 'We're going to transfer her up to ICU very soon. Best you go with the baby. I'll come and update you as soon as I can.'

And wherever the baby was being taken, whether it was a maternity ward or the paediatric ICU, it would be a more private place, Jet's tone suggested. They would be able to talk about this. Hopefully, they might even be able to sort out the mess Max had created.

It seemed a reasonable plan. Max wasn't due on duty

here in the emergency department until first thing tomorrow morning. They had a whole night to sort things out. Stepping back from taking any responsibility for Ellie might be a good first step. He took another step towards the baby and nodded.

'Let's go,' he agreed.

'How would you feel about holding her?'

'Ah…I'm not sure that's a great idea right now, is it?'

The paediatrician also took another glance at the monitor where the newborn baby's heart rate was slowing down yet again.

'It could help. Have you heard of kangaroo care?'

'No.' Max was staring at the baby in the plastic crib. It was lying on its side, a soft white hat covering the dark whorls of hair on its head. One arm was bent, a tiny starfish hand resting on its cheek.

Max hadn't spent this long in the company of a baby this small…ever. He'd participated in a fair few deliveries, of course, throughout his training and then in a short run on O and G but it was a rare occurrence in Emergency and the babies were always whisked off to places like this paediatric intensive care unit. He'd never had a reason to stay involved. He didn't now, except as a fraud.

He shouldn't really be here at all.

'It's been around since the late seventies,' the paediatric consultant broke into his guilt. 'But it's gaining quite a following. It's basically skin-to-skin contact with a parent. As long as the infant is medically stable, there's no reason not to use it and it's been shown to improve oxygenation and respiratory rates. It can actually make a significant difference to something like bradycardia.'

'Skin-to-skin?' Max couldn't keep the dismay out of his voice. 'Are you kidding me?'

'You don't sit around naked.' The doctor smiled. 'In fact, the baby needs to be under your own clothing to help maintain body temperature stability.' Her smile became reassuring rather than amused. 'I know she looks tiny and fragile and that her arrival was a bit unexpected…'

'You have no idea,' Max murmured.

'And I know you're worried about Ellie,' she continued, 'but this is a way to help everybody, including—maybe especially—yourself.'

'Oh?' Max was listening now. He needed to help himself. Fast. 'How, exactly?'

'You'll be doing what Ellie can't do at the moment, which is caring for her baby. You could well make a big difference medically for this little one.' She was watching him and a tiny frown line appeared. 'If you're really not comfortable, then I can get one of the nursing staff to do it, but it's far better if it's a parent. It can be a way of bonding that could make all the difference to the stress of the next few days.'

Max had the sensation of being trapped in a kind of glass box. He was being watched. By the paediatrician and her registrar. By the nurse who was hovering near the crib. Even by other nurses in this unit as they went about their own tasks. They all seemed to have paused right now to hold their breath and see what he was going to do.

They all believed that he was this baby's father and what kind of a father wouldn't want to do something that might help his kid? If it became obvious that he had no need—or, let's face it, desire—to bond with this infant, people might start asking questions. Gossiping at the very least, and the less any of this was talked about the better. For Ellie's sake.

Which was how all this had started, wasn't it?

He really would have to be more careful next time, he decided with a wry inward smile as he found himself nodding and then being guided to the comfortable armchair rolled into this corner of the PICU.

A nurse took the layers away from the baby. They left her with a nappy and her hat on, an oxygen saturation monitor clipped to a minuscule toe and some unobtrusive sticky dots and soft wires that connected her to a cardiac monitor. She was mostly naked, Max noted with some alarm. Small and pink and awkward-looking, with stick-like arms and legs.

'Keep her prone and upright,' the paediatrician advised. 'The nurses will keep an eye on you both and levels are set for an alarm to go off if the oxygen levels or cardiac rhythm need interventions.'

Max had sacrificed the neck of his T-shirt so that he didn't need to discard any of his own clothing. The vertical cut allowed him to fold the neckline down so that the baby's face would be uncovered. He heard the whimper of the baby as she was picked up.

Good grief…he really didn't want to do this. Was it too late to back out?

An alarm began to sound. A slow bell that pinged

ominously. Maybe the baby didn't like the idea, either. Her heart rhythm was jumping erratically.

'Does she need to go back in the crib?' Max tried not to sound too hopeful.

'Let's see how we go for a minute or two.'

With an inward sigh, Max held up the bottom of his old, soft T-shirt while a nurse positioned the baby and then covered her. A layer of the leather jacket came next and then she helped him put his arm in the right place for support. He felt awkward. Uncomfortable.

He could feel the baby wriggle against his chest, moving tiny limbs as if in protest. He could feel the miniature chest heaving as she attempted to breathe and cry at the same time but the effort seemed exhausting and the movements diminished.

Max took a cautious glance downwards and found the baby's eyes were open. So dark they looked black and they were fixed on him. He took a deep, careful breath and let it out very slowly.

'Look at that.' The paediatrician sounded delighted. 'Heart rate's coming up and it's steady.'

They waited another minute as Max sat as still as humanly possible.

'Looking good,' came the expert verdict. 'We'll leave you to it, Max.'

'Ah...' He watched as staff began to disperse. To stop watching, even, from all over the unit. Any second now and he would be virtually on his own. 'How long should I stay here?'

'The longer the better,' a nurse said cheerfully. 'As long as you can, anyway.'

Max tipped his head back and closed his eyes. He

breathed. In and out. He could feel the baby breathing. In that first long, quiet minute of being left to himself he could even feel the baby's heart beating. A soft, rapid ticking against his chest. Almost on top of his own heart.

Weird.

He opened his eyes and tilted his chin so he could look down again.

The baby was still awake. Still watching him with a curiously intent gaze that managed to look utterly bewildered at the same time.

'Mmm,' Max murmured sympathetically. 'I know just how you feel. But don't worry. We'll get it all sorted out in no time.'

'Whoa! What are you *doing*?'

'Oh, *man*…'

Rick, closely followed by Jet, had come into a now dimly lit PICU to find Max still in the armchair, with a tiny baby nestled on his chest beneath his leather jacket.

'Shh…don't wake her up.'

Rick's eyebrows were sky high. 'I bumped into Jet as he was coming out of the big people ICU,' he said in a stage whisper. 'Thought I'd come and say hi and…' His grin widened. 'I'm sure glad I did. Wouldn't have missed *this* for quids. What *are* you doing?'

'Being a kangaroo,' Max muttered. 'Go away.'

Jet was looking at the monitors. 'Kid looks stable enough,' he said. 'Why don't you put it back to bed and we'll go get a coffee or something.'

Max sighed. 'Because every time I try and put her

down she goes into a bradycardia and the oxygen levels drop.'

The nursing staff hadn't missed the arrival of Max's friends. More than one of them was finding a task that necessitated getting a lot closer to this extraordinary scene. Three large men and one very small baby.

'She loves her daddy,' the closest one said with a smile directed at Rick.

He smiled back. 'And who wouldn't?'

The nurse giggled. Max could swear she even batted her eyelashes at Rick. He sighed again.

'What's the story, Jet? How's Ellie doing?'

'On dialysis,' Jet said grimly. 'Renal function hasn't picked up yet and there's still some concern about her lungs. They're going to keep her sedated and on the ventilator, at least overnight.'

'Prognosis?'

Jet shrugged. 'She's hanging in there. Could go either way.'

Max swallowed. What was going to happen to this baby if Ellie didn't make it? He should be worried that he'd put his hand up as her only available relative but, instead, he found himself more worried about what life might have in store for this tiny girl.

Rick was leaning closer. 'Kinda cute, isn't it?' He was grinning again. 'You know, I think I can see the family likeness.'

Jet snorted. He took a glance over his shoulder as if his scowl might be enough to ensure that the staff minded their own business for a while.

'How long are you going to keep this up, Max?'

Max said nothing. He was quite used to the feel of

the baby against him now. In fact, at some point during the last couple of hours he'd experienced an odd sense of relief when the contact was re-established and things had settled down again. He wasn't going to make another attempt to put the baby back in her plastic crib any time soon. Maybe it wouldn't feel right until he knew whether or not her mother was going to survive.

Rick's smile had finally faded. 'Jet told me what happened in ED.' His mouth quirked again briefly. 'And if he hadn't told me, I would have found out pretty damn quick. The whole hospital is buzzing with the news of your sudden fatherhood, mate.'

'I'll bet.'

'I mean, it was one thing to tell the weasel you were the father so that he'd go away but...' Rick sucked in a long breath, an eloquent sound that encompassed the depth of the trouble Max had got himself into here.

'The guy raped her,' Max said quietly.

There was a moment's silence. Max could feel an echo of his own reaction to that information. The way it changed things. The anger on Ellie's behalf. On behalf of all women, really. They all liked women. A lot. He could sense the way his friends stilled. He saw Jet's hands curl into fists.

'And then he got her fired,' he added. 'When she tried to get away from him. He's been stalking her ever since.' He cleared his throat. 'And I told her she was safe.'

Another moment of silence as Rick and Jet absorbed and then accepted the implications.

'She won't be safe until she's well enough to look after this baby and get away.'

'She'll never be safe.' Rick's eyes were narrowed. 'The *bastard*.'

'Anyway…' Max didn't want to consider the future right now. The present was more than enough to deal with. Especially given that the baby was stirring. Woken by the intense conversation around it, perhaps. Or maybe it could sense the tension in the body it rested against.

The whimper became a warbling cry that made both Rick and Jet shift their feet uncomfortably. It also brought a nurse, who was carrying a bottle.

'Looks like it's dinnertime,' she said. 'Here you go, Daddy.' She handed Max the bottle.

'Maybe you better do this,' he muttered.

The baby's cry strengthened. Jet's pager sounded and he reached for it to read the message with obvious relief as Max fumbled with the bottle, trying to fit the teat into the tiny mouth.

'Gotta go,' Jet said. 'Sorry, mate. I'll get back later.'

'I'll come with you,' Rick said. Clearly this experience was rapidly losing its entertainment value.

Jet slanted a backward glance at Max. 'You want me to arrange cover for your ED shift tomorrow?'

The baby's mouth had finally closed over the teat and she was trying to suck. Max tilted the bottle to help. The baby sucked harder, her dark gaze fixed on the man who didn't seem to know what he was doing. But then she tasted the milk and the sucking settled into a rhythm.

'Max?' Jet prompted.

'Yeah…cover would be good.' Max couldn't break the eye contact with the infant so he didn't even try and look up. 'I'm not going anywhere for a while.'

CHAPTER FOUR

SHE was lost.

It was dark. *So* dark. And maybe she was in a forest. There was danger. Animals or tree branches that scratched and bit. Things to trip over so that she landed hard enough to hurt herself because there was pain that wouldn't go away.

And fear.

She was running but so confused she couldn't tell whether she was running away from something that terrified her or towards something that she wanted so badly it was worth going through this terrible journey.

Weirdly, in spite of the pain and the fear, she felt protected. As though something…no, some*one*…was watching over her. A guardian angel but one so dark it was invisible. She thought she could detect a ripple in the inky shadows at times but then it would vanish, often under the onslaught of new pain, and then she would be in the dark again. Utterly forlorn.

Time was irrelevant. She had been in this place for ever so when it changed and light began to filter in, the new development was even more confusing. Scary.

'Ellie? Can you hear me?'

Yes…but she had no idea who this voice belonged to. She'd heard it before, she knew that much. And she liked it. She liked it very much because it made her feel…safe.

Talk some more, she begged silently. I want to feel your voice.

No…shouldn't that be hear? Except she *could* feel it. It wrapped around her like the softest blanket to keep her warm and yet it had a rough edge that rumbled its way through her ears and brain and into every part of her body. Through places that hurt and somehow it softened the pain so that it became no more than a background ache. Unimportant. The voice went right into her bones.

'Can you open your eyes?' it asked.

Ellie tried but they felt glued shut. Her eyelids were made of something so heavy it was impossible for tiny muscles to lift them. She could feel something, though. An encouraging kind of flutter.

'Wake up, Ellie.' The voice was also encouraging. 'There's someone here who would love to meet you properly.'

She tried again. Tried really hard because the owner of the voice wanted her to and that made it important to succeed. So important that nothing else mattered for the moment and even the ache deep within was forgotten. And slowly she achieved her goal. Her eyes were open and it was bright. Too bright. Her eyes stung and all she could see was a blur.

A very large, dark blur that reminded her fleetingly of the nasty place she'd been in for ever. The flash of memory was disturbing but the remnant of fear was gone just as quickly, leaving something oddly pleasant in its wake. This blur was like the shadow of that guardian angel. The one she'd tried so hard to catch sight of properly but which had always been just out of reach. Evaporating into the darkness.

The dreamlike wisp evaporated as well as Ellie blinked, adjusting to the light and letting the face swimming above hers come into focus.

Dark hair. Waves that were almost curls with small ends here and there that refused to behave and created a roguish frame for a face that had very definite lines and a jaw that was dark and rough and hadn't seen a razor for several days.

Dark eyes that were watching her very intently and a mouth that was tilting into a soft smile. The most beautiful smile Ellie had ever seen in her life.

'Hi, there,' the voice said. 'How're you doing?'

Ellie's lips felt stiff, as though they hadn't been used in quite a while. She tried to say something but her throat hurt and the only sound that emerged was a rusty squeak. She swallowed carefully and blinked again. Cautiously but very quickly in the end, just in case this was a dream and the man with the beautiful smile would vanish if she closed her eyelids for too long.

Her head was swirling with incomplete images and thoughts. She knew she was in a bed. In a hospital because she knew that familiar smell so well and there were equally recognisable sounds like the soft beeping of pagers and monitoring equipment. She could see the sharp edges of that equipment in her peripheral vision and she could hear echoes of voices that had long since stopped speaking. Urgent voices. Saying things like '*massive haemorrhage*' and '*Trauma One*' and '*blood group and cross-match. Stat*'.

Paralysed by the kaleidoscope happening inside her head, Ellie focused on those intent dark eyes above her.

'You're in the intensive care unit,' the voice said calmly. 'You've been pretty sick for a couple of days but you're going to be all right. You're off the ventilator now and your lungs are doing well. So are your kidneys. How's your throat? It's probably a bit sore after having a tube in it for so long.'

There was a frown in those eyes now. He was worried about something. *Her?* That was nice. Ellie liked that she was important enough for him to be worried about her. Maybe he'd smile at her again.

'I'm Max—remember? You came to the apartment to find Sarah but she wasn't there. And then you got into trouble. You went into labour and—'

Ellie could feel her eyes widening. Her skin was prickling as though the blanket the voice had provided was being stripped off, leaving her exposed to the elements. The sense of safety was gone, too. She could feel the fear of that awful forest place crowding around her. Something was happening in her brain. An almost painful series of jolts as pieces fell into place.

Sarah. Marcus. Her *baby*…

'She's fine,' Max said softly. 'See?'

His head tilted and Ellie's gaze followed the downward trajectory of his. Down his body to where his arms were cradling something. She couldn't see what it was until Max tipped forward and there, nestled in blankets, was a tiny face. A sleeping, newborn baby.

'*Oh*…' The sound forced its way past her sore, dry throat. 'Is that…?'

She knew it was. She could *feel* it but she needed to be told as well. To make sure she wasn't dreaming.

'Sure is,' Max said. 'This is your daughter, Ellie. Would you like to hold her?'

Ellie nodded. She couldn't say anything because her already tight throat was now entirely choked by tears. She could feel them rolling down her face as Max carefully placed the baby on her chest and then helped her move her arms to cradle the infant. He pushed IV tubing attached to her arm to one side and then he looked up, past Ellie.

'Could you grab an extra pillow or two?' he asked someone. 'Let's try and prop Ellie up a bit more.'

Her arms felt so weak Ellie was frightened she'd let go but Max seemed to understand because he kept his hands on top, supporting her. A nurse came and tucked another pillow beneath her shoulders and an extra one under her head. A rush of dizziness faded and Ellie found she could blink her tears away and actually see her baby properly for the first time.

Her eyes were still closed, a fan of dark lashes sitting on each cheek like butterflies. A tiny button of a nose and a mouth pursed into a perfect cupid's bow.

'Isn't she beautiful?'

There was a note of wonder in his voice and something more. Something that was enough to make Ellie lift her gaze for an instant but Max was intent on the tiny face in her arms and he didn't look up so she couldn't get any clue to that confusing undertone.

She didn't have the energy to try and understand. Didn't even have the inclination to try because there was something far more important to think about. Something so wonderful that really it was no surprise that Max seemed to share what she couldn't begin to put into words.

This was her baby.

Her daughter. It was a *girl* and she was—

'Is she—?' Ellie's voice caught. Suddenly, she was too scared to ask.

'She's perfect.' Max sounded…good grief…*proud*? 'Ten little fingers, ten little toes. She's feeding well. Fifty grams up on two days ago.'

'*What…?*' Again, this was disturbing enough to make her stop feasting her eyes on the perfect features of her baby. 'My God…how long…?'

'Have you been in here?' Max looked up this time and there was sympathy in his eyes as he completed her horrified question. 'Three days, Ellie. This little button was born at seven minutes past six on Sunday.'

It was too much to take in. Ellie could have accepted feeling like this if she'd been coming round from, say, a general anaesthetic for an emergency Caesarean but her precious baby had been in the world for three whole days without her mother's knowledge, let alone her care and protection.

Panic was edging closer and Ellie found she was struggling to take a breath. She had to take in enough air to warn Max. To demand that they let her out of this bed so that she could be with her baby and take care of her. Or at least for them to bring the baby in here so that she could watch over her. Every second of every hour.

'*Ellie.*'

The tone was firm enough for her to realise this wasn't the first time he'd said her name. '*Listen* to me.'

The words were a command but were delivered in what was virtually a whisper. What Max was about to say was imperative.

And private.

Gulping like a stranded fish, Ellie blinked frightened tears into submission and fixed her gaze on Max. He took a quick look around them and then back at her.

'Remember how I told Marcus I was the baby's father and it made him go away?'

Ellie managed a nod.

'Well, I told them that here too and everyone believes it.'

That's what it had been, Ellie realised. That odd note in his voice. The way he'd been holding this tiny baby. He had looked and sounded for all the world like a besotted new father.

So he had been acting? To protect them?

Ellie blinked again, this time in bewilderment. He was either an incredibly good actor or her brain wasn't functioning at anywhere near normal levels of acuity. No, it had to be acting if everyone else believed it as well.

'There's more.' Max leaned closer. He could have been admiring the baby and he even used the tip of his middle finger to stroke the infant's cheek gently but his intention seemed to have been to put his mouth close enough to Ellie's ear to ensure that no one overheard.

'I didn't give them your real name,' he told her. 'And…um…I wasn't thinking too straight at the time so I told them…'

He sounded almost embarrassed, Ellie thought. What kind of weird name had he come up with?

'I told them that your surname was McAdam.'

Nothing wrong with that, Ellie decided with relief. It was a perfectly nice name.

'OK,' she whispered.

There was a moment's silence. Ellie could feel how still Max was. So still she was only aware of the tiny movements in her arms as her baby breathed and stirred slightly in slumber. She was used to the feel of those tiny limbs moving. It was like she'd lost part of herself but had found it again only now the movements were on the outside, instead of safely enclosed in her womb.

Max was still quiet. He seemed to be waiting for something. A breath audible enough to be a sigh escaped his lips.

'That's *my* name, Ellie.'

'Oh…' Well, that was OK, too. She didn't mind borrowing his name for a little while. As long as he didn't mind. But maybe he did. The continued silence was starting to feel uncomfortable.

'I…ah…told them we were married,' Max said, so softly Ellie was sure she hadn't heard correctly.

She could remember what had happened at the apartment. That he'd claimed he was the baby's father and that he and his fellow dark angels had made sure Marcus had gone away and that she was safe.

And he'd obviously kept up the charade in order to keep protecting her when she had been totally help-less, presumably in the emergency department of what-ever this hospital was. He'd even gone an extra mile in giving her a new name so Marcus wouldn't be alerted to where she now was. Not just any name, either. He'd loaned her his own, along with the additional protec-tion of allowing people to think she was his wife.

His *wife*.

Ellie took another look at this extraordinary man. He was a hero, no doubt about that. Maybe he wasn't wearing his motorbike leathers right now and he looked tired and unshaven but he was still absolutely gorgeous. And he was capable of bestowing the most beautiful smiles in the world.

The woman who would be his real wife one day was the luckiest woman in the world. She just didn't know it yet.

Gratitude for all that he'd done for her was filling Ellie's heart. Competing—no, meshing with the over-whelming love she already had for the tiny person she still held in her arms. It was all too much and it seemed to be getting hard to breathe again. So hard, it was ut-terly exhausting.

A pinging sound came from somewhere above her head and then there was the sound of footsteps ap-proaching rapidly.

'Oxygen saturation level's way down,' a nurse ob-served. The alarm was silenced.

'Hardly surprising. First time she's been awake and it's been an emotional reunion for these two.'

'Of course it has. But I need to put some oxygen on and she needs to rest. I think you'll have to take baby back to the PICU, Dr McAdam.'

'*No.*' The word was ripped out of Ellie in a gasp.

'Just for a while, Ellie.' Max's hands were moving under her arms already, preparing to lift the precious bundle. He was still bent over her. 'She's being taken good care of, I promise.' His mouth was so close Ellie could see every nuance of the words being made. 'She's safe, Ellie. Believe it and rest. We both want you to rest and get better.'

'Of course you do.' The nurse had a smile in her voice. 'Don't worry. I'll take good care of Mrs McAdam for you.'

Mrs McAdam?

This *was* a dream. Or maybe a nightmare, Ellie decided as Max took her daughter from her arms. But then he leaned in and kissed her. Softly, on her lips, and Ellie found her eyes drifting shut. This was most definitely a dream.

'Sleep well, darling,' he said clearly. 'I'll be back very soon.'

This time when Ellie woke her eyes snapped open and focused instantly. The wave of disappointment at finding the space beside her bed empty was enough to make her cry out.

'What's wrong?' The nurse was on the other side of the bed and Ellie could see a cotton bud in her hand as she turned her head. 'Sorry, I didn't mean to wake you but your lips were looking so dry and uncomfortable.'

'Where are they?' Ellie knew she sounded frightened but she *was*, dammit. She was alone apart from a nurse she didn't recognise. Was her baby alone too? Feeling unprotected and vulnerable?

'It's two a.m., Ellie,' the nurse said kindly. 'They'll be asleep. I expect your baby is safely tucked up in her crib and that Max is sprawled in the armchair beside her.' Her voice took on a wistful note. 'Or maybe he's holding her right now. He won't let anyone else feed her, you know.'

Ellie stared at the nurse. No, she didn't know and she didn't understand. 'But…it's been days,' she said finally, her voice wobbling. 'Days and days.'

'I know.' The nurse, an attractive blonde with a name tag that said 'Tori', took a deep breath and let it out in a sigh. Then she smiled at Ellie. 'We were all gobsmacked to hear that Max had got married secretly, but you know what's blown everyone away even more?'

Ellie shook her head slowly. So it hadn't been a dream. She had to pretend she was Max's wife for the moment. Oh…Lord!

'What an amazing father he's turned out to be,' Tori said. 'He was wearing his leathers when he came in with you, do you remember?'

Ellie found herself smiling. Oh…*yes*…

'I don't think he got out of them for the next thirty-six hours. He was sitting up there in the PICU doing kangaroo care. I've got a friend who works in there and she said that none of them could take their eyes off him. There he was, in those mega-masculine clothes, with a newborn baby skin to skin with him on his chest. Tucked under that leather jacket. Can you imagine?'

Ellie could. She remembered that jacket. And that chest. Maybe her contact had been very brief but she would never forget how solid it had felt. How safe. There'd been layers of clothes over it, of course but, oddly, it was all too easy to imagine how it might feel skin to skin. It gave her a sharp twinge in a painful place deep down in her belly. Painful but far from unpleasant.

She went back to picturing her baby and she knew how protected she would have felt and it was enough to bring tears to her eyes. She loved Max for what he'd done for her daughter. She would never, ever be able to thank him enough.

'He didn't have to keep it up for so long,' Tori continued as she poured water from a jug on the bedside table into a cup that had a built-in straw. 'A few hours at a time would probably have been enough to get all the medical benefits for the baby but he wouldn't leave her. He got his shifts in Emergency covered and stuff brought in from home. He's practically moved in.' Tori was smiling widely now. 'Not that any of the nursing staff are complaining, mind you. Would you like a drink of water?'

'Yes, please.'

'Just a sip to start with. Your tummy hasn't had anything in it for a while and I don't want you throwing up.'

Ellie sipped the cool water and it tasted wonderful.

She drew in a deep breath. And then another. It felt easier.

'Any pain?' Tori queried.

Ellie thought about it. That was better too. 'I feel good…I think. Can I sit up? Or go to the loo or something?'

'You don't need to. You've still got a catheter in. I think they're planning on taking it out tomorrow and you might be able to have a shower, even. Word is that if you stay as stable as you've been today, they'll shift you out of ICU and onto the ward. The maternity ward,' the nurse added with another smile. 'You can have your baby right beside you. How good will that be?'

But Ellie was frowning as she remembered something Tori had said earlier. 'Why is she in the PICU? Max said she was fine.' Her mouth trembled. 'He said she was p-perfect.'

'She is,' Tori assured her hurriedly. 'On the small side, but there's nothing wrong with her. She went there initially because she needed watching but now it's more like staff privilege, I guess. It was a private space for Max to do the kangaroo thing. I think he might have been a bit embarrassed to be seen bonding with his baby like that, you know?' She chuckled. 'Men, eh?'

'Mmm.' Of course he would have been embarrassed. It wasn't even *his* baby.

What on earth had made Max go this far to help her? A total stranger. He had to be the most extraordinary person she'd ever met. Never mind how lucky his future wife would be. *She* was the lucky one right now.

'Would you like a bit of a wash, seeing as you're awake? I could help you clean your teeth.'

'That would be wonderful.'

'And then you can catch some more sleep and when you wake up in the morning, I'll bet your family will be back in here.' Tori paused as she headed off for supplies. 'Have you guys got a name for the baby yet?'

'No…I kind of expected it would be a boy.'

A boy that she would always have worried might turn out to be like his father. But what had Max said? That her baby might be a girl and pretty, just like her mum.

Max thought she was pretty? Ellie could feel the flush of warmth in her cheeks.

'You're looking so much better.' Tori sounded satisfied. 'And there's no rush to come up with a name. Legally, I believe you've got a month before she has to be registered.' She grinned. 'Her dad started calling her "Mouse" and everyone else is now. Mouse McAdam. Bit different, anyway.'

Yes. Different. Untraceable.

Safe.

The end was in sight.

It should be a huge relief. It was a huge relief.

'How 'bout that, Mouse?' Max looked down at the bundle he was carrying in the wake of the nurse who was pushing the plastic wheeled crib. 'You're going to the maternity ward. Your mummy's so much better that she's going to be able to look after you now. How good is that?'

It was very good. Excellent, even. He would be able

to go home and get a full night's sleep. He'd be able to get back to work and he couldn't wait for a full-on, exhausting shift in the emergency department. The last few days had been an unexpected and disturbing disruption to his life and the sooner it was back on track the better. Maybe he'd suggest a weekend bike ride to the guys. Rick might stop laughing at him, finally, for playacting being a father. Jet might stop glaring at him and muttering under his breath about how crazy he was.

They were almost there now. Ellie had been put in a private room at the end of the ward. She'd only been on her feet for the first time that morning and was so weak she'd need constant help for the next few days but the nursing staff would be there for her. It was what they were paid to do, after all, and they'd do it well because everybody fell in love with Mouse.

The weight in his arms was so familiar. The kangaroo care wasn't needed any more, of course, but Max would never forget the feel of that tiny body against his own. Or the moments of a satisfaction like no other he'd ever experienced. Like when he'd got her to take the bottle that first time. Or when she had only stopped crying when a nurse had placed her back in *his* arms.

'Here you go,' she had said, clearly reluctant. 'It's her daddy she wants.'

Daddy.

Was this what it felt like to be a father? He'd known what level of responsibility it would come with. And the kind of background anxiety that something bad could happen that had led to an urge to protect that was very disruptive to say the least. It had been crazy, hadn't it, to take time off work to guard this infant? And if he'd felt this strongly about a baby that wasn't even his, heaven help him if he ever got one of his own. If anything, he could take this whole experience as a warning.

The baby didn't seem to approve of being relocated. She was whimpering by the time they reached the room where Ellie was sitting, propped up on pillows. She looked pale and her long hair lay in limp, dark strands but the IV lines and the oxygen mask had gone and when she saw Max coming through the door, carrying her baby, her face lit up with a smile that made him catch his breath at its brilliance.

She held out her arms and Max handed over the bundle. He hung around, though, because Mouse was crying and, well, he might be the only one who could settle her down properly. He knew this baby better than anyone, including her mother. They might need him. Just for a bit longer.

The staff busied themselves.

'She's hungry,' a nurse declared. 'I'll go and fix a bottle for her.'

Max nodded. She *was* hungry, he could recognise the cry. He couldn't leave yet because he'd be able to help Ellie with her first feed. He was good at bottles. He knew just how Mouse liked it to be held and how far to tip it and when. How you knew it was going well because her eyes would find yours and stare at you with that intense concentration that made you feel like the most important person in the world.

'I…I thought I'd try feeding her myself,' Ellie said.

She must have noticed his expression because a faint blush spread over her cheeks.

'I'm drug-free, and the midwife who came to see me this morning showed me how to express milk and she said it hasn't dried up and there'll be plenty once I start feeding. And if there isn't…' Ellie sounded a little defensive now. 'I can top up with a bottle but it's going to be good for both of us if I give it a try.'

'You want some help getting her latched on?' the nurse queried.

'Um…I'd rather try by myself.' Ellie ducked her head, embarrassed. 'The midwife gave me the *Don't Panic Guide to Birth* to read and it's great. There's a technique in it that should work just as well for a baby this long after birth as if I'd done it straight away.'

'I've read that.' The nurse nodded. 'It's about being skin to skin and letting the baby latch on by itself, isn't it?'

Ellie nodded, shy but eager.

'That's supposed to be between the mother and baby, unassisted, but…' The nurse was frowning. 'Given that you've just come from the intensive care unit, I'm not happy leaving you entirely by yourself with baby.'

Mouse was crying in earnest now, sounding distressed, with a warbling cry Max hadn't heard before. It was making *him* feel tense.

'Maybe if the father stays,' the nurse suggested. 'That's allowed, isn't it?'

Ellie was rocking the baby. 'Shh, shh…' she crooned. 'It's all right…'

Except it wasn't all right. Max could see his own tension in Ellie's face and hear it in the escalating misery of the baby's cry. Someone needed to sort this out.

'Of course it's allowed,' he snapped. 'Why wouldn't it be? Might be a good idea if you all left us to it.'

They went, closing the door behind them. Max drew the curtains over the windows on the corridor side of the room.

'What should I do?'

'Nothing,' Ellie said. She was peeling away baby blankets. 'I need to undress…her.' She was fumbling with the ties on the baby's gown but then she looked up and Max could see the tears in her eyes. 'She hasn't even got a name,' Ellie choked out.

'Yes, she has.' Max stepped closer. He knew how to take that gown off. 'She's Mouse. Because she's tiny and cute and sometimes she twitches her nose. Do you need the nappy off as well?'

'I…I don't think so.'

'Skin to skin, right?'

Ellie didn't meet his eyes. 'Mmm. I need to put her…um, Mouse, between my breasts.'

Max swallowed. 'OK. I'll hold her for a tick while you sort *your* gown.'

He was used to holding this baby when it was virtually naked. The movements of small, unfettered limbs no longer triggered alarm. He held the baby against his chest and, by some miracle, it calmed her. He could feel the rub of that tiny nose against his shirt and the high-pitched cries softened into noisy snuffles.

'She likes you,' Ellie said.

'She just knows me. Maybe it's a smell thing.' Max was busy not looking at Ellie as she took her arms from the sleeves of her gown and pushed it down to her waist.

'Mmm.' Her voiced sounded oddly strangled. 'That's what the book said. The baby needs to see and hear you and smell and taste. I put her face down between my breasts and stroke her back and she learns my smell and then she should start moving her head around until she finds the nipple all by herself.'

'Really?' Max was surprised enough to look up and there was Ellie with her breasts exposed. Small and round, like the rest of her. Pale and firm looking, with a tracing of blue veins and nut-brown nipples.

Max had to swallow hard again. He shouldn't be doing this. He really shouldn't. He could see the same discomfort in Ellie's eyes when he hauled his gaze away, a flush of something like guilt warming the back of his neck. For two pins he'd give her the baby and leave her to it but he couldn't do that, could he? They wouldn't let her do this alone and if she had a complete stranger watching, the chances of this going well might be greatly diminished.

So, instead, he smiled. 'You look like a Madonna,' he told her. 'You ready?'

'Mmm.'

Max had to position Mouse and that inevitably meant that his hands had to touch her breasts. He tried to ignore the awareness. The odd tingle it gave him deep in his gut. At least it didn't take long and then he could step back and simply observe. Be there in case Ellie needed rescuing.

It seemed to be going well. The baby stopped even snuffling as it lay there against its mother's skin. Ellie stroked her gently down the middle of her back and then raised her hand slowly to repeat the motion. Again and again.

So softly. Her fingers tracing a miniature spine. The movement had to be soothing.

It was certainly soothing Max.

Mouse was moving now, pulling her little legs up and then pushing them down again.

'Do you think she needs a blanket?' Ellie spoke in a whisper.

'It's pretty warm in here. See how she goes.'

The baby had looked up at the sound of Ellie's voice.

'She's watching me.' There was wonder in the whisper now.

Max watched Mouse. He saw her put her hands up to her mouth and then fling an arm sideways to make contact with a breast. She started to move her head from side to side, rubbing her nose on Ellie's skin the way she had been doing on Max's shirt not so long ago.

He opened his mouth to make an encouraging comment but then shut it again. He didn't want to break whatever magic was happening here. Voices and other noises from beyond the door faded into irrelevance and there was a silence in this room that had a very different feel to it. Both Max and Ellie were watching the baby, totally caught up in something they had no need to interfere with. Something primaeval and instinctive.

Something very wonderful.

Mouse was bobbing her head now. Then she

stretched her neck and her whole head jerked so that it landed on top of Ellie's breast. With a tiny gasp, Ellie moved her hands to support the baby who had opened her mouth to poke out her tongue and lick the skin right beside a nipple.

Max held his breath. He could swear his heart stopped in that final moment when the baby's mouth closed over Ellie's nipple. And then he could hear the sound of sucking. When a tiny hand came up and pressed against the pale skin of Ellie's breast, he actually had to swallow past a constriction in his throat that felt horribly like tears were not far away.

Ellie looked up then and she had tears she wasn't bothering to swallow away. They rolled down her cheeks and her eyes shone with more of them but Max had never seen such an expression of joy in anyone's face. He couldn't look away. Couldn't swallow quite hard enough either but it didn't seem to matter that his own eyes got so wet.

This was a moment he would remember for the rest of his life. This joy. This connection. Between Ellie and her baby. Between Ellie and himself.

It made everything that had happened in this crazy week worthwhile because if he hadn't pretended to be the father of this baby, he wouldn't be here right now. He wouldn't have witnessed that little miracle of nature.

He and Ellie had shared the magic. No one else could be part of it or even begin to understand it. It was Ellie who finally broke that eye contact and he could sense what an effort it had taken. She looked down again. So did Max.

And there was Mouse. Sucking blissfully and staring up at her mother. Ellie wouldn't look up at him again. Max knew what it felt like to be caught in *that* gaze. He could blink away the moisture in his eyes now. Take a deep breath and let it out very slowly. He could even smile.

His work was done.

CHAPTER FIVE

'HAPPY birthday, dear Mouse… Happy birthday to you.'

Ellie was laughing. 'She's only a week old!'

Max was holding a bunch of rainbow-hued balloons. He tied them to the doorhandle and then ducked outside the room again. Ellie's jaw dropped when he returned moments later with his arms overflowing with parcels. He put them on the end of her bed where there was plenty of room because Ellie was sitting cross-legged, her back against her pillows and her baby in her arms, seemingly engrossed in being fed.

'Max…what have you *done*?'

The intent look she received from those dark eyes was out of kilter with the satisfied smile that was fading a little.

'You didn't have a whole lot of baby stuff ready, did you?'

'No.' Ellie bit her lip. 'I thought I had plenty of time and…and I had other things on my mind.'

The smile brightened again. 'I thought as much. And they're talking about letting you guys escape so I thought you'd need a few things to start you off.'

'Oh…Max…' It was embarrassing how easily tears came to her eyes these days. Ellie had never been one to cry much. 'As if you haven't done enough for us already.'

Max shrugged. He stepped closer and peered down at the baby. 'Is she done? Looks like she's asleep.'

'She is.' Ellie slipped her little finger into the corner of the tiny mouth to break any remaining suction. It also exposed her nipple to Max but any embarrassment over something like this had long since vanished. It had probably evaporated that very first time, in fact, when they had shared that amazing experience of Mouse finding Ellie's breast by herself.

'Maybe I could hold her for a bit, while you open her presents.'

'OK.' Max was the one person in the world that Ellie could hand her baby to without a qualm. He took Mouse and positioned her upright against his shoulder and he began rubbing her back gently.

Ellie opened a parcel to find a selection of tiny stretch suits in pink and yellow and the palest green. Another had tiny singlets and hats and one was full of bootees, including a soft yellow pair that looked like ducks. There were toys. Rattles and small, stuffed animals and a brightly coloured play rug. Sleep suits that buttoned up like tiny sleeping bags at the bottom and even a dress that was a smocked white affair with a scattering of exquisite, embroidered flowers and a matching bonnet.

Ellie had to blink back tears yet again as she held it up. 'It's *gorgeous*.'

'I know it's probably a bit big but, hey…she's growing pretty fast.'

'Max…I don't know what to say.'

Mouse did. She gave an impressively large burp that made both Ellie and Max laugh and broke the potentially awkward moment.

Except that she had caught his gaze as they laughed and the eye contact held and became something else. Something huge that squeezed Ellie's heart so hard it was painful. It was Max who looked away first and she hurriedly dropped her own gaze and bit her bottom lip as the silence took on a heavier feel.

Max cleared his throat. 'I've been thinking,' he said.

'About?'

'You.'

Ellie's heart gave another squeeze and it was a noticeable effort to draw a breath.

'And Mouse, here.' Max had tilted his head so that his chin was touching the top of the baby's head.

'I know. I really have to decide on a proper name.' For some reason Ellie was feeling nervous now. What was Max about to say? Give her some last advice before disappearing from their lives? 'I'm thinking maybe Amelia? Or…or Charlotte?'

He frowned. 'Definitely not Amelia though I'm sure Jet would approve.'

'Why?'

'You know, Amelia Earhart? The famous female pilot?'

'Oh…' Jet had been up to visit once in the last few

days and Ellie had had the impression he didn't approve of her at all.

'I wouldn't be in a hurry,' Max said. 'The longer it takes the better, really.'

'Why?'

'Because if you can't think of the right name, you won't be able to register the birth and the longer you leave that the better.'

'Mmm. I've been thinking about that myself. I'll have to use her real surname for that and if Marcus found me because I bought a plane ticket, he might well be able to trace that.'

'Especially seeing as he had an idea of when the baby's due.' Max smiled at Ellie. 'Good thinking, having her a few weeks early. Gives you a bit of time to play with.'

'Except that I'll be registering her birth at about the time she was really due.'

Max nodded but he wasn't meeting Ellie's gaze. 'What if you could legally register her as McAdam?'

'You mean, change my name by deed poll or something?'

'No.' Max turned his head and his gaze locked with hers. 'I mean I could marry you.'

The world stopped turning for a heartbeat. Ellie had to close her eyes and then open them very slowly just to make sure she hadn't fallen into some parallel universe.

'Did…um…did you just say you could *marry* me?'

'Yep.'

'So that Mouse could have your name?'

'And you. You need a new name, too. It's not as if

I'd be giving away anything I couldn't still keep myself as well. The perfect gift, if you put it like that.'

'Apart from ruining your single status.' Ellie's breath came out in a huff of laughter. 'I've seen the way the nurses around here look at you, Max. There's more than a few disappointed by your *pretend* marriage. A real one might take a lot more explaining.'

'Hey, am I complaining?' Max flashed her a grin. 'To tell the truth, I'm quite glad of an opportunity to be unavailable. Could be the making of me, being celibate for a while.'

'A while? That's like a piece of string, isn't it? How long were you thinking?'

Max looked serious again. 'As long as it takes, just like the string. How long do you think it will take you to settle into motherhood? Find a place you want to be and get your life on track?'

Ellie was silent. The future was huge and blank. The only goal she could focus on was to look after her daughter and keep her safe.

'Six months?' Max prompted. 'A year, maybe?'

Still Ellie said nothing.

'Think of it like an insurance policy,' Max suggested. 'Think *about* it, anyway. The offer's there and I don't offer anything I'm not prepared to follow through.' He got to his feet and Ellie watched his hands as he shifted Mouse. One hand was under her small bottom and the other cradled her head to protect her neck. He moved her so gently she didn't stir in her sleep. 'I have to go,' Max said quietly. 'I'll leave you with the birthday girl but I'll be back later. We can talk about it when you've had a chance to think.'

Left alone, Ellie unwound her legs and climbed very carefully off her bed. She should put Mouse back into her crib to sleep but, instead, she found herself walking slowly around her room.

Thinking hard.

'You did *what*?'

The CT scan technician glanced sharply sideways at the two doctors standing in front of the screens that were about to show images of their patient's head and neck.

'We're almost good to go,' she said nervously. 'I'll just check on Stephen.' She ducked behind the glass screen to where two nurses were preparing a teenaged boy for the scan.

'I suggested that Ellie married me,' Max repeated patiently. 'It's no big deal.'

'Are you *kidding*? It's a huge deal. *Marriage?*'

'Keep your voice down. I'm supposed to be married to her already, remember? This would just make it legal as far as the paperwork goes. I'm talking name only. Ellie needs a new name. The mouse needs a name. I'm trying to make sure the poor kid doesn't end up being a "Jones".'

For once, Rick wasn't smiling. 'I suppose you're planning to put your moniker on the birth certificate, too?'

Max shrugged. 'I've gone this far. What's the harm in going a bit further?'

Rick whistled silently. 'The kid is going to grow up thinking that you *are* her biological father.'

'Not necessarily. I'm sure Ellie will tell her the truth

when she's old enough to understand. It's not as though she'll remember me. I'm talking about a limited time, here. A few months maybe and then we'll get a quiet divorce. No harm done.'

'And fifteen years down the track? When a teenager you've forgotten about turns up on your doorstep because nobody got round to telling her the truth? What then?'

Max was silent for a moment. He wouldn't have forgotten about Mouse. No way. Rick cleared his throat as a prompt. '*I'll* tell her the truth.'

'Don't forget to tell your wife and the three kids of your own you'll probably have by then. Might throw a bit of a dampener on a peaceful evening at home otherwise.'

'I won't have a wife and three kids.' He could sound quite confident about that. Was it because the prospect was distinctly uninviting? An as-yet-unknown woman. Babies. Good grief, he'd been through more than enough in the last week to put him off babies for a very long time. Quite possibly for ever.

'What if it turns up with an adoptive mother?' Rick continued relentlessly. 'Like that Sarah who had your apartment? And they're there because you're the last hope to save the kid who desperately needs a bone marrow–transplant or a kidney or a bit of liver? How are you going to feel then? I'll tell you, mate. You'll feel like crap. Like you made a very big mistake a very long time ago.'

Max sighed. 'If you thought the worst-case scenario was going to happen you'd never do anything in life.' He wanted to change the subject. 'Like that kid in there. Stephen. He wouldn't have even started playing ice-hockey if he'd thought about getting tripped up and head-slammed into a wall.'

Rick gave a huff of laughter. 'Your logic's flawed. You're supporting my side of the argument, here.'

Max ignored him. He looked at the technician who was still sending anxious glances towards the windows he and Rick stood behind. He pressed the microphone button. 'Good to go in there?'

She nodded and started the scanner. The bed began to move slowly into the mouth of the huge machine.

'We'll be right here, Steve,' Max heard her say reassuringly. 'Keep as still as you possibly can.'

A nurse ushered Stephen's frightened mother away. 'He'll be fine,' she was saying. 'It won't take long and his doctor's right here to watch him. He's got an expert from Neurosurgery to check the results as well. Try not to worry.'

The scanner whirred and clicked as it set itself into the programmed position to begin the scan. Rick's attention was on the patient file in front of him.

'Knocked out cold for approximately thirty seconds,' he read aloud. 'Retrograde amnesia, headache, repetitive speech and nausea. Sounds like a good going concussion.'

'Let's hope that's all it is,' Max said quietly.

'You've ruled out a C-spine injury?'

'X-ray looked OK. I wanted something a bit more definitive. Same with the brain injury. Watch and wait didn't feel right.'

'Gut feeling, huh?'

'Yeah.'

Just like his gut feeling that doing something extra was needed to protect Ellie and the baby. He knew it was crazy, dammit. He didn't need Rick chewing his ear off about it and heaven help him when Jet found out. He'd had second thoughts himself but if he'd learned anything in all his years of dealing with emergencies it was to listen to that gut instinct.

Sometimes, it saved lives.

Images began appearing slowly. Black and white maps of the interior of Stephen's body. So far, things were looking good. Maybe, this time, his gut feeling had been wrong.

'C-spine looks fine,' Rick pronounced.

'Mmm.' Just the brain to check now.

'Isn't Ellie due for discharge soon?' Rick asked as they waited for new images to appear.

The technician was seated at the far end of this bench under the windows and Rick was talking quietly enough.

'Yeah,' Max confirmed. 'Probably tomorrow.'

'Where's she going to go?'

The scanner was making enough noise to cover his response. 'It would look a bit weird if she didn't come home with me,' Max muttered. 'I've trumpeted the fact I'm involved, here. Anyway—' he knew he sounded defensive now '—I've got a spare room. It's no big deal.'

'You'll be living with her. She might find she likes it.'

Max said nothing. He thought about having company in his apartment. About coming home from work and finding Ellie and the mouse there. It wasn't beyond the realms of possibility that he might quite like it himself. For a while, anyway. Wasn't a change supposed to be as good as a holiday?

'What if…?' Rick leaned closer. 'She decides she might like to be a *real* wife?'

'Not going to happen.'

'You mean you could live in the same house as an attractive woman and not take advantage of the situation?'

Max tried to shut down the mental picture of Ellie sitting on the bed that day, naked to the waist. He'd known the gut feeling he'd experienced then had been highly inappropriate. It was worse now. For God's sake, Ellie had just had a baby. Maybe the last time she'd been with a man had been when she'd been raped. This was sick.

And yet it hit him with all the force of a kick from a small mule. Suddenly Max was angry. With himself. With the situation he found himself in. Most of all, with the bastard who'd done this to someone like Ellie in the first place.

'Of course I can,' he hissed at Rick. Couldn't his friend see how far he was going in order to protect her? Suggesting he might try something that had the potential to hurt her was an insult.

'Hmm.' Rick was staring at the screens again. 'Good luck with that, mate.' His tone was distracted and Max focused on what his colleague was seeing. He knew the significance even before another one of Rick's silent whistles. 'Look at that. Your gut's on the money again. Subdural bleed…right there, see?'

Max could indeed. 'And another one there. Look.

It's a coup-contrecoup injury.' The brain had bounced in the skull on impact and created an area of damage at both the front and back. 'Guess I'll be handing him over to your team, then.'

Rick nodded, still studying the images, any personal exchanges forgotten. 'Could well be heading for surgery. Good call, Max.'

Yes. Sometimes listening to that gut instinct could save lives.

What was Ellie's instinct telling *her* in regard to whether or not to take up his offer?

Would she say yes?

As crazy as it was, Max hoped she would. He just knew—for the same kind of inexplicable reasons that had made him insist on further investigations for his patient—that it was the right thing to do.

For everybody.

Had he been serious?

Marriage?

Ellie had no reason to think Max hadn't been serious given that he'd already claimed paternity of her daughter and given her the pretence of being his wife for the last week.

But this was huge. This would mean going through at least some form of a wedding ceremony with him to make it legal.

And that was wrong. Just so wrong.

She would say no, of course. He might be hugely relieved but he might ask her why not and what could she say to that?

That the offer was too over the top? Amazing? *Perfect?*

Except it wasn't and that was the problem. He wasn't talking about anything like a real marriage here. He was offering her the gift of his name so that she would be legally entitled to use it. It was an abuse of what marriage was and that cut too deeply to be acceptable to Ellie.

She'd grown up with a single mother and had dreamed of being part of a 'real' family for her entire life. It wasn't that she'd had an unhappy childhood, it was just that she had seen what others had had and had known there was something missing. And then she'd been given a stepfather when she'd been ten years old. He'd been willing enough to take on someone else's child but the truth that there was never any real connection there had become blindingly obvious when they'd had their own child a couple of years later. Despite her mother doing her best to ensure she was an integral part of the household, Ellie had always felt she was on the outside, looking in on a real family.

At some point in her teenage years, childish fantasies of her real father turning up in her life had been abandoned in favour of her making her own family one day. Finding a man she could love with all her heart who loved her just as much. Having their own children. A home that was a *family* home. Full of laughter and love and the occasional smell of baking. A dog and maybe some hens out the back so she could collect her own eggs for that baking.

OK, so she'd messed up on part of it and the man who was the father of her baby was totally wrong but that didn't mean it had to be completely over, did it? She could make a home for her child. She could have the dog and even the hens, dammit. And one day she might find a man who would love her *and* her child. He would offer marriage and become a part of her family. Having to explain that she'd become pregnant by a man she didn't love would be bad enough. Telling him that she'd married the first time in name only would be even more shameful.

It would belittle something that meant the world to Ellie. Make a mockery of her accepting a proposal and saying vows that included 'till death us do part'. She couldn't…*wouldn't* do it.

Was it fate that made Max appear at the very instant she knew why she couldn't possibly accept his offer?

'Hey…how's it going?'

Ellie smiled. 'All good. Very quiet. Mouse has been asleep for hours and I've been enjoying the view. I love how hilly Dunedin is.'

'It's a nice little town. I haven't been here that long myself but I'm getting to know it. It's a good place to live.'

'Mmm.' Ellie was trying to find the right way to tell him that she wasn't going to be living here.

'I went past the office and had a chat to your nurse. Looks like you'll get the all-clear for discharge after rounds tomorrow morning. You can get out of here and go home.'

Ellie stared at Max.

Go home?

Where was that, exactly?

Most of her belongings were in storage in Wellington

and all she'd come here with had been an overnight bag
and her passport. If that became known it would ring
alarm bells for the medical staff for sure. The kind of
alarms that would set wheels in motion. Social service
type wheels because they couldn't let a mother who
was only just on her feet after a life-threatening event
go off and provide sole care for a newborn baby.

And if she got sucked into that system there would
be no hiding her real identity. Marcus would be able to
trace her in a flash. He would turn up and she would
be weak and vulnerable and wouldn't have Max or his
friends to stand up for her. She could go further north
to the town where her mother and stepfather were but
they had a small house, two teenage boys and their
own worries. Ellie hadn't even told them she was pregnant. Turning up on their doorstep with a baby was an
option that was definitely a very last resort.

Max was watching her. 'You're going to need help
for a while yet, Ellie. You know that, don't you?'

Ellie nodded. 'I don't expect you to provide it, Max.
I've got to start standing on my own two feet. This is
my fault, because I didn't plan ahead. I was so busy
taking it all one day at a time and relying on some airy-
fairy plan that I would go and start a new life in a new
place.'

'You can still do that. Just not tomorrow.'

The small squeak from the crib was a welcome
distraction from having to face a reality that had
very scary blank patches. Ellie reached into the crib
and gathered her daughter into her arms, holding her
close enough to bury her face against her body for a
moment.

The rush of love she felt for this tiny creature was enough to bring tears to her eyes and feed a seed of determination. She had someone more important than herself to think about now. Someone she loved who would love her back. As she carried the baby to the towel on the bed in preparation to change her nappy, Ellie had a moment of clarity that was as welcome as the distraction had been.

It didn't matter that Marcus was her father. Maybe she would even thank him one day for being responsible for this incredible gift. Max had been right. Anything negative on the paternal side had most likely been due to nurture, not nature. This little girl was going to be brought up with the kind of love that would make her into a person Ellie knew she would be very, very proud of.

She was already. Taking hold of two tiny hands, Ellie bent to kiss her baby.

'Isn't she beautiful?'

'Yeah.' The word was gruff. Not that Ellie looked but she wouldn't have been surprised if Max had glanced over his shoulder to make sure no one overheard.

Not that she was fooled. He might have tried to hide it over the last few days, with that casual dropping in to see how things were going, but Ellie hadn't missed the sidelong glances into the crib or at the bundle in her arms. He might shrug as though it was unimportant when he was offered a cuddle but she hadn't seen him refuse one yet. And there'd been that time when Mouse had been crying and crying and Max had turned up and taken her and she'd snuggled in to his chest and settled.

There'd been more than satisfaction in the look Max had bestowed on the baby he'd held and the look had gone on for long enough for Ellie to recognise it as the kind of connection she had found in breastfeeding. And what about that shower of gifts for her one-week birthday this morning? She was wearing one of the tiny stretch suits now and Ellie eased the small legs out, bending again to kiss a miniature foot.

She hadn't known Max very long at all but she owed him her life and the chance to start again properly and she loved him for that along with everything he'd done since then. As a friend. She wasn't *in* love with him.

But she *could* be. Heavens, this was turning into a series of revelations. Was it just that she was well on the road to recovery now and her brain was waking up? Yes. It would all be all too easy to fall in love with Max McAdam and what would that get her? A broken heart, that's what.

She'd seen the way women looked at him and knew why they looked that way. He was gorgeous and successful and she knew better than any of them how kind he was. He could have anyone he chose so why on earth would he be interested in someone as ordinary as her? Someone with someone else's child in tow, what's more, and she knew better than most what kind of heartache that could result in.

She didn't dare look at him for a minute. Just in case she found herself looking for something it would be very unwise to look for. Like the possibility that she was wrong. That there might be a scrap of hope that he *could* be interested. She needed a new distraction.

'She really does need a proper name,' she said, rolling up the dirty nappy to discard.

'That's what I came to talk to you about.'

Oh, help. As if she could get her head around explaining why she wasn't going to accept his offer of marriage when she was trying to suppress the knowledge of how easy it would be to fall in love with this man.

'I meant a first name. Can't see myself enrolling her at school as Mouse.' Ellie tried to make light of changing the subject. Cleaning the small bottom in front of her was helping. 'It needs to be a special name, though.'

'What's your mother's name?'

'Joan.'

'Oh…' Max was watching as she put a clean nappy in place. 'That doesn't sound right.'

'No.'

'How 'bout your grandmother?'

'Beatrice.'

'That's not so bad.'

'Except that she disowned my mother when she became an unmarried mother.'

'Oh.' Was he going to make a comment about history repeating itself? Ellie hoped not. 'There must be someone that's special. A name that you'd like to honour?'

Ellie looked up. 'Yes.' Her heart gave an odd little flip. 'You're right. There is. Someone I have no idea how to thank.' She smiled at him. 'I'm going to call her…Maxine.'

The look on his face was priceless. 'Are you *kidding* me? No. You can't do that. It's totally wrong for her.'

Ellie had picked up Mouse again. 'Maybe I was kidding about the name but I wasn't joking about having no idea how to thank you.' Suddenly the words fell into place easily. 'You've done so much for us, Max, and I can't believe you offered to marry me. I really appreciate the offer but I can't do it. It's...' He'd even given her words to borrow. 'Totally wrong.'

'But what are you going to do tomorrow?'

'Find a motel, I guess. Just for a week or two until I've got myself sorted out properly.'

Max shook his head. 'No way. You're not a hundred per cent yourself. I won't let you do that.'

'This is my life, Max,' Ellie said gently. 'My responsibility. You can't stop me doing what I want to do.'

'Wanna bet?' Max could feel himself scowling at her. 'I'm a consultant on staff here. You think they won't listen to me when I tell them you have nowhere to go that's suitable for a convalescent mother and a neonate?'

Ellie was biting her bottom lip. Mouse was rubbing her nose against her T-shirt and making noises that emphasised her need for some dinner.

'I'll have to go to my mum's, then.'

'And where's that?'

'A little town near the bottom of the Coromandel peninsula. Couple of hours by bus from the airport.'

Max shook his head. 'You can't travel that far yet. You've had adult respiratory distress syndrome, Ellie. Your lungs still need time to recover properly. Flying anywhere is out of the question.' He wasn't sure it was contraindicated but delivered in such a decisive tone, it certainly sounded plausible and it should work as a means of preventing Ellie just getting on a plane and vanishing from his life.

What are you doing? The small voice in his head sounded astonished. Wasn't this the perfect way out? He could almost hear Rick and Jet applauding the voice but Max was determined to argue. She wasn't going to marry him and that was fine. Oddly disappointing but probably for the best given the kind of potential unseen complications Rick had enlightened him with. But to just vanish into nowhere? Not acceptable because… because…

'How did Marcus trace your whereabouts last time?'

Ellie went pale. 'OK. No flying, then. I'll get a car. I've got enough money saved to keep us going for a while.'

'A three-day journey with a week-old baby? For goodness' sake, Ellie, what are you trying to prove? I've got a spare room and it's no big deal.' Max stalked towards the window and then turned, rubbing his forehead as he took a quick glance at the closed door. 'Look…I've gone out on a limb here and everybody thinks I'm your husband. That I'm Mouse's father. How's it going to look if word gets out that you don't come home with me? That this has all been some kind of fraud?'

Ellie was backing away from him, Mouse in her arms. She sank into the armchair beside the bed and for a long minute, as she arranged her clothing to put her baby to her breast, there was nothing but the hungry infant's cries. And then there was silence.

'I don't want people to know,' Ellie admitted quietly. 'I don't want questions being asked or…or social services or someone getting involved but…but I can't just come and stay with you, Max.'

'Why not?'

In the instant before Ellie averted her gaze, Max caught a flash of something.

Embarrassment, given the flush of colour in her cheeks now? No, that didn't make sense. She hadn't hesitated to start breastfeeding in front of him and why would she? They'd been through a far more intimate session that first time.

Something Rick had said rang in his head like a warning bell. Something about her wanting to be a 'real' wife. Oh…*hell*. Was Ellie attracted to him? That could certainly make things a bit awkward. He wanted to help, not set her up to get hurt. He wasn't offering to settle down and take on an instant family.

Perish the thought.

But he'd offered marriage.

What *had* he been thinking?

This was a mess. Max stared at Ellie's bent head, her hair falling like a screen to frame the baby, who was pushing on her breast with her little hand and staring up at her mother with a rapturous expression.

A warmth curled through Max. She was such a cute baby with her dark hair sticking up in spikes and eyes that still looked black. They'd got to know each other pretty well, him and the mouse. They were kangaroo buddies. And that gave him an idea.

'Ellie…we're friends, aren't we?'

She nodded. 'Of course. I owe you so much.' She looked up and her eyes shone with moisture. 'I'll never ever forget what you did for us.' Her smile was wobbly. 'A week ago you'd never met me. We don't know each other, really, do we? Not well enough to live together.'

They knew each other well enough, Max wanted to tell her. She knew he was looking out for them. He knew that she had been through a rough time and had the guts and determination to get through whatever life threw at her. But maybe she had a point. The offer of marriage had been misguided. Maybe living together, even temporarily, was also unwise.

'How 'bout a compromise, then?'

'Like what?'

'There's a motel about three doors down from my apartment block. I could give my address for discharge details and take you to a unit there. That way, you'd be independent but I could drop in a couple of times a day to make sure you were OK and I'd only be a phone call away if you had any problems.'

'Y-you'd do that?'

'Of course.' Max nodded slowly. 'Hey...I told you you were safe, remember? You're not. Yet. You will be, but if you go steaming off on your own right now and something happens to you, or Mouse, how do think that would make me feel?'

Just terrible, he answered for her silently. Never mind fifteen years down the track like Rick had warned. He didn't want to feel bad tomorrow, thanks very much.

Ellie held his gaze and seemed to read the correct

answer to his question. The tense lines in her face softened and she smiled.

'The motel would be perfect.'

CHAPTER SIX

THE motel was a long, long way from being perfect.

'I guess it's clean enough,' Max said, somewhat dubiously.

It was also completely without any character to give it warmth. Bland, white walls, grey carpet and tiles and no decoration other than a ghastly abstract print over the bed. There was a small couch, also grey, a television set and a kitchenette. An internal door opened to a bathroom that was as basic as the rest of the unit.

Max opened a cupboard beside a microwave oven. There was a single pair of everything. Two plates, two glasses, two cups and saucers. The cutlery drawer was just as sparsely furnished. He made a less than impressed sound.

'It's fine.' Ellie was sitting on the end of the bed, holding Mouse. She looked pale and tired and no wonder.

'I shouldn't have made you stop at the baby shop. You look done in.'

'I just need to sit quietly for a bit. And I needed to go shopping. I couldn't have managed without getting the crib and nappies and everything.' She smiled. 'I'm glad you brought your car. I had visions of me leaving the hospital on the back of your bike.'

Max gave a huff of laughter. 'As if! The bike's a toy since I grew up a bit. I'll go and get the rest of the stuff.'

He went through the sliding glass door to where his SUV was parked directly outside. He had requested a unit near the manager's office for Ellie so that she had help nearby if needed it but also for security. Maybe it was better that she was here even if it lacked a little in material comforts. Marcus Jones knew where his apartment was and if Ellie was there, she'd be alone a lot of the time while he was at work. At least here she had the manager in residence and other patrons who would be coming and going.

It was just a shame it seemed so much more second rate in the daylight. He hadn't noticed how much traffic noise you could hear from the main road last night, either. Still…safety was paramount. He pulled the large, basket-style bassinette from the back of the car, throwing in the packs of disposable nappies and other purchases. A door slammed overhead and then a man's angry voice drowned out the traffic noise.

'Don't blame me, woman.'

'Don't blame *you*?' The female voice was shrill. 'It's *your* fault I'm stuck in this scummy motel with three kids. It was you and your drunken mates that got us evicted. It was you and your noise that made the neighbours complain.'

'*My* noise?' Max looked up in time to see the man kick the wall of the upstairs unit. 'Can you hear *yourself*, you stupid cow?'

From somewhere behind the woman came the cry of a frightened child. The man swore loudly and turned his head, to see Max looking up.

'What are *you* looking at?'

Max simply stared back, saying nothing. He noted the tattoos and the piercings. The hunted expression on the face of a man who was far too young to have three children and housing problems. With another oath, the angry man took off, heading for the metal stairway at the end of the block.

'If you're going to the pub,' the woman yelled after him, 'don't bother coming back, you hear me?'

Max took the bassinette inside. Ellie had heard her, judging by the flicker of dismay in her eyes.

'You sure you want to stay here?'

She nodded. She even smiled. 'It's only for a week or two. I've coped with worse.'

Good grief, she was a determined soul and good on her. She'd need her courage and determination to be a good single mum and she would be good, Max was quite confident of that. She would be the best and Mouse was a lucky kid. He made one more trip to the car to get Ellie's bag.

'And you're sure you don't want the daily midwife visits? I'm not sure we did the right thing saying they weren't needed.'

'It would have been a bit tricky to have her visit the motel when you put your address down for me on the discharge papers.'

'Hmm. I forgot to tell you I registered you here under my name, too. I told the manager you were my sister.' Max was still bothered by the dismissal of the home visits most new mothers relied on. It was supposed to be getting less complicated to maintain the deception now that Ellie was back in the real world. He had to get rid of this gnawing sense of responsibility.

'How will you know if Mouse is getting enough milk without her getting weighed every day?'

'She won't sleep if she's hungry. I've got the bottles and formula if I need it and I've got the outpatient appointments for us both in two days. We'll be fine, Max, honestly.'

'Well, I'm only a phone call away, don't forget. I'll be working for the next few days to make up for the time I took off last week but it's day shift. I'll pop in on my way to work if it's not too early for you and I'll come again on my way home. I can bring you some takeaways so you don't have to worry about cooking.'

'You don't—'

Max overrode her intended objection. 'What kind of food do you like? Chinese? Indian? Burgers?'

Ellie conceded defeat graciously, with a shy smile. 'Fish and chips. I haven't had any for ages.'

'There's a little shopping centre just round the corner on the main road. About five minutes' walk, I guess. It's got milk and bread and all the basic stuff. Make a list and I can run down and get the things you might need for the rest of today.'

Ellie wasn't about to agree to any more assistance. 'A five-minute walk won't be a problem. I'll get sorted here and have a rest and then I'll try out that baby sling I bought and take Mouse for her first outing.'

It was ridiculous to feel like he was being excluded from something important. What did he want? To accompany Ellie and Mouse to the shops so that people would think it was his baby? So he could feel some kind of fatherly pride?

This had to stop.

'I'd better get back to work. My couple of hours' cover for this morning has about run out. Text me if you need anything other than fish and chips when I'm on the way home. You've got my mobile number?'

'Yes.' Ellie was smiling again. 'Go, Max. You're needed at work.'

Meaning he wasn't needed here?

This was good. One step closer to discharging the responsibility he'd taken on when Ellie had stepped into his life.

Max went. Quickly. Before he had time to register any more inappropriate reactions let alone try to analyse them.

Ellie watched the SUV pull away, leaving the space in front of her unit empty.

It felt empty inside, too. She was alone with her baby. Really alone this time. No bell to push to summon assistance. No medical staff walking past her door at frequent intervals or the familiar, safe sounds of a busy hospital.

Max would be back later, though, and Ellie was determined to show him how well she could cope. That she was worth the effort he'd already put in to helping her.

For the next few hours, Ellie coped very well. She arranged her things in the unit, which made it feel more like her own space. She made up the bassinette with the cute sheets that had little, yellow ducks embroidered on the edges. She arranged baby clothes in a drawer and positioned nappies and wipes beside the padded change mat. When Mouse woke up, she fed and then washed her, putting her into a new set of her birthday clothes. She took her daughter around the unit, telling her about every item of furniture and what grown-ups used them for and when she fell asleep again, she was happy to go into her new bassinette and Ellie flopped onto the big bed and slept deeply for some time herself.

She was woken by the sound of a television set coming on loudly next door. For a moment, she lay totally bemused by where she was and desperately wanting to simply roll over and go back to sleep but then she remembered and staggered into the bathroom to splash water on her face, hoping to wake herself up properly before Mouse needed attention or, worse, Max turned up with dinner.

The cold water didn't seem to help much. Ellie's legs felt like lead, her eyes were gritty and her brain distinctly foggy still. She pushed damp strands of her fringe out of her eyes as she dried her face. She was well overdue for a haircut. Maybe she should just chop it all off because finding the energy to brush it right now was just too hard. Dropping the towel, Ellie raised her gaze wearily to the mirror to consider the option.

Oh…Lord, she looked *awful*.

She'd lost a lot more weight than she should have by giving birth, thanks to being so ill for several days. Her face looked pale and pinched. Her hair was lank and the oversized sweatshirt that had been useful in helping disguise her pregnancy was totally swamping her now. She looked like a street kid. A homeless person. About as far from a competent new mother as it would be possible to look. It was a pathetic picture and, for a long moment, Ellie was swamped by more than the sweatshirt.

She *was* homeless. The future was a chasm of the unknown. She wasn't even here under her own name and she couldn't afford not to hide her existence. Until she escaped the country she was going to be afraid of discovery. Terrified of Marcus tracking her down. Of something happening that might separate her from her precious baby.

A door slammed upstairs and the sound of angry pounding began again. The wail of a siren could be heard from the main road advertising the urgency of some emergency situation. The tension was contagious. In a sudden panic, Ellie dashed from the bathroom. How could she have left Mouse unattended, even for a moment? Had she even locked the sliding door before she fell asleep?

Her heart pounding, she stood by the bassinette and looked down at the peaceful, innocent face of the sleeping baby. She had to fight the urge to snatch Mouse up into her arms so she hugged herself tightly instead.

Huge, hot, painful tears rolled down her face.

She wanted to be somewhere else. She wanted to feel healthy and full of energy. She wanted, more than anything, just to feel *safe*. To know that her baby was safe.

She wanted…Max.

Nothing felt this bad when he was close. He gave

her strength. Made her feel…too much. Alive. Optimistic. *Safe*.

As if to underline the difference in the space she was in without Max, the noise overhead increased. There were crashing noises, an ominous moment of silence and then a cry of pain. A moment later, simultaneously, came a woman's scream and a large, dark shape hurtled down past Ellie's glass door.

The screaming continued but, by some miracle, it wasn't waking Mouse. Ellie ran to make sure her door was locked but, when she tugged the net curtain aside to expose the doorhandle, she gasped in horror.

The dark shape hadn't been a piece of furniture being tipped over the balcony, as she'd assumed. Sprawled exactly where Max had parked his car earlier was the body of a man, one jeans-clad leg at an awkward angle and a heavily tattooed arm bent under his head. Ellie could see the manager running from the motel office. The older man stopped and stared, his jaw sagging. The woman upstairs was still screaming.

The scene looked frozen. The man on the ground wasn't moving. Neither was the motel manager. Ellie yanked her door open.

'Call an ambulance,' she shouted at the manager. 'And the police.'

'*No-o-o…*' The screaming upstairs morphed into words. 'It was an *accident*. I didn't mean to… Oh, my God…*Nigel…*' Ellie heard the footsteps of the woman as she ran along the balcony to the stairs, sobbing now. 'You're not dead. Please don't be dead…'

Was he dead? Ellie's blood ran cold. She didn't want to be here with her innocent child with a dead man outside their door. The motel manager had vanished back into his office, presumably to call the emergency services. Other people were emerging from their units but they all looked unsure of what they should do. Maybe she was the only person here who had any medical training.

With a desperate glance at her sleeping baby for another heartbeat, Ellie stepped through her door and pulled it closed behind her. The least she could do was make sure the man had a patent airway and to keep his C-spine protected for the few minutes it might take for an ambulance to arrive.

'Hello…' She crouched beside the sprawled figure and touched his shoulder. 'Can you hear me?'

She hadn't expected a response. Falling from the second floor onto concrete was a recipe for a severe head injury and spinal trauma, if not instant death. Carefully, she tilted his chin just far enough to ensure his airway was open and then she bent, her cheek close to his mouth to feel for a puff of breath, her fingers on his neck to feel for a pulse and her eyes watching for any chest movement.

The woman was beside her now, sobbing uncontrollably as she dropped to her knees.

'Don't touch him,' Ellie warned. 'We don't want to move him in case he's got spinal injuries.'

'He's dead,' the woman sobbed. 'I killed him. Oh… God…'

'He's not dead. He's breathing quite well and he's got a good pulse.' She looked up at the gathering crowd. 'Can someone find a blanket, please? And maybe some towels? And check that an ambulance is on the way.'

'It's coming.' The motel manager appeared again. 'They'll be here as soon as they can.'

'Good. Can you put your hands on his head, like this…?' Ellie showed him how to support the man's neck. 'Keep him as still as you can. When we get a towel I'll make a padding to help. I'm going to check for any bleeding.'

Someone ran towards them with a pile of towels and some plastic shopping bags.

'I couldn't find any gloves,' the middle-aged woman said breathlessly, 'but I did a first-aid course and they said bags were good.'

'Thanks.' The word was heartfelt. Ellie hadn't thought enough about her own safety. She put bags over her hands and a heartbeat later one was covered in blood. The man was bleeding heavily from a wound on the underside of his arm. Ellie turned the limb and a spurt of blood from a large laceration made it obvious an artery was involved. She covered the wound with her hand and pressed down hard. The rest of her survey would have to be visual. She couldn't see any more blood but there was an obvious, open fracture to his ankle. She needed something to cover it to help prevent infection. The man needed covering as well. If he was going into shock he needed to be kept warm.

'How did it happen?' someone was asking in a hor-rified tone.

'I saw him having another fight with his missus,' an-other voice answered. 'She went at him with something and he kind of rolled over the balcony railing.'

'Probably a knife, by the look of that arm. Has someone called the cops?'

'They're on the way.' The motel manager sounded grim.

'They've got kids, haven't they? Maybe someone better check on the poor little blighters.'

The woman had buried her face in her hands and was rocking back and forth, crying hysterically.

'Mummy?' A frightened voice came from overhead. 'What are you doing? Darren's crying. He's scared…'

Ellie glanced up to see the terrified face of a small girl who was crouched down and peering through the railings. It was a stark reminder that there were children involved here. She couldn't afford to forget about her own child either. Mouse was due to wake up any time now and the thought of her being alone in the unit and crying for *her* mother was unbearable. But she couldn't leave. She had pressure on an arterial bleed and she couldn't let go.

The voices of the people surrounding her began to blur into a muttering that merged with the wailing of the distraught woman and the cries of the children upstairs. Ellie's fingers in the plastic bag slipped for an instant and a fresh well of blood appeared. It made her feel faint. Dizzy.

And then she felt a firm touch on her shoulder. She knew it was Max well before she heard his voice. She could feel his presence. Solid and commanding. The dizziness faded.

'Hang on for a tick,' he said, close to her ear. His voice rumbled into her body and she could feel the awful tension retreating. 'You're doing great. I've got gloves here in my pocket.' He was pulling them on as he spoke. 'OK. I've got this.'

He crouched right beside her, close enough for his thigh to be pressed against her hip. A solid rock of a man. His hand pushed hers aside as he slipped it into position to apply pressure to the wound.

'Arterial bleed?'

'Yes.'

'Head injury?'

'Presumably. He's been unresponsive since he fell.'

'Fell?' Max flicked a gaze upwards. 'Good grief… anything else you've noticed?'

'Compound fracture of his tib/fib. I haven't moved him to check his chest or abdomen because I was worried about his C-spine. Breathing was OK. I've been kind of stuck with this bleed…'

The sound of an approaching siren was abruptly cut off. Flashing blue and red lights appeared over the heads of the crowd of bystanders as the ambulance backed in past the motel office.

'Make some room,' someone yelled. 'The paramedics are here.'

Max caught Ellie's gaze. 'You OK?'

Ellie wasn't at all sure about her emotional state but he was probably asking about her physical shape. She nodded.

'And Mouse?'

He must have seen the flash of panic in her eyes. 'Go inside,' he directed, turning his gaze to the paramedics who were climbing out through the open back doors of the ambulance. One carried a large, soft backpack of gear. The other held an oxygen cylinder in one hand and a lifepack in the other. 'We'll take over now. Hey…' He obviously recognised the crew. 'Good to see you guys. This chap apparently took a tumble from the balcony up there. GCS of three and I'm sitting on an arterial bleed here.'

Ellie edged back as the paramedics moved in.

'Grab a collar,' one told the other. 'And a scoop stretcher.'

She slipped through her door, not pausing until she stood beside the bassinette. The light had faded fast while she'd been outside and she had to blink for a moment to readjust. Because it was quiet in here, she had assumed Mouse was still asleep but her heart skipped a beat when she realised that the baby was awake. Not crying but staring up at her mother. She could imagine she saw recognition in that intense gaze. Trust. She hadn't been afraid because she knew that the person who loved her the most was coming back.

Ellie swallowed hard. She found a smile. 'Everything's going to be OK,' she whispered. 'Max is here. Let me just give my hands a quick wash and then I'm going to pick you up and I'm not going to let you go, I promise.'

With Mouse in her arms a short time later, Ellie went to stand in her doorway to watch the ambulance crew working under the direction of the emergency department consultant. They had a collar in place and an oxygen mask covering the man's face. IV lines were in and the motel manager was holding a bag of fluid aloft. A pressure bandage was in place on the lacerated arm and a splint was being applied to the broken ankle.

The police were here as well. A female officer went upstairs to the children and another two officers were taking charge of the woman, who had stopped crying and now looked so stunned she was making no protest at being led away.

The scoop stretcher was made ready to use. The paramedics then adjusted the man's position slightly so that he was completely on his back with his spine correctly aligned. It wasn't quite dark out there yet so there was more than enough light to see what had been hidden on one side of the man's lower chest.

A knife handle was protruding. Had he been stabbed before he'd fallen or had he been holding the knife and fallen onto it? Either way it was shocking.

The paramedics went into action smoothly and swiftly. They made a doughnut-shaped padding to go around the impaled object and stabilise it.

'Let's load and go,' one of them ordered.

'I'll leave you to it. He's looking stable.' Max stepped back as they clipped the scoop stretcher into place on either side of the man. He looked up as they lifted it and his gaze went straight to Ellie, standing there with Mouse in her arms.

The crowd shifted as the stretcher was carried to the ambulance. People wanted to see the end of this drama with the ambulance departing, hopefully with its lights and sirens activated. The police cars would be going soon, too, taking the woman and children away.

Max didn't go with them. He stripped off his gloves and dropped them onto the considerable pile of wrappings and other debris the paramedics had left behind. Then he walked straight towards Ellie. His face was grim. So was his tone of voice.

'Pack your stuff,' he ordered. 'There's no way you're staying here. I'm taking you home.'

CHAPTER SEVEN

'SHE can't go.'

'Excuse me?' Max flicked his gaze up from where he was slotting the bassinette, stuffed full of baby clothes and nappies, into the back of his car.

'Your sister,' the motel manager said nervously. 'The police might want to talk to her again. She's their best witness.'

'She's already given them a statement. They can talk again later. Preferably tomorrow. We're only going to be just down the road. I gave you my address on the registration form.'

The manager looked bewildered. Things were happening in his establishment that were far more than he had any desire to cope with. Max took pity on him.

'I know it's a bit weird. She should have come home with me in the first place but she's kind of independent is my sister. Extremely capable but she likes to manage things on her own.' Not that she was putting up any kind of resistance to him having taken control for now. Ellie was sitting in the back seat of his car, with Mouse in the baby seat strapped in right beside her. She had to be listening to this exchange but she was sitting very still. Looking tense enough to snap at any moment.

Max didn't want any further delays. He smiled at the manager and lowered his voice. 'She doesn't really approve of me, you know? I like to ride motorbikes and have parties. Not the best environment for a new baby, is it?'

'N-no, I guess not.'

Max shut the back hatch of the SUV so that Ellie couldn't hear him. 'But this hasn't turned out to be a very good environment either, has it? I can't leave her somewhere where people get stabbed and thrown off balconies.'

'Nothing like this has ever happened before.' The manager was almost wringing his hands. 'All the police here…all that blood… They're putting up tape, did you see? In case that guy dies and it becomes a crime scene. What's *that* going to do to my business?'

Max had seen the tape. Luckily he'd moved so fast he'd got most of Ellie's possessions out of the unit before it became impossible to access the door. Now he needed to get her away from here. The last thing Ellie needed was the police asking too many questions. They would be wanting to talk to him at some stage and *he* needed to think about what he was going to tell them concerning his relationship with their chief witness.

Talk about weaving a tangled web of deception. The strands were winding themselves ever more tightly around him and it was getting hard to think straight. All Max could do was run on instinct and hope that it served him as well as it always had when it came to out-of-control situations. He wasn't at all sure that it had worked particularly well over the last week but he had no choice other than to continue to go with it. No way could he leave Ellie here to fend for herself. She was in a fragile state anyway and this nasty incident must have shaken her up badly.

Max ignored the manager's anxious fluttering around the back of his vehicle as he climbed into the driver's seat. He had to manoeuvre to get out through the extra police cars that had arrived on scene and a glance in his rear-view mirror showed the manager now talking animatedly to an officer, pointing at his departing car. He suppressed a sigh. How much time would they have before someone official came knocking at his door?

For a wild moment, Max considered driving right past his own address. Finding somewhere else to put Ellie and Mouse. Somewhere nobody could find them. The police *or* Marcus Jones. But then what? They'd be totally dependent on him, wouldn't they?

And why on earth did that ridiculous scenario hold some kind of strange appeal? It was crazy. This whole week had been crazy and by the time Max had formed that inescapable conclusion, he was outside his apartment.

'Here we are.'

The statement, admittedly uttered with some resignation, fell into silence. Max turned his head to find huge eyes in a very pale face.

'I'm really sorry, Max.' The apology was a whisper. 'I'm a lot of trouble, aren't I?'

Yes. She was. She and the mouse had turned his life completely upside down in the blink of an eye and the worst of it was that Max was still lying awake at night, haunted by what could have happened if he hadn't become involved. She'd got under his skin. Maybe it had happened in that first moment, when she'd stumbled into his arms and growled at him to let her go.

Or maybe it had been Mouse who'd really got under his skin. Seeped in, probably, which was hardly surprising when they'd spent so much time with their skins touching.

Whatever. He was in this up to his neck. He couldn't get out until that fierce Ellie appeared again. The one who would shove him away and growl at him in a brave stand for independence and autonomy. There wasn't a hint of fierceness in her face right now. Max could see fear and uncertainty. But when his gaze slid down and he saw her hand resting on the edge of the baby seat, holding a tiny hand in her fingers, he could see the bond between a mother and child. The love.

He could see the courage that came with that as a given.

And it was a gentle kind of fierce.

Max could only smile. A poignant tilt to his lips that felt nothing like any smile he'd ever produced in his life.

'Hey…' He moved his gaze back to Ellie's face. 'I like trouble. Keeps life interesting. They didn't call us the "bad boys" at school for nothing.'

He carried the baby seat into the apartment and then he ferried in the baby gear.

'Uh-oh…where's *your* bag, Ellie?'

'I must have left it behind. I was only grabbing baby stuff.'

'So you don't have a change of clothes or any-thing?'

'No.'

They both looked at what Ellie was wearing. The horrible, shapeless sweatshirt and jeans that looked five sizes too big. And then Max frowned.

'Your clothes are covered in blood.'

'Oh, my God…' Ellie stared down at her stained jeans. 'They're saturated. What if he had hepatitis? Or HIV?'

'Get them off,' Max said crisply. 'Get into the shower. Have a really good scrub. I'll throw these into the laundry and soak them in bleach. Check that you don't have any open wounds…on your legs, in particu-lar. Did you get any blood on your hands?'

'No. Someone gave me plastic bags.'

'That's right. I wondered what you were using when I arrived. That's good.' Max stepped towards the baby seat where the mouse was beginning to squeak. 'I'll look after her. The bathroom's just down the hall. First door on the left.'

'But she sounds hungry.'

'I'll give her a bottle. She's had them before, I don't think she'll mind.' Max didn't mind either, he real-ised. He had enjoyed those feeding times up in PICU. Missed them, almost.

'But—'

He raised his eyebrows at Ellie as if surprised by her insubordination. 'Shower, Ellie,' he ordered. 'For Mouse's protection as much as your own.'

Ellie gave an audible gulp. 'But…I won't have any clothes.'

'I'll find you something and leave it outside the bathroom door. Go on. There are clean towels in there and plenty of soap and shampoo so wash your hair as well. A thorough scrub from head to toe, got it? Decontamination.'

He had undone the safety belt around Mouse and was lifting her into his arms. Ellie stood indecisively for a moment longer, watching him. And then, with a noise that could have been a tiny sob, she turned and fled towards the bathroom.

It was a good twenty minutes before she emerged. Her hair lay in damp strands over her shoulders, spikes of her fringe hanging into her eyes. She had rolled up the sleeves of that salmon-coloured shirt he rather liked even though it was too close to being pink and the tail hung down far enough to almost cover the red silk boxers he had also provided.

With her face scrubbed clean and her bare legs and feet, she looked like a teenager. A malnourished one at that. She also looked far shyer than Max had anticipated. She was in his house and now in his clothes and she was clearly discomfited by the turn of events. She not only looked incredibly young but rather too vulnerable as well.

'Squeaky clean?' He tried to sound casual but he could *smell* how clean she was, dammit. Had she discovered some soap he didn't know he had? Or was that vaguely floral, gorgeously feminine scent simply coming from her exposed skin? He hadn't seen her this uncovered since that day she'd breastfed Mouse for the first time.

Oh, *God*... Why did that scene keep ambushing his brain, not to mention other regions of his anatomy?

Ellie was nodding. 'How did it go with the bottle?'

'See for yourself.' Max couldn't help a proud grin as he waved at where he'd placed the bassinette, tucking it into a corner of the living area, away from any draughts from the windows. 'Fed, burped, changed and back to sleep. I reckon she's had enough excitement for one day.'

The nod was heartfelt this time. 'Me, too.'

'Hungry?'

'Starving.'

'Me, too.' This was good. Something to focus on that took his mind off Ellie's bare legs and the knowledge that she wasn't wearing a bra under that soft, old shirt.

'The fish and chips are stone cold. I was just waiting for you to get out of the bathroom so I could go and get a fresh lot.'

'*No.*'

Max stopped in his tracks even though he was already halfway to the door. Escape into some fresh air had been the perfect plan but the anguish in Ellie's whisper made him feel as though he'd come up against a brick wall.

'What's wrong?'

'I...um...I'd rather you didn't go. What if...the police come? What do I tell them?'

Her expression suggested a belief that Max would have all the right answers and her trust undid something deep within. So did the thought that she didn't want to be left alone. That she wanted *him* to stay with her.

'Oh…Ellie…' Her name was almost a groan.

An admission of defeat?

He walked back towards her, one step at a time, feeling as if he had no other choice at all. He gathered her into his arms and then realised that this was the first time he'd held her since she had stumbled on his doorstep—a lifetime ago. She'd been covered in shapeless clothing then and all he'd really been aware of had been the baby bump between them. Now it was just Ellie with a mere layer of silky material between them. He could feel the real shape of her body and the way it fitted against his. The length of her back. Firm, round little buttocks, all slippery under the silk. Her nose was buried against his chest and it even rubbed against him, a bit like Mouse when she was hungry or upset.

Max held Ellie with one arm around her back and with the other he smoothed the damp strands of her hair.

'It's OK,' he heard himself murmur. 'I'll look after you. I'm not going anywhere for a while.'

The words seemed to echo. Where had he heard them before?

Oh…yeah… Back when he had started the skin-to-skin thing with Mouse, that's when. When he'd known he was caught for as long as it was going to take because to do anything else simply wasn't an acceptable option.

Ellie tipped her head back far enough to look up at him. Her face held a look of astonishment.

Of hope.

But a question lingered in her eyes. Was it possible he really mean what he'd just said?

Max couldn't think of anything more he could say to reassure her. Words seemed to have deserted him, in any case, as he looked down at those toffee-coloured eyes. At a nose that Mouse would undoubtedly share when she grew up. At lips that were parted just a fraction.

He tried to smile but that ability had clearly deserted him along with the power of speech. So he did something that seemed to come naturally. He bent his head and brushed her lips with his own. A kiss that wasn't really a kiss. Only reassurance. The kind you could give any female friend.

So why did it *feel* like a very different kind of kiss? The first stroke of something he wanted to dive into headlong. He was so aware of the scent of this woman in his arms. The feel of her body. He wanted to taste her. To hear the kinds of sounds she might make when she wasn't scared or shy. When she was more than merely happy, in fact. Max was good at eliciting sounds that came with intense physical stuff. A sigh of pure pleasure perhaps or the groan of ultimate satisfaction.

He could—

Whoa! Max managed to stop his mouth descending again. He even managed to straighten up. To suck in enough air to resuscitate his brain.

'How—'bout I put them in the oven, then?'

'Huh?' Ellie's eyes snapped open. When had she closed them? And *why*?

'The fish and chips. Would they be all right if we

reheat them, do you think? I'd hate to give you food poisoning.'

'Oh…' Colour was flooding Ellie's cheeks and she wriggled free of his arm. Or maybe he'd dropped it already. 'I'm sure they'd be absolutely fine.'

'Right. I'm onto it, then.' Of course they'd be fine.

He would be too as soon as he was far enough away from the feel and scent of Ellie.

It hadn't been a kiss.

Not a real kiss.

It didn't mean anything. Not to him, anyway.

To Ellie?

The world had tilted so sharply beneath her feet at the merest touch of his lips on hers that she knew she was in real trouble. She'd seen it coming, though, hadn't she? She'd known how easy it would be to fall in love with him. She'd tried, God help her, to maintain some distance. Just a shred of independence—both physical and emotional—and where had that landed her?

Here. In his apartment. In his clothes, for heaven's sake.

In love.

But just because you felt that strongly about someone it didn't mean you had to act on it, did it? It didn't mean that Max was going to guess how she felt and run for the hills. And he would run. Why wouldn't he? He was a gorgeous bachelor, part of a group of them, and they all played with toys like powerful motorbikes and had women lining up for their attention.

Ellie couldn't afford for Max to want to run. She needed him right now. So did Mouse. They both needed his friendship and his protection. Not for ever. Just for a week or two. Surely she could keep the way she felt hidden for that long? And then she could step out of his life and keep the basis of a friendship that would last for a lifetime.

She had to try. Friendship with this man was an infinitely preferable option to scaring him off so that she never saw him again. They could stay in touch. Visit occasionally, even. It wouldn't be beyond the realms of friendship to ask him to be a godfather to her daughter and, that way, they would have a link for life. Not that she'd ask him just yet.

With their dinner reheating in the oven, Max had taken himself off to a laundry space. He'd insisted that it was no trouble to disinfect Ellie's clothing and put it through the washing machine and dryer. It would be good to go in the morning. He'd been so keen, in fact, it had been difficult to avoid the impression that he found her wearing his clothes as disturbing as Ellie did, albeit for very different reasons.

He seemed to keep himself very busy for the rest of the evening as well. He made up the spare bed and helped Ellie sort the baby gear and then he made more than one phone call to speak to Jet, who was on duty again in the emergency department.

'That guy Nigel looks like he's going to make it,' he informed Ellie eventually. 'He's been to Theatre. The knife skated over his ribs and the damage was pretty superficial. His ankle's been fixed. He's got a good concussion but his C-spine checked out clear.'

'Oh…thank goodness for that. If it had turned into a murder investigation, I would have had to stay in the country for court appearances or something, wouldn't I?'

Max gave her an odd look. 'Yeah…I guess. But you weren't planning on leaving immediately, were you?'

'As soon as I can.' Ellie found a smile to give Max. 'Don't worry. We won't be messing up your lifestyle for too long. We might even be able to go back to the motel tomorrow.'

The look she got now was almost a glare. 'I don't think so. Not with the type of clientele that place attracts. The police will be swarming around for days, I expect.'

'If Nigel's going to be all right, maybe they won't need to talk to me again,' Ellie said hopefully. 'I was worried about what to tell them.'

'The truth,' Max suggested.

Ellie's eyes widened. 'You mean my real name?'

'No, not that bit.' But Max looked less than sure. Then he gave his head a slight shake. 'It's not doing any harm,' he said. 'And it seems to be working so far. I'd stick to McAdam if I was you.'

Ellie had reason to remember the advice the next day, well after Max had gone to work and she was alone in the apartment with Mouse. She had her baby in her arms when the knock came at the door. For a moment, panic set in. It could be the police. It could also be Marcus. What if he'd had someone watching and had been informed that she'd moved in with Max? He'd had enough time to catch a plane from Auckland and find her here, without any protection other than a locked but probably flimsy door.

Heart thudding, she went to peer through the peep-hole on the door.

'Max?' A feminine voice called. 'You home, babe?'

The image through the peephole was distorted. Ellie could see what appeared to be the longest pair of legs she'd ever seen. Long and sleek and black. Like the hair that flowed from the woman's head. She opened the door and then wished she hadn't. The woman really was long and sleek. She towered above Ellie, thanks to the stiletto heels that finished the look of her tight leather pants. Ellie was back in her newly cleaned maternity jeans and baggy sweatshirt that had both gone a rather odd, patchy colour from being bleached. She had never felt so short and dumpy and dowdy.

'Ahh…' The woman's rapid up-and-down glance said it all. 'Is Max here?'

'No. He's at work.'

'Damn. I've got something I think he'll be quite excited about.'

Ellie didn't doubt that for a second. This woman would be just his type. Heavens, she already had biker chicks' pants on. She could sling a leg over the back of his bike and put her heavily bangled arms around his waist and ride off into the sunset at a moment's notice.

'I'm Gina,' the woman said. 'I'm a…friend of Max's. And Rick's,' she added with a confident smile.

Ellie nodded. She tried, and failed, to smile back.

'And you are?'

It was right then that Ellie remembered the advice and it was simply too tempting not to use it.

'I'll Ellie McAdam,' she said.

'Oh…' Perfectly sculpted eyebrows shot up. 'Max's sister?'

'No.' This time, Ellie managed a smile. 'His wife.'

Maybe the advice hadn't involved using the fraudulent relationship as well as the name but Ellie couldn't resist. She couldn't even summon sympathy for how Max was going to explain his way out of this after she'd gone.

'And…' Gina's gaze dropped to the baby in Ellie's arms. 'Oh, my God…'

Ellie didn't say anything. She didn't need to. Gina was obviously having no problem coming to her own conclusion.

'Um…' Her visitor had been holding something in her hands, which she now held out. 'I can see why he's on the lookout for a new property. This one might be really great for you guys.' Gina wasn't one to let an opportunity slip past, evidently. 'I met Max…and Rick at a bike show recently. I'm a real estate agent and Max gave me his details. Said he was on the lookout for a new property. This just came into the office and it's kind of special so, of course, I thought of Max.'

'Thanks.' Ellie's smile was genuine now. Sympathetic, even. She could well believe that Gina had thought of Max. What woman wouldn't?

Max didn't appear to have returned the interest, however.

'Gina? Gina who?' He'd brought Chinese food home with him and the aroma was seriously tempting as he unpacked the carry bags.

'She didn't say. Gorgeous looking, though. Leather pants and long, dark hair. Said she met you and Rick at a bike rally or something.'

'Oh-h.… We did pop in on a Ducati show a couple of weeks back. Yeah…rings a bell. We swapped cards but I gave hers to Rick 'cos he was thinking he might give her a call.'

'She left you brochures. Said you were looking for a property to buy?'

Max grimaced. 'I should be but I really can't be bothered. I might just move back in with Rick when Jet gets another stint away with the army.'

'What's wrong with this place?'

'I've only got a sub-lease for three months. Sarah reckoned she wouldn't be away any longer than that, though I can extend it if she doesn't come back. She took this on as a two-year lease.'

'Oh?' Ellie was distracted, both by the tubs of hot food now on the table and the reminder of her old flat-mate. 'I must email her and see how things are going with Josh.'

'Good idea. Might give me a shove in the right direction.'

'Which is?' Ellie pulled the disposable chopsticks apart. Max was opening the tubs and she'd never felt so hungry in her life. She must be getting better, she decided. Her body was coming back to life.

Max saw her practically drooling and he grinned. 'Good to see you looking hungry. Steak with black bean sauce in that one. This one's chicken and ginger and that's stir-fried veggies 'cos it looked healthy. There's a bucket of rice so dig in.' He dipped his chopsticks into the first container and started filling his plate. For a minute or two they were both preoccupied with their food but after a few mouthfuls Max paused and glanced at Ellie.

'I guess the right direction is settling down,' he said sadly. 'I'm thirty-six. I can't ride round on my bike and move from place to place for ever. I like it here in Dunedin so maybe I need to put some roots down. Buying a house seems like a good first step. What do *you* think?'

A settled-down Max? With a home of his own? Would a wife and children and maybe even a dog be on the agenda as well?

Stupid to feel that bubble of hope but irresistible not to take the opportunity to soak in the expression on Max's face. To enjoy that rough look his jaw always had at this time of day that made her fingers itch to touch it. To make direct eye contact and feel it all the way to her bones.

'Couldn't hurt to look,' she offered. 'The picture's lovely and Gina seemed to think it was something special.'

'But it's way out on the peninsula. Long way to work.' Max ate in silence for a while again. 'Mind you, it's a great road for a bike ride. Good twists and turns and it runs right along the harbour's edge.' He ate another mouthful. 'I've got a couple of days off coming up. Why don't you come with me and help me look?'

'On your bike? Not on your life, mate.'

Max laughed, a wonderfully rich sound that made Ellie feel warm all over and happier than she could remember being in such a long time.

'Hardly. Not with the mouse to take into account. We'll take the car and it'll be as safe as houses, I promise.'

Ellie still shook her head.

'Why not?'

'Um…I kind of told Gina that I was your wife and she assumed that Mouse was yours as well. She looked kind of disappointed.'

Max was grinning. 'Is that so? I'll tell Rick. She's just his type.'

'Not yours?' Ellie knew she sounded surprised.

Max shrugged. 'Used to be. Maybe I'm growing up a bit. Thinking about house buying does that to a man, you know.'

Ellie wanted to ask what he thought his type was now but she didn't dare. This wasn't a conversation she really wanted to have because the little spears of wishful thinking were too delicious to want to give up. It couldn't hurt to indulge a small and very private fantasy for a little while, could it?

But Gina used to be his type and Ellie couldn't help remembering the way she'd felt that morning. Dumpy and dowdy.

'I still couldn't go.' It was her turn to grimace as she looked down at herself. 'Even if I went back to the motel for my bag, I didn't bring any non-pregnancy clothes with me. I look like I've been rummaging through the unwanted stuff from a charity shop. You really wouldn't want to be seen out with me, Max.'

'So wear something else.'

'Don't think your boxers and shirt would work either.'

'So…go shopping.'

'What?' That hadn't even occurred to Ellie.

'You're feeling better, aren't you? You're certainly looking better.'

Ellie nodded.

'So, take a taxi and go to one of the big department stores in town. You could take Mouse in the car seat and they'd have everything under one roof. Not too much walking about to tire you out. You've got those outpatient appointments tomorrow afternoon, haven't you? So you have to go out anyway.'

Ellie continued to nod. Everything under one roof? Clothes, lingerie, shoes. A hairdresser, maybe?

How long had it been since she'd worried about her appearance? Or had a reason to want to look good? This was a kind of hope that was permissible. Part of her fantasy, maybe, but one that was grounded in reality. It could happen. She could make a dramatic improvement to the way she looked. It was exciting.

'If I go to a bank, I won't even have to use my credit card.'

'Is that a problem? You want some cash?'

Ellie shook her head hurriedly. 'I've just been careful for so long because people can trace where you are if you use cards, can't they? I've seen it happen on those crime shows.'

The reminder of why she had come here in the first place and the continued need for care dampened the atmosphere.

'I'm sure it'll be fine,' Ellie muttered. 'It's not as if he doesn't know where I am now anyway.'

He could be waiting. Biding his time. Probably quite

confident that he would receive information about the birth of his child and he would, eventually, because time was running out. The birth had to be registered. Mouse had to be given a name.

'The offer's still open, you know,' Max said quietly.

'To see the house?' Ellie's smile was a little tight. 'Sure. Sounds like fun.'

'No.' Max had stopped eating. He was watching her face. 'The name. Marriage.'

Ellie stopped eating, too. Her appetite had vanished.

She wouldn't marry Max to give Mouse his name. Or to take it herself.

To marry Max knowing that it was in name only and that a very amicable divorce was already pencilled in?

No, thanks.

CHAPTER EIGHT

GINA the real estate agent did a double-take when she saw Ellie for the second time on the Sunday that was Mouse's two-week birthday.

Max wasn't surprised in the least. He'd been kind of stunned himself when he'd got home from work the other day after Ellie had been on her trip into town. She'd been wearing jeans that actually fitted and a soft, russet-coloured knit top that made her eyes and her hair seem the most astonishing mix of copper and chestnut shades. She'd looked…amazing and it was confusing because it wasn't so easy now to dismiss errant thoughts by reminding himself that she wasn't his 'type'.

She still didn't fit with the kind of athletic, leggy girls who were out for little more than a good time. She was different all right. Dangerously different because there was an attraction there that went a lot deeper than sex. He and Rick had always favoured blondes, too, but Ellie's hair was so *rich*. She'd said she'd only had her hair trimmed and that the hairdresser had put some rinse through it to bring out natural highlights but it *glowed* in some mysterious fashion and it looked *so* soft. His fingers had itched to bury themselves in it.

He hadn't, of course. He was being very, very careful ever since that kiss that hadn't been a kiss. Ellie valued her independence. She had some definite plans for her future that didn't include him and he didn't want to be involved. It would only complicate her life. Not to mention his. Coming to see this house was an aberration that was making him distinctly nervous for some reason. It had only been intended as an outing. There were lots of tourist attractions out here on the Otago Peninsula. Larnach Castle and the aquarium. The lighthouse and the world-famous albatross colony. It was just a bonus that he could make a foray into the world of real estate that he knew he should enter and now was probably as good a time as any.

Maybe it was because it was something he'd never done before. Or maybe it had something to do with the way Gina had been staring at Ellie as if she couldn't believe she was the same woman and Max could sympathise with the confused expression. Things were changing and Max wasn't sure about the direction they were taking. Some of it was good. He was delighted that both Ellie and Mouse had passed the assessments given in their outpatient appointments at the hospital. He could have predicted how pleased the doctors would be because he could see Ellie's strength returning day by day. She had a sparkle about her that couldn't be attributed entirely to a new wardrobe or a clever hairdresser.

Pretty soon now she'd disappear out of his life. She'd already been on the internet, checking out discount flight fares to Australia. She'd been exploring job opportunities as well and rental accommodation that might suit. The next step was to update her passport to include her child and that was only on hold until she decided on the name she wanted for her daughter.

She'd bought a book of names when she'd been in town and it had come out again last night.

'Annabelle? Bella? I quite like Bella. Oh, look… here's Maxine. It means "greatest".'

'You're not calling her Maxine.'

'She's probably going to end up being Mouse for the rest of her life,' Ellie had said mournfully. 'Mouse Peters. Doesn't have the best ring to it, does it?'

Mouse McAdam didn't sound too bad. Not that he'd pointed that out, mind you. Funny how the idea of marriage to Ellie to provide a legal name had suddenly lost its appeal. Why? Was it because he could finally see that it would be such a sham and not what any marriage should be about? Especially a marriage that involved someone like Ellie. Not that Max had ever given that much thought to the institution but, deep down, he had principles and one of them was obviously that marriage was not something that should be taken that lightly.

Who knew?

Perhaps house hunting was another aspect of grown-up life that shouldn't be taken lightly but they'd driven out along the windy peninsula road on this sunny afternoon, admiring the shards of light playing on the ruffled harbour waters. They'd had a bit of trouble locating the address, despite his satellite navigation device, because this house was set on a hillside and hidden from the road by a thick stand of native bush. Sunlight filtered through the canopy of these private woods, which effectively killed any traffic or other noise from the outside world and there was an atmosphere that made Max pause when he climbed out of the car. He had an odd feeling that he was being pushed towards something he really wasn't ready for. He gave himself a mental shake. Anyone would feel like that with a smiling real estate agent bearing down on them. He was only a potential buyer here. He could say no and he already knew he *would* say no.

The house itself was a wonderful, rambling old villa with a wisteria vine adorning the deep veranda and a view of the harbour and the green hills on the other side that would probably make it sell in a flash. They all stood for a moment at the top of the steps, their backs to the front door.

'That's Port Chalmers over there,' Max pointed out to Ellie. 'That's where Rick's place is. He's got a converted warehouse loft close to the container terminal. Very industrial. Trendy.'

'Bit different from this, then.'

'Mmm.' It was a bachelor pad all right and it hadn't had the space for the three of them when Jet had come home for a spell. Why had he offered to move somewhere else? Had he seen his new apartment as a stepping stone from bachelor pad to family home? If so, he hadn't had his feet in the interim space for nearly long enough.

'You'll love this place,' Gina said, turning to unlock the door. 'Come on. I can't wait to show you around.' She waited for them to enter the wide hallway. 'Such a cute baby,' she said as Ellie went past. 'What's his name?'

'It's a she,' Max said. 'And her name is Mouse.'

Gina giggled. 'What's her *real* name?'

There was a moment's awkward silence and then Ellie spoke. 'We haven't decided. Max doesn't like my choice so I'm waiting till he comes up with something better.'

'Fair enough.' Gina was heading for a sweeping stairway at the end of the hall. 'Let's start upstairs with the master bedroom. It's got the most amazing view.'

Max followed in silence. It was just part of the pretence, wasn't it? Ellie wasn't really expecting him to come up with a name for Mouse, was she? That was a responsibility he wasn't happy to take on but what if he didn't and she ended up calling the poor kid Maxine?

'Vacant possession,' Gina told them as they came back downstairs. 'The owner was hoping not to have to sell but he's decided to stay in Europe and he needs the capital for his business venture.'

'It's big,' was Max's verdict as they completed the tour.

Gina nodded happily. 'Four bedrooms and the office, two bathrooms, the games room in the basement and the guest suite over the garage. It's a perfect family home.'

But he didn't have a family. Gina glanced to where Ellie was standing with Mouse in the baby sling near the French doors that opened from the open-plan kitchen living area to a terrace that flowed into a large, sloping garden. Max followed her gaze. Was Ellie admiring the backdrop of the bush or deliberately avoiding having to keep up the deception that they were just the kind of family that this house was crying out for?

'I know it might seem a bit big compared to your apartment at the moment but think of it as future-proofing,' Gina said with a smile. 'Who knows? You might end up with a few more little ones and this is the kind of house you'd want your grandchildren visiting, isn't it?'

Grandchildren? Good grief! Max saw his life tele-scoping inwards with him as an old man, rocking on that veranda. No, thanks. He had a hell of lot more living to do before then.

'This would be paradise for children,' Gina added, blithely unaware of the effect her comment had had. 'Tree huts in the bush. There's a little stream on the boundary and it's not much of a walk down to the har-bour. You could have a boat. It's great for swimming in the summer. Or you could go fishing off the jetty.'

With the grandchildren. Ha!

Max tried to sound businesslike. 'The house is pretty old. It needs repairs as it is and would take a lot of maintenance to keep up.'

Gina smiled again. 'I'll bet you're good with a hammer and paintbrush, Max.'

'Never tried to find out.' His precious time off was put to far more enjoyable uses. Like a blast of fresh air on an open road bike ride. Or drinking time with his mates. Or a hot date. Yes, he still had a lot of living to do out there. To give up that time to work on a house? To build tree huts or mess about with boats? He needed to get out of here.

He didn't have a family. He didn't even have the prospect of one.

Carefully, Max avoided even a glance in Ellie's direction.

'I'll think about it,' he told Gina, 'but I don't think it's what I'm looking for at the moment. Thanks for showing us around, though.'

'No worries. It's not on the market just yet so you've got time to think. I'll be listing it next week, probably.' Gina ushered them out and locked the door behind them. 'I've got to dash.' She winked at Max. 'I've got a date with your friend Rick tonight.'

Max watched her slide into her little sports car and take off with a spurt of gravel beneath the tyres.

Dammit. *He* wanted a date with Rick. A fast ride to nowhere. Or, rather, somewhere that had a few icy lagers on tap. He wanted to step out of this parallel universe he'd fallen into that contained big houses and tree huts and babies that needed real names and sweet-smelling, *different* women.

What the hell had happened to his life?

Max was very quiet on the way back to the apartment.

So was Ellie.

She'd seen that look on his face as Gina had driven off, having announced her upcoming date with Rick.

Max had been envious. *He* wanted to be out with Gina. Having fun. Instead, he was stuck with her. And a baby. He was probably realising just how effectively he had scuttled any chance he might have had with Gina because she believed he had a wife and child. If she hadn't already been getting the vibes during the house tour, that look on Max's face had made it very clear that the deception was past its use-by date.

Any fleeting hope that Max might even consider family life was firmly relegated to fantasyland.

Just like that perfect, perfect house with its magical setting that made it a world of its own.

Why did Mouse choose to become so grizzly as soon as they arrived home? It was almost as though she was trying to chase Max away. He certainly didn't seem inclined to hang around. A few text messages and a change of clothes and he was off.

'Going on a bike ride with Jet,' he told Ellie, when he came out of his room wearing the leather gear she hadn't seen him in since the day she'd arrived.

Sexy, sexy gear. She stood there with a howling baby in her arms and knew she didn't stand a chance with this man and she never would.

Max pulled a helmet down from above the coat rack in the hall. 'Don't wait for me for dinner. We'll probably eat out at a pub somewhere.'

Somewhere there'd be lots of people. Attractive women who didn't have babies. There'd be music and dancing and the kind of atmosphere that was just what young doctors ordered for their time away from work.

Yes. Max couldn't wait to escape but, to his credit, he paused at the door.

'You OK being on your own for a while?'

'I'm fine. Have fun, Max.'

'Don't open the door to anyone. Text me if you get worried.'

'I'll be fine.' She could imagine what Jet's reaction

would be if Max received a text from her requesting assistance. She could see that dark scowl and it was easy to imagine what he'd say to his friend.

For God's sake, man, get rid of her. She's been nothing but trouble since she got here.

It took a long time to get Mouse happy. A feed and cuddle, a bath and change of clothes. Ellie was tired by the time her daughter was asleep in her bassinette but she didn't rest herself. She got busy.

An hour later, she had printed out and filled in an application form for a job in a Melbourne hospital that boasted a nearby crèche that took babies from six weeks old upwards. She found an envelope, stuffed the form inside and then sealed it and then she closed her eyes and breathed out a sigh of relief.

She knew where she was heading.

She had a future again.

Knowing that, and knowing that her time of being close to Max McAdam was limited, there really wasn't any harm in enjoying every moment she had left.

Was there?

Something else had changed.

Max couldn't quite put his finger on what it was but maybe that night out with Jet had cleared his head. Which was weird, seeing as he'd ended up leaving his bike at a mate's house, getting a taxi home in the early hours of the morning and waking up with a mother of a hangover.

Ellie had been very considerate the next day, keeping well out of his way with a shopping trip that resulted in a pushchair that she then took Mouse for a long walk in. He'd barely noticed them and it wasn't until several days later that he realised he still wasn't noticing them.

No, that wasn't quite right. He knew they were there well enough but it wasn't creating any negative-type tension. Yes, that was what it was. For whatever reason, after he'd burned off the fear of ending up rocking on a veranda having had his entire life sucked away, a new serenity had slipped into his life.

Max came to this satisfactory conclusion as he watched over Mouse while Ellie had a shower and washed her hair late one evening. Mouse was awake and he'd picked her up but she didn't seem to be uncomfortable or hungry so he was sitting on the couch with the baby lying on his lap, the back of her head resting on his knees. She was gripping his forefingers with those miniature fists and looking up at him with an amusingly serious expression.

'How's it going?' Max asked. 'I've had a good day. How 'bout you?'

It had been a good day. A good week, actually, with a huge variety of interesting cases. Having someone to come home to who was genuinely interested in hearing about everything he'd been doing was the best way to debrief he'd ever come across. Living with Rick and Jet, the last thing any of them felt inclined to do out of hours was rehash a working day but Ellie seemed to revel in it. She could ask the kind of questions that made him realise what a good job he'd done or sometimes make him think about how he could do it even better next time. And sometimes, best of all, he could make her laugh.

Like he had tonight.

'So this guy comes in like the hounds of hell are chasing him. He's as white as a sheet. Bloodstained tea-towel wrapped around one hand and a bag of frozen veggies in the other. Tells us he's chopped his finger off and it's in with the frozen peas and then he faints into a puddle on the floor.'

'Oh, no! What did you do?'

'Cleared Trauma One. Put out a call to Neurosurgery and Rick happens to be in the department for something else so he gets all excited about the possibility of reattaching a finger and then…'

'What?'

'We unwrap the tea-towel and find he's only nicked the very top off his finger. Flesh wound. All he needed was a sticky plaster.'

And Ellie had laughed. A wonderful ripple of sound that made Max feel proud of his ability to entertain. Made him feel…important, somehow. Made him feel really good, anyway.

'I miss it,' Ellie had confessed. 'Maybe it's just as well I can't afford to be a full-time mum for too long. It'll be good to get back to work and you know what?'

'What?'

'I think I'll go into Emergency this time instead of going back to Theatre work.'

'Join the Band-Aid brigade?'

'The reason that's so funny is because it's so far towards the other end of the spectrum for the kind of life-and-death stuff you deal with every day. The variety is amazing. Challenging. I can see why you love it so much.'

And Max could see why Ellie might want to be a full-time mother for as long as she could afford to.

He was watching a play of facial movements in the tiny features in his lap. A furrowed brow that made the mouse look cross and then a wrinkled nose as if she'd smelt something particularly offensive. The tiny cupid's bow of a mouth was open and the tip of a pink tongue emerged and then disappeared again.

Max found himself poking the tip of his own tongue out to mirror the action. Mouse's eyes widened. Max widened his own eyes. And then he found himself sitting there, holding the hands of a three-week-old baby, making the most ridiculous faces he could.

Mouse seemed to love it. He could swear she was trying to copy him. She definitely followed a tongue-poking manoeuvre. It was fascinating. Just as rewarding as making Ellie laugh. He was making sounds without realising what he was doing for a while. Clicking his tongue and talking—God help him—in baby talk. And then it happened. The corners of that little mouth stretched and curled.

Mouse smiled at him.

Ellie didn't believe him when she came back. She sat on the end of the couch, combing out her hair, and paused to shake her head.

'She's too young to smile. They're not supposed to do that until they're about six weeks old.'

'She did. She smiled at me. Didn't you?' Max lifted the tiny hands and clicked his tongue again, trying to elicit a repeat of the miracle smile.

'Maybe she had wind.'

'Nope. It was a smile. Look…*look*…she's doing it again.'

Sure enough, she was, even if it was just with one side of her mouth this time.

'Oh, my God,' Ellie breathed. 'She *is* smiling.'

They both stared at Mouse. And then they looked up to stare at each other and after a long, long moment, they both smiled.

Max had to look away. He needed to move, in fact. Handing Ellie her baby, he stood up. He walked aimlessly across the room towards the bookshelf where his gaze fell on the 'bad boys' photograph. The four of them.

Slowly, he turned back to Ellie.

'What about Mattie?' he asked quietly.

'Your friend?'

'No. The name.'

She got it. She looked down at Mouse and then back up at him and she still looked like she had after seeing her baby smile for the first time.

'Short for Matilda,' she whispered. 'Mattie. It's perfect, Max, but are you sure?'

'Sounds good to me.'

'But I'd be naming her after someone that was very special to you.'

It was kind of difficult to swallow. 'It's what I'd choose for her name,' he said gruffly. 'If she was mine.'

Ellie's gaze slid away and she seemed to be blinking fast. 'Matilda it is, then.' She leaned down to kiss her baby. 'Hello, Mattie.'

* * *

He had given Mouse her real name.

The name he would have chosen for his own child.

The joy of what was a priceless gift was still with Ellie when she had tucked a very sleepy baby into the bassinette in the room they shared. She had a dreamy smile playing on her lips when she went back to the living area to find Max turning out all the lights. She could see him illuminated only by the soft glow coming from the hallway behind her.

'I thought you'd gone to bed,' he said.

'I wanted to say thank you.'

'Hey…no worries.'

If he hadn't smiled at her she could have just said something else and turned away but that smile… So real. So heartbreakingly tender. It was enough to undo her utterly. Ellie stepped forward, closing the gap between them, standing on tiptoe as she reached up to hug Max. Instinct told her she could communicate how much that gift meant—how much his friendship meant—far better through touch than words that could only be inadequate.

His arms went around her and pulled her closer. His head was bent over hers and she heard the deliberate, indrawn breath—as though Max was revelling in the scent of her hair. Of *her*.

She could feel his body against hers. The solid wall of his chest on her breasts. The imprint of every finger against her back. A pressure on her belly that brought a shaft of desire so intense she had to close her eyes tightly and try—desperately—to remember why it was she couldn't let Max know how she really felt about him.

Maybe she wasn't succeeding very well. When the hug finally loosened—way after it should have, given a status of friendly gratitude—and Ellie cracked her eyes open, she found Max watching her and she could see what appeared to be a reflection of exactly how *she* was feeling in the dark depths of his eyes.

'Ellie...'

Her name was a whisper. A half-groan. A warning perhaps. Or a question.

She didn't respond. Not verbally, anyway. Instead, she allowed her body to overrule any conscious thought. She kept her arms around Max's neck, went back on tiptoe and tilted her head, parting her lips.

Offering him her mouth.

Her body.

The sound Max made was most definitely a groan this time. His mouth covered hers and it was no casual brush. His lips found the shape of her mouth, locked onto it and then took it on a journey like none Ellie had ever experienced. A roller-coaster of movement. Pressure that built and then fell away into shards of sensation she could feel way down low in her belly. The most delicious sliding of his tongue teasing hers as his hands cradled her head, his fingers buried deep in her hair.

Finally, she could do what she'd been itching to do for so long and feel the roughness of that shadowed jaw under her fingers and then her palms as she slid her hands up to loosen the waves of his hair and glory in the silky slide as she explored the shape of his whole head.

And then his lips dropped away from hers to touch

the side of her neck and Ellie tipped her head back to offer him her throat.

Her life.

'Ellie…' This time her name was a growl of frustration. 'We can't do this.'

Ellie froze. She couldn't ask why not. She couldn't even *think* why not.

'It's too soon.'

The statement was bewildering. How could it be too soon when she felt like this? So totally in love with him. But she couldn't tell him that because then he would run and this would *never* happen. She'd be gone soon and she'd never know what it could have been like, except in her fantasies.

'You only gave birth a few weeks ago. If we don't stop this, I won't—'

'I'm fine,' Ellie interrupted. She held the eye contact without wavering. 'I'm fine,' she repeated in a whisper. 'I didn't need stitches. I—' Oh, God… What could she say that wouldn't sound like begging? If he wanted to stop, she had to respect that. 'I'm fine,' she repeated simply, her voice trailing into silence.

I want this, she tried to tell him with her eyes. *As long as you want it too.*

Max must have picked up at least something of her unspoken message. He closed his eyes for a heartbeat and then he picked Ellie up. Swept her into his arms effortlessly and carried her into his room.

Into his bed.

Their next kiss took them to a whole new level and with it came the shedding of clothes and the touch of skin on skin. A new roller-coaster that was as much of an emotional as a physical ride.

Ellie offered Max her heart.

Her soul.

You could give someone a name and still keep it.

You could give someone your heart when it was still right there inside you, keeping you alive.

Such gifts were treasures that were the most precious things you could own and nobody could take them away from you.

Ellie was musing on the wonder of it all as she took Mouse…no, Mattie…for a ride in her pushchair late the following afternoon.

She was walking slowly, a little weary after her amazing night, but she'd never been this happy.

Ever.

Not even when she'd seen her baby for the first time or felt her suckling at her breast. Or when she'd felt the first stirrings of her love for Max in that moment of connection when he'd been there to witness her feeding Mattie for the first time. And when he'd chosen a name that meant so much to him and offered it to her daughter. Or even when she'd held him in her arms last night when he'd come apart and cried out her name in the wake of her own astonishing climax.

No. This feeling was bigger. A combination of all of those things and it encompassed all the people involved. Herself. Max. Mattie.

Even if it only lasted a matter of days. Even if Max had no idea he was such an integral part of it, *this* was what family felt like. Separate beings welded together by love. By the gifts that you could give and still keep.

She and Mattie were only going as far as the corner shop. Ellie was cooking dinner for Max and wanted it to be very special. She'd been to the supermarket earlier and thought she had everything, right down to the bottle of champagne chilling in the fridge.

Max didn't have to know what she was really celebrating. She intended to tell him it was a name-warming for Mattie. And then she thought it could be her one-month birthday but that needed a cake and when she went to start baking one, she discovered they had run out of butter. No big deal. It was a short walk to the shop and, now that she thought about it, there was a postbox there as well. She could buy the butter *and* finally post that application form. Silly to keep putting it off when it might mean she missed out on the opportunity altogether.

The walk took her past the motel where she'd spent her first day away from the hospital. The place she'd never gone back to, not wanting to claim the old clothes that were part of a life she intended leaving well behind. The memories of her brief stay there were decidedly unpleasant. Echoes of the abuse being shouted still hung in the air. If she looked down the driveway as she walked past she'd be able to see the spot where Nigel had landed in front of her unit. Had the bloodstains been cleaned away?

Not that she really wanted to know but it was inevitable that her head turned in that direction as she reached the motel's entranceway. What she saw made her stop in her tracks. Blink hard and look again because she couldn't believe what she *was* seeing.

Right there—in the exact spot Nigel had been sprawled after his fall from the balcony above—lay another shape. A small one.

A *child*?

Ellie could feel the blood draining from her head. A curious buzzing sound filled her ears, which probably explained why she hadn't heard the woman crying out for help. A woman who was now running towards her.

Was this one of Nigel's children? Had they been climbing on the balcony? Had it been damaged by the accident and never repaired? She hadn't taken much notice of his wife that night. It could be her rushing down the driveway.

'*Help*,' the woman begged. She grabbed Ellie's arm. 'Please…he's fallen. Can you help?'

'Of course.' Ellie jerked the pushchair to turn it but the wheels were locked somehow and it almost tipped.

'I'll take care of her,' the woman gasped. 'Please… I don't know what to do. I don't know if he's breathing…'

Ellie ran to the child, pulling her phone from her pocket. She'd just check the boy's airway and then call for an ambulance. She knelt down and tipped the child's head back carefully. His eyes snapped open and he grinned up at her.

'Do I get my ten dollars now?'

'*What?*'

Ellie's heart was pounding painfully and her head

was still buzzing. What kind of *stupid* prank was this? He'd scared her half to death. Had scared his mother. She flicked her head sideways, opening her mouth to call out. To reassure the woman that this child was fine and there'd been no need to panic.

And that was when her heart stopped.

Because the woman was nowhere to be seen.

And neither was the pushchair containing her own child.

CHAPTER NINE

Of all the events that had occurred to turn his life upside down in the last month, this was by far the worst.

It was an unimaginable horror.

Max had received the call at work just as he'd been due to finish his shift. He'd been having a coffee with Jet and Rick, in fact, and the other two men had stiffened to attention as they'd heard his stunned silence and the staccato questions of a man intent on gaining control of an unacceptable situation.

'What's happened?

'What's being done?

'Where *is* she right now?'

They had all ridden their bikes to work that day. They might have arrived at different times but they left as a single unit. Three powerful machines with black-clad men hunched over them as they sped towards the same destination.

The motel where the police had been talking to Ellie.

She looked like a ghost. A small, terrified wraith.

If Rick and Jet were surprised by the way Max

strode into the motel manager's office, pushing through the throng of uniformed police officers to gather Ellie into his arms, they did no more than exchange a loaded glance.

Every occupant of the room watched the embrace that followed. The way Ellie clung to Max as though her life depended on it. The way the tall, leather-clad man curled his body so protectively over hers.

The bond was unmistakable.

So powerful that Rick sent another glance at the man standing at his shoulder. Jet merely quirked an eyebrow and then nodded, albeit with resignation. The significance had been noted. The importance of this mission had just been upgraded to a red alert.

'You're Dr Max McAdam?' A senior police officer had apparently decided enough was enough when it came to a comforting embrace.

'Yes,' Max growled.

'And you've been posing as Ms Peters's husband? The father of this missing child?'

'He told *me* he was her brother.' The motel manager looked up from where another officer was taking his statement.

Max took a deep breath. He moved so that he could face the senior officer but he didn't let go of Ellie. He tucked her against his side with an arm that enclosed her completely.

'That's correct.' He held the gaze of the man speaking to him. He was more than prepared to defend his actions and if anyone threatened this woman he held, they'd better be prepared for a battle. 'And you are?'

'Detective Inspector Jack Davidson.' The officer

was taking Max's measure. 'Jack,' he added, his tone suggesting that he was impressed by what he was seeing. His gaze slid to Ellie. 'We've been told about the behaviour of Dr Marcus Jones. I believe you were a witness to his pursuit of this young woman? Following her to Dunedin?'

'Also correct.'

'The man's a weasel.' Rick's drawl floated across the room.

Jack Davidson ignored the interjection. 'You're also aware that he's the real father of Ms Peters's baby?'

Max scowled. No, he wanted to say. The real father would have been there to do the kangaroo care his baby had needed at birth.

He would have been the one to witness the miracle of that first breastfeeding.

He would have seen that first smile.

He would have cherished Ellie, dammit. Realised what an amazing woman she was and won her trust so that he could have experienced the joy of making love to her, not forcing her because he'd decided that was what *he* wanted.

Max could feel his blood beginning to boil. A real father wouldn't have separated his baby from her mother. He would have moved heaven and earth to keep them together. To keep them safe. The way he had every intention of doing, so help him.

'Dr McAdam? Max?' The tone was impatient.

'Biologically, yes,' Max snapped.

But Mouse's *real* father?

He was that person. And he always would be as far as he was concerned. Would it make any difference to

Ellie if she knew how he felt? That he loved her child and would protect her with his life, if necessary? He gave her the softest squeeze to try and convey that he was there. Heart and soul.

'We've confirmed that it was Marcus Jones who visited Mr Grimsby, the manager here, yesterday and obtained all the details he could regarding Ms Peters's stay here and the incident that prompted her departure.'

'He said he was a lawyer,' the manager protested. 'That Miss Peters was planning to sue. That he could get a court order if I didn't co-operate and that he could make sure my business got wrecked.'

Max ignored the interruption. 'I still don't understand how this happened. How he managed to take Mouse.'

'Mouse?' The detective inspector frowned. 'You mean—?'

'It was my fault,' Ellie said quietly. Her voice was oddly calm. Expressionless. 'I left her. I practically handed her over. I—'

'This *wasn't* your fault,' Max told her firmly. He could be perfectly sure about that without knowing any of the details.

'Ellie was taken in by what appears to be a carefully set-up ruse,' Jack Davidson told Max. 'We're currently trying to track the woman involved who offered to look after the baby while Ellie went to the aid of a child who seemed to have fallen from an upstairs balcony here.'

Max tightened his hold on Ellie. The *bastard*. He must have heard the details of the accident and known exactly what kind of buttons it would push for someone who had the training to help. Especially using a child. There was no way Ellie wouldn't have been sucked in. He would have been himself.

But she pulled away from his touch. She wrapped her own arms around herself and looked as though she was staring at something a million miles away.

'It was *my* fault,' she whispered.

'We've got a good description of the woman from several people and—' The detective broke off as the radio clipped to his shoulder crackled into life. He answered with a call sign.

'Jack?' Everybody could hear the voice on the other end. 'We've located the pushchair.'

Ellie gasped but everybody else seemed to be holding their breath.

'Any sign of the baby?' the detective snapped.

A moment's silence and then came the response.

'No.'

How could one of the smallest words in existence create such agony?

Ellie couldn't move. She couldn't speak. She couldn't even cry. The atmosphere in the room was changing. People were moving and things were happening but she couldn't focus on what was being said. This was a nightmare and she had no control over any of it.

After a bewildering length of time, she found herself being led out of the motel office.

'Keep her in your apartment, then,' she heard someone say reluctantly. 'Don't go anywhere.'

'If any contact whatsoever is made,' another voice

ordered, 'let us know. Immediately. We'll keep you informed of any developments on our side.'

Max walked her to his apartment. He tried to put his arm around her again but Ellie couldn't bear it. She had to hold onto herself because her heart was ripped open and this was the only way to hold the pieces together. If she let go—relaxed even the tiniest bit—she might actually die.

When she entered the apartment and saw the table that she'd set for the special dinner she'd planned for Max it all morphed together into the same, ghastly nightmare.

If she hadn't fallen in love she wouldn't have set the table like that. With candles and glasses ready to fill with champagne. She wouldn't have thought of baking a cake and wouldn't have gone on that fateful walk to the shop.

She wouldn't have lost her baby.

'He won't hurt her,' Max said gently. Did he want to believe that because the alternative was simply unthinkable?

Ellie spun around. '*You* don't know that.' She knew more than he did. The fear lying like a dead weight inside her was growing. Starting to send tendrils right into her veins.

'I know it's you that he wants.' Max raised his hands as though he wanted to touch Ellie. She took a step backwards. She couldn't cope with being comforted. Didn't *deserve* to be. Max dropped his hands by his sides. 'He's using Mouse as bait. He can't afford to hurt her.'

Why not? How would she know what he was doing? Maybe he was just doing this to punish her.

'He'll call,' Max said. 'And then we'll know where he is and the police can get him. They'll find Mouse and bring her back safely.'

She was Mouse again. Not Mattie.

Why? Because she was so tiny and defenceless? Or because the person she'd been named for had died a dreadful, and possibly unnecessary, death?

Ellie squeezed herself more tightly to try and hold back the wave of pain. She tried to shake the black thoughts away. The effort was so great that her breath escaped in an agonised sob and her legs felt so much like jelly she had to let herself sink onto the couch. She pulled her legs up beneath her, curling into the corner. She could hear the rumble of motorbikes outside. She could even feel it, against her skin.

No…that was her phone vibrating. Oh…*God*…was this it? *Contact?*

She fumbled for her phone as Max was moving to open the front door. Rick came in.

'Jet's gone back to get your bike,' he told Max.

Ellie had managed to open her phone to find a text message.

Don't talk to anyone, it said. *Or you won't see her again.*

She snapped the phone shut as Max turned but he hadn't missed the action.

'You got a message?' There was an urgency in his voice that she'd never heard before. Pain, even.

Every instinct Ellie had was to tell Max. To show him the message. To share the horror and have these men help to make a plan and deal with it. They would protect her and Mouse. The dark angels.

But, if she did, Marcus might know somehow and he might hurt her baby. He was capable of it, she knew that better than anyone. He'd hurt *her*, hadn't he?

'N-no,' Ellie stammered. 'I was just…hoping.'

Max held her gaze with a look that broke her heart all over again. He understood. He was feeling this, too. Then he gave a single, curt nod.

'He would have got the landline number from the motel records. He'll probably ring here.'

The phone in the apartment did ring a short time later, after Jet had joined the tense group. Ellie uncurled her legs, ready to jump from the couch, but Max got to the phone first.

'They've traced the woman and arrested her,' he reported after what seemed an interminably long conversation. 'She was paid to set it all up and snatch Mouse. She handed her over to Marcus at the corner shop as arranged. He abandoned the pushchair and took off in a vehicle. One that he rented at the airport and apparently requested a baby seat for. The police have the details. They've got all the manpower they have available searching now.'

Ellie could feel her phone vibrating silently in her pocket again.

'They've got the airport covered,' Max continued. 'And they're watching the main roads in and out of the city.'

Ellie managed to nod. Then she stood up. Three men stilled. Three sets of dark eyes were fixed on her.

'I…um…need to go to the loo,' she said.

In the privacy of the bathroom, she opened her phone with trembling fingers. The text message this time was an address. A road she'd never heard of.

Come alone, the message finished. *Or else.*

Ellie splashed cold water on her face, trying to rinse away the nausea that made her stomach roil. She had to try and think. What the hell was she going to do now?

Tell Max.

No. If she did, he would go instead of her. Probably without taking the risk of including the police. These guys didn't always follow the rules, did they? Not when someone's life was at stake and they might be able to do something themselves. And if he went instead of her, Marcus would hurt Max. And if he hurt Max, what would stop him from hurting Mouse? To punish her for sending someone else. For disobeying him.

She stood to lose the two people she loved most in the entire world.

But if she went herself, there was a chance she could sort this out. What if she could persuade Marcus that she'd made a mistake? That she wanted to be with him and their child? He couldn't keep her isolated completely and she could use the first opportunity she had to call for help.

To call the police.

And Max.

Yes. The more she thought about it, the more the idea seemed the best choice she had. Maybe the only choice because the safety of her baby had to be her first consideration and what did she have to go on?

The knowledge that Marcus had Mouse.

The fact that he wanted *her*.

All she had to do was convince him that he'd won for long enough to save Mouse.

And then what?

Would Max still want to have anything to do with her given the amount of trouble she'd caused? There was a new pain to be found going down that track so it was just as well she couldn't afford to think that far ahead. She couldn't handle thinking of anything more than how to get where she needed to be. To where Marcus was. And Mouse.

The ache in her breasts went up several notches to become unbearable. They were heavy with the milk that Mouse must be getting desperate for by now. Marcus might have requested a baby seat in the rental vehicle but had he thought to provide a bottle? Or nappies? Highly unlikely.

Another reason why she had to be the one to go. And surely Max would be grateful that she hadn't made things worse for him and his friends?

But how could she get out of there without giving herself away?

How could she find where this address was?

How could she get there?

Think, she ordered herself. Take a deep breath and think. *There has to be a way.*

A minute later, with shaking fingers, she managed to send a return message.

I'm on my way.

Something had happened in those couple of minutes that Ellie had been in the bathroom, Max decided.

She'd gone in there looking as though she couldn't string two coherent thoughts together and she had come out looking…focused.

Weirdly calm.

He went into the kitchen to make coffee. Ellie sat on the couch. Rick and Jet sat at the table which had place settings for two, he noted belatedly. And, good grief… candles?

Had Ellie been planning a romantic dinner tonight? Food, in various stages of preparation, was scattered over the bench top. A fresh-looking salad. Mushrooms, sliced and ready to sauté. Was there steak in the fridge? And, if so, how had Ellie known what his all-time favourite dinner was? Not that he was remotely hungry right now. And a romantic dinner seemed like a bad-taste joke.

Had it only been last night that they had stepped over the boundaries of friendship and into the realm of lovers?

It didn't seem real. Maybe Ellie was regretting it and that was why she didn't want him touching her any more. Perhaps she considered him some kind of distraction now and if she hadn't been distracted she wouldn't have become separated from Mouse.

Mattie.

Oh…God. Silently, Max placed mugs of coffee in front of Rick and Jet. What would they think if they knew he'd given their missing mate's name to the baby who was now also missing?

Rick would probably shake his head sadly.

Jet would give him a look that would tell him he'd been crazy getting into any of this in the first place.

Max went back into the kitchen for the other two mugs. He walked towards Ellie, trying to decide if she'd want him to sit on the couch with her or join the others at the table, leaving her separate. Alone.

He couldn't do that. Max sat on the couch beside her. She was still hugging herself and he noticed the way her hands were shaking.

'You cold?'

'Mmm.'

'Drink this. It'll help warm you up.'

But Ellie shook her head, declining the coffee. 'No, thanks…I think I might have a shower.'

'Good idea.' Odd, but maybe it would distract her from this awful waiting as well as warming her up. He wasn't surprised Ellie was feeling cold. Dread was sitting in his own gut like a block of ice.

'Will you call me if…if someone rings?'

'Of course.' Max watched helplessly as Ellie went into the hallway, closing the door behind her. Leave it open, he wanted to call, but why would she want to when the house was full of men?

With a heavy sigh, Max got to his feet again. He took the unwanted coffee into the kitchen and tipped it down the sink. Then he took the other mug and joined his friends at the table.

The conversation was spasmodic.

'Maybe he won't call,' Jet suggested. 'Maybe it's the kid he wants.'

Rick shook his head. 'Nah. Didn't you *see* the way he looked at Ellie that day? Hear the way he spoke to her? The creep thinks he owns her.'

'He doesn't give a damn about the baby,' Max said

through gritted teeth. 'Or he wouldn't have taken her away from her mother.'

'He'll call.' Rick sounded confident. 'And I intend to be there when they corner the bastard.'

'We're not doing anything that could put Mouse in any danger,' Max said fiercely. 'No way.'

The phone rang again and Max activated the speaker.

'Max?'

'Yeah.'

'Jack Davidson. There's been a possible sighting of the vehicle Jones hired but…' The detective sounded puzzled. 'It's way out on the peninsula. Does that make any kind of sense to you?'

'No.' It didn't. It was a dead-end road. Miles away from any kind of escape from the city unless it was to be by boat and even Marcus Jones couldn't be that crazy, could he? 'Ellie's never even… Oh, wait…we did take a drive out there recently to look at a house that was for sale.'

Jet's eyebrows rose eloquently.

'They were just looking,' Rick told Jet in a stage whisper. 'Gina told me all about it.'

'We'll follow the lead up,' the detective finished. 'Any contact been made at your end?'

'No.'

After the call, silence fell amongst the three men. Jet got up and paced the living area.

'Bit poky in here, isn't it?'

'I've gone off the whole area,' Max admitted. 'And I'm going to have to move soon in any case. Sarah sent me an email to say she's coming back.'

'Who? Oh, the chick who sub-leased you this place?' Jet paused to stare out the window. 'Wasn't she going to the States to find the father of her sick kid?'

'Turned out he wasn't the father after a DNA test.'

'Bummer.'

'Yeah. He put Sarah onto another possibility, though. Josh's mother had just broken up with another guy when he met her. He was also a doctor who worked at Auckland Central. Thinks his name is Richard some-one. Or someone Richard.'

'How old is the kid?' Jet was pacing again.

'Dunno.' Max had only one child on his mind right now. 'Around seven or eight, I guess.'

Jet's teeth gleamed as he grinned at Rick. 'Guess that lets you off the hook, mate.'

'Get off the grass. I'm careful about stuff like that.'

Another silence fell. Maybe they were all thinking about a time a little further back in their lives. Ten years ago, when they'd all dealt with their grief over Matt in different ways. Jet had taken up martial arts. Max had taken on some intensive postgraduate stud-ies. Rick had been drinking a lot. And partying. Hard. Being careful might not have been high on his agenda for a while there so it was just as well the timeframe wasn't compatible.

Max's thoughts drifted back to what was threatening to overwhelm him but did he want to start a conversa-tion about Marcus Jones and what he might be capable of doing to a baby?

What he might do to Ellie if he ever got close enough to her again.

It wasn't the first time a kind of telepathy had oc-curred between these men.

'She's taking a hell of a long time in that shower, isn't she?'

'Yeah...' Max shoved his chair back. 'I might go and check on her.'

He could hear the shower running as he stepped into the narrow hallway but he got no response when he knocked on the bathroom door.

'Ellie? You OK?' He opened the door to a wall of steam.

For a moment, it was hard to see anything in the small room but when Max stepped in, he could see quite well enough through the condensation on the glass walls of the shower.

The water was running but there was nobody stand-ing beneath it and in that split second of realisation Max knew there never had been.

With an oath, he shut off the water. Three long steps was all it took to get him back to the door of the living room.

'She's gone,' he said, his tone as hollow as his gut.

'*What?* Where?'

'To meet the weasel, of course,' Jet said impatiently. 'How does she know where to go?'

'Her phone.' Max breathed out another soft curse. 'I *thought* she'd got a message but she denied it.'

'She was probably following instructions.'

'But how can she go anywhere? Unless it's on foot?'

Max took a swift glance at the hook beside the coat rack. 'My car keys are gone.'

He moved towards the phone. 'I'd better call Davidson.'

'Wait.' Jet wasn't pacing any longer. He was standing very still. 'We know where she's going.'

'Yeah…to meet some deranged bastard who's got her baby.'

Jet shook his head impatiently. 'His vehicle's been sighted on the peninsula road, yes?'

Max and Rick stared at him.

'How hard could it be to catch up with an SUV on that road?'

An exchange of glances was all it took.

The three men reached for their helmets. Seconds later and they were outside the apartment, kicking their bikes into life.

With a roar of intent, they sped off into the night.

CHAPTER TEN

VALUABLE time had been lost while Ellie tried to remember how to programme the satellite navigation
device in Max's car but now she was well on her way.

But where on earth was she going?

It seemed to be the route she and Max had taken the
day they'd gone to view that house. Along Andersons
Bay Road. Onto Portobello Road with the dark expanse
of the harbour on her left. But why would Marcus want
to come way out here?

Because it was isolated?

Was he planning to *kill* her?

No. While the thought was terrifying, Ellie didn't
believe it. Marcus Jones was a respected surgeon. His
reputation and career meant everything to him. He
was obsessive, yes, and very, very angry that she was
refusing to do what he wanted her to do, but murder?
Unthinkable. And even if she was in danger—and she
knew perfectly well that she was being stupid going off
on her own like this—what mattered was the safety of
her child. If she lost her own life in saving Mattie, so
be it. The drive to protect her baby was strong enough
to override everything else.

She couldn't go as fast as she wanted on this road because of its twists and turns but she was keeping ahead of any other traffic. The frequent glances into the rear-view mirror, fearing the flashing lights of an overtaking police vehicle, showed nothing very close at all. There were lights behind her but they were going at much the same speed she was and they disappeared for a while each time she took a bend. Nothing to worry about.

Max would have found the shower running without her by now and Ellie felt a twist of remorse at deceiving him. He didn't deserve that. But he did deserve her protection and keeping him well away from Marcus Jones was the best thing she could do as far as not causing him any further trouble. He wouldn't have hesitated to jump in boots and all. That was one of the things she loved most about him. His strong sense of right and wrong and the absolute need to help someone in trouble. He'd be frustrated right now because he wouldn't have any idea of where she was going. She didn't even know herself. Even if he'd told the police she was missing they would have no clue as to where to begin looking either.

The image of Max, on the phone maybe, rubbing his forehead and frowning with concern...for *her*...sent a wave of longing through Ellie. A desire to reassure him. A desperate need to feel his arms around her.

She gripped the steering-wheel so tightly her fingers started losing sensation. She had to concentrate. She had bought some time but would it be enough? Marcus was hardly a patient man and this journey seemed to be going on for ever. She had gone past Portobello and onto Harrington Point Road from where they had turned up the hill to that house. The fleeting thought that Marcus had somehow known how much she loved the property and had purchased it as some kind of bribe could be dismissed because this was obviously nowhere near the end of this road where she'd been ordered to go.

She lost sight of the harbour. The countryside her headlights picked out was barren. Dry, rocky grass-covered hills with patches of gorse but little else. The harbour might be invisible but there was a new vast darkness on her right. The open sea, well below some dramatic-looking cliffs. No flashing lights behind her, though she did catch a glimpse around one corner of a vehicle's lights. Maybe two cars were following because there seemed to be more than two lights. Who would be travelling this road at night? A farmer? The person who looked after the lighthouse? Wildlife officers who had work to do at the albatross colony maybe? That thought was comforting. It would be nice to think there was someone else not too far away when she reached her destination.

Finally, she got to where Harrington Point Road ended. In a car park for people who wanted to visit the tourist attraction of the albatross colony. A cluster of buildings had security lights on but there were no signs of any activity so the only other car in this area had to belong to the person who had brought her there. It was too dark to see if it was occupied but then came a flash of light. And another. The bright, white glare of an automated lighthouse signal.

Ellie could see the other car was empty. Of adults, at

least, but was Mouse in there? She killed the engine of Max's car and fumbled for her safety belt, her feet hitting the ground at a run the instant she'd climbed out. Her path took her straight to the other vehicle, to peer in through the windows in the desperate hope of seeing an occupied baby seat but the interior was empty and in that moment of utter desolation Ellie felt the buzz of the phone in her pocket.

Walk towards the lighthouse, the message read. *You'll see where I am.*

The gust of wind Ellie stepped into was cold but nothing on the ice that was running in her veins as she followed the new instruction. She stumbled on the rough roadway because, in between the flashes of the lighthouse beacon, it was so dark. On and on she went. She could see the lighthouse clearly with its white walls and the darker dome of its tip but she couldn't see anyone standing nearby.

With each brief illumination, she turned her head further, frantically searching for the man who was waiting for her. He wasn't close to the lighthouse at all. He had gone past signs warning of the danger of the nearby cliffs and he was standing very close to where the land beneath his feet appeared to vanish.

Ellie was much closer when the next flash of light came. She saw that Marcus was holding the handle of a baby's car seat in one hand.

And he was smiling.

They had to kill the engines of the bikes as soon as they saw the vehicle Ellie was driving pull to a stop but they could coast some distance down the hill in silence. They had already switched off their headlamps before rounding the last bend in the road.

'We'll go the rest of the way on foot,' Jet told his companions. 'How fit are you guys feeling?'

'Fit enough,' came Max's terse response. 'Let's go.'

'Got a phone call to make first,' Jet said calmly. 'Not a good look to have the back-up arriving too far past the action.'

Abandoning the bikes, the three men travelled fast on foot but they were still well behind Ellie when she got close to the lighthouse. They paused as they saw her turn off the pathway.

'Where the hell is she going? There's nothing but cliffs over there.'

'*He's* there,' Max hissed. 'Wait for the light. See?'

They saw. The lone figure and the small shape of the car seat.

Ellie a matter of metres away.

Open ground around them. No chance to get behind Marcus and take him down and if he saw any of them approaching, he could drop that car seat—and Mouse—over the cliffs beside him.

If Ellie got close enough, she could meet the same fate.

And there was nothing at all Max could do about it.

He'd never felt so helpless in his life. There was fury, there, too. At Ellie, for putting herself in danger like this. What the hell was he going to do if something happened to her? His life wouldn't be worth living.

Why?

Because he *loved* her, dammit. He loved Ellie and he loved Mouse and it didn't matter that they had turned his life upside down. He wanted it to stay that way. He didn't want to lose either of them. He *couldn't*…

Don't move, Ellie, he prayed silently. *Don't get any closer. Wait…*

'The lighthouse,' Jet said softly. 'It's as close as we can get and it'll give us cover. Wait for the light to go past and then run like hell.'

'Marcus?' Ellie stopped. Instinct was telling her not to get close enough to be touched. Not yet, anyway. Not unless she had no other choice. 'What are you doing?'

'Waiting for you, Eleanor.'

She closed her eyes for a heartbeat. How was she going to play this? Would he want her to seem weak and helpless? But hadn't she just demonstrated she wasn't by getting here at all? There was only one thing she wanted to say right now.

'I want my baby.' She swallowed hard. 'Please… give her back to me.'

'*My* baby, too, Eleanor. *Isn't* she?'

No, Ellie wanted to scream. She's mine. And…and Max's. He gave her the name of his special friend. The name he would have chosen for his own child.

'*Isn't* she?' The snarl was almost a shriek.

'Y-yes. Yes, she is.'

'No lies this time. You haven't got your let's-pretend-we're-tough-guy-bikie doctor friends around to help you this time, have you?'

'No.' Oh, dear Lord…she wished she did. All three

of them. In their black leather gear. Tall and menacing and ready to protect her. But she didn't have her dark angels. She had to protect herself. And her baby.

'I'm sorry, Marcus,' she said shakily. 'I didn't mean to lie to you.'

'Yes, you did. You're lying now, you stupid cow.'

'I…I was scared. I'm still scared…' No problem sounding genuine now. '*Please,* Marcus. I'll do any-thing you want. Just…don't hurt her.'

The icy wind was gusting. Biting through her cloth-ing. Was Mouse freezing? Ellie could hear a thin whimper of sound but it was unlike any noise she'd ever heard from her baby before. It sounded…ex-hausted. Alarming.

'She's cold, Marcus,' Ellie said desperately. 'And hungry. I need to feed her. Please…'

'Come and get her, then.'

She couldn't do that. She had to get Marcus away from the edge of the cliff but she couldn't think of any way to achieve that. Paralysed by fear, Ellie simply stood there. Waiting for another flash of light. Listening to… What was that?

Marcus heard something too. 'What the *hell* is that?' he yelled. 'You told someone where you were going, didn't you?'

'No. I promise. I didn't tell anyone.'

The noise was getting louder. She looked over her shoulder and up at the sky. The tiny flashing lights of an aircraft were clearly visible and the sound was taking on the recognisable 'chop' of helicopter rotors. Was help coming? Did she simply need to find some way of stalling Marcus? Distracting him, maybe?

'We need to go somewhere they won't be able to see us, Marcus. We have to hide. Quickly!'

'What? No…I—'

'It's all right. Listen, we'll get away from here. I'll tell the police it was all a mistake. That you didn't kidnap anybody. That we're together. You know, engaged…' She turned towards the lighthouse. 'Come with me.'

The helicopter had activated a powerful searchlight. An area that included the car park was being looked at while it hovered overhead.

'You don't want me,' Marcus sneered. 'You want *him*. You think I don't know what you've been doing? Playing happy families. Going to look at houses to buy?'

'No. It's you I want, Marcus. Only you.'

The helicopter was moving again. It was almost directly overhead. Ellie dipped her head and groaned aloud. This wasn't going to work. She couldn't lie convincingly enough. But then she raised her face and saw Marcus running towards her.

Empty-handed.

The spotlight from the helicopter came on again and the terror that Marcus had thrown the car seat over the cliff proved unfounded. The seat was on the ground where he'd been standing. He'd simply abandoned it.

'You *bastard*.' All that terror and an unholy fury that someone could frighten her that much went into the shove Ellie gave Marcus as he reached out to grab her. He stumbled backwards, stepped onto a rock and fell hard.

Ellie ran. Not towards the relative safety of the

lighthouse but back towards the cliff. She reached the car seat. The safety-belt mechanism was open and there was nothing to slow her from grabbing her baby with both hands and clutching her to her breasts. But, just as swiftly, Marcus was getting back onto his feet.

The roar of the hovering helicopter filled her head. The spotlight was almost blinding her. Could she really see what she thought she was seeing?

Three dark shapes well away from the shadows of the lighthouse. Moving at astonishing speed towards Marcus. And further away, flashing blue and red lights. So many of them. Emergency vehicles speeding along the road towards this scene.

The knowledge that somehow Max had followed her here and was trying to protect her was unbelievable but maybe he was too late. Everybody was too late. Marcus was on his feet, his face so twisted with fury it was virtually unrecognisable. He was launching himself in her direction. Screaming words that were incomprehensible. He wasn't going to stop. He was going to send them all over the cliff.

Ellie curled herself over the precious bundle in her arms. Curled herself so forcefully she rolled forward, landing on her shoulder and then her back. She felt the impact of a foot on her thigh and then saw Marcus tumble to land on her other side. She heard the thump of his body land and then he rolled again, unable to slow the momentum he'd built up. Another roll and then he vanished. She heard an unearthly scream that got drowned by the whine of an aircraft engine being shut down after landing.

The moment that sound began to fade she could hear the sound of the voice she loved the most.

'*Ellie*. My God, Ellie, are you all right?'

CHAPTER ELEVEN

IT WAS over.

The car park was crowded with emergency vehicles. Police cars and vans. Ambulances. Even a fire engine had been dispatched.

The police had been less than impressed by the way the three doctors had taken off after Ellie by themselves. Detective Inspector Jack Davidson was having words with Max while his deputies took statements from Rick and Jet somewhere else.

'Just what the hell did you think you were *doing*, exactly? What do you guys think you are? Doctors or members of some elite SAS branch?'

'Jet's actually done a lot of work with the SAS.' Max was trying to see past the solid figure of the detective. Into the back of the ambulance where he knew Ellie was. With Mouse. He'd had no time to do more than make sure neither of them had any obvious physical injuries before others had begun arriving and taking over this scene.

The helicopter was lifting off again. This time its spotlight would be used to locate Marcus Jones. Surviving the fall was an impossibility, but someone would have to be winched down to recover the body if it hadn't made it as far as the ocean.

Marcus Jones was gone. Ellie was safe.

It was over.

She would no longer need his protection.

She hadn't wanted it at the end, anyway, had she? She'd chosen to come here alone. She must have been scared stiff but she still hadn't included him.

That hurt. Enough to make him angry. Or sad. Or… *something* that was powerful enough to feel like it was eating him up inside.

Detective Inspector Davidson wasn't helping.

'You could all be charged, you know that? Interfering with police operations is a serious offence.'

Rick walked towards them, Jet by his side. 'You done yet?' he queried.

'Yes,' Max said.

'No,' Jack Davidson said. 'Not by a long shot.'

Jet stared at him. 'What's the problem? Case solved. Victims are uninjured. You'll get the credit. You wouldn't have been anywhere near here if I hadn't called it in.' He shoved his hands into the pockets of his leather jacket. 'Bloody cold, isn't it? Don't s'pose there's any coffee to be had?'

Max had more important things on *his* mind. 'I'm going to see how Ellie's getting on,' he muttered.

He put his own hands in his pockets and hunched his shoulders against the wind. It was only a short walk to the ambulance but he was flanked by Rick and Jet.

'Hey…' Rick gave his upper arm a friendly thump. 'Cheer up. It's all sorted. The weasel won't be bothering anybody ever again.'

'Yeah…' Jet sounded just as cheerful. 'Your work is done. Life, as we know it, can resume.'

Rick was nodding. 'Did I ever get round to telling you he offered to marry Ellie?'

'What?' Clearly, Jet hadn't caught up on that titbit. He shook his head in disbelief but then he grinned. 'Every cloud has a silver lining, man. You don't have to even *think* about getting married or being some kind of stand-in daddy now. How good is that?'

The voices had been carried on the wind through a back door that was slightly ajar and Ellie had had no choice other than to overhear the end of that exchange.

She'd been crying. Trying to get her baby to feed, which would be the best way to warm her up, but Mouse was having none of it. She was wrapped in several blankets but was still making that odd, plaintive whimpering that was quiet enough to frighten Ellie.

She still hadn't processed everything that had just happened. She wouldn't believe that Marcus was actually dead and no longer a threat until someone proved it to her. She was cold and still afraid and…despite the attention of all the capable professionals around her… she was lonely.

Hearing Rick and Jet celebrating the fact that the trouble was over and that she had no further claim of any kind on Max pushed her misery to the point where her tears dried up. She probably seemed quite calm by the time Max climbed into the back of the ambulance and sat on the stretcher beside her.

'You OK?'

'I'm…OK.'

'What about Mouse?'

'She's not hurt but she's very cold. She won't feed…' Ellie's voice cracked. She wanted to say she didn't know what to do and she was scared but that would just be asking for help all over again, wouldn't it? Max wouldn't want that. He was free now. His best friends thought that was a silver lining to the cloud she had generated by coming into his life. Max probably agreed with them.

'We'll get going,' a paramedic decided. 'Get her into the emergency department where they've got all the gear to get her properly warmed up.'

'You tried the kangaroo thing?' Max had caught Ellie's gaze and was holding it with an odd intensity.

'I'm cold, too. It might make things worse and I couldn't give her to someone she doesn't know.'

'She knows me,' Max said softly. 'Can I try? I'm as warm as toast in here.' He unzipped his leather jacket and smiled at Ellie.

He *was* warm. Ellie could feel his body heat from where she was sitting. She could *see* it in his smile. He had such a warm heart, this man.

She loved him so much.

Enough to trust him with her precious baby.

'What do we do?'

'Undress her. Down to her nappy.'

'What?' A junior ambulance officer sounded horrified. 'She's hypothermic.'

'Out,' Max ordered. 'I'm an emergency department specialist and I'm taking over treatment of this patient for now. Crank the heater up, shut all the doors and go away for a while. Thank you,' he added politely.

Ellie undressed Mouse. She heard doors opening and then slamming shut, more than once. It wasn't until she looked up to see if Max was ready for Mouse that she realised Rick and Jet had climbed inside. Jet sat in the driver's seat and Rick was in the front passenger seat but they were both sitting sideways so they could see what was happening in the back of the vehicle.

Max had been wearing a work shirt under his leather jacket today and he unbuttoned it. He took Mouse from Ellie and positioned her against his chest, tucking the shirt around the small body and then pulling his jacket over to cover everything but her face.

'I was kind of nervous the first time I did this,' he told Ellie. 'But you know what…?'

'What?'

Ellie's voice came out as a whisper. She was totally captivated by what she was seeing. This gorgeous, big man with a tiny baby nestled against his heart, wrapped up in the black leather jacket with its macho zips and buckles. He'd done this when Mouse had first entered the world but she'd never seen it.

And it was…beautiful.

'I've kind of missed it,' Max told her.

He hadn't had any idea.

It had seemed such an imposition at the time. Something he'd been obliged to do because he'd stuck his neck out and tried to protect the woman who'd landed on his doorstep in big trouble.

He'd done it and he'd been proud of his success. He'd known that a bond had been formed but, until tonight, he'd had no idea how deep it ran. Faced with the possibility of a life that didn't include Mouse or Ellie, he'd discovered just how empty it would be. Meaningless.

'Hey…I think she's stopped crying.'

'Has she?' Ellie leaned closer. Close enough for her head to be touching his shoulder. She had a blanket around her shoulders but Max saw her shiver. At least that bone-deep misery in her face lifted a little as she peered down at the tiny face against his chest. Mouse had, indeed, stopped that sad whimpering. She was snuggled in as though relishing the body heat.

Rick and Jet were leaning further into the cabin, trying to see for themselves.

'Aw…' Rick was smiling. 'Cute little mouse, isn't she?'

'Her name's Mattie,' Max said quietly.

He could feel the way his mates stilled. Without looking up, he knew they'd be exchanging a glance. Silent communication. Checking with each other whether this was acceptable, given its significance to them all.

'Max chose her name,' Ellie said nervously into the silence. 'He said…he said…'

'That it was the name I'd choose for my own child,' Max finished for her. He looked up. 'It had to be that special,' he explained to the others. 'Because…she feels like my own kid.' His smile felt very lopsided. 'Guess I fell in love.'

Rick cleared his throat. 'Saw that coming,' he muttered. 'Only I thought it'd be with the mum, not the munchkin.'

'Yes…well…there is that.' Max looked down at

Ellie. 'It was. *Is*. Ellie...I love you. I don't ever want to have to face the possibility of losing you again. I don't ever want a day that you're not a part of. You *and* Mattie.'

Ellie's eyes were huge. Shining with tears that he hoped like hell were caused by joy. There'd been way too many of any other sort for her.

'I love you, too, Max. But...' Ellie's glance slid sideway. '...I heard you...talking about that silver lining. About how good it was that you didn't...'

'Have to marry you?' Max supplied. He glared at Rick and Jet, who inched backwards. 'No. I don't *have* to marry you. But I *want* to. Those idiot friends of mine have no idea what they were making fun of but I know. I've never wanted anything as much in my entire life. Except maybe for one thing...' Max jerked his head. 'Like a bit of privacy. Would you guys like to get lost for a minute or two? There are some things a man needs to do on his own.'

'Yeah...' Rick grinned at Jet. 'Like propose. Shall we let him get on with it?'

'Don't see we've got much choice,' Jet grumbled. 'All right, I'm going.'

But he paused to look back. Not at Max but at Ellie. For a moment, he just held her gaze and then he smiled. 'Mattie's a cool name,' he said gruffly. 'Good choice.'

Ellie held her breath as the door shut, leaving them alone.

'She's doing that nose-rubbing thing,' Max said. 'I think she might be ready for something to eat.'

'I don't want her to get cold again.'

'How 'bout if you hold her and I hold *you* and keep you both warm?'

It sounded like heaven. 'Do you think your jacket's big enough?'

'My heart is,' Max told her. 'I'm going to look after you, Ellie. Both of you.'

Somehow, they managed it. Tucked against Max's chest, with Mattie in her arms and Max's arms around them both, Ellie was able to feed her baby. And it *was* heaven. She tilted her head back so that it rested under Max's shoulder and she could look up at him.

'I love you, Max. I think I have ever since you opened the door that day.'

He held her gaze. 'And I've been wanting to hold you ever since you fell into my arms. I just didn't recognise what it was all about until tonight.'

Strange how easy it was to push the trauma of the last few hours away. She'd have to deal with it all properly but not yet. Not while she was in this blissful little bubble.

'I feel so safe with you.'

'You are safe. You always will be if I have anything to do with it.' Max bent and kissed her lips gently. 'You and Mattie.' He moved his hand to stroke a thumb softly over the baby's dark spikes of hair. 'My family.' The hold around Ellie tightened. 'Marry me?'

'Of course I will. Yes. Yes and yes and—'

He kissed her again. Deeper this time and with a tenderness that melted any lingering chill she might have had after the night's events.

'Shall we buy that house? Would it make a good place to live for our family?'

'I think it would be a perfect place.'

A knock came on the back door of the ambulance. 'You OK in there?' a voice called.

Max and Ellie looked at each other. They both looked down at Mattie.

'We're good,' Max called back. He caught Ellie's gaze again and smiled. 'Aren't we?'

'Oh, yes…' Ellie smiled back through tears of joy. 'We're very, very good.'

EPILOGUE

'OH, ELLIE…you look stunning.'

'Do I?' Ellie turned a little so that she could see the row of intricate buttons running down the back of her dress, keeping the beaded bodice hugging her body and then fading into the soft folds of the gathered, silk skirt. Her hair fell loose to her bare shoulders, except for the twisted strands making a band of intricate coils that were studded with tiny, silk flowers.

She grinned. 'I do look OK, don't I?'

'Stunning.'

'Thanks, Sarah. You look amazing, too. I love that dress.'

Her bridesmaid looked down at herself. 'It's as old as the hills. A ballgown left over from a life I don't even remember any more.'

'It's perfect. As blue as that sky out there. Now… I've got lots of leftover flowers. Let's tie a bit of your hair back and give you a matching Druid look.'

'Hmm. Not sure about that. What do you think, Josh?'

Both women looked to where a small, dark-haired boy sat on the bed, propped up against the pillows, watching the proceedings.

'Yes. You should have flowers too, Aunty Sarah. They look pretty.'

'Right. You feeling OK, hon?'

'Yeah.'

'Up to throwing a few rose petals?'

Josh made a face. 'It's a stupid thing to do.'

Ellie gave Sarah a ghost of a wink. 'Max doesn't think so,' she said casually.

'Oh…'

In the space of only a short meeting last night, Max had become Josh's hero. Ellie had seen the look of adoration creeping onto the child's face and had had to blink away tears.

Tears of sadness, because she could understand the indescribable pain Sarah was having to deal with given the possibility of losing this child but there was joy there as well. Enormous gratitude that things had worked out as they had. Mattie was safe. She was going to grow up with Max as her father. She would look at him with that same kind of wonder before she was much older.

She was safe, too. She had nothing more to fear from Marcus Jones. She couldn't imagine ever being truly afraid again, with Max by her side.

Today she was going to make a public commitment to share the rest of her life with the man she loved. That was the most amazingly joyful prospect in itself but, like icing on the cake, there was more happiness to be found in contemplating what the future might hold for Max and herself as Mattie grew up. That she would have a whole family—the kind she had always dreamed of. That she might be joined by a brother or sister one day.

The thought of Mattie was enough to propel her towards the windows of this upstairs bedroom, as Sarah deftly twisted sections of her long blonde hair and fastened them at the back of her head. Ellie stood carefully out of sight as she peered down into the garden and then she smiled and had to blink hard again.

She would have sworn that nothing could make Max look more irresistibly sexy than his motorbike gear but the dark dress suit was the polished version of a bad boy. The other side of the coin and it was, most definitely, equally irresistible.

Especially given the small, white bundle he was holding. Three-month-old Mattie was wearing that pretty, smocked dress with the embroidered flowers that Max had given her that day, on her one-week birthday. It was still a bit big and her face was entirely hidden by the matching bonnet but it was perfect for today for all sorts of reasons.

'Is he here yet?'

'Um…no.' Ellie felt her forehead crease with a tiny pang of anxiety. If she'd known what she had learned only last night, would she have asked Sarah to be her bridesmaid? It had seemed the obvious choice. The news about Marcus had hit the papers just as Sarah and Josh had returned from the States and it had been enough to re-establish contact between them, albeit via email and phone calls while Sarah had been in Auckland. Catching up on all that had happened to both of them since they had shared a house had been enough to re-establish their friendship so, yes, she had been the obvious choice.

'You…won't say anything, will you?' she added quietly. 'Not today?'

'I promised, didn't I?' Sarah was threading the stems of the flowers into her hair. 'Besides, it's a great opportunity to meet him first. To have him meet Josh.'

'Who's going to meet me?' Josh was climbing off the bed.

He was wearing a scaled-down version of Max's suit and looked absolutely adorable. Sarah was right. This would be a perfect introduction because nobody could meet this child and be unmoved. And if what Sarah suspected was the truth then a huge amount was riding on what could happen after this meeting. A life was at stake, no less. No wonder Sarah was lost for words.

'Lots of people,' Ellie said into the short silence. 'Doctors and nurses from the new hospital that Sarah's going to be working in soon. And…and Max's friends, Jet and Rick. You know… You saw that picture of them all with their motorbikes last night.'

'Oh, yeah… Cool.' He had a real urchin grin, this kid. 'Can I have a ride on a bike?'

'Not today,' Sarah said firmly.

'Tomorrow?'

'We'll have to see.'

'That means no, doesn't it, Ellie?'

'Not necessarily.' Another sneak peek through the window showed that final arrangements were being made on the lawn. Max was standing by the flower-covered gazebo with the marriage celebrant. Rick was standing beside them and…good grief, Mattie had been given into the care of Jet. Ellie smiled.

'Is he there?' Sarah asked again.

'Who?' Josh demanded.

'The best man,' his aunt responded.

Ellie's gaze was back on Max. She hadn't realised she'd stepped into view until he looked up. He was seeing her a tad too soon but what did it matter? He would be seeing her every day for the rest of her life and if he always looked at her the way he was right now she would be the happiest woman on earth. For a delicious moment, she basked in that love, in the strength of the connection between them. It was time to go downstairs and into the garden of their family home. Time to tell the world just how much she loved Max McAdam.

'Oh, yes…' she murmured.

The best man was definitely there.

He was waiting for her to arrive by his side. To stay there for ever.

She took a deep breath and smiled brightly at Sarah and Josh.

'Let's go.'

THE UNSUNG HERO

BY
ALISON ROBERTS

CHAPTER ONE

TIME stood still.

Rick Wilson had never actually understood that phrase before this moment but, man, he did now.

It was kind of like one of those three-hundred-and-sixty-degree shots in a movie where something was frozen in space but the rest of the scene continued around it. He was part of that scene but where he was and what he was here for became suddenly and completely irrelevant.

It seemed extraordinary that nobody else had noticed but why would they? The only thing that had really stopped was in his head. A stun-gun effect on his thought processes from that first sight of…perfection, that was the only word for it.

Some kind of goddess in a floaty blue dress. Long, long blonde hair, some of which had been wound around her head and adorned with tiny, white flowers. She was tall and slim and he'd put good money on her eyes being blue. Dark blue.

Who was she and where the hell had she been? Nowhere near his world, that was for sure, because he would have remembered.

More than his brain had been stunned but it wasn't until the need for oxygen made Rick suck in a rather deep breath that he realised his chest had also been immobilised. The sound he made elicited a nudge from the man standing close by his side. And a look. He might as well have had a bubble over his head like a cartoon character as well. One that said, *Do me a favour and try and keep your hands off her for the duration of the ceremony at least.*

No worries. Rick's grin flashed back. How long could a ceremony last, after all?

Suddenly, the annoyance of wearing the ridiculous bow-tie and the vaguely trapped feeling that weddings in general, and this one in particular, always gave him became worthwhile. He was actually pleased he was dressed up to the nines. That he would be here for hours and that one of his official duties was to partner the bridesmaid. The goddess, no less.

She was much closer now. With a supreme effort, Rick tried to stop staring. He managed to switch off the mental zoom lens and take in some of the wider picture. He could hear the music and see the way the small gathering of guests in this garden setting had twisted in their seats to watch the bride and her bridesmaid approaching. A small boy was in front of the two women, throwing handfuls of rose petals from the basket he was carrying.

The sight of the child triggered a process of recalling snatches of conversations he now wished he'd paid more attention to. Worry over the choice of a bridesmaid because…that's right, she had a kid who was very sick. Only it wasn't her kid, exactly. He was a nephew or something but she was his only family and she was clearly some sort of saint because she'd been travelling the globe trying to track down his biological father so that the kid's leukaemia could be treated with a bone-marrow transplant.

What was her name?

Rick was thinking hard as he watched the boy being directed to sit in an empty seat in the front row.

Sarah.

That was it. Nice name.

He had to wait while the bridesmaid positioned herself beside the bride and took charge of the bouquet but, finally, she looked up and caught his welcoming smile. Her eyes widened a fraction and she held the eye contact for a heartbeat longer. Then she looked away as the celebrant began to speak and welcome those gathered to witness the ceremony. It took Rick a few seconds to realise why he was feeling oddly poleaxed again.

She hadn't smiled back, that was why.

Sarah had to take a deep, deep breath.

It was good that she had the bouquet to hold because it effectively hid the slight tremor she could feel in her hands. She hadn't expected him to look at her like that—as though he couldn't wait to launch a campaign to jump her bones. A stupid oversight, really, because she ought to be used to that kind of reaction from men by now. It was just so wildly inappropriate at this moment that she had an insane urge to slap his face. So she held on to that bunch of flowers for dear life and listened to the familiar words of a traditional wedding ceremony.

'I, Maxwell McAdam, take thee, Eleanor Peters, to be my wife. To have and to hold…'

Maybe she'd misinterpreted the look. He was probably just a nice guy, as Ellie had assured her he was. He was the best man and it was his job to look after the bridesmaid, wasn't it? To be friendly.

'To love and cherish from this day forward. This is my solemn vow.'

Sarah found her gaze drifting sideways in the tiny pause as the bride, her friend Ellie, prepared to take her turn to recite the vows. If Rick was doing his job properly, he'd be focused on the ceremony. Thinking about the rings he would need to produce very soon. To her consternation, however, she found herself catching his direct gaze again. How long had he been looking at *her*?

At least he was looking suitably serious this time, with no hint of that confident, playboy smile but there was a question in those dark eyes that had nothing to do with what they were a part of at this moment and if she simply turned away it would be a rebuff that could have repercussions.

Enormous repercussions.

Her tiny smile might have been hesitant but it was enough for that unspoken question to vanish. For Rick's face to soften a fraction in that split second before they both looked away.

'I, Eleanor Peters, take thee, Maxwell McAdam, to be my husband. To have and to hold…'

The first kiss as husband and wife was a moment that would be etched on Rick's brain for ever. The way Max and Ellie looked at each other. The soft intensity in the way their lips touched to seal their commitment. The way the kiss went on...and on.

Impossible not to feel the power of the link between this newly married couple and it was strong enough to give Rick an odd twisting sensation in his gut. A combination of recognition and...loss?

Recognition was automatic. He'd known Max since high school. Since, along with Jet and Matt, they'd formed a brotherhood that had become true family for all of them. Labelled the 'bad boys', they'd had the kind of bond that meant you'd put your life on the line for them in a heartbeat and life without the strength and power of that support crew was unimaginable.

Loss came from the uneasy feeling that the order of his universe was changing because one of the 'bad boys' was no longer a single entity. He had a ready-made family, in fact, what with Ellie's baby Mattie. Fast bike rides and nights out with fabulous women were a thing of the past. Max was now committed to sharing his life with a woman and the bond between them was clearly cemented with the same kind of soul-deep glue that Rick had only known with the brotherhood.

Was it really possible to feel that way about a *woman*?

The guests were clapping and cheering. A whistle or two could be heard. Rick glanced sideways to where Jet was seated in the front row. The third 'bad boy' had been given the responsibility of caring for baby Mattie during the ceremony and he was still holding her with the kind of expression that made Rick think of a bomb-disposal expert in the middle of a dangerous mission. A focused scowl that suggested appreciation of both the significance of the mission and its less-than-desirable potential.

Noticing the direction of Rick's gaze, Jet rolled his eyes as the kiss finally wound up. It took him back to the conversation they'd had only last night, over a few beers. To them both vowing to avoid the kind of commitment Max had chosen. They'd keep their bikes, thanks very much. They'd work hard and play hard and take all the fun life had to offer because they knew damn well how short it could be.

The boy beside Jet was making a disgusted face but then he grinned repentantly at Sarah, who had also looked away from the couple. It was inevitable that their gazes brushed as they turned back to their duties. With the image of that kiss still burning itself into Rick's memory cells, along with the reminder of that vow to play hard and get the most out of life, it was just as inevitable that his gaze dropped from Sarah's eyes to her mouth.

Such a soft-looking, deliciously kissable kind of mouth.

He felt his breath leave his lungs in a soft sigh as he wondered…

No, make that anticipated. And, knowing he could trust that very pleasant curl in his gut, he knew that kissing Sarah was something he had very good reason to look forward to. All he needed now was a smooth opening line and that shouldn't be a problem given the amount of practice he'd had over the last decade or more.

First, there were the congratulations to be given to

the newly married couple. Rick thumped Max on the back to accentuate his hug and then kissed Ellie, whose eyes were shining with joyous tears.

'Thanks, Rick.' She turned from him to receive Sarah's hug. ''Bout time we introduced you two,' she said. 'Rick, this is—'

'Sarah,' he cut in, smiling. 'I've heard all about you.'

She looked disconcerted, turning back to Ellie, but the bride was being taken to a small table on one side of the flower-covered gazebo to deal with the paperwork.

'W-what have you heard?'

'You're an old friend of Ellie's.'

'We were flatmates in Auckland.'

'And didn't you sublet your apartment here to Max?'

'Yes. I was away in the States for a while.'

Rick nodded. 'So, really, you're responsible for this wedding happening. If Ellie hadn't come looking for you, she would never have met Max.'

And *he* would never have met Sarah. Now, that could have been a smooth opening gambit except that he didn't have time to deliver it. The signatures of the witnesses were now required and both Rick and Sarah had duties to perform. After that, group photographs were taken with the lovely backdrop of this garden that Max and Ellie's new property boasted, the photographer's attention focused on the bride and groom. Rick had more time to think but, annoyingly, inspiration wouldn't strike.

Maybe that had something to do with the munchkins.

Mattie was back in her mother's arms now, much to Jet's obvious relief, and the boy was glued to Sarah's side as they watched some family shots being taken. Ellie held Mattie and Max held Ellie and nobody who saw those photographs in years to come would ever guess that Max wasn't Mattie's biological father.

It didn't even seem that crazy any more, though Rick certainly couldn't see himself putting his hand up to adopt an infant. He took another glance at the boy standing beside Sarah. Weird that her living accessory wasn't the deal-breaker it would have been even a few months ago but this was a kid, not a baby, and, anyway, he was a special enough case to make allowances for.

'Let's get a photo of all the boys in their suits,' Ellie suggested. 'Josh, come and stand with Max and Rick.'

'Do I *have* to?'

'Yes.' Sarah gave him a stern look but then smiled winningly. 'Please? For me? And Ellie?'

Oh, man…That was a real smile. One that no man could possibly resist. Even a half-grown one.

'All right. I s'pose,' Josh grumbled.

He was soon standing between the groom and the best man, a miniature version of the two tall men in his small suit and bow-tie. He had dark hair, too. What was left of it. Rick could see the pale skin of the boy's scalp and knew it wouldn't be long before he was completely bald. He could also see that Sarah was watching him watch Josh and she had an odd look on her face.

Did she know that he knew the history? Was she worried that it might colour the way he talked to the boy? She needn't worry. Rick dealt with a lot of seriously ill children and he wasn't about to talk down to the lad or exude sympathy. The smile he gave Sarah was intended to reassure her but, strangely, she looked distinctly uncomfortable.

If it hadn't been too weird a thought to entertain, he might have even interpreted her expression as vaguely guilty.

Did she think he was directing sympathy at her, maybe? As if. He had enough sensitivity to know that she wouldn't appreciate that. She was clearly a strong and capable woman. Someone who'd taken on the responsibility of a child who wasn't her own. Who was having to cope with the disaster of that child becoming gravely ill and who was doing everything she possibly could to put things right.

He respected that. Good grief, she'd gone to the other side of the world to try and track down the boy's dad and when she'd discovered he wasn't the one, she'd headed back to chase up another lead. Hopefully, that had proved successful. What with all the drama of Max and Ellie in recent months and then getting them shifted to this house and the wedding being planned, Rick hadn't caught up on any further news about that. He had heard that Josh had been in hospital again in Auckland, which was why Sarah had only just made it to Dunedin in time to be Ellie's bridesmaid. Maybe that had been for the transplant.

'Hey, buddy.' He winked at Josh as they positioned themselves near an old sundial in a corner of the garden. 'How's it going?'

Josh eyed him warily.

'I'm Rick.'

'I know. You're Max's friend.'

'Yep.' Both men spoke together and then Max put his arm over Josh's shoulders as cameras whirred. 'Rick's got a Ducati too. Just like mine.' He raised an eyebrow at Rick. 'Josh was looking at that photo of us last night. With the bikes.'

'Max said he might give me a ride one day.'

'Cool.' Rick had no trouble smiling for the camera. Maybe this was it. His ticket for getting to know Sarah. Max was going to be very busy settling into married life. *He* could offer to give Josh that ride.

'I don't think so.'

Sarah held out her hand to accept the glass of juice she had requested at the drinks table, congratulating herself on being so restrained.

Had Rick been waiting for a moment when she was away from everybody else to make his unwelcome offer to give Josh a ride on his motorbike?

Over my dead body had been the words that first sprang to mind but she had managed—with difficulty—to stop them emerging. She didn't want to antagonise this man. OK, maybe this *was* a long shot but it was the only shot she had left and she couldn't afford to throw it away. And maybe she should have been as prepared for something like this as for the way Rick was making no secret of finding her attractive.

He was totally irresponsible. The kind of good-looking—well, OK, make that *great*-looking guy who skated through life getting everything he wanted and to hell with any less than pleasant consequences. How old was he? Thirty-five or -six? High time he woke up and smelled the coffee, that's for sure, but what was she going to do if he simply refused?

'I'm not suggesting anything remotely dangerous.' Rick pulled a can of lager from the nest of ice in a big silver tub. 'Just a slow crawl around the block, or something.'

The smile revealed that Rick Wilson usually got what he wanted and no wonder. It was a winning smile, for sure. Confident and lazy. Softening a face of definite lines and a shadowed jaw that had 'bad boy' stamped all over it. Soft, dark hair that had been neatly combed into place a while back but the breeze in this outdoor setting had detached a single lock that almost touched an equally dark eyebrow. Eyes that had a hint of mischief that any woman would have trouble resisting.

Any other woman, that was.

'I don't think so,' Sarah repeated, trying very hard not to put a punctuation mark between each word. She even added a smile of her own. 'But thanks anyway.'

His smile faded. A tiny frown appeared between his eyes.

Oh…help.

As if in answer to the silent plea, there was a rustle of silk beside her and Ellie reached for one of the cans in the tub of ice.

'For Max.' She grinned in response to Rick's raised eyebrows. 'He's got his hands full of baby at the moment.' Then she looked from Rick to Sarah and she paused, her eyes widening.

Sarah gave her head a tiny shake. No, she hadn't broken her promise.

'Rick was just offering to give Josh a ride on his bike,' she said, her tone carefully neutral.

'Oh…' Ellie bit her lip, giving Rick an oddly sympathetic glance. 'Um…Josh's mother was killed when she was a pillion passenger on her boyfriend's bike,' she said quietly.

Rick winced visibly. 'Sorry.'

'No worries. You weren't to know.' Sarah could see Josh approaching. 'Here's your juice,' she said brightly. 'Want something to eat as well?'

'Nah. I've already had heaps. Can we go down to the beach? Max says there's a jetty and you can go fishing.'

'Maybe another day. We're here for the wedding, remember? And not for too much longer, either. You don't want to get too tired when you're going to be starting school again this week.'

This wasn't going well.

If it wasn't his wedding day, he might have given Max a bit of stick for setting him up for that little disaster of offering Josh the opportunity to get maimed or worse.

He still could, if he made a joke of it, but there was something even more disturbing that needed his attention urgently.

Sarah was talking to Jet now. Smiling and nodding at something he was saying. Rick broke off the conversation he was having with some theatre nurses he knew and moved in their direction. The clock was ticking here because who knew how long it would be before she whisked Josh off home? And what if she was busy agreeing to a date or something? No. Rick could be pretty sure he was safe on that score. Jet wouldn't go near a woman who had a child. The mere mention of babies had been enough at times for his mate to hold up crossed fingers and make a hissing sound to ward off bad voodoo.

'We'll have to see how it goes,' Sarah was saying as he got close enough to hear. 'One step at a time.'

'Hey…' Jet seemed happy enough to include Rick in the conversation. 'Did you know Sarah's a special-ised ICU nurse? She's coming back to work at Queen Mary's next week.'

'Just casual to start with,' Sarah added. 'I'm not sure how it'll go. All depends on Josh, of course.'

'Of course.' Rick gave up trying to find a smooth opening line. Instead, he went for something much more mundane. 'Our paths will be crossing. I spend quite a good percentage of my time in ICU.'

'You're a neurosurgeon, yes?'

'Yes.' This was good. Had she been asking someone about *him*? Even better that she would be working in that department. Given that neurosurgery was often the main specialty involved in cases like head injuries, he often spent considerable periods of time in ICU. But then he frowned.

'Coming back? You've worked there before?' Surely he would have spotted her. In the unit or the cafeteria. Even the car park, dammit. He was absolutely certain he would have noticed.

Sarah's expression was rueful. 'I applied for a job and got it but I never actually did a shift. That was when Josh got diagnosed.'

'ALL?' Jet queried.

Sarah's nod was grim. Acute lymphoblastic leukaemia was the stuff of parental nightmares. 'The next few months were a bit of a blur. All the invasive diagnostic tests and then induction chemotherapy. I lived in the children's oncology unit.'

'Good response to induction?' It was Jet who spoke again.

Sarah shook her head this time. 'Slow enough to be a real concern. We finally achieved remission but that was when I was told he was a candidate for an early HSCT.'

Rick was listening carefully despite being fascinated by watching Sarah's face as she spoke. She was genuine all right. Nuances of emotion played across her features and he could feel the agony she'd been through. God help him, but he had an insane urge to wrap her into his arms and hold her close. He shook it off and focused on what she'd been saying.

HSCT. Haematopoietic stem-cell transplant. More commonly known as a bone-marrow transplant.

'And that took you to the States?' he asked. 'To try and locate a donor?'

Sarah's gaze flicked in his direction. She hesitated before responding but he couldn't read her expression this time. It was almost as if shutters had come down but he could tell she was struggling with *something*. Then she looked away from both her companions, her gaze raking the small crowd now scattered throughout the garden.

Many were holding champagne glasses and some had plates, having helped themselves to a sumptuous afternoon tea from the table laden with silver, tiered stands that held everything from savouries and sandwiches to tiny cupcakes decorated with hearts. Imitating Sarah's observation, Rick spotted Josh, who was sitting on the wide steps of the terrace beside Max, who was feeding Mattie with a bottle.

Of course. She wouldn't want to be discussing this if Josh was within earshot.

'We heard that didn't work out,' he said gently. 'But Auckland was more successful, yes?'

'What?' Those dark blue eyes flashed with… what?…*alarm*? 'What makes you say that?'

Rick sighed inwardly. He was only trying to be interested here. Supportive. Was she always this prickly?

'Ellie mentioned that Josh was in hospital, that's all. And that was why there was some doubt about whether you'd make it to the wedding. I knew you'd gone to Auckland because of another donor possibility so I was hoping that was due to a transplant happening.'

'No.' He could see the deep breath Sarah took. 'He got sick. Pneumonia. A bug he probably picked up from the plane trip home.'

She was watching Josh again. Ellie had gone over to the steps and was sitting beside her brand-new husband but leaning forward, talking to Josh on his other side. Then she stood up and began walking towards Rick. He glanced at Jet but there seemed to be nothing to say to break the suddenly tense silence enclosing the three of them.

Josh's condition was fragile. He might or might not still be in remission but even if he was, he was at risk due to his suppressed immune system that the maintenance drug regime would cause. Any bacterial, viral or fungal infection could be potentially fatal. Ellie joined the group but it didn't relieve the tension. If anything, it went up a notch or two even before she spoke.

'Sarah…I'm sorry but Josh isn't feeling very well. He says he's got a headache and he thinks he's going to be sick.'

'Oh, *no*!' Rick saw the colour drain from Sarah's face.

'It could just be too many chocolate éclairs and sunshine but…'

The tiny word hung in the air. It could be an infection of some kind. It could even be a sign of a central nervous system relapse, which would not only take away the status of remission but could escalate the progression of this boy's disease.

'I'll have to get him checked.' Sarah's eyes were bright. Too bright. Glittering with unshed tears? 'Oh, *God*… We've only just got over the last setback. He was so desperate to stay well enough to go to school again.'

'I'm so sorry.' Ellie was biting her bottom lip. 'Jet could take you into Emergency.' She turned. 'You've got a shift starting later tonight, haven't you?'

'Yeah.'

'He knows everyone,' she said to Sarah. 'He'll make sure Josh gets the best of care.'

'I'll go too,' Rick announced.

The others all looked at him in surprise.

'Jet and I came together,' he said quickly. 'In my car. It's not as if you guys are planning formal speeches or anything, are you?' He didn't give Ellie time to respond. 'Jet can look after Josh and everything that needs to happen. I can look after Sarah.'

It felt good to say that. And he meant every word. Smooth opening lines or first kisses were the last thing on his mind right now. This was about a potentially sick kid and the woman who was, effectively, his mother. There was no hidden agenda or ulterior motive.

The 'bad boys' weren't being disbanded by this marriage, he realised in a moment of sudden clarity. The tribe was simply expanding. Ellie was a part of it and, by association, Sarah came under the same protective umbrella. That was what this was about. Solidarity. A tribe thing.

So why did Sarah and Ellie exchange a glance that made him feel as if he'd stepped into a minefield?

'I think…' Ellie spoke after a loaded pause and her voice sounded strange. 'That might be quite a good idea, don't you, Sarah?'

Equally strangely, Sarah had closed her eyes as though offering up a silent prayer. She opened them slowly, stared at Ellie for a second and then turned her head towards Rick.

The gaze was so intense it rang alarm bells that were positively deafening. What the hell was going on here?

'Yes.' Sarah sounded perfectly calm, which was weird in itself. 'It *is* a good idea. Can we go now, please?'

Josh had been diagnosed with leukaemia here at Queen Mary's and it became rapidly obvious that he was a favourite patient amongst the paediatric oncology staff that got summoned to the emergency department. One of the registrars even called his consultant, Mike Randall, who said he would be coming in to see what was happening.

A lot was happening. Numerous blood tests and a chest X-ray. An exhaustive physical examination, abdominal ultrasound and a lumbar puncture. Jet changed into scrubs and simply went on shift early but Rick was left with little to do but be there and observe, feeling somewhat ridiculous in his dinner suit and the bow-tie, which had come undone but he wasn't about to bother retying it.

Sarah would have probably felt absurdly overdressed, too, in that long frock and with the flowers still in her hair but it didn't seem to occur to her. As pale as her nephew, she was there by his side for every moment. Holding his hand for the blood tests and curled protectively close to his head throughout the lumbar puncture procedure. Rustling in her long dress as she walked beside his bed when it was rolled to a different area. She said little but seemed grateful to have Jet and Rick there to smooth the admission process and the transition of care to the oncology department.

Josh was just as stoical as Sarah. The hospital environment and these frightening and painful procedures were a part of life for both of them now and they were in it together. With every passing minute, Rick became more aware of the striking bond between these two. Of their courage. Josh didn't cry, even once, and Rick was left convinced that Sarah was a vital component of any treatment for this child. The gentle way she touched him, almost constantly, and the way she held direct eye contact throughout the worst moments, infusing him with both strength and comfort, touched something very deep in Rick.

All his younger patients had families that loved them and would do anything they could to help but he'd never witnessed a bond quite like this. They were both special but Sarah…she was astonishing.

By the time the consultant, Mike, arrived, the early testing was complete and Josh had been moved to a private room in the children's ward. Surprisingly, Max turned up at the same time.

'What are you doing here, man?' Rick asked. 'It's your wedding night!'

'Ellie sent me in with some clothes for Sarah and to find out what's happening. How's Josh?'

'I think we're about to find out.' Rick tilted his head to where Mike was gripping Sarah's hand.

'I hoped it would be an outpatient appointment when we got to see you again,' the older doctor was saying. 'You've only just come down from Auckland, haven't you?'

'Yesterday,' Sarah confirmed wryly.

They both looked at the still figure of the sleeping child on the bed beside them. He had a pulse oximeter on a finger and an IV line snaking up from a heavily bandaged elbow to the stand supporting bags of medicated fluids.

'Let's step outside for a minute so we don't wake him up,' Mike suggested. 'He'll be worn out by now, I suspect.'

He raised his eyebrows as they reached the two men standing by the door. 'Rick…this is a bit out of your field, isn't it? And, Max…didn't I hear you were getting married today?'

'I did. Sarah was our bridesmaid and Josh was the pageboy.'

'Ahh…' Mike's smile was warm. 'And there I was thinking you'd all dressed up on my account.'

He pulled the door almost closed behind him and they drifted closer to the window where they could still see Josh. The ward was quiet ant the corridor dimly lit, with evening visiting hours well over. A baby began crying somewhere and a child's voice called out for her mother. It was a subdued and slightly miserable background.

Mike spoke softly. 'We still haven't got all the results back yet, of course. And I've scheduled a bone-marrow biopsy and MRI scan for tomorrow morning.'

Sarah made a low sound of distress that cut Rick like a sharp blade. Mike's face creased in sympathy.

'I know. I'm sorry. The good news is that his fever's dropped and his lungs are clear. There's no significant change in the size of his liver or spleen and his kidney function's looking good. Even better, this doesn't look like CNS involvement. I think the symptoms are probably due to a virus and we've got treatment under way to deal with it. Antivirals and antibiotics to cover all the bases.'

'He was going to try and go back to school this week. Said he'd wear a mask even if it made him look like a freak.'

Mike shook his head, dismissing the possibility. 'We'll have him in here for a bit. I want to make sure he's still in remission. If not, we're going to have to get back into a pretty aggressive chemotherapy programme.'

Sarah closed her eyes and Rick could sense her struggle in trying to find the strength to face what was coming. He felt helpless.

'What about HSCT?' he asked Mike. 'That's going to be the best option, isn't it?'

Mike's expression was grim. 'No siblings, unfortunately. Sarah's the only family and she's nowhere near a match. Nothing's come up on the bone-marrow register and she hasn't been able to trace Josh's father.' He turned to Sarah. 'You didn't get any further in your hunt in Auckland, did you?'

Her eyes were open now. She was staring at Rick but her gaze flicked back to Mike.

'Actually, I think I did. Quite by chance and only because of Josh being admitted for the chest infection. One of the nurses in the ward had been working there for ages and she seemed to know everybody.'

'And?' There was an undercurrent of excitement in Mike's tone.

'I've got a possibility to chase up. I…I'm just not sure how co-operative he might be.'

'You think he'd refuse to help?' Rick could hear more than a hint of outrage in his own voice.

'He might. He doesn't even know he's got a son yet.'

Rick gave a dismissive snort. 'Tough. It's not as if he's had to take any responsibility so far, is it?'

'No.'

Sarah's agreement was cautious. She was giving him an odd look, as though wondering why he was pushing this, but there was an element of something like hope in her face and that made Rick feel good. Very good. He was helping here.

'But that's not exactly his fault,' she added. 'He didn't know. I don't think Josh's mother even knew.'

'Doesn't matter.' Rick was confident now. He ignored the way Max was staring at him as though he was about to step off a cliff or something. He could support Sarah in this quest. Help her. Maybe help Josh as well. 'If he's a decent human being,' he said firmly, 'then getting tested is the least he can do.'

Sarah looked away from him to Max who gave her a slow nod of encouragement. She looked back at Rick.

'I hope you meant that,' she said softly. 'How soon do you think you could arrange to have the test?'

CHAPTER TWO

'What?'

He was looking at her as if she was some kind of alien species, clearly unable to make any sense of her request. Sarah glanced at Max but he was watching his friend and had an expression of sympathy that made her heart sink. He knew how hard it would be for Rick to accept the idea he could be Josh's father. And maybe he wasn't. Maybe she was making life difficult for all sorts of people unnecessarily but she had no choice, did she?

This was about Josh.

Mike Randall was frowning. 'I'm confused,' he confessed. 'What's Rick got to do with this, Sarah?'

'Absolutely nothing.' Rick held up his hands in an eloquent gesture of denial. 'Look, I'm sorry, Sarah. I've got no idea where this is coming from but you couldn't be more wrong.'

Sarah swallowed hard. She directed her next words at Mike rather than Rick. 'I was chasing someone I thought was called Richard. Known as Rick. I couldn't find any Richard. Then someone suggested that Rick could be short for Eric and…bingo.'

She heard an angry huff of sound from Rick. He turned, walked a couple of jerky steps, shoving his sleeves clear of his wrists as though preparing to do battle. Then he swung back to face them all, shaking his head incredulously.

'I mean, I know I haven't exactly been a monk but… for God's sake, I wasn't even in the country at the time Josh would have been conceived…what, eight or nine years ago? I was in Sydney on a postgraduate surgical course for two years. Wasn't I, Max?'

'Ah… Yes, but—'

'There isn't a "*but*".' Rick was staring at Max with lines of bewilderment creasing his face now. He was being attacked here. Where was the back-up he clearly expected? Max looked as though he was in physical pain. He wanted, more than anything, to be able to provide the support his friend desperately wanted but he couldn't do it because he knew something Rick didn't.

Sarah waited, knowing that Rick would turn back to her eventually. She was the one initiating this attack, wasn't she? So she watched him, seeing the way he straightened his spine and the way his hands curled into fists of frustration. It was the bewilderment that really got to her, though. A window of vulnerability in a man who might otherwise seem invincible. Big. Strong. Clever. Impossibly gorgeous right now with the sleeves of that dinner jacket shoved onto his forearms and the top button of his shirt undone with the ends of that black tie hanging on each side.

Sure enough, he turned to make eye contact with her and it was like a physical blow. As though she had betrayed him.

She had to swallow hard. 'How old do you think Josh is, Rick?'

'Seven,' he said promptly, dredging up another fragment of a conversation in past weeks. 'Or maybe eight.' He flicked a challenging glance at Max.

'That's what I thought,' Max said apologetically. 'But it was a guess, Rick. I—'

'I know he's small for his age,' Sarah interrupted, trying to let Max off the hook. 'But he's nine. Coming up to nine and a half. He was conceived in Auckland a bit over ten years ago.'

Rick was still glaring at Max. 'You *knew* about this, didn't you?'

'Only since last night.' Max sighed heavily. 'It's not as if I've had a chance to talk to you. Sarah promised not to say anything until after the wedding. I was going to warn you, mate.'

Sarah caught Mike's glance. Friction on a personal level between these two men wasn't going to be helpful. He raised his eyebrows and Sarah nodded.

'I went to the States,' she said, 'to find the man who was on Josh's birth certificate. The man my sister genuinely thought *was* Josh's father as far as I could tell. He thought he might be, too and actually got excited by the idea. He couldn't wait to do the DNA test and he was gutted when it turned out that Josh couldn't possibly be his son.'

Rick snorted. 'You'll get the same result from me,' he said coldly. 'Except I won't be pretending *I'm* gutted.' He shook his head. 'You're wasting your time. And *mine*.'

Sarah was finding it hard to stay calm. He was

simply going to refuse to accept the possibility, wasn't he? This might turn into a dead end that could haunt her for ever.

'My sister's name was Lucy,' she said with a tiny wobble in her voice. 'She was two years older than me and we looked very alike.'

He couldn't deny he found her attractive, surely? His interest had been flashing like a neon sign from the first moment he'd laid eyes on her. The kind of physical attributes people found attractive in the opposite sex didn't change that much. She had always been drawn to tall, dark men. Like Rick.

She sighed again, inwardly this time, at the regret that tugged deep inside. In another lifetime she might have been having a very different kind of conversation with Rick Wilson.

'Lucy Prescott?' she prompted. 'Ring any bells?'

'No.' The word was a growl.

'The man who wasn't Josh's father remembered her. It had only been a brief affair but he'd been in love with her. He'd said he'd known he was failing to measure up to the previous man in her life. Only a one-night stand, Lucy had said, and it was never going to go anywhere, but it was all too obvious that she would have preferred it to.'

And Sarah could understand why now. She could also begin to understand why her sister had always kept it a secret. A private fantasy that might have been discredited by sharing it with anyone, even her sister. Rick was one of a kind and he would have been completely out of her league back then when Lucy had been just a shy, country girl starting out on her nursing training.

'He went to the States a month or so later,' she finished. 'He never knew Lucy was pregnant. She refused to tell him. Or say who the father was. I only found that out when I requested Josh's birth certificate after he got sick.'

Silence fell as she finished speaking. Through the crack in the nearby door came a soft whimper.

Sarah tensed and then breathed out with a sigh of resignation. She had to go back to Josh, to be there when he woke up, but it wasn't as if there wasn't any point in saying anything more right now. She had dropped the bombshell. The best thing she could do was give Rick the space to get his head around it.

It was hard not to add a plea of some kind before she turned away. Especially seeing as Rick was giving her his undivided attention. Or maybe he was hoping he could make her go 'poof' and disappear from his life by sheer willpower. She held his gaze for a long second.

Please, she begged silently. *Just…please.*

Mike followed Sarah back into the room to check on his young patient and Rick was left in the corridor with just Max for company.

He turned on his heel and began to walk away.

'Hey…' Max sounded alarmed. 'Where are you going?'

'To find someone to talk to,' Rick snapped. 'A mate who might genuinely be in *my* corner.'

'*I'm* in your corner.' Max caught up with him well before he reached the elevators.

That hadn't been the impression he'd just got. Rick

didn't pause to push the button or wait for a lift. He didn't want to give Max the chance to say anything else. Shoving the fire-escape door open, he took to the stairs, ignoring the sound of the footsteps following him. He didn't even look over his shoulder as he barged into the emergency department.

Jet was listening to a patient's chest in a cubicle near the internal doors. He glanced up, took in the expression on Rick's face and smoothly unhooked the earpieces to hang the stethoscope around his neck.

'You're quite right,' he said to the registrar beside him. 'Order a chest X-ray and start some diuretics. I'll be in the office for a few minutes. Page me if I'm needed.' With a commanding jerk of his head, he led both Rick and Max into one of the consultants' offices.

'What the hell's the matter with you two?'

'Why don't you ask *him*?' Rick growled. He glared at Max.

Jet hooked one leg up to perch on the edge of the desk. He studied Rick for a moment and then turned his attention to Max. And then, surprisingly, he grinned.

'Takes me right back, this does. Remember when the headmaster caught you two fighting on the dorm floor? You got detention for a month and had to pick up rubbish on the rugby grounds. Matt and I used to fall over ourselves laughing, watching you with your spiky sticks and bags.'

His smile faded, his gaze settling on Max. 'What? What did I say?'

Max sighed. 'This has kind of got something to do with Matt, that's all.'

'For God's sake,' Rick exploded. 'How can you say that? It's got *nothing* to do with Matt.'

'Of course it has. And if you calmed down and tried using your brain for half a minute, you'd see why. *Think* about it.'

'What does he need to think about?' Jet's tone was wary.

'Matt,' Max said heavily. 'What life was like for us all when he died.'

Rick looked up at the ceiling. He didn't realise how hard his fists were clenched until the ache reached his elbows.

Unbearable, that's what it had been like. Matt had been the final member of their group. The youngest by a few months and a bit smaller but he'd made up for his lack of height with an extra dose of daring and humour and intelligence. Life had been the ultimate adventure for Matt but he had died, tragically, when a brain aneurysm had not been diagnosed in time to save him, despite the warning symptoms. They had all been newly qualified doctors at the time. The remaining three, aching with such a loss, had all blamed themselves in some way for his death.

'You hit the books, I seem to remember,' Jet said slowly. 'We hardly saw you.'

'And you burned off your grief getting your black belt in that martial arts thing.' Max nodded. 'And Rick? Do you remember what he did?'

'Drank a lot,' Jet said promptly. 'And partied like there was no tomorrow.'

'Exactly.'

The satisfied note in Max's voice was more than irritating.

'There's no "*exactly*" about it,' Rick informed them. 'I'm careful. Even if I'm drunk I'm careful.'

'Can you honestly put your hand on your heart and swear there might not have been an occasion then when you found you didn't have anything on hand or were just too blasé to care?'

Rick said nothing. The truth was that that period of time was pretty much a blur now. He'd been trying to forget and it had been a successful mission. He closed his eyes slowly.

Too many parties. Too much alcohol. Way too many girls and most of them had been blue-eyed blondes. Max had married a woman with chestnut hair. Jet thought the darker the better but Rick had always gone for blondes. That particular period wasn't an indication of how he usually treated women, however, and even now he could feel shame at the way he'd used those girls.

One-night stands had been all that he could do. He'd had enough emotional rubbish to deal with without inviting any more into his life. All he'd wanted had been the temporary release that sex could provide and if it wasn't enough for the partner, she'd got brushed aside. Names? As much of a blur as the faces. Pick a girl's name, he thought wearily. Any name could be a contender. Annabelle or Casey or Lisa or…or *Lucy*. Yes. If Sarah's sister had been at one of those parties and had been willing, he would have taken advantage of her.

Of course he couldn't swear to anything and his friends knew it. Maybe talking about this wasn't such a good idea. It certainly wasn't helping. Any second now and Jet was going to be taking the side Max was on. The dark side. Rick needed to be alone. A stiff drink or two and some peace and quiet and maybe he could parcel up this feeling of dread and make it go away somehow.

'Condoms aren't a magic bullet, anyway,' Max continued. 'You know that. They can fail. Or break. How many times have we congratulated ourselves on our hassle-free record? Or so we thought.'

Jet whistled silently. 'Oh, man… Is this going where I think it's going?'

Max didn't seem to have heard him. He was still talking directly to Rick. 'Lucy looked just like her sister. Maybe your memory of ten-plus years ago is understandably hazy but what about a few hours ago? Your tongue was practically hanging out of your mouth the instant you clapped eyes on Sarah.'

'Sarah?' Jet was sitting very still now. Making sense of what was happening around him.

'Lucy was Sarah's sister,' Max said more quietly. 'Josh's mother.'

'Holy cow! And she thinks Rick's the father?'

'He could be,' Max agreed.

'She's wrong,' Rick said at the same time.

'How do you know?' Jet asked Rick.

'I just *do*.' Rick knew his tone was desperate. He didn't know, did he? He just couldn't begin to imagine the repercussions if she was right. To be presented with a nine-year-old kid? A *sick* kid? To know that the boy had been in the world for so long and he hadn't even known he'd existed? No. There was no way to get his head around this.

Max and Jet exchanged a glance.

'The solution's simple,' Jet said. 'Three letters, mate. DNA.'

Max stepped towards Rick and gripped his upper arm. 'He's right. The possibility is there and a kid's life might depend on it. If nothing else, you can set the record straight and Sarah can keep hunting.'

Yes. There was definitely a possibility there. One that might let him off the hook completely.

'Fine. I'll do the damn test.'

The thought that it might exonerate him kept him going until he reached home. The long hours of a solitary, sleepless night, however, put a far more negative spin on the plan.

Maybe fate had it in for him. Perhaps this was his punishment for that wild, irresponsible few months until he'd got both his head and his act back together. And what a punishment it would be. The effect it could have on his life was potentially catastrophic. Having a child could have a major impact on career choices, finances, relationships…

Being a father.

Oh, man…that was a minefield and a half. He couldn't do it. He had no idea of how a father should behave. He only had to think of his own father to know how they *shouldn't* behave but that was no help. His mates wouldn't be able to help either, would they? They'd all had way less than perfect family lives, which was why they'd all been sent off to boarding school and ended up forging their bond. The kind of family that meant something.

Max would think he'd know but he was getting in on the ground floor with Mattie, wasn't he? He hadn't been presented with a child who was old enough to judge performance and find it lacking. Old enough to get *hurt*, dammit.

It would be a disaster for everybody involved but most especially Josh, who most certainly didn't need that in his life on top of everything else. He couldn't do it to him. But if he did turn out to be Josh's father, he'd have no choice.

The endless merry-go-round of thoughts and emotions finally slowed as dawn broke and in those quiet minutes as a new day was born, Rick found a solution.

If his irresponsibility had created a child and fate had decreed that he could help him in some way, then of course he would do it. Josh didn't have to know where the bone marrow was coming from. If he didn't know that his biological father was involved, Rick wouldn't have to try and be the person Josh would want his father to be. He wouldn't have to hurt the kid by trying...and failing. It would be kinder all round, really.

Much kinder.

The attraction had been snuffed out. As cleanly as a lamp being switched off. There wasn't even a flicker of it to be seen when Rick came to the ward the following morning.

He didn't come into Josh's room. Just gave Sarah a curt nod through the window and then waited for her to join him in the relative privacy of the corridor.

'I've sorted the tests,' he told her. 'DNA, blood and tissue typing. You'll have to wait for the results.'

'Thank you.'

It was such an inadequate thing to say. She could see how huge this had been for him. Rick looked as though he hadn't slept a wink. There were shadows under his eyes and more lines around them than she remembered. It really wasn't fair that it only added to his appeal or that his appeal for her was still there when it had totally gone from his side of the equation.

She'd done her own share of thinking last night. Imagining Lucy with Rick. Feeling disturbingly… envious.

Just as well that Rick had shut off that static of sexual awareness. They could be colleagues now. A step up from total strangers but new enough to still have to earn trust. And that wasn't going to be easy because Rick's demeanour suggested she'd already had his trust and couldn't have broken it more effectively.

Fair enough. She had tipped his life upside down. Taken away his carefree existence. Put a huge spoke in the entire wheel of his universe, probably.

'Don't go getting your hopes up too much,' Rick warned.

'I won't. But...'

'But what?'

Amazing that his eyes could darken even further. They were like coals now. Remnants of a fire that had long since died out. Sarah had to look away.

'Have…have you given any thought to the next step, if…if…?'

Oh, Lord. She couldn't even say it out loud.

'If I do turn out to be his father?' Rick's mouth curled but it couldn't be considered any kind of smile. 'Give me some credit, Sarah,' he drawled. 'I'm not stupid.'

'I wasn't suggesting you were.' The putdown sparked something that felt like rebellion. Didn't he know by now that she was more than prepared to fight for what was right?

'If I'm his father and there's enough of a match to make my bone marrow compatible, then of course I'll be a donor.'

Sarah let out a breath she hadn't noticed she'd been holding. This was precisely what she'd wanted to hear. So why was she left with this oddly unsatisfied sensation?

'If—and it's a mighty big *if* as far as I'm concerned,' Rick continued, his voice low and intense. 'If things do turn out that way and I'm a donor, then that's the end of it.'

'Sorry?' Sarah wasn't following.

'I had no idea he existed,' Rick said. 'He's nine years old. It's a bit late to step into the role of being a father. So I don't want Josh to be told. Is that clear?'

Sarah's mouth opened but no words came out.

It was clear all right. But acceptable? That was something else entirely. If she called him on this, however, he might back off and he'd already agreed to being a potential donor. That was all that mattered right now, wasn't it?

One step at a time.

It wasn't the first time in their brief acquaintance

that she'd had the impression Rick Wilson was a man used to getting what he wanted from life.

He had taken her silence for acquiescence.

'Good,' he said. 'I'm glad we understand each other.'

And with that, he turned and left. Mission accomplished.

That spark of rebellion flared. Any kind of fan could easily see it flame into anger but Sarah had her own mission to deal with.

Intravenous sedation had made Josh sleepy enough not to notice his bed being wheeled into the treatment room of the ward. Or even being rolled onto his stomach and having the skin around his lower spine swabbed with disinfectant and then covered with a sterile drape that had a square hole in its centre.

Sarah positioned herself close to his head and took a small hand in hers.

'All set?' Mike was gowned and gloved. He had a syringe full of local anaesthetic in his hand.

Sarah nodded. She focused on Josh's face rather than watching the needle. She saw the crease on his forehead that let her know he was aware of his skin being pierced. The deeper frown and tiny whimper that told her the bone was now being frozen.

Despite the sedation and all the local anaesthetic, the next part of the procedure was painful. Not that Josh would remember any of it, thanks to the medication, but Sarah would. The sleepy groans and embryonic sobs brought tears to her own eyes and she ended up having to sniff audibly.

'You OK, Sarah?'

'Yes.'

'Not much longer.'

'That's good.'

It was probably just as well that Rick had backed away from any involvement with Josh at the moment. If he was watching this, he'd know exactly what was in store for him if it came to donating bone marrow. There'd be more than one puncture site, too, because they'd need a couple of litres of his liquid marrow. Josh only needed a tiny amount to cover the slides a technician was ready to prepare at the nearby trolley.

Would Rick opt for a general anaesthetic? Hardly likely, given the small but significant risk. IV sedation like Josh had had? That also didn't seem likely. He was a surgeon and having to abstain from making any important decisions or doing medical procedures might be a huge inconvenience. She wouldn't be at all surprised if he opted to just tough it out with local and that thought was enough to make her shudder inwardly.

She couldn't do it. Of course, it would be his choice but it was a lot to ask of anyone. Except that if it came to that, Rick wouldn't be just anyone. He'd be Josh's father. His *dad*. And it was a small thing to ask if it could save his son's life.

Mike had finished aspirating the marrow. Now he needed to do the biopsy.

'Almost done, short stuff,' Sarah whispered. 'You're being a wee hero.'

As he always was. He was such a brave kid. As if it hadn't been enough to lose his mum when he was only six and have to go and live with an aunt he hadn't seen nearly enough of. She wished she'd been there more for him when he'd been little but Lucy had gone back to their small home town after their mother had died and it had been her older sister who'd pushed her to stay in big cities and keep taking her career to the next level. Not to make the same mistakes she'd made.

At least she hadn't been a total stranger when tragedy had struck. Her love for Josh had been genuine but, even if she hadn't loved him as her nephew, he would have captured her heart totally over the last year with his courage and resilience.

'I'll get better,' he often reassured her. 'Don't worry, Sarah. One day I'll be big and I'll look after *you*.'

Sarah had to sniff again. A nurse passed her a tissue and Mike looked up to give her a sympathetic smile.

'We're all done. Looks like a good sample. Not too much cortex.'

'Great.'

'We'll head on up for the MRI before the sedation wears off. I'll give him some pain relief, too. He'll be a bit sore when he wakes up.'

'He'll be OK,' Sarah said. 'I don't think he's ever really complained after one of these.'

Rick would be in even more pain after this procedure but he'd get over it soon enough and as far as he was concerned, that would be the end of his involvement. And…dammit, that really wasn't acceptable, Sarah realised.

'He's an amazing kid,' Mike was saying warmly as he pressed a gauze swab to the puncture site. 'One out of the box.'

So true. And if Rick was Josh's father, he needed to spend enough time with him to see what an incredible person his son was. Everyone who knew this child fell in love with him. Josh deserved to know that his own father was amongst that number.

If Rick thought he could make up for refusing to acknowledge his son merely by going through a medical procedure then he had another think coming his way, courtesy of her. *This* was what had been niggling at her ever since he'd walked off earlier. Where her anger was stemming from. He was dismissing Josh as a person without seeing how special he was. He should be *proud* to claim him.

And surely Josh had a right to know who his father was? But how could Sarah tell him if there was rejection in store?

One step at a time, she reminded herself, walking beside Josh's bed on their journey to the radiology department for the MRI scan. She squeezed his hand, reassuring herself as much as the drowsy child. The next step couldn't happen until the test results came through and that gave her plenty of time to think about exactly what that step should involve.

The thirteen-year-old boy lay, white and still on a bed in the intensive care unit. Flanked by monitors, IV tubing, medical staff and two distraught-looking parents.

The mother was crying again. The father put his arm around her. 'He's still alive,' he said, his voice raw. 'It'll be OK, you'll see. The doc knows what he's doing. It'll be OK.'

He looked down at his son but the glance was brief. The sight was still too horrific. The swathe of bandages around the head. Eyes so swollen you couldn't see eyelashes even, and then there was the awful bruising and a split lip to cap it off. He must be virtually unrecognisable even to his closest family.

This was the kind of case Rick found particularly gruelling. A whole family torn apart because of a dreadful accident. Simon had been on his way home from school and had been knocked off his bicycle by a speeding delivery van. He had a badly fractured leg, supported by a slab of plaster and padded by pillows until the boy's condition was stable enough for further surgery. It was much less of a concern than his head injury at this point in time. Right now, Simon was on a ventilator, unable to breathe on his own, and the surgery Rick had just performed held no guarantees for either survival or a good long-term outcome.

Simon's parents were a mess. Shocked and terrified but desperate to be with their son. This had to be every parent's worst nightmare and Rick had seen it all too often.

Was this why he'd never given serious thought to having a family of his own? He wasn't totally averse to the notion like Jet was, but neither could he imagine embracing the concept as Max had done. He was somewhere between the two. The desire was there but still dormant. Weighed down, perhaps, by the legacy of his own childhood.

Along with the logistics of attaining the state of parenthood, the motivation to deal with the downsides of parenting had made it all too easy to shove the whole concept into the 'too hard' basket and leave it there. And if it stayed in there so long it was too late to do anything about it, the whole issue might just quietly go away and he'd be able to take comfort in the thought that he couldn't have really wanted it badly enough in any case.

It was getting late by the time Rick left the ICU, but for a while he hung around the wards, reviewing his inpatients. He was reluctant to head home because it would mean a visit to his office to collect his keys.

Had it only been a few days ago when he'd been less than happy with the company of his mates and had wanted time alone to get his head sorted? Now, when he'd had enough of himself, there was no opportunity to obtain the kind of company he needed.

He'd assured Max that he would be absolutely fine. That Max couldn't possibly postpone the week in Rarotonga that he and Ellie and Mattie had lined up for their honeymoon. He'd meant every word of it at the time, of course, but then he hadn't known that Jet would receive a summons back to his elite army medical unit. A three-month stint that would see him involved in training exercises and deployment to any areas that might need the specialised skills of the unit. He'd left town yesterday, with his personal belongings in a backpack, his bike under cover in Rick's garage and the satisfied gleam of impending adventure lighting his features.

Rick had no one to talk to.

About the rough day he'd had at work.

Or about the envelope that had landed in his in-box this afternoon, seconds before the call to the emergency department where Simon had been waiting.

He knew what was in that envelope.

The DNA results.

The slip of paper inside could be a passport to freedom but it could also be a life sentence.

Being a father might not be a choice he had the luxury of making. It might be about to blindside him and, despite thinking he had found a solution that would work for everybody involved, he still had no idea how he was going to react if he discovered he really was Josh's father.

Maybe he didn't need his mates around to talk to. He could almost hear Jet's impatient voice.

Only one way to find out, man. For God's sake, just get on with it.

With a grim smile, Rick dropped the set of notes he was holding back into the trolley and headed for his office.

Minutes later, he was staring at his hands in disgust. He was a surgeon, for heaven's sake. With a reputation he could be justifiably proud of. He operated on people's brains and spines. Tricky surgery that required absolute precision and he'd never known his hands to falter. To tremble.

They were damn close to trembling now, as he ripped open that envelope.

CHAPTER THREE

'Do you want the good news or the bad news first?'

Josh rolled his eyes and sighed theatrically. 'Gimme the bad news, then.'

'You're in for new treatment stuff next week.'

'More chemo?'

'Yeah.' Sarah was trying hard to sound upbeat but it wasn't easy and she had to blink rapidly a few times. Josh was watching her.

'That's OK, I s'pose. Like last time?'

'Not exactly. They're going to bring the big guns out this time and try and shoot all the cancer cells. You'll get some radiation treatment as well as the drugs.'

Josh's eyes widened. 'I'm gonna be radiated? Will I go green or start glowing?'

Sarah grinned. 'No. And don't go expecting to get some superpowers or anything, either. It's more like having a whole bunch of X-rays all at once.'

Josh was a smart kid. He understood far more than most people gave him credit for and Sarah had always been honest with him. Not that she gave him every detail, of course, but if he asked a question, she told him the truth. Josh seemed to know how much information he could handle and, like many children who faced life-threatening disease, he had a wisdom way beyond his years.

He put Sarah to shame, sometimes, with his acceptance of how things were. He understood death better than any child should. He wasn't afraid of it but he loved life and instinctively made the most of every moment. Right now, however, he was having a flash of being just an ordinary little boy and his bottom lip jutted out.

'Will it hurt?' he asked in a small voice.

'No.' Sarah badly wanted to gather him into her arms but she knew better. Josh was getting well past wanting hugs or slobbery kisses. She often caught hints of the man he could become, in fact. Like now, as he squared bony shoulders and lifted his chin.

'That's OK, then.' The glance he gave his aunt was steady. 'Is that it?'

'Not quite. You're going to have a Hickman catheter put in again.'

He'd had one before, in his first run of chemotherapy. The indwelling catheter would be inserted into a central venous line and stitched in place. It meant that all the drugs and blood products could be administered and samples taken without the pain or risk of infection that came from multiple puncture sites.

'But I'll be asleep when they do that, right?'

'Oh, yes. Of course.'

'Am I going to get real sick again?'

It was hard to maintain the direct eye contact. 'You might. They'll give you stuff to stop you throwing up.'

'Is this going to be the last time I have to do it?'

'We're all hoping so, hon.'

'When is it going to start?'

'Well, that's the good news. Not for a few days and you're allowed to come home until then. You get to choose whatever you want to do and we can go to the shops and get a supply of DVDs and books and anything else you want to bring into hospital with you.'

'They've got tons of stuff here already. Will I be in this room again or can I go in with the other chemo kids? Oscar's got ALL like me and he said there's an empty bed in his room.'

Sarah took a deep breath. The 'good' news had come and gone in a heartbeat. 'You won't be in this ward, Josh. You're going to a special unit. You'll have your own room and everything you need but it's...' Oh, God. How could she sound upbeat in telling him that he would be kept in strict isolation? For weeks? 'It's bug-free. To protect you from getting any kind of infection.'

'But I'm better. I haven't got a temperature or anything now.'

'This treatment is different. You know how the bad leukaemia cells happen in your bone marrow?'

'Yeah. That's why they stick holes in my back. To get the marrow and look at the cells under the microscope and count them.'

'This new treatment is designed to get rid of all the bad cells but it kills off the good ones as well. Doctor Mike will be able to draw you some nice pictures of what happens but it means that, for a while, you won't have any bone marrow that does its job of making new blood or protecting you from bugs.'

'And then what happens?'

'They give you some new bone marrow. When it's had enough time to get right into your bones and settle down, it'll start making new blood. Nice, healthy blood.'

Josh took that in, frowning with concentration.

'So I'll be fixed?'

'That's the plan.' Sarah's smile broke through as she took out that shiny, new hope to show Josh. 'This is it,' she told him solemnly. 'The chance we've been waiting for.'

'So you've found my dad, then?'

Sarah's breath caught. She'd never told Josh that she was trying to trace his biological father. He'd never asked. As far as she'd known, he thought that the trip to the States had been so that he could go to Disneyland and the visits to a hospital and the doctor who used to live in New Zealand had been simply to look after him while they were away.

Had he overheard something?

Oh…Lord… Had he done more than play games on her laptop? Read her emails, maybe?

'Who is he?'

Still, words failed Sarah. Rick had made his wishes very clear on this subject. It wasn't that she didn't have the courage to defy him, more that she hadn't been able to come up with any plan that didn't involve Josh facing rejection, and she couldn't bring herself to inflict emotional pain on top of the physical ordeal he was facing.

'It's OK,' Josh told her kindly. 'I already know.'

'*What*?'

'It's Max's friend. The man at the wedding. Rick.'

Sarah's jaw dropped. 'How do you know that?'

'I heard you talking to Ellie. Promising that you wouldn't say anything until after the wedding. And… you kept looking at him kind of funny. Kept watching him.'

'Did I?' Sarah felt helpless. How on earth was she going to explain *this* to Rick? She could hardly expect him to believe that Josh had figured it out for himself without her saying anything. He'd be furious.

'How come he didn't know?' Josh asked.

'That he was your dad?'

Josh nodded.

'It happens.' This was more information than a nine-year-old should have to deal with. But Josh wasn't any-nine-year old, was he? 'A girl can get pregnant and have a baby but if she doesn't tell the father and they're not together any more, there's no way for him to know.'

'But he knows now?'

It was Sarah's turn to nod.

'Why hasn't he come to visit me, then?'

Good question. As good as the very similar one she'd asked Mike Randall herself, not very long ago, when the oncology consultant had been the one to tell her the amazing news of what a close genetic match Rick had turned out to be for Josh. But Mike hadn't been able to give her an answer and she had to be very careful with what she said to Josh.

'You know what?' she asked finally.

'What?'

'I think he's scared of you.'

Josh looked puzzled then shook his head. 'I'm just

a kid. He's a grown-up and he rides a motorbike. Why would he be scared of *me*?'

'Being a parent *can* be scary,' Sarah tried to explain. 'Especially if it just happens. One minute you're not and then—*bang*—you've got someone else to be responsible for and take care of and…and love. It can change your whole life.'

'I s'pose.' Josh was watching her carefully. 'Were *you* scared of me?'

Sarah smiled. 'You bet I was. But I still wanted you and you know I love you to little pieces, don't you?' She had to hug him now. And give him a big kiss on the top of his head.

Josh made a disgusted noise. 'He'll have to come and see me,' he said decisively when he had wriggled free.

'How's that?'

'When he gives me his bone marrow.'

Sarah was silent again. It was quite possible that the only part of Rick Josh would get to meet would be the bone marrow donated arriving for infusion. The frustration was familiar now, the anger still simmering quietly on Josh's behalf. The desire to protect this lad from rejection was redundant. The fact that he knew the identity of his father and was waiting for a visit that might never happen meant that the rejection was already real.

'You can tell him it's not so scary,' Josh said.

'Oh, Josh…' Sarah gave a huff of laughter. If only it was that easy. 'I will,' she promised, 'but don't get your hopes up too much. Rick might be more scared than I was and…it just happened for me, didn't it? You turned up on my doorstep, pretty much. And...' she smiled at this little boy with all the love in her heart '...it was the best present I ever, ever got.'

Josh's nod was thoughtful. 'Maybe you should give me to my dad, then,' he said calmly.

'*What*?' For the second time in the space of only minutes, Sarah was utterly shocked.

'Not for ever.' Josh was frowning again, thinking things through. 'If *he* found me on his doorstep, he might stop being scared.' Big, brown eyes were alight with sparks of both determination and what looked worryingly like hope. '*He* might think I was a good present, too.'

Sarah had to close her eyes. Out of the mouths of babes. The countless scenarios she had played with in the last few days paled in comparison to the bold genius Josh had just come up with. But she had to shake her head.

'He um...might not be too happy about that, hon.'

Except that she could hear Ellie's voice now. The conversation they'd had just before she'd taken off for her honeymoon. When she'd given her Rick's address in case she needed help while they were away.

He'll help if he possibly can, she had said with complete conviction. *He's a great guy. They all are. I'd trust any one of those three guys with my life. With Mattie's life.*

That's what Sarah would be trusting him with, wasn't it? Because Josh *was* her life these days.

'It'd be OK,' Josh was saying. 'He'd see I'm not so scary. And, besides, I'd kind of like a ride on his bike. He said I could have one.'

Sarah's eyes flew open. 'No way!'

Josh looked mutinous. 'You said I could do anything I wanted to do before I have to come back into hospital and I want to ride a bike.'

'Why? They're horrible, dangerous things.'

'Mum said my dad rode a bike. She said he had a leather jacket and he was the nicest, handsomest man in the world.'

Good grief… Had Lucy known the real identify of Josh's father all along? Or had she seen something in Josh as he'd grown older that had reminded her of the man who'd been her secret? Or…maybe…she'd just wanted to give him a hero image to feel proud of. Sarah could understand why. She could only hold her breath and hope like hell that Rick would live up to his status.

'I might die,' Josh said matter-of-factly. 'What if that happens and I never got to find out what it's like?'

Sarah groaned inwardly. Talk about emotional black-mail.

But Josh was grinning now. He had her over a barrel and they both knew it.

He'd been thinking about Simon when the doorbell rang.

His young patient in Intensive Care was starting to breathe on his own and it looked like he'd be able to come off the ventilator very soon. Survival was seeming more likely but at what cost? How brain damaged might he be? His parents had adapted to their new environment remarkably quickly and they'd actually been overjoyed at the news of progress today but how happy would they be further down the track if their son couldn't talk or walk? Or maybe not even recognise them?

To see the bright, inquisitive eyes of an intelligent child looking up at him when he opened the door was light years away from where his thoughts had been. It was so unexpected that Rick was totally floored. His brain was having difficulty joining the dots.

'Josh? What on earth are you doing here?'

'Sarah dropped me.'

'Huh?' Rick looked over the boy's head. A small, red car was at the end of his driveway. It was a tricky manoeuvre at this time of day to back out onto what was essentially a main road. It could well take a minute or two.

'I've come to visit,' Josh said.

Rick dropped his gaze. Josh had a look on his face that could only be deemed supremely confident. Triumphant, almost. It was a look that said, *You can't send me away cos I'm your son*. He also had what looked suspiciously like an overnight bag at his feet.

'Hang tight for a tick, buddy.' Rick pulled his lips into the best semblance of a smile he could manage. 'I'll be right back.'

He'd never walked down that driveway with such powerful strides. Driven by outrage. What the *hell* did Sarah think she was playing at here?

He almost missed his opportunity. She didn't see him approaching because she was looking over her shoulder and she'd found a gap in the traffic and started to back out. As she turned the wheel to change direction, Rick stepped out in front of her car. It was a pretty stupid thing to do but Rick was past thinking clearly. Did he really think he could stop the vehicle from running him over by thumping his fist on the bonnet like that?

Whatever. It worked. Sarah jammed on the brakes and the car stalled with a lurch. Rick took another two strides that brought him to the driver's window, which had been rolled down to aid visibility. Sarah was staring straight ahead, still gripping the steering-wheel.

'What's going on here?' He kept his tone quiet. Deliberately dangerous.

Sarah flinched but didn't meet his unfriendly stare. 'Josh wanted to visit you.' Her voice was high and tight. 'He seems to think that you offered him a ride on your bike and he wants to take you up on it.'

This didn't make sense. When he'd suggested that at the wedding, Sarah had acted as if he was planning to murder her nephew. Not that he was going to be distracted by trying to find out why she'd changed her mind. There were more pressing issues to get sorted.

'So you just left him on my doorstep? What kind of guardian *are* you? What if you'd got the address wrong? If I hadn't been home?'

The flinch had become semi-permanent. Sarah radiated tension.

'I got Mike to check your roster. I already knew your address. And…and I waited until I saw you open the door.'

She slid him a sideways glance that was an oddly appealing mix of defiance and guilt. Rick recognised something in that glance from way back. Teenage stuff. When you were doing something you simply had to do but knew damn well you would get into trouble if you got caught. Again, Rick wasn't going to be distracted and certainly not by some misguided feeling of empathy for this woman.

'Is this some kind of game? You think I'm going to change my mind about telling him I'm his father just because we're face-to-face?'

Sarah turned her head this time. He could see the movement of muscles in her throat as she swallowed. 'You don't have to change your mind. Josh already knows.'

Rick made an incredulous sound. 'You *told* him? After I specifically said that I didn't want—'

'No,' Sarah interrupted fiercely. 'I didn't tell him. I thought he had a right to know but I didn't tell him because I didn't want him to know that you didn't want to acknowledge him. Josh told *me* and I couldn't lie about it.'

Something cold was folding itself around Rick. Fear? Or maybe it was actually something hot. Like fury.

'I don't believe you.'

'Your prerogative.' Sarah's tone was clipped. 'But for what it's worth, Josh wanted to meet you. This was his idea.'

'It's a very *bad* idea.' Rick's words were just as clipped as hers had been. 'I don't like being pushed around.'

'No. I don't suppose you do.'

Another glance and he had the impression there was a spark of…what, sympathy in her eyes? It *could* be amusement. Rick's anger strained at the leash.

'Did it not occur to you the risk you were taking? I'm not exactly happy about this, Sarah. What if I back out of this whole donor thing?'

'You wouldn't do that.'

Her calm assumption only pushed him further.

'How can you be so sure of that?'

His menacing tone did the trick. He saw the flash of fear in her face. Oddly, getting the upper hand wasn't as satisfying as it could have been.

'I'm trusting my instinct,' Sarah admitted. 'I don't think you're someone who'd break a promise.'

She wasn't talking about an offer to give a kid a ride around the block on the back of a bike here and they both knew it. Of course he wouldn't back out of being a donor when a life was at stake but this had just become a lot more complicated.

Messy.

Full of emotional fishhooks that Rick could already feel catching in his gut. And he was angry. Angry at having his life disrupted by having to think about any of this at all. At being manipulated by a woman and a kid who were making assumptions when they didn't know him at all. He didn't want them to know him, he realised. That was what this was all about. If he let them into his life, nothing would ever be the same.

He was fighting for his life here. Life as he knew it, anyway. And he had the horrible feeling that he wasn't going to win this battle. He folded his arms and stared down at Sarah. The anger was still fierce.

'Bit of a gamble, though, isn't it?'

'Yeah...' Sarah's tone hardened, as though she was catching his anger. Or maybe because she was disappointed in what he was revealing about his character. 'I'm gambling on you being a decent human being.'

He'd used those words himself to assure her that Josh's father, if he was located, wouldn't be able to refuse to do the right thing. Sarah's tone suggested that she was prepared to find out she'd been mistaken in believing him. That he was about to break her trust.

The car was making a partial obstacle on the road. A motorist made a point of coming to a halt and leaning on his horn to advertise the inconvenience. Rick was still stinging from Sarah's tone. He turned to glare at the driver and the man shook his head and pulled out to go around them.

'If you back out,' Sarah told him, 'Josh will die. I'll be working at Queen Mary's and you'll be reminded of him—and what you didn't do—every time you see me.'

'I could go somewhere else.' Rick knew he sounded immature. Petulant almost but there was something close to desperation hovering over him. There was a small boy on his doorstep right now who knew that Rick was his biological father. When he went back up that driveway, he would *be* a father, whether he wanted to be or not.

Sarah's gaze had softened. There was definitely sympathy in her eyes. 'You'll still remember,' she said quietly. 'Probably every time you see a kid.'

Another car went around them. Sarah was fiddling with her gear stick. Putting the car in neutral. Preparing to start it again and drive away?

'What on earth do you think you'll achieve by

leaving him *here*? Just how long were you planning to abandon him?'

Sarah answered his second query first. 'Josh was going to text me. I would have come back very soon if he wasn't happy. What did I think I might achieve?'

Sarah's gaze was locked on his and Rick couldn't break the contact. 'Josh has the right to know what kind of person his father is. *You* need to know what you're missing out on if you don't know what kind of person your son is.' She gave a heavy sigh. 'You're already involved in this, Rick. I think you need to be invested in it as well.'

'Why? He's got you. That's been enough so far. It's still enough.'

'No. It isn't.' Sarah's voice rose. 'Not for Josh *or* for me.' Her voice shook now and her eyes flashed. 'Have you any idea how much I've been ripped apart by all this? No, of course you don't. You'd rather not even think about it. Keep it all at a nice, safe distance. Well, let me tell you something…'

She sucked in a quick, shaky breath. 'This sucks. You said you don't like being pushed into things. Newsflash, Rick—none of us do. And what did I get pushed into? Not only being a parent but having to deal with the kind of things that no one wants to face. It's not that I don't love Josh. He's a loveable kid and I adore him but it *hurts* like hell watching him go through all this. Knowing he might die in the end in spite of it.'

Sarah had tears on her face. She scrubbed at them angrily. 'I'm only his aunty,' she said, her voice raw. 'You're his *father*.'

Still, there was no way Rick could break that eye contact. Spare himself the accusation in her face.

'Grow up and take some responsibility,' Sarah snapped, turning the key and revving the engine of her car. 'You owe this much to Josh. Hey…maybe you owe it to me, too, for doing *your* job for so long.'

It was Sarah who broke the eye contact. The car was moving now and all Rick could think to do was to step back and let it go.

And when it had gone, he had a clear view up his driveway.

To where a small boy was sitting on his doorstep.

Sarah had to pull off the road just as soon as she could find a space that would be out of sight.

She could barely see with the tears flooding her eyes and her hands were shaking so hard she couldn't steer the car safely.

Having come to a halt, she sat there, gripping the wheel with both hands together at the top, her forehead resting on them.

What she'd just done—leaving Josh alone with Rick—was the hardest thing ever and she wasn't even sure she should have done it.

The thought of Josh being given a ride on Rick's motorbike was bad enough. Terrifying. His body was so fragile and would be far too easy to break. But leaving him with a man who could break his heart was infinitely worse.

She couldn't even stay and watch because if she had, the whole point of this exercise would have been negated. So she couldn't know what was happening and all she could do was wait.

She had to have faith, she told herself.

And she did. She had the utmost faith in Josh. In his intelligence and courage and maturity.

As her sobs subsided and she got her breathing under control again, Sarah was aware of something else.

For some unknown reason, she also had faith in Rick.

CHAPTER FOUR

THE confidence had vanished from Josh's face.

He couldn't have overheard anything that had been said down at the end of the driveway and he couldn't have even seen any facial expressions because Rick had been bending down on the far side of the vehicle and Sarah had turned in his direction, but he must have sensed the tension and he would have seen the car driving away. Had he noticed that Sarah hadn't given him a backward glance?

It might explain why he was looking so bereft.

Rick felt an odd pang in his chest that morphed into a kind of squeeze. He took in how pale Josh was. How he had less hair than he'd had even a few days ago. This kid was sick. There was a real possibility that he could die in the not-too-distant future and he was, essentially, an orphan. You'd have to have a pretty black heart not to respond to that package. And he might look a bit lost and vulnerable right now but he still looked determined.

Rick felt his lips twist into a lopsided grin. He had to admire the kid's guts. Not to mention his enterprise. If he could apply the same tactics to beating his disease as he must have to get something he wanted—like the bike ride—he might have a good show of succeeding.

The car had taken Sarah away physically. Rick was making a supreme effort, as he walked back up the driveway, to push her out of the considerable mental space she was still occupying. This was about him and Josh. It would be totally unacceptable to take out any of his anger for Sarah on this child.

This was no big deal, really. It wouldn't even take that long. He'd give him what he wanted and then Josh could text his aunt and get taken home.

'A bike ride, then?' he offered.

OK, maybe he was sidestepping the major issue here but he could hardly jump right in and talk about their biological relationship. Josh wasn't to know that *he* knew Josh knew the truth and at least he could sound casual about a bike ride. Friendly, even.

'Yeah…' That lost look was wiped from Josh's face as he grinned. 'That'd be awesome.'

'You'd better come inside, then, and dump your bag.'

The loft apartment was a warehouse conversion and the door led into a massive living area with a wall of glass that looked straight down on a busy wharf. Container ships were being loaded and unloaded. Trucks and cranes and forklifts and people wearing hard hats and bright orange high-visibility vests made the scene a hive of activity. Josh walked over to the windows and his jaw dropped. Rick was happy to let him stand there and take it in.

He needed a moment himself. He walked to the kitchen that was part of the open-plan area and eyed

the bottle of beer he'd uncapped just before the doorbell
had sounded. With a sigh of regret he screwed the cap
back on and put it back in the fridge. It would have to
wait until after the joy ride and by then he might need
something a good deal stronger. He took a sideways
glance at the small boy, who was still staring at the
view with rapt attention.

A small boy's dream, having something like this to
watch on tap. Was that why he loved it? Had he never
really grown up? Sarah's stinging words were still
sounding in his head.

Grow up and take some responsibility.

Maybe she had a point.

With an inward sigh this time, Rick pushed himself
to walk closer to Josh. It felt incredibly awkward, which
was weird because he was good with kids, but this was
different. Hugely different. Unprecedented. It became
slightly easier when he wasn't looking directly at Josh.
They stood side by side to admire the view.

'Pretty cool, huh?'

'What's that little boat doing?'

'That one's a tug. It'll be going out to the heads to
guide another big ship in. The one over there is the
coastguard boat. They go out for rescues sometimes in
really rough weather. That's fun to watch.'

Josh nodded but was busy watching massive logs
being taken off the back of a truck. A crane was attached to chains in the middle of the logs and they
tipped like a seesaw. 'What happens if they drop
them?'

'It could cause a nasty accident, I guess. But they

know what they're doing. I've never seen them drop any yet.'

Josh looked as though he could happily stand there for a long time but Rick was feeling edgy. Too aware of this small person standing so close. Of the fact that they were alone together. That he might have to talk about the fact that he was Josh's father.

'How 'bout that ride, then?'

'OK. But I don't mind waiting. If you're busy or something.'

'Nah. We can't go too far, though. It'll be getting dark before too long and I don't want you getting too cold or anything.'

'Where's your bike?'

'There's a garage space underneath here. The stairs are over by the kitchen bit.'

'Do you live here by yourself?'

'At the moment, I do.' Rick led the way to the internal stairwell. 'Max used to live with me and so did Jet.'

'Who's Jet?'

'You sat beside him at Max and Ellie's wedding. He was holding the baby.' The memory cheered Rick up but it also reminded him of the moment he'd set eyes on Sarah. Still being mad at her didn't seem to diminish his appreciation of the way she looked. She was gorgeous. Her sister had probably been gorgeous as well but to his shame Rick had no concrete memory of her. As he'd had to concede she would have been one of many in that period of his life he had no desire to remember in too much detail.

'Where is he now?'

'He had to go back to the army. He works as a doctor for the soldiers sometimes. Rides around in helicopters and rescues people and stuff.'

'Wow. That'd be cool.'

'Bikes are cool, too. See?' Rick stepped into the garage. This was another big space. His SUV for routine travel was parked on one side and on the other his bike stood in solitary, gleaming black glory. 'It's a Ducati,' he told Josh. 'Sportclassic GT1000. Not bad, huh?' He stroked the seat. 'Jet's got a Superbike, which is over there under the tarp while he's away. It's a bit more powerful but this is my baby.' He pulled his hand away from the machine with a final pat and then looked up to find Josh looking at him rather intently. Curiously.

As though he was behaving in an unexpected way. Was it possible Sarah had told him that she thought Rick had a lot of growing up to do?

'We'll need to give you a jacket and helmet,' he went on hurriedly. 'We'll use Jet's, he won't mind. They'll be miles too big for you but we can pad up the helmet and that's the most important bit of protection.'

Josh looked like a little kid playing dress-up by the time Rick had him kitted out to his satisfaction. His hands were lost in leather mittens and barely emerged from the sleeves of the jacket. His head was equally lost in the helmet and all Rick could really see was a pair of dark eyes staring at him as he rolled the bike out of the garage.

'Sarah says that motorbikes are horrible, dangerous things,' he informed Rick.

'Sarah's not a boy,' Rick responded, as though that excused her.

She wasn't a girl, either, he thought as he helped Josh climb onto the back of the bike. She was all woman, was Sarah. He was still puzzled as to why she was allowing this ride to go ahead. She'd be terrified that Josh would get hurt. The fact that she could put her own fears to one side to let Josh do something he wanted to do said a lot about her strength of character.

That she was letting him be the one to give Josh the ride said a lot about how much she was trusting him. Rick wasn't about to let her down.

'Put both arms around my waist and hang on tight,' he instructed Josh. 'Don't let go for any reason, OK?'

'OK.'

'We're not going very far. We'll get a bit closer to the wharf so you can see the ships and then we'll go up the hill but that's all. And we're not racing anything. Got it?'

'Yep.' Josh's skinny arms came around Rick's waist and the grip was reassuringly strong. 'Let's go.'

They went.

Sarah wasn't any closer to getting home.

She was still sitting in her car in the lay-by but she wasn't crying any more. Staring out at the choppy, grey water of the harbour was soothing. Knowing that she was still close enough to Rick's apartment to go and rescue Josh in a matter of minutes was even more comforting.

Besides, she had a lot to think about. She could make a mental list of everything she needed to get done in the next couple of days. Washing and ironing so that Josh could pack everything he would need to move into the bone-marrow unit. Sorting the games and books and DVDs he'd want for the next few weeks. Shopping for treats. Arranging schoolwork, perhaps. And then there were all the other things that were a level away from Josh but still vital. Stuff that needed doing around the apartment. Going to the bank to try and arrange another loan. Paying the bills that were mounting up by the day.

She had to go back to work soon. A lot sooner than she might have chosen to but they weren't going to survive financially if she didn't. The trip to the States and then staying in Auckland had virtually wiped out her savings. If Josh settled well enough in the unit she might be able to start doing some shifts at night while he was asleep. It could be the ideal time in some ways, because he would have expert care when she wasn't around.

That wouldn't be on tap when he came out. Even if the bone marrow took successfully, he wouldn't be able to attend school normally for months yet. Paying someone to be with him while Sarah worked might take so much out of what she'd be earning that it would be pointless.

One day at a time.

The mantra arrived automatically these days, when the spiral of thoughts and worries threatened to overwhelm her. All that mattered right now was tackling this next, huge hurdle. When they were through it would be the time to worry about what was going to happen next. Sarah was practised in reversing the time telescope. She shrank it from the months ahead to weeks. Then into days and finally only hours.

Josh was with Rick. He was probably on the back of some horribly big motorbike while she was sitting here watching seagulls bobbing on tiny waves. She hoped he was hanging on tight. *She* certainly would be.

In fact, she could imagine it. Pressing against the solid back of Rick's body, her arms around his waist and the hum of a powerful engine beneath them. Bizarrely, the notion wasn't nearly as alarming as it should be. Instead, it had an appeal strong enough to quicken her pulse and send a curious warmth into her limbs.

A huff of laughter escaped Sarah. If she went any further down that track, it would be her begging for a ride next. But at least the awful tension was easing and she felt better. Not relaxed enough to want to drive the fifteen kilometres or so to her apartment in the city but more than enough to start wondering if she'd been a bit too hard on Rick.

Had she really told him he needed to grow up?

That he owed her something because she'd been doing his job as the sole parent figure for Josh?

That was unfair, given that he hadn't known of his child's existence.

He was a bachelor. One with a demanding job and probably precious little free time to enjoy other things like his bike. Or his home. Sarah hadn't taken much notice of her surroundings in finding Rick's address but now she found herself curious. Why did he choose to live out here? In what looked, from the outside, like an old warehouse? The whole area had given an impression of being old. Kind of rundown, which didn't quite gel with the image she had of Rick being a glitzy, playboy type.

It wouldn't hurt to go back, would it? To drive around and see if she'd missed something? She might find a café somewhere that could provide a good cup of coffee and, heaven knew, she could do with a caffeine boost. It would distract her for a while, too. If she hadn't received a 'come and get me' text from Josh within the next hour or so, she could assume that the visit was going well and then she would drive home and throw herself into some housework or something.

Sarah checked the road in both directions, put on her indicator and did a U-turn.

For the first time ever, Rick was feeling nervous about riding his beloved bike.

Good grief…even when he'd had his first solo ride when he'd been fifteen he hadn't felt like this. So aware of the unforgiving tarmac laid out beneath the speeding wheels. Padded leather could only do so much to protect skin and flesh and wasn't much protection at all when it came to broken bones. And how many head injuries had he dealt with over the years resulting from accidents involving motorbikes?

If Jet could see him riding this cautiously, he'd be grinning from ear to ear. Making some smart remark about him trading in the Ducati for a walking frame. But Jet had never taken a kid as a pillion, had he?

It felt weird. Nothing like any of the girls Rick had taken for a ride. Weightwise, he could have been alone so it made no difference to cornering or anything. He was acutely aware of the arms around his waist. A sensation that had always been a bonus with a pretty girl on the back, but this was a kid.

His kid.

Those tiny arms felt like prison walls. Starting to close in and trap something that was unrecognisable but important and Rick had the sinking feeling that it could be a big ask to ensure its freedom. The sooner this was over with the better.

They went as close to the wharf as they could get and went past acres of stored containers. He took them along the coast road for a mile or two after that, heading for Carey's Bay. Traffic was light and the road conditions were good and Rick found himself relaxing a bit. If they had more time, he thought, they could have gone a lot further. There were some fabulous beaches out this way, like Long Beach and Warrington and Murdering Beach. Surf and huge sand dunes that you could bodysurf down.

What was he thinking? Josh was nowhere near well enough to go swimming or play in sand dunes and he didn't want to spend hours in his company anyway. He turned them around and headed up a hill to give them a good view of the harbour and the bush-clad hills and crowded streets of Port Chalmers and then headed back.

The seaport was really a suburb of the city of Dunedin but it was more like a quirky little township in its own right. Industrial, thanks to the busy port, but it was also trendy for those wanting a slightly alternative lifestyle. It attracted artists and musicians. Very close to all the city amenities but most definitely outside its limits. On the edge, and Rick loved it.

He took them along Beach Street and then George Street, through the small town centre with all its cafés and galleries. He felt Josh loosen his grip around his waist. Fortunately, he was coming to an intersection when he needed to stop and give way. Before he could turn and tell Josh to hang on tightly again, he felt a small fist thumping his back.

'What's up, buddy?'

'That's *Sarah's* car,' Josh shouted.

'What? Where?'

Josh pointed. Then he waved.

With a sinking heart, Rick looked from the small car to the window of the café it was parked in front of. Sure enough, sitting on a high stool in front of a counter in the window was Sarah. Staring back. Looking as though she'd been caught out. Completely busted, no less.

The reddened cheeks and guilty expression made a nice change. Put Rick back on the moral high ground, even. He revved the bike engine gently. Just enough to give him the momentum to turn and roll into the vacant spot beside Sarah's car. It was too tempting not to rub her nose in it just a little.

'Let's go and say hello,' he suggested to Josh. 'I could do with a coffee.'

Sarah had known it was them as soon as she'd seen the bike rolling past the café window, slowing down for the intersection. Her heart had skipped a beat, seeing the reality of the small figure on the back of the black monster of a bike.

Josh had spotted her and there had been that awful moment of waiting for Rick's head to turn, knowing that he would think she was hanging around, spying on his lifestyle if not his person.

Her discomfort increased when she saw him turn the bike and park beside her car. Then he got off and pulled off his helmet and she saw this rugged man in his leather jacket and pants and heavy boots. The dark hair all tousled from the helmet removal. She couldn't drag her gaze away as he stripped off his gloves and stuffed them into the helmet. He wasn't smiling as he reached to lift Josh from the back of the bike but, perversely, that only made him seem more attractive.

A bad-boy biker. Dark and dangerous. But she could see the care he took in lifting Josh. The way he made it seem no big deal and not a putdown because of the boy's size or physical capabilities. Sarah's breath caught in her throat somewhere. She hardly knew Rick but she was getting the distinct impression that he was something rather unique. Special.

Josh looked tiny in his oversized clothes, needing both arms to carry the helmet inside, but there was something about them being dressed alike. It was more than the clothes, as it had been at the wedding. Something about the way they walked, maybe. An air of owning the space they were moving through. Sarah had the strange feeling that she was merely a guest in *their* café. That she was privileged to be here, in fact. Even the smiles that the man and boy greeted her were oddly similar.

I did it, Rick's said. *See? I'm not as bad as you think I am.*

I did it,' Josh's said. *See? It's not as dangerous as you thought.*

Rick ordered a short, black espresso and didn't add any sugar. The remains of Sarah's sweetened cappuccino suddenly seemed frivolous and feminine. Josh opted for a milkshake but Sarah shook her head when he asked if he could have some food from the cabinet.

'It's not that long till dinnertime,' she said, despite feeling like a party-pooper. 'You need proper food, not cakes.'

'What's on the menu, then?' Rick queried.

They had taken the other stools at the counter and sat in a row, with Josh in the middle, but the boy was leaning forward, intent on holding his straw with no hands so Sarah and Rick had an almost clear space between them. Close enough to touch each other if they reached out, Sarah surprised herself by noticing.

'Whatever Josh fancies,' she said hurriedly. 'As long as it's real food and not junk.'

'A hamburger,' Josh said. 'They never give you hamburgers in hospital.'

'Hmm.' Sarah put off having to debate the nutritional value of Josh's choice. She smiled at him instead. 'How was the ride, short stuff?'

'Awesome. We went *really* fast.'

She couldn't help firing an accusing glare at Rick but he was shaking his head slowly, unseen by Josh. The wry smile made it perfectly convincing.

'I like the jacket.'

'It's Jet's. He's away rescuing soldiers in a helicopter.'

'Wow. That sounds exciting.'

'You should see Rick's house, Sarah. He gets to watch the ships and cranes and everything. It's cool.'

'Is it?' Sarah avoided looking at Rick this time. He might think she was angling for an invitation to visit his home. And she wasn't. This was about him and Josh. She was only involved as a facilitator and that was fine by her.

Absolutely fine.

Had he said anything to Josh about their relationship? Unexpectedly, Rick saw the question in her gaze, as though he could read her thoughts. He looked uncomfortable and the subtle movement of his head was negative. Sarah jerked her gaze away, disappointed.

A silence fell. Josh's initial enjoyment of the milkshake had waned and he seemed to become aware of the silence around him.

'I have to go back into hospital on Monday,' he announced.

'I know,' Rick said.

Of course he did. He would have an appointment to have his bone marrow collected within days of Josh's admission. He was watching Josh at the moment, his expression curious.

'Do you know what's going to happen this time?'

'Yeah. I'm gonna get radiated. I'll prob'ly go green and start glowing.'

Rick grinned. 'Maybe you'll get a superpower at the same time and be able to hear stuff from miles away.'

'Or go invisible.' Josh nodded. 'Or fly. That'd be cool.'

'Sure would. Closest I get to flying is going fast on my bike.'

'Like *we* did.'

'Mmm.' Rick's glance at Sarah assured her he was only agreeing so he didn't shoot Josh down. 'Do you know why you're getting the radiation?'

'To kill my bone marrow,' Josh told him. 'I've got ALL. D'you know what that is?'

'Tell me,' Rick invited.

There was genuine interest in his tone. He wanted to know how much Josh knew about his illness. Sarah peered into her coffee cup and caught a bit of leftover cinnamon dusted froth on her finger. She licked it off and went back for more.

'It's acute lymphoblastic leukaemia,' Josh said with careful pronunciation and obvious pride in his ability to remember.

'What's that?'

Josh rolled his eyes. 'You should know. You're a doctor.'

Rick grinned. 'I do know. I was just wondering if *you* knew.'

''Course I do. I've got it.' Josh sighed with exasperation but co-operated anyway. 'It means that my white blood cells are wonky and I get too many of them, which means there's no room for good blood cells and it makes me really sick.'

Rick nodded. 'Wish they'd made it sound that easy at med school.'

'I might get fixed this time,' Josh continued.

'Because if I get good bone marrow, it might make white cells that aren't wonky.'

Sarah watched Rick drain his small coffee cup as though he needed fuel.

'It's my bone marrow that you'll be getting,' he said to Josh. 'It's always done a pretty good job for me.' A muscle in his jaw bunched. 'You know why it's *my* bone marrow that you'll be getting, Josh?'

'Yeah. You're my dad.'

The statement was completely matter-of-fact but it hung in the air with all the presence of an unexploded bomb. This could be it, Sarah realised, unable to expel the breath she'd sucked in. Josh could be in for a rejection of anything but a genetic similarity.

'Yeah…' Rick said quietly. 'I'm your father.'

The correction was subtle but significant. A dad was involved. Part of the son's life. A father didn't have to be.

'I never knew,' Rick added.

'I know.'

'It's been a bit of a surprise, really.'

'I know that, too.' Josh tilted his head to scrutinise Rick's face. 'I don't think you're really scared, though.'

'Who said I was?'

Josh turned away, clearly avoiding the need to make a response. He stared out of the window and his face suddenly lit up.

'Look at that dog, Sarah.'

She looked. The dog was large and very scruffy. It sat on the footpath with its nose almost touching the glass, staring up at Josh.

'Isn't it *cool*?'

'Hmm.'

'Can I go and pat it? *Please*?'

'Josh, you know you have to be careful of—' *Bugs*, she stopped herself saying. *Infection that could kill you so fast you wouldn't know what hit you.* 'Strange dogs,' she carried on in a slightly strangled voice. 'They might bite.'

'*He* wouldn't bite,' Josh said with absolute conviction. 'Look at him.'

She took a second glance. The dog's tongue was hanging out. Its tail was sweeping a patch of the footpath clean. Josh was sliding down from his stool and Sarah was aware of Rick's stillness. She could feel him staring at her. Clearly, he hadn't been distracted by the dog's appearance and was still stewing about who had told Josh he was a coward. Maybe an apology of some sort was due.

'OK,' she told Josh. 'Just for a minute, though, and be *careful*.'

The small boy streaked out of the door. Sarah met Rick's gaze.

'I told Josh how scary it was to have a kid land on your doorstep,' she said cautiously. 'To have your life tipped upside down and everything.'

Rick's closed expression was a warning that he had no intention of letting that happen. It was a clear reminder of the terms he had set out and let her know that if the repercussions of those terms being broken were unfortunate, it wasn't going to be his fault.

Sarah merely raised an eyebrow to remind him that the repercussions would affect him as well.

They both looked out of the window to where Josh was crouched beside the dog, hugging it. The dog wriggled with joy and sent a vast, pink tongue across the boy's face. Sarah couldn't help herself. She leaned forward and knocked on the window, shaking her head as Josh looked up. She could see the huge sigh he heaved and the difficulty with which he prised himself away from the dog. He even went back for a final stroke before he came back into the café. The dog watched until the door swung shut and then trotted away out of sight.

'Come and finish your milkshake,' Sarah told Josh. 'We should probably head home. We've got a big day tomorrow.'

'He didn't have a collar,' Josh said unhappily. 'And he shouldn't be running around on the road by himself, should he?'

'Lots of dogs do that around here,' Rick said. 'I wouldn't worry about it, buddy.' He raised an eyebrow at Sarah, which seemed like a query about whether it would be a good idea to change the subject. Her nod of agreement was subtle.

'So what's on the agenda for tomorrow?' Rick asked brightly.

'Shopping, mainly,' Sarah responded. 'We've got some Harry Potter episodes to stock up on amongst other supplies. And I'm going to try and get hold of Josh's teacher, Miss Allen, to get some work to pass on to the hospital tutor.'

'What?' Josh stopped leaning on the counter to peer hopefully out the window. He sounded aggrieved. 'Do I have to do extra schoolwork?'

'You don't want to get too far behind, do you? For when you go back to school?'

'I s'pose not. The other kids would think I'm dumb.'

'You're not dumb, buddy.' Rick's statement was firm and Sarah could see the way Josh straightened his back with pride.

'Can we get a hamburger on the way home?'

'Maybe.'

'You said I could have whatever I wanted.'

'As long as it's proper food. Hamburgers are more like junk.'

'Not all of them,' Rick put in. 'There's a gourmet hamburger joint not too far from where we're sitting, in fact.'

Sarah frowned. Was he trying to undermine parental boundaries that were hard enough to get established anyway?

'You get things like fresh chicken breast with avocado and bacon,' Rick said calmly. 'Or steak. The one I like is grilled lamb with mint and cucumber yoghurt. And you can get kumera wedges instead of chips.'

Sarah's mouth was watering.

'I just want an ordinary hamburger,' Josh complained.

'These are better,' Rick said in a tone that brooked no further argument. 'Healthier. You can still get a beef and cheese burger.'

'You seem to know the menu off by heart,' Sarah said.

Rick shrugged. 'Jet and I didn't always have the time

or inclination to cook. And these are seriously good, take my word for it.'

But Sarah looked at her watch. 'I don't think we can,' she said. 'We need to get your bag, Josh. You're due for all your pills.'

Rick barely hesitated. 'How 'bout we all grab some burgers and take them back to my place?'

Sarah's hesitation was far more pronounced but Josh was nodding vigorously.

'Yeah…that's what *I* want to do. Please, Sarah? Can we? We might see that dog again near the hamburger shop.'

It had been the polite thing to do, inviting them back.

Maybe the invitation had been a form of expressing his relief at how easily a potentially awkward situation had come and gone.

Josh simply accepted the fact that Rick was his father as steadily as he appeared to deal with his illness. No recriminations. No promises extracted regarding future involvement.

It was easier to get along with the boy than his aunt but what prompted the invitation also included a kind of peace treaty. He could let go of the anger he'd been holding for Sarah. Yes, she had pushed him. Manipulated him. But he'd never have offered to spend time with Josh voluntarily, would he? And now it was done and there were no dark secrets and it all seemed much more straightforward and less threatening.

She had done the right thing, with no assistance from him, and Rick could only respect that.

So, here they all were, lounging in the comfortable

armchairs near the window, eating the enormous burgers and watching the lights come on all over the wharf as work continued into the night.

A bit different from sitting here with his mates, as he'd done so many times in the past, but it wasn't as bad as he'd thought it could be. The company was quite pleasant, in fact. Not that he'd want it all the time, of course, but…now and again didn't seem like it would be too much of a hardship.

Especially if Sarah came with Josh. There was most definitely a pleasure to be found in watching her. Rick knew he was going to be haunted later by the memory of her sitting in that café, sucking coffee froth off her finger. There was a slight moral dilemma here, in that he knew it wasn't exactly appropriate to find himself turned on by his newfound son's guardian, but he'd grapple with that later as well. As long as he didn't act on it, and kept hold of the new level of respect he had for Sarah, it was probably no problem.

They left soon after eating because Josh was clearly exhausted. Rick followed them out. Sarah got Josh installed in the front passenger seat and his eyes were closing even as she shut the door. Rick touched her shoulder to make her pause before she headed for the driver's seat.

'Is he OK?'

'He'll be tired out. It's been quite a day for him.'

Rick could understand that. It had been quite a day for him as well. 'This stuff you're going shopping for tomorrow?'

'Yes?'

'They're things Josh will need for his stay in hospital?'

'Yes.' Sarah was watching him, her eyebrows raised.

'I'd...um...like to help pay for it.'

The moment's silence was heavy. Sarah held his gaze. 'It's not necessary,' she said.

But she didn't sound convincing. About to argue, Rick was stopped by the continued eye contact. The intensity behind it.

'What Josh needs from you is something money can't buy,' Sarah said softly. 'He needs something he's never had. A dad.'

Rick could feel every muscle in his body tense. 'I can't just morph into a dad, Sarah. I wouldn't have a clue where to begin.'

Sarah smiled. 'There's no "how to" manual.' She looked away. 'You just do your best for as long as you can.' She captured his gaze again. 'It might not even be for very long. Couldn't you at least give it a go?'

Part of Rick wanted to back away. As fast and as far as possible. He thought of Jet and his action to ward off bad voodoo and the idea of doing it himself had momentary appeal before being dismissed as inappropriate, not to mention immature.

There was another part of him that couldn't turn away from this. Not now. Something had changed today, thanks to both Sarah and the remarkable kid who was his son.

Maybe he'd grown up a little as well.

His nod was slow, but sure. He even managed a smile.

'I'll give a shot,' Rick said. 'I can't promise I'll be any good at it but I'll do my best.'

'That's all you need to do.' Sarah's smile lit up her eyes. She stood on tiptoe and put her arms around Rick's neck to hug him. 'Thank you.'

It was only a brief hug.

Weird the way he could still feel it, long after she had driven away into the night.

CHAPTER FIVE

JOSH was readmitted to hospital early on a Monday morning.

He received sedation to have the Hickman catheter inserted just under his collarbone and by lunchtime the intensive chemotherapy course to destroy his own bone marrow had begun.

The room in the bone-marrow transplant unit that was to become their world for the next few weeks felt remarkably like a prison to Sarah. It contained a bed for Josh and two armchairs of the kind that had controls to raise a footrest and tip back so they could be slept in comfortably. A small *en suite* bathroom a few steps away from the foot of the bed had a shower, toilet and handbasin.

There were windows on the corridor side of the room, directly opposite an identical room that had yet to pull the curtains on their internal windows. On the outside wall was another window but the view was of another wing of the hospital. Dozens more windows that seemed like blank eyes staring back.

With a determinedly bright smile, Sarah turned away from the less than inspiring outlook. Josh was propped up on his pillows but still looked sleepy. The leg of a favourite soft toy poked out from under the covers beside him, one of the few personal items that gave this room a little bit of colour. The top buttons of his pyjama jacket were undone to reveal the dressing over the indwelling catheter. Close to that were rather complicated-looking connections that provided several ports. If necessary—and it probably would be—he could be infused with drugs and fluids and blood products all at the same time and there would still be access available to take blood samples.

Currently, Josh had sticky electrodes on his chest and wires that connected them to a cardiac monitor by his bed. A blood-pressure cuff was wrapped around his upper arm and inflated automatically at intervals to make recordings. A clip that measured the oxygen saturation in his blood completely covered the middle finger of his other hand. The steady beeping was a sound Sarah was well used to. It had been a comforting background, more than once, in the lonely hours of so many nights when she had been sitting alone beside a bed that looked just like this one. Wondering if Josh would still be alive in the morning.

Déjà vu of the worst kind. Pulling her back into something she would have done anything to be able to avoid. A sinking sensation that carried her on waves of heartbreak. Loneliness and frustration and unbearable sorrow.

A soft tap on the door advertised the arrival of a visitor and Sarah looked up to see the green gown and white mask that everyone who entered this room would have to wear from now on, including herself. It made everyone look the same and added an element that might end up being the worst aspect of this new admission so far. It felt like she and Josh had been sucked into something faceless. Impersonal.

Less caring.

She knew that was totally untrue. If anything, the opposite was the case but the dampening of an important sense in removing most of the features and facial expressions from the staff was hard to get used to. It made a person's eyes incredibly important as an avenue of communication so it was the first thing her gaze sought. This time, however, she recognised the new arrival even before he'd turned round as he manoeuvred something large and bulky into the room.

'Rick!'

His eyebrows rose. 'Is this a bad time to visit?'

'No…not at all. I just…' Hadn't expected the visit, that was all. Yes, he'd said he would get involved. Give being a father figure his best shot. But…

The voices had woken Josh. 'What's that?' he asked.

'Hey, buddy.' Rick's swift glance took in the bedside equipment. The monitors, the indwelling catheter and the bags of suspended fluid with their bright stickers to warn of the toxic drugs they contained. 'How're you doing?'

'I'm not being sick yet.'

'That's great.'

'What's that?'

'This?' Rick picked up the large object resting against his leg. 'It's a cork board.'

'You can't bring things like that in,' Sarah said.

'There's a risk of infection, especially from plant material, and that's—'

'Been decontaminated,' Rick interrupted. 'Sprayed to within an inch of its life. Like this other stuff.'

She hadn't noticed the box. Now she was as curious as Josh.

'That looks like the best spot.' Rick tilted the board and propped it against the wall beneath the window on the corridor side of the room. 'Easy viewing level when you're lying in bed, I reckon. What do you think, Josh?'

'I can see it all right.' Sarah could understand why Josh sounded dubious. A cork board? Was he supposed to draw pictures to pin on it like a five-year-old? Or wait for get-well cards from relatives he didn't have?

'Cool. Now...' Rick was opening the box. 'I've got something else in here.'

Josh's eyelids had started to droop but then he frowned and pushed them open again. 'What's that thing?"

'A camera. I know it looks a bit weird. It's an old-fashioned kind, not digital. Which is why I managed to acquire it. We used to use them in the old days. It's Polaroid and it takes instant pictures.' He aimed the camera at Josh and it clicked. Almost at once, a piece of white card began appearing from its base. 'This is the picture,' he told Josh. 'You have to wait for a minute or two for it to develop. See?'

He was beside the head of the bed now, holding the card for Josh to watch. Sarah watched them, feeling absurdly pleased that Rick had come to visit so early on and that Josh was looking interested. Too distracted to be thinking about anything else, in fact. She felt the same way. The fear and the loneliness and the sense of confinement was gone. Tucked away in some part of her brain that she had no need to access while Rick was there.

'Hey…that's *me*.' Josh sounded delighted.

'Sure is.' Rick glanced at Sarah, including her in the conversation. 'It's a picture of your first day in here. Tomorrow we can take another one. I thought you might like a kind of photo album on the wall so you can see all the milestones on the road to getting better.'

Josh turned to Sarah. 'You can take a picture of me throwing up.'

'Cool. Not.'

'There might be some pictures from home you could stick onto the board,' Rick suggested. 'To remind Josh of the good stuff he can look forward to when he gets out of here. Maybe even a picture of something extra-special that could be a reward.'

'A dog,' Josh said promptly. 'That's what I want. My own puppy.'

'Oh, Josh…you know we're not allowed to keep pets in the apartment.' Sarah could feel the slide of an emotional roller-coaster. A moment ago she'd been blown away by the thought Rick had put into this gift. The promise of his involvement in saying *we* could take another picture tomorrow and every day after that. Now he was making her the bad guy here. Letting Josh reveal a dream that she had no hope of fulfilling even if everything else went perfectly.

Josh was not only looking awake right now, his eyes

were shining and his lips were curved into a dreamy smile. Thinking about the puppy he'd wanted for ever.

A dog would be my friend, he'd told her once. *Then it wouldn't matter if I was too sick to go to school.*

'You might not live in that apartment for ever.'

Rick's gaze was on Sarah now and there was a question in his eyes that she could read remarkably clearly. Was it really a bad thing to let Josh dream about something that might help him get through the worst of this? Even if it didn't eventuate? Yes, part of Sarah wanted to respond. She'd always been honest with Josh. False hope wasn't necessarily better than no hope. Except… except that Josh was looking happier right now than she'd seen him look in ages. He wasn't counting down the hours until he started throwing up or found himself in unbearable pain. He was thinking about something that might actually make going through everything that was to come worthwhile. And it wasn't totally dishonest. It was highly likely they wouldn't have to live in that apartment for ever, especially if she could start working again.

'We could get a house,' Josh said happily. 'With a garden. Couldn't we, Sarah? One day?'

'Absolutely we could,' Sarah found herself saying. 'We'll find a picture of one we might like, shall we? And stick it on the board?'

'Yeah…' But Josh sounded sleepy again. His eyes drifted shut and he seemed to melt further into his pillows but he still had a smile tilting the corners of his mouth.

Rick pinned the Polaroid snap onto the corkboard. 'I'll show you how to use this camera,' he said to Sarah.

'Then you can take pictures when I'm not around. I'll show Josh how to use it tomorrow.'

'It was a wonderful idea, Rick. Thank you.'

'No worries.' Rick shrugged off the praise. It took only a few moments for him to demonstrate the workings of the camera. 'I've got a ton of the blank cards,' he told her. 'It all became redundant ages ago and ended up in my office for some reason. It's nice to have a use for it. And now...' the corners of his eyes crinkled as he smiled beneath the mask '...I've got to run. I've got a mountain of stuff to get through in the next couple of days so I can take some time off.'

'Oh...of course. When is your procedure scheduled for?'

'Wednesday, at the moment. Depends on how Josh goes with the prep.'

'Are you going to get knocked out?'

'No. I don't want a general anaesthetic.'

Sarah nodded. She had expected he wouldn't. 'What about the IV sedation? I think I'd go for a bucket of that.'

'They have offered me some jungle juice but I declined.' A flash of something like embarrassment showed on Rick's face. He had clearly been attracted by the prospect. 'It would mean I couldn't drive for twenty-four hours afterwards and I don't want to have to spend the night in here.'

'I could drive you home,' Sarah offered. 'And pick you up the next day.'

Rick didn't meet her eyes. 'I can cope with the local.'

He'd prefer not to have to, though, wouldn't he?

Anyone would. 'Why make it worse for yourself than it has to be?' she asked carefully. 'Heaven knows, you're doing enough as it is. It's no big deal if I give you a ride home and pick you up the next morning.'

'You wouldn't want to leave Josh.'

'It wouldn't be for long. He'd be fine. I'd really like to…' Sarah held Rick's gaze. 'What you've done…are doing for Josh. It's really…'

The pleasure he had given. A chance to dream. Hope for a future.

It was beyond price. Beyond anything Sarah could find words to thank him for. She had to blink hard and turned slightly to look at Josh so that Rick wouldn't see how affected she was. She almost missed the shrugging movement Rick was making for the second time in that visit. She heard the rustle of his gown as he headed for the door.

'I said I'd give it my best shot,' he muttered. 'I'll let you know…about Wednesday.'

Rick headed for the intensive care unit. He had time to check on how young Simon was doing before he was due in Theatre for what would be a long and probably difficult surgery on a two-year-old girl who had a brain tumour with tentacles surrounding her spinal cord.

He was very pleased with the effect his brain wave about the old Polaroid camera had had. It had obviously distracted Josh from what was happening around him, albeit for only a short time, but, even better, he'd seen how Sarah had reacted. That initial surprise that he had actually come to visit. The quiet respect that he'd thought of a gift that could make a difference to how difficult this admission would be. There'd been that bristling at what she'd seen as stepping on her toes as a parent when he'd suggested that dreaming of a time when he could have his own dog wasn't so farfetched but then he'd seen…what?…acceptance? *Relief?*

No, that wasn't quite it but there'd been something. A connection. Maybe she believed now that he was prepared to try being a father figure for Josh and that she now had someone who was stepping up to share the burden. A partner.

Yes. Rick liked that idea. Sarah was more of a parent to Josh than he'd ever been but he had applied for a job-sharing arrangement and, so far, it was going well.

Better than he'd anticipated, in fact. Maybe this being a father thing wouldn't be so bad.

Josh was a good kid. He had looked pale and sick and had been through a fairly major procedure that morning. He was also confined to a small room where his only visitors had to be shrouded like alien beings and he was going to be in there for what must seem like an eternity to a nine-year-old, but he hadn't been whinging about any of it. He was a tough little nut. He'd wanted a photograph of him throwing up, for heaven's sake. Rick found himself grinning as he walked into Intensive Care.

Simon's parents were beside his bed. They both looked pale and were sitting very still. Their world had caved in on them, hadn't it? They were used to being in here now. Familiar with the machines and the new kind of care their son needed. Small things had become incredibly important but their focus was entirely on what was happening in here. World War Three could have broken out but they would still be totally focused.

Watching for any signs that their precious child was going to survive and be all right.

Simon still lay like a small, reclining statue. Breathing on his own now but not showing any sign of coming out of the coma. Josh had been this pale but what a difference to be able to see the spark of life in a child's eyes. To be able to make them smile.

It wasn't that Rick had ever lacked any sympathy for the parents of his young patients. He would be going from this room to talk to the distraught family of the very sick toddler on his theatre list for this afternoon. He had seen too many parents suffering through this kind of experience. He'd seen the courage with which some of them faced inevitable failure and the agony of dealing with its aftermath. But he'd never felt quite like this. As though he knew the real level of pain it could cause because he could imagine what it would be like if it was Josh, lying here in Intensive Care. Or waiting in the ward to be taken for surgery that might save his life but could, quite possibly, end it.

He barely knew his own child but he knew that Josh had dreams. He wanted to go back to school. He wanted to live in a house that had a garden and a dog to play with. And Rick wanted him to have all those things. The desire to make it happen was sudden and fierce and almost threatened to overwhelm him.

He had to clear his throat as he looked up from reviewing Simon's chart.

'The intracranial pressure is coming down,' he told Simon's parents.

'That's good, isn't it?'

'Of course it is, honey,' the father said.

Simon's mother looked like she was holding her breath, too frightened to accept good news unless it could be trusted.

'It's very good,' Rick told her. 'Along with every-thing else that's settling down, it means that Simon's condition is stable. We'll be able to send him to Theatre to have his leg dealt with properly.'

'And will he wake up? After that?'

'I don't know,' Rick had to admit. 'I'm sorry, but I can't give you any definite time when that might happen. It's a matter of continuing to look after him and waiting to see what happens as the swelling keeps going down.'

'But it's a step in the right direction, isn't it?' Simon's father had covered his eyes with his hand. He gave a huge sniff and his wife reached out to hold his other hand. Then they smiled at each other and Rick could actually feel the strength being passed from one to the other.

They were a partnership. They could help each other get through this and because they had each other, they were far more likely to cope. Whatever happened.

He wanted it to be like that for him and Sarah. A partnership that really meant something. A support that would get her through whatever was coming. It gave him a good feeling, imagining himself in that sup-portive role. Being her rock. A hero, even. And who knew? It might end up being one of the most worth-while things he would do in his life.

He was going to give it his best shot, that was for sure. For both Josh and Sarah.

* * *

The combination of a heavy drug regime and the radio-therapy were taking their toll on Josh.

By Wednesday he was running a temperature and his platelet count was so low he'd needed a blood transfusion. His joints hurt enough to need some serious pain relief and the nausea and vomiting were only just under control.

He was miserable.

'Katie's on duty today. She's your favourite nurse, isn't she?'

The assent was reluctant.

'Do you want to look at the book Rick brought yesterday? The one about dogs?'

Josh said nothing. His eyes looked blank, as though nothing mattered any more. Sarah covered up her need to blink and swallow back the tears by reaching for the *Encyclopaedia of Dogs* that Rick had apparently found in the well-stocked hospital bookshop. She edged her chair even closer to Josh's bed and laid the book where he could see it, flicking through the pages and showing him pictures.

'Look at that! It's an Irish wolfhound. It's twice the size you are, short stuff. Imagine how much it would need to eat. I think something a bit smaller would be better, don't you?'

Josh gave a half-hearted shrug that reminded her rather strongly of the way Rick had reacted to praise the other day.

'It's Wednesday today,' she said, after a moment's silence. 'Rick's going to have his bone marrow collected this afternoon. Do you think he'll be as brave as you are with that kind of thing?'

That got a reaction. A look of disgust almost.

''Course he will.'

Was there an element of hero-worship in there already? It wouldn't surprise her in the least. Rick had appeared in Josh's life like a thunderbolt. Larger than life. Tall and handsome and clever. He lived in what would have to be a small boy's paradise with a constant live action show of trucks and ships and machinery doing important things. He had taken Josh for a ride on his motorbike. He'd become a regular visitor to this room and often arrived with a surprise. Like the camera and the book about dogs.

Was it a bad thing, that Josh might see his father as the new sun in his universe? It certainly added a very new dimension to his life. The visits were something to look forward to in an otherwise bleak environment and the new development of having a father who seemed to care about him was…absolute magic.

As long as Rick kept up his promise of involvement. Sarah didn't want to contemplate the consequences if he changed his mind and disappeared from Josh's life for whatever reason. Not that he was showing any sign of regretting his choice. He'd be taking the next step in a matter of hours, in fact. Going through what would probably be a painful and unpleasant medical procedure.

'You haven't forgotten that I'll be out for a while later? When I drive Rick home?'

Josh stared at her, that frightening blankness still in his face.

'It won't be for long. And Katie's going to stay in here to keep you company. That's OK, isn't it?'

The telltale wobble of a bottom lip made her heart sink like a stone. She couldn't leave him if it was going to cause further distress but she had promised Rick and she didn't want to let *him* down either. What was she going to do?

Trying to think, Sarah's gaze went back to the book lying on the bed cover. She turned a random number of pages.

'Good grief, look at that. Looks like a rat with a wig on, doesn't it?'

Josh barely glanced at the photograph of the hairless Chinese crested dog. Sarah's level of desperation increased.

'I might see that other dog again when I drive Rick home,' she said. 'You know, the one that was outside the coffee shop?'

That did it. The spark of interest made Josh's face come to life. Sarah's heart gave a painful squeeze.

'What will you do if you see it?'

Uh-oh…She was getting into dangerous territory here but she couldn't bear to see that blank look return.

'If it doesn't have someone looking after it, it might be lost. Or abandoned or something.'

Josh nodded. 'It would need someone to take it home, then, wouldn't it?'

'I guess.' Sarah mentally crossed her fingers, hoping that she might see the dog wearing a collar and lead. Being walked by a responsible dog owner.

'So you'll look out for it?'

'Yes.'

'When are you going?'

He actually wanted her to go now. If nothing else, it had solved her most immediate dilemma. 'Not till this afternoon. You'll be asleep, I expect.'

He was looking ready to sleep again now. Struggling to keep his eyes open. 'But you'll wake me up when you get back? And tell me?'

'Absolutely.'

Josh gave a big sigh and his eyes drifted shut. 'That's good,' he mumbled.

'I didn't see it.'

'See what?'

'The dog.'

'What dog?' Rick wanted to make that crease on Sarah's forehead disappear but he had no idea what she was talking about. It probably had something to do with the dramatic increase in his level of pain, having had his long frame folded into her small car for what seemed like a long time now. Or maybe his brain was fuzzy due to the after-effects of the IV sedation. No wonder you weren't allowed to drive for a while.

'That scruffy mutt we saw outside the coffee shop that day. Josh is worried about it. He wanted me to keep an eye out and rescue it if I saw it wandering around.'

'And take it to the pound?'

Sarah's laugh was a little hollow. 'I think he'd prefer me to take it home.'

It was Rick's turn to frown now. 'Might be just as well you didn't see it, then.'

'Yeah…I guess.'

'What, you think you could cope with having an illegal hound in your apartment as well as having Josh in hospital?'

'No, of course not. It's just…'

'What?' Rick had to suppress an urge to reach out and touch Sarah to encourage her to keep talking. He smiled at her instead, which seemed to do the trick.

'Well…he was so unhappy today. Sick and sore and miserable, and I've never seen him look quite like that. Blank, you know? Like he would just give up on everything if he was given half a chance. But when I mentioned the dog, he…came alive again. It was…it was…' Sarah pressed her lips together and squeezed her eyes shut.

Rick did touch her this time. Just a friendly squeeze on the arm still holding the steering-wheel.

'I get it,' he said. 'Hey, I'll keep an eye out for it myself. I often go past there, on my way to the hamburger shop.'

'Oh…that reminds me. Have you got something for your dinner?'

'I'm not exactly hungry. Might just take some of the nice painkillers they've given me and wash them down with a shot of something tastier than water.'

Sarah's eyes darkened with sympathy. 'Poor you. Um…do you need a hand getting up the steps?'

He didn't, of course. Sure, he was pretty sore but it wasn't about to incapacitate him. But he rather liked the way she was looking at him right now. As though how he felt mattered enough for her to be sharing his pain. Jet would have given him a thump on his arm and told him to 'harden up, man'.

'That would be nice,' he heard himself saying in a

voice small enough to make him very glad Jet wasn't around to overhear. 'If you've got the time, that is. You must be wanting to get back to Josh.'

'He's fine. He had a big dose of painkillers himself just before I left and went out like a light. His nurse thought he'd be asleep for a good few hours.'

She put her arm around Rick when he started climbing the steps and that felt so nice he probably went a lot slower than he actually needed to go. And then they were inside and there was no reason for her to stay any longer but Rick didn't want her to leave just yet.

'Can I make you a cup of tea or something?'

Sarah hesitated, gave Rick a long glance and then took a deep breath. 'Why don't I make one for both of us? That way I can make sure you feel OK after you have your pills. I don't want to rush away and have you fall over and hit your head or something.'

They both went into the kitchen. Sarah boiled the jug and found some mugs while Rick threw down a couple of pills with a shot of whisky. He couldn't help noticing the glance she threw at him.

'Don't worry, I'm not about to down the whole bottle. The faster these pills work the quicker I'll get to sleep. A good night and I'll be as right as rain by the morning.'

'If you say so.' Sarah took the steaming mugs to the low table near the chairs.

Rick lowered himself very carefully.

'Is it really bad?'

He shrugged. 'Feels a bit like I came off my bike and landed on my bum.'

Her lips twitched. 'On a scale of zero to ten? Zero being—'

Rick laughed. 'You're such a nurse. I'm fine. Let's stop talking about it. Tell me something about you instead.'

'Like what?'

Like what, indeed?

He could ask about her childhood but that would inevitably mean talking about her sister and Rick would end up feeling guilty. He didn't want to have to think about how his irresponsibility might have derailed a young woman's life.

He was making up for it now, wasn't he? Trying to, anyway.

He could ask about her career but that would mean talking about medicine. Work. The experience of being on the patient's side of the equation was a little too fresh to make that appealing. It would be nice to forget about hospitals for a while.

What did that leave?

Sarah herself. In the present time. Yes…that was definitely what he'd like to talk about. If he could think up a question. It seemed oddly difficult to catch what was inside his head and make it come out in words.

'How bold are you?'

'Sorry?' Sarah came very close to slopping her drink all over her clothing.

'I meant how *old* are you?'

'Twenty-seven.'

'And how long have you been…? How long…' Rick narrowed his eyes to help him concentrate '…with Josh?'

Sarah understood. 'Coming up to three years now. He was six when the accident happened and Lucy was killed.'

Oops. The sister. How could he divert the topic?

'Mmm. The motorbike.' No. That wasn't a good direction. 'Boyfriend,' Rick muttered experimentally. That seemed to be an improvement. Relief made him smile at Sarah. 'Have you got a boyfriend?'

'No.' The word was clipped.

Rick looked away. He didn't want to be caught looking pleased about that or anything. He eyed the mug of tea. He'd rather have another shot of whisky but that probably wouldn't be a good idea. He was feeling pleasantly numb around the edges already. The pain was rapidly becoming very distant.

'I did,' Sarah said into the growing silence. 'He took off after Josh arrived. He wasn't about to include someone else's kid in his life.'

'Creep,' Rick said helpfully.

'Not really. It's a big ask.'

It wouldn't be for *him*, though, would it? He liked Josh. A lot. Which was good because he was *his* kid after all. Weird how proud that was making him feel right now. Rick could feel himself smiling broadly.

'What's funny?' Sarah had an odd note in her voice. It also sounded as if it was coming from rather a long way away. 'Rick…are you feeling all right?'

'I'm fun.'

'Hmm. Maybe you should go to bed.'

'Mmm.' This was the best idea yet. He kept smiling at Sarah. 'Come with me?'

'Oh…*God*,' Sarah muttered. She stood up, helped

Rick to his feet and put a firm arm around his waist. 'Come on. You need to sleep.'

Rick's feet felt like dead weights but he could walk just fine. Until he got to the stairs leading to the mezzanine level where his bed was. Sarah turned him round after his attempt at the first step nearly had them both on the floor.

'Couch,' she said. 'I'll get a pillow and some blankets. You're not safe with stairs.'

She was right. Rick was still with it enough to be able to keep himself safe. He even managed to pull his shoes off and lie down on the couch by the time she returned.

Sarah put a glass of water and his mobile phone on the table nearby. She covered him with the duvet from his bed and then bent down to ease a pillow under his head.

'You're a wonderful woman, Sarah,' he said, pleased at how clearly the words came out. Lying down was good.

'Are you going to be all right on your own, do you think?'

'Just need to catch a few zeds. I'm fine. You go.'

She hesitated.

'The phone's there.' Rick flapped a hand. 'I'll call you if I need rescue, OK? I'm not totally away with the fairies. Just…just…' He let himself float for a moment. 'Just happy.'

'Hmm.' It sounded like Sarah was smiling. 'I can see that. I guess the pills are at maximum effect by now. They'll wear off while you sleep.'

'Ni'-night.'

'Sleep well, Rick. You're a hero.'

He opened one eye. 'Do I get a goodnight kiss, then?'

Sarah shook her head as she gave a huff of laughter. 'You're a rogue,' she told him.

But then she bent and gave him a swift, soft kiss on his lips. She was standing again before he could even think of making his arms move to catch her.

'I'll see you in the morning,' she said. 'Sleep tight.'

It didn't matter that he hadn't been able to catch and hold Sarah. He could imagine exactly what it would have been like. And what might have happened if her lips had stayed in contact with his a little longer.

The pleasant fuzziness of the painkillers morphed into something so delicious that Rick could only heave a sigh of pure contentment and go with it. To paradise.

He had no idea how long Sarah sat watching him and he didn't hear a thing when she finally slipped away, closing the door softly behind her.

CHAPTER SIX

RICK's text message to Sarah the next day sounded faintly embarrassed.

Max back in town, it said. *No need to collect me.*

Sarah wouldn't have been surprised if Rick had found an excuse not to visit Josh. After the twenty-four-hour stand-down period he would have some catching up to do on his patients and by the time he'd been on his feet that long, he might well be sore enough to want to head straight home again. It was to his credit that he turned up late that afternoon.

He did, however, avoid direct eye contact with Sarah. And he muttered an apology about 'last night' before he got close enough to Josh's bed to be overheard.

'No worries,' Sarah said calmly. 'You were…um… happy.'

'High as a kite, more like.' His tone was rueful. 'I should have stuck to the local.'

Sarah turned back to the window. She could understand him feeling embarrassed about how friendly he'd been but he didn't have to rub it in. Unless, of course, he wanted her to be absolutely sure he saw her as Josh's aunt-cum-mother and nothing else.

Well…fine. She saw him as nothing more than Josh's father. Inappropriate words or touches on his part that might have occurred as the result of close proximity and inhibitions being stifled by medication could be forgiven and forgotten. Along with that oddly protective urge she'd experienced that had led her to sit and watch over him last night. And the way she'd unconsciously found herself touching her own lips softly, more than once, as though reliving that brief kiss.

At least Josh wasn't picking up on any weird vibe.

'Does your bum hurt?' he asked Rick.

'Kind of…you know.'

Josh did know. He was eyeing Rick with new respect. He nodded importantly and, with a visible effort, straightened up against his pillows. A deliberate imitation of Rick's solid stance?

They were watching each other. Man and boy. Both had to be thinking about the physical discomfort of a procedure they had both endured recently. Sarah could almost feel the way their mutual respect grew. She saw the smile of quiet pride on Josh's exhausted face and the way the creases around Rick's eyes deepened as he returned it. She could feel the connection then. Still new and nebulous but definitely there, and her own lips curved into a slightly wobbly smile beneath her mask.

Oh, yes…She could forgive Rick anything. Even the stirring of things far better left to lie still that his request for a goodnight kiss had achieved. This was more than simply fronting up and trying to act like a father. There was a growing bond that went far deeper than going through the motions. Right now, Rick and

Josh might both be proud of themselves but, far more significantly, they were also proud of each other.

Rick made that casual shrugging gesture she was coming to recognise as shying away from being praised. It suggested an appealing modesty. 'Take any photographs today?' he asked Josh.

'Yeah.' Josh managed a faint grin. 'Me throwing up. See?'

Rick dutifully took note of the new addition to the cork board. It wasn't graphic—just Josh with his face attached to the rim of a vomit container, but he'd been happy and maybe he'd been right. The picture deserved a slot in the visual diary. Maybe later they would look back and be able to see how long ago it had been since he'd felt so awful.

Sarah wasn't feeling so great herself. Josh had still been asleep when she'd finally come back last night after her vigil over Rick but she'd been unable to sleep. Now, when she moved to go and sit down on one of the chairs, she had to catch the rail at the end of the bed to steady herself.

How on earth had Rick managed to catch her elbow so fast?

'Are you all right?'

Oh…Lord. That expression in those dark eyes threatened to undo her completely. When had somebody last demonstrated real concern for *her*? When had anybody *ever* looked at her quite like that? Stupidly, it made her want to cry.

'Are you going to throw up?' Josh asked with interest.

'No…' But Sarah was still caught by Rick's gaze.

'I mean, yes. I'm all right. I'm fine. Just…a bit tired, I guess.'

'How much have you had to eat today?'

'Only lunch so far.'

'You didn't eat your lunch,' Josh reminded her. He yawned. 'It came while I was throwing up, remember? You said it didn't look so good after all.'

Rick was frowning. 'And you didn't have breakfast?'

'I had coffee.'

'And last night? After you got back from tucking me in?' At least he could sound casual about it now. 'Did you have a proper dinner?'

What would he say if she told him it had been far too late to visit the cafeteria because she'd sat watching him sleep for so long? That would bring the embarrassment back with a vengeance, wouldn't it? She didn't want to do that.

Rick shook his head. 'Ellie's coming in to say hi soon. You should both go out and get some food. There's a nice bistro only a block or so away from here. They do great pasta.'

Josh spoke with his eyes shut. 'Is Ellie coming to visit *me*?'

'She won't be allowed in here,' Sarah said apologetically. 'Sorry, Josh, but there's a strict limit on who gets in to visit you. At the moment it's just me and Rick and your doctors and nurses.'

'Cos you're my mum now,' Josh mumbled.

'That's right, short stuff.'

'And Rick's my dad.'

Sarah's hesitation was imperceptible. She didn't dare

look at Rick. She bent down and kissed Josh's head instead. 'Yeah...'

Josh made a very sleepy sound of approval. When Sarah straightened, she saw the door opening to admit a nurse who was coming in to do the vital-sign monitoring that was due. She also saw Rick slipping out. And beyond him, as he stripped off the mask and gown, she could see Ellie, looking anxious.

The cringe factor was still there.

Every time he caught direct eye contact with Sarah, Rick had the very uncomfortable feeling that she might be able to see remnants of those incredible, drug-fuelled dreams he'd had about her last night.

He had been fairly confident this morning that he could remember where reality had left off and fantasy had taken over, but what if that was merely wishful thinking on his part? What if it hadn't been as chaste a kiss as he thought? Had he actually tasted the sweet scent of her mouth? Felt the slide of her tongue driving him into a passion that had been as overwhelming as it had been unrecognisable?

If so, either Sarah had been totally unmoved by the experience or she was an extremely good actress. Even now, watching her greet Ellie, catch up on news of the honeymoon and relay an update on Josh, he couldn't detect any tension. Or any of those secret female, tele-pathic-type messages about something personal that needed private analysis and resolution.

Ellie was apologising again for having béen out of the country when her friend had needed support.

'We've been fine,' Sarah assured her. 'Rick's been absolutely wonderful.'

Ellie's eyes widened.

So did Rick's. His chest might have puffed out just a little as well. He shrugged it off.

'Haven't done much,' he muttered. 'It's my kid in there, after all.'

But Ellie was biting her lip and smiling at the same time. She hugged Sarah. Then she stood on tiptoe and threw her arms around Rick's neck, hugging him tightly.

'I knew you'd end up being a hero,' she whispered. 'Thank you.'

He'd 'ended up' being a hero? She was thanking him? Sarah's expression was softened by heartfelt gratitude as well. As though he'd done something they'd wanted badly but hadn't really expected him to do.

Fair enough. He hadn't exactly behaved very well when first confronted by the possibility of Josh being his son, had he? But he hadn't known anything about these people back then. Was it really such a short time ago? They were part of his life now. Important. Special.

Oh…hell. These two women looked like they were about to start crying. He didn't want any more gratitude or talk about heroics. He was no hero. If he hadn't been so irresponsible and uncaring in the first place, none of this would be happening to any of them. Including the innocent kid in the room right beside them who was suffering most.

This was *his* fault. All of it.

'Sarah's starving,' he informed Ellie. 'She hasn't

eaten all day and she was so wobbly in there she almost fell over. I thought you could take her to that nice bistro down the road and fill her up with pasta or something.'

'Oh...' Ellie looked stricken. 'Max is looking after Mattie but he's covering for someone in ED for a few hours yet.' Her glance at Sarah was very apologetic. It became inspired when it returned to Rick.

'*You* could take her,' Ellie said.

'It's OK,' Sarah said hurriedly. 'I can get something from the cafeteria. That way I can get back to Josh faster.'

The odd combination of relief and disappointment Rick was experiencing got interrupted by the door of Josh's room opening. His nurse, Katie, poked her head out.

'Josh wants a rerun of his Harry Potter DVD and I haven't seen all of it so I'm going to stay with him. Why don't you have a good break, Sarah? A nice meal and a shower and so on. Do you good.'

'But—'

'I've got your mobile number. I'll ring if Josh needs you.'

Katie disappeared back into the room. They could all see the screen of the television set that angled down from the ceiling in the corner of the room. They could also see Josh, his eyes only half-open but already glued to the images of his favourite movie.

There was a moment's silence in the corridor as Rick struggled to eradicate the last of that cringe factor. But, suddenly, he stopped trying. Maybe it was a good thing. A kind of penance. He could learn from it and maybe even continue the process of finally growing up that seemed to have started under Sarah's orders.

'I can recommend the ravioli,' he said, raising his eyebrows and letting a smile curve one side of his mouth. 'How 'bout it? My treat… I owe you a thank-you for your kind taxi service yesterday.'

Sarah looked back through the window. There must be a scary scene happening judging by the wide eyes of both Josh and Katie and the way they were holding hands. She looked at Ellie, who nodded with firm encouragement.

'Go on,' she urged. 'A break from here is exactly what you need. I know I'm a much better mum when I've had a bit of a break from Mattie. Speaking of whom…'

'You go,' Sarah told her. 'I'll call you tomorrow and…' she flicked a glance at Rick '…tell you whether the ravioli lives up to its reputation.'

Sarah had known this might be awkward.

She also knew that unless they could get past it, it might grow into something a lot worse than mild embarrassment. If Rick started to avoid her, he would, by default, be avoiding Josh and she couldn't let that happen.

Not now, with that new bond developing. Having a father he could be proud of—who was proud of *him*—had to be the best gift Josh could ever receive. Whatever it took, she had to make sure he didn't lose that gift or have its value undermined in some way. Any private feelings she might have in the matter of including Rick in their lives were irrelevant. Or had to become so in a hurry.

So she did her best to chatter brightly as they walked the short distance to the bistro. About Josh, of course, and the happenings of the day.

'He's doing pretty well, all things considered,' she was saying as they reached their destination. 'Totally exhausted but Mike says that's only to be expected. He thinks we're on track to do the transplant tomorrow. Or the next day.' She couldn't help the tiny gulp that punctuated the prediction.

'Nervous about it?' Rick's hand was on her elbow as he steered her through the door into a small, dimly lit establishment, made cheerful by its warmth and the tempting smell of hot food.

'Yes. He ran through the list of things they'd be watching for while the transfusion happens. Fever and chills and hives and chest pain and so on. It's a big deal. I'm not sure I can hold my breath for that long.'

She stopped talking as they were shown to a table tucked into the corner of the room, with two old wooden chairs on the available sides. It had a checked cloth and a slim candle stuck in an old, misshapen wine bottle that carried the dribbles of wax from years of service.

Sarah had to smile. 'This takes me back to my student days. I didn't think places like this existed any more.'

Tables around them were rapidly filling up.

'We'd better order soon or we might end up being here for a while.' Rick signalled the young waitress.

Sarah ordered a wild mushroom ravioli with

roasted red pepper sauce. Rick chose the individual ravioli lasagne.

'Garlic bread?' The waitress flicked a lighter and leaned in to light their candle.

'Please.'

'Anything to drink? Do you want the wine list?'

Sarah caught Rick's questioning glance. 'Why not?' she decided aloud. A glass of wine would be a rare treat these days.

'I think I'd better stick to water,' Rick said when Sarah had made her choice. His grin was endearingly self-deprecating. 'After last night, I mean.'

Sarah sighed but smiled at the same time. 'Don't make such a big deal out of it, Rick. It was kind of cute, really—asking for a goodnight kiss.'

She looked up and then wished she hadn't because she got caught. Candlelight flickered and Rick's eyes were very dark and watchful. The echo of the last word she'd spoken seemed to dance in the space between them and all she could think about for a moment was kissing.

Kissing Rick.

'Hardly a grown-up thing to do,' he said softly.

Good heavens... Her angry words that day she'd left Josh on his doorstep must have really hit home.

'Just as well I'm used to boy stuff, then,' she said lightly. 'Let's forget it.'

'OK.' But Rick still seemed on edge. 'Guess I'll have to add it to the list of things to do with you that I'm not so proud of.'

'A whole list?' Sarah was very thankful that her wine had arrived. A large first mouthful on her very empty stomach was having an instant effect in relaxing her. 'Oh, come on…you're doing something you have every right to feel *very* proud of.'

'Being a donor?' Rick was toying with his water glass. Running his thumb up the side to wipe off condensation the iced liquid had caused. Sarah couldn't take her eyes off the movement. His long, surgeon's fingers. The delicate, intense touch.

'Has it occurred to you that it's actually my fault that Josh is going through this whole business?'

'*What*?' Sarah shifted her gaze from his hands to his face. 'Don't be daft. You can hardly take the blame for Josh getting sick.'

'But I can for him being here at all. For the way I treated your sister.' Rick looked away. 'All I can say in my defence is that it was a bad time. Self-destruction seemed like the only escape route I could find.'

'I know.' Seemingly of its own volition, her hand stretched across the table to touch Rick's. His skin felt more than alive. It tingled and burned under her fingers and she had to pull her hand back in case it showed. 'Ellie told me about your friend Matt. I'm sorry. It must have been a terrible time for all of you.'

Rick merely nodded. He took a gulp of his water and Sarah followed his example and picked up her wine glass again.

Oh…help. This was a vast topic and not one Sarah had expected Rick to bring up. She didn't want him feeling guilty, though. Or feeling like he owed Josh something just because he was sick. She wanted Josh to have a father he could look up to and love. Who would love him back with the kind of unconditional love that could only be tainted by things like guilt or pity.

She took another mouthful of the wine, set her glass down again and then spoke slowly and carefully.

'Lucy was a big girl. It was her choice to sleep with you, Rick. She was hardly behaving that well herself, was she, if she jumped into bed with someone else fast enough to assume the baby was his when she found out she was pregnant.'

'She really didn't think it was me?'

'Apparently not.' Should she tell Rick about what she'd said to Josh? About his father riding a motorbike and being so handsome? Sarah swallowed hard. 'She never said anything to me about you. I had no idea you even existed.' She couldn't help letting her gaze rest on his face for a moment and she certainly couldn't stop the smile that tugged at her lips. 'Seems weird now.'

Why was that? With a sinking sensation, Sarah realised that it was because he had already made such an impact on her life that she would always be aware of him in some way. And she'd as much as told him so.

But Rick only made a grunting sound that could have been agreement. Thankfully, he seemed to have missed the implication. Except he *was* frowning.

Sarah held her breath, waiting for him to speak.

'Do you think it wrecked her life?' he asked abruptly. 'Getting pregnant?'

Sarah was given time to consider her response by the arrival of their meals. The food was the most delicious she'd tasted in a very long time and she had to eat a couple of mouthfuls despite being aware of Rick waiting anxiously for her to speak.

'Sorry. I was starving.'

'No worries. I probably shouldn't be asking you anyway. It's just…I've been thinking about it, that's all.'

'Of course you have.' Sarah rested her fork on her plate and gave him her full attention. 'Being pregnant didn't wreck Lucy's life. It changed it but I think she was happier for that change.'

'Why?'

'She was a country girl at heart. We grew up in a small town and she was quite intimidated by the city. I think she felt pretty lost. Lonely, even.'

'She must have gone through hell, then, finding she was pregnant and wondering what to do.'

'She was tough.' Sarah's smile was fond. 'She coped. She didn't even tell me until well down the track. And neither of us told our mother.'

'Why not?'

'She had a very strict moral code. She raised us on her own after Dad died and I don't think she found that much joy in the process. Her church was more important than anything. When she eventually found out, she never spoke to Lucy again.'

'God…*families*…'

Sarah ignored the undercurrent of his tone.

'When Josh was born Luce fell in love with him and he was all that mattered. She wasn't going to let anyone take him away from her and that meant never involving the father. He was her family. Her future. When Mum died, she left me her house. I was going to sell it and give Luce the money but she decided that being out in the country would be a good place to raise Josh. She was so excited about it.' Sarah took a deep breath.

'You didn't wreck her life, Rick. You gave her a dream. Like…like telling Josh that he could have a dog one day, you know? It's kind of like hope that the perfect life is there, just waiting for you. And maybe…'

She stopped talking, appalled at what she had been about to say. That maybe Lucy had been dreaming of finding a father for Josh who would be just like Rick. She choked back both the words and the sentiments they represented. Absurdly, she found herself close to tears. She tried to pick up her fork but her hand was shaking so she dropped it with a clatter and reached for her wineglass again.

She knew she should say more but how could she without revealing far too much about the way she was reacting to Rick? She didn't want to talk any more about Lucy right now either.

Why is that? an insistent voice in her head queried. *Because you don't want the ghost of your sister standing between you and this man?*

Sarah drained her glass and made of a show of returning her attention to her food. Rick was watching her very intently but he didn't say anything other than offering her another glass of wine, which she refused.

In fact, neither of said very much for the rest of the meal or the walk back to Queen Mary's, and Sarah had no idea whether she'd been successful in trying to abort the guilt trip Rick had embarked on.

She was making a map of a rather similar kind of journey herself. Along the lines of cashing in on a fantasy Lucy could no longer even dream about. Good heavens, wasn't being attracted to a man her own sister had slept with unacceptable enough all by itself?

Of course it was. This had to stop.

'Let me know when they schedule the transplant,' Rick said as they reached the main doors of the hospital. 'I'd like to be there.'

Sarah nodded. 'I will. Thanks.'

'What for?'

'Oh…the meal. Being here…' Being *you*, she couldn't help adding silently. 'You know…'

Rick had that watchful look again. 'Maybe it should be *me* thanking you.'

Sarah blinked. 'What for?'

'Oh…I don't know. Making me grow up, perhaps? Being…' He hesitated for a heartbeat. 'Are we friends yet, Sarah?'

'I think so,' she said gravely. But then she smiled. 'Don't grow up completely. Keep a bit of that boy stuff.'

'What, like asking for a goodnight kiss?'

It was a light-hearted comment. They were standing right in front of the entranceway. Any moment now and Sarah would go inside and back to the bone-marrow transplant unit. Rick would head for the car park and home. All they needed to do was share a smile and any embarrassment from last night would evaporate for ever and they could part on a new level of friendship.

The smile was there already. The intention to leave at that was also there. So why on earth did she stay exactly where she was?

'I'm the one who had the wine,' she heard herself saying. 'I think it's my turn to ask.'

She didn't have to.

'Fair enough.' Rick was smiling as he dipped his head and touched her lips with his own.

It was a brief kiss. The kind that friends could exchange. There was nothing more in its length or pressure than the token gesture she had given Rick last night but it was different. Very, very different.

Dangerous.

The electric sensation of touching his hand with hers had nothing on this contact of their lips.

Sarah was playing with fire here, and she knew it was wrong. She could blame it on exhaustion, or the wine, or stress, or the fact that her hormones were in flood after the longest drought, but no excuse was going to make it any less wrong.

Summoning every ounce of strength she possessed, Sarah broke the contact almost the instant it had happened and turned away.

'See?' Her tone was so light it floated. 'No big deal. Goodnight, Rick.'

The doors slid open with admirable swiftness. She knew Rick was still standing there but no way was she going to risk a backward glance.

It wasn't going to happen, she told herself fiercely, increasing her speed. She wasn't going to allow it to happen.

Sarah could not, *would* not, fall in love with Rick Wilson.

He was Josh's father.

Quite possibly the most important person right now in a small boy's life.

A small boy she loved with all her heart.

A life that was hanging in the balance.

CHAPTER SEVEN

THE tension in that small room could have been cut with a knife.

'Drip, drip, drip,' Josh said, looking up at the bag of dark, red fluid hanging above his head. 'It looks like blood.'

'It's better than blood,' Mike told his young patient. 'It's the stuff that *makes* blood.'

'How's it going to get inside my bones?'

'Through the blood vessels. The same way the new blood gets out.'

'How does it know to stay in there? Why doesn't it just keeping floating round and round?'

'It's smart.'

Mike was watching Josh intently for any sign of an adverse reaction to the transfusion. The boy lay with only his pyjama pants on. His chest was bare, partly so they could watch for the beginnings of any rash and also because it was well plastered with electrodes for the continuous ECG monitoring every beat of his heart. Blood pressure was being recorded automatically every few minutes and Josh's favourite nurse, Katie, was standing with a clipboard, noting down everything that was being tracked.

Sarah was there too, of course. She was sitting beside the bed but Josh had refused to have his hand held.

'I'm not a baby,' he'd said. 'And it doesn't even hurt.'

Rick was standing beside the window. A part of this procedure but outside the inner circle with nothing to do but watch. And feel the atmosphere pressing in on him. Was this tension only due to the importance of this procedure going well?

Not for him.

He'd been over and over it in his head ever since Sarah had walked through those doors last night but he was no closer to making sense of any of it.

What the hell had been going on last night?

Things had been going so well. That bistro was one of his favourite places with its unpretentious, laid-back atmosphere. Kind of casual but intimate at the same time. The food had been up to its usual standard and he'd found himself thoroughly enjoying the company. Especially when Sarah had seemed intent on making him feel better about the notion that had been haunting him. That he might have completely derailed her sister's life by being the cause of an unwanted pregnancy.

She'd almost been telling him he'd made her life better, for God's sake. That he'd given Lucy a whole new direction. A *dream*… And then she'd clammed up and had had that look of struggling *not* to say what was on the tip of her tongue.

He'd seen that look before, he'd realised last night, sitting at his window watching a night shift in action on the wharf and puzzled by the mixed signals he seemed to have been given. Right back when they'd first met at the wedding. He'd asked her about her trip to the States. About searching for a possible donor for Josh. She'd known she was talking to that person right then but she'd promised not to say anything, hadn't she, so she'd buttoned her lip.

What did that have to do with what she'd been saying about Lucy? She'd dreamed of a family. Raising her kid in the country and having a dog. The perfect life. Except it hadn't been, had it, because her precious son had been missing something important. A father.

Him.

Whatever she'd said, there was still blame to be found. He'd changed the whole direction of her sister's life and then abandoned her because it had meant nothing to him. Left her with a child and a dream that was never fulfilled. Of course she would blame him, and fair enough.

He could handle that but he'd thought they'd got past it and the beginnings of a real friendship were there. She'd forgiven him for the stupid, drug-induced pass he'd made at her. *No big deal*, she'd said.

She'd even kissed him to prove it.

Except it *had* been a big deal. For him. That fleeting contact of her lips… Being close enough to smell her scent and feel the warmth of her breath… Oh, *man*…

It was still there in the room. That kiss. Like an elephant. Sarah probably didn't even see it. Partly because her attention was entirely on Josh but also because it had meant nothing to her.

Was this karma? He'd slept with her sister and the repercussions were still crashing into his life like a tidal wave. His attraction to Sarah was just part of it and the

whole picture was laced with emotion that pulsed like
a life force. A network of vessels like the ones inside
Josh that *his* bone marrow was now a part of. Things
were too mingled to separate. Him and Josh. Him and
Sarah. It was…

Confusing, that was what it was.

'Why doesn't my dad come and visit me any more?'

'He *does*. Every day.'

The hesitation was telling. So was the plaintive note
in Josh's voice. 'Not so much.'

Sarah's hands stilled in her task of sifting through
DVDs to try and find something that might interest a
bored child. It was true. Ever since the transplant had
happened, the number of times per day that Rick came
in to see them had dropped dramatically. OK, it had
only been a few days but the hope that only she was
noticing was something she could no longer cling to.

It was disturbing to say the least.

Did Rick feel like his duty was done now? The donation of bone marrow had been made and apparently
accepted by Josh's body so far, with no sign of rejection
issues. It was probably too early to stop worrying about
the onset of graft versus host disease. Or was it? She
needed to ask Mike about that when he came in on his
rounds. She could ask Rick but the routine visit from
Josh's consultant was more likely to occur first. Rick
seemed to be leaving it later and later in his day to pop
in and the visits seemed to be getting shorter.

Less…personal.

Or maybe that was only from her point of view because Rick was so focused on Josh when he *was* in the

room. The man and boy seemed to be getting closer and more comfortable with each other every day. She felt like she was being shut out. Rick was perfectly polite and friendly to her but she could feel the distance between them like a solid barrier. Kind of like the way he'd been after she'd first broken the news that he could be Josh's father and he had switched off that initial interest in *her*.

Was that part of it? The way she'd brushed him off after dinner the other night? Was he backing away from Josh because of *that*? Oh…why on earth had she given in to that temptation to kiss him? Maybe he thought she was playing games. Flirting and then playing hard to get. It might have been misguided but all she'd been trying to do was take the significance out of that first kiss. Put them on friendly terms but nothing more.

But now she seemed to be in exactly the scenario she'd been trying to avoid by not letting herself get too close to Rick. It wasn't supposed to backfire like this.

'Do you want to watch Harry Potter again?'

'No.'

'How 'bout we look at some of the maths Miss Allen sent in?'

'*No-o-o.*' Josh shook his head with miserable jerks. 'I'm too tired. I feel sick.'

Sarah's heart skipped a beat. It was so hard to stop her voice getting instantly tighter and higher. 'What kind of sick?'

'I'm hot. And my back hurts.'

Oh…God. They were living on such a knife-edge now. These few weeks following the transplant were the most critical. It took time for the transplanted bone marrow to migrate into the bone cavities. To engraft and start doing their job of producing normal blood cells. Until then, Josh was at high risk of infection or excessive bleeding. Blood samples were being taken daily to monitor whether engraftment was taking place and to watch organ function. Josh was being given multiple antibiotics along with anti-rejection drugs on top of what had become his normal drug regime. He would also receive blood and platelet transfusions as required.

Mike had warned them that it was normal for a bone-marrow-transplant patient to feel very sick and weak. Josh would experience nausea and vomiting, diarrhoea and extreme weakness. The possible complications he had talked to Sarah about included infection, bleeding, graft versus host disease and liver disease. Mouth ulcers and temporary confusion seemed minor in comparison but could still add a new level of misery.

So many things could go wrong and even the slightest symptom Josh experienced created a wave of panic that was pointless but inevitable. He said he felt hot. Was he running a temperature? Could he have already picked up a bug of some kind? A sore back might indicate a problem with his kidneys. Or maybe his liver. He was pale and tired enough to look as though a blood transfusion might be on the cards. Sarah fought the panic. She even managed to keep her voice sounding perfectly calm.

'I'll get Katie to call Doctor Mike and he can come and have a look at you.'

Josh nodded. He lay on his bed and stared at the ceiling.

'Shall I take today's picture for the cork board?'

He shook his head.

'We could put a different picture up. Do you want to choose one from the ones I cut out of the house magazines? The kind of house we might want to live in one day?' Sarah was feeling desperate. 'The one with the garden for the dog, remember?'

Josh sighed. His lip quivered. 'I like Rick's house,' he said in a small voice.

'It hasn't got a garden.' Sarah kicked herself mentally for the negative comment and searched wildly for a way to repair the unhappy silence that fell. 'There's lots of houses that would be close to Rick's house though. In Port Chalmers.'

Would she want to live that far away from work? Practically on Rick's doorstep? Yes…if it made Josh happy.

'That might be OK.' He seemed to be thinking about it but then he pushed at his bed cover. 'I want to go to the toilet.'

Sarah nodded. 'Come on, then.' She stood on the pedal at the end of the bed to lower it as far as it could go. Then she drew the covers back to free his legs. She put her arm around Josh to support him as he began to stand up but he pulled away irritably.

'I don't need help.'

'OK.'

This was the hardest part. The way Josh was so determined to be independent when it was obviously getting to be more of a struggle every day. He'd lost so much weight in the last week and his strength was not up to making his body move the way he wanted it to.

Sarah could only hover by his side as he hung on to his IV stand, pushing it slowly ahead of him to get to the bathroom. He hated using a bedpan or bottle so much that if he ever agreed to it, Sarah would know he was dangerously ill. So it was good that he was still insisting on taking these steps to look after things himself.

'Don't come in.'

'Only if you leave the door open just a little bit.'

He conceded half an inch of a gap. Thank goodness the door didn't have any kind of lock. Sarah hated being even this far away where she wouldn't be able to catch him if he fell. He let Katie go in with him but no one else. Sarah rested her forehead against the wall and took in a slow breath.

Rick might have been allowed to accompany him.

Josh needed him here. Nobody could say how much of an effect someone's psychological wellbeing had on their physical condition but it was obvious that the happier someone was, the better they could heal. And even if it didn't have a measurable effect on the kinds of things they could monitor with all this high-tech equipment, it would make these weeks that much more bearable. For everyone.

She had to talk to Rick about this, but how? She couldn't do it in the room with Josh because it was quite likely that the conversation would have to include being open about the attraction between them. If he was asleep it might be OK but the last time Rick had come through the door and seen Josh asleep he'd said he'd come back later and he'd slipped out again too fast for Sarah to say anything. Non-verbal communication even to indicate the need to talk to him was going to be difficult as well, given the way his gaze seemed to slide away the instant it caught hers.

Sarah heard the sound of the toilet being flushed and breathed a sigh of relief. In a short time she would have Josh safely back in his bed where she could watch over him.

With the relief came a new thought. Would it make a difference if she was honest about finding Rick attractive? That she was being pulled so close, so fast that she knew she could fall in love with him far, far too easily?

But then what? She'd feel like she was selling herself for Josh's sake. Forcing Rick into playing the role of being a father. Never knowing if he was around because of Josh or because of her. What if Josh somehow sensed that Rick's interest had to do with more than being a dad?

Back to square one. He would be devastated.

She couldn't win. What was best for Josh, what *she* wanted, what was possibly going through Rick's head, was filling her own mind. Endlessly going round and round. Confusing her. Ramping up a tension that was quite bad enough all on its own.

The dog was the last straw.

Sitting there, outside the gourmet hamburger shop, with its big, sad eyes fixed on Rick while he waited for his order to be filled.

It reminded him of the look on Sarah's face when he'd gone to visit Josh on his way home. The gazes had held a plea he couldn't respond to. Wanted something from him that he wasn't capable of delivering even if he'd *wanted* to. Which he didn't.

Dammit. As if today hadn't been hard enough already.

That session, with Simon's mother sitting in his office in floods of tears. Simon's coma had lightened a little and the boy was responsive to painful stimuli but he hadn't opened his eyes in nearly two weeks. Hadn't responded to his mother's voice or squeezed his dad's hand or given any hope that he might come back as more than a physical shell of the child they'd known and loved.

It was early days yet, Rick had reassured the mother. Simon was young and healthy. His EEG showed a good amount of brain activity. It was too soon to give up hope.

But fear and exhaustion had taken a huge toll. Simon's mother was facing the possibility of having a severely brain-damaged son.

'I should have made the most of every moment,' she'd sobbed. 'Why did I waste those moments by telling him off about how messy his room was or sending him outside to scrape the mud off his rugby boots? Why didn't we take him to Disneyland years ago instead of worrying about how fast we could pay off the mortgage? What if…?' She'd stopped, staring at Rick in utter desolation. 'What if I never hear him say "I love you, Mum" again?'

The words had haunted Rick all day.

What if there came a time when Rick knew he'd never see that smart, funny, brave kid who happened to be *his* son again? If he found himself having an agonised conversation with Max or Jet and saying *he* should have made the most of every moment?

But how could he when he was so aware of Sarah every time he even walked into the bone-marrow unit? Knowing that she would be there in the room? That he would have to keep his guard up and make sure he didn't give out any signals about the effect she had on him? Knowing that if he did, she'd just brush him off as unimportant. No big deal. He wasn't worth a position of anything more than Josh's father because he'd treated her sister so badly he'd made sure that she would never realise her dream of a complete family.

Well, that was fine. He didn't want it to be a big deal. Having a sick kid was enough of a complication in his life. He just didn't want the aggravation of having to be so close to the untouchable Sarah adding its own tension.

'Here you go, mate. Lamb burger and kumera wedges. Extra mint yoghurt on the side.'

'Cheers.' Rick managed a smile. 'Now I'll just have to get past the potential ambush at the door.'

The man serving him looked over his shoulder and groaned. 'That mutt back again? I'll have to ring the council in the morning. I called them last week and they're obviously not doing their job properly. Typical! Why do we bother paying our rates, huh?'

No doubt he'd give the council an earful tomorrow. They'd make an extra effort to find the dog and lock him into a cage. They'd wait the required length of time for someone to claim it, was it ten days? And then, if nobody came, they'd dispose of it. End of story.

An old bell clanged as Rick pushed open the door

and stepped into the street. He couldn't help glancing down at the dog.

At least Josh would never know what its fate had been.

The dog grinned up at him, flattening its ears and waving its tail.

'Oh, for God's sake…' Rick opened the bag he was holding and fished a piece of the lamb steak out of the burger. He threw it and the dog caught the food with a flash of white teeth. It practically inhaled it.

Rick walked on. It wasn't far to the warehouse and he'd felt the need to stretch his legs so he hadn't bothered to bring a vehicle. Half a block later, he realised he wasn't alone.

'Go home,' he told the dog sternly. 'You must have one.'

It had been stupid to give it any food. The dog clearly thought he could solve all its problems now. It was staying a respectful distance behind him but it was still there as he turned up his driveway.

'Look, I'll give you some more food,' he said. 'And then you can go home. OK?'

He wasn't going to sacrifice the rest of his dinner but he emptied half the bag of kumera wedges onto the side of the driveway and then resolutely went inside and closed his door. The dog would be gone by morning. At least it wouldn't still be miserably hungry when the dog catcher found it and it wasn't as if he could do any more to help the mutt.

So why did he feel that, despite doing his best, he was still somehow failing everyone?

The dog.

Simon.

Sarah.

Josh.

Himself...?

Life never used to be this complicated. If this was what finally growing up was all about, maybe he'd had the right idea in postponing it for so long.

She was waiting for him this time.

This was the fourth time Sarah had slipped out of Josh's room to hover in the unit's reception area. The desk was only staffed during working hours so it had been deserted for quite some time now. The nursing staff were either busy with patients or in the central office further down the corridor. If any of them knew where she was, they would assume she needed a bit of peace and quiet and room to stretch her legs just a little after the strain of a long and difficult day.

Josh had developed pain that needed more medication but that had made him vomit and he'd needed yet more drugs to control the nausea. There'd been a blood transfusion this afternoon and along with new pain and the monitoring and extra tests, Josh hadn't had a chance to rest properly. He'd been awake and fretful and asking, at regular intervals, when his dad was going to come and visit.

And now it was 7:00 p.m. and Rick still hadn't showed his face. If he didn't appear in the next few minutes, Sarah was going to call him at home and give him a piece of her mind about letting a sick little boy down. She was furious. Pacing back and forth across the reception area wasn't helping at all. Seeing Rick finally come through the double doors that led to the main hospital didn't help either. If anything, it bent and broke the last of her self-control.

'Where have you *been* all day, Rick? Josh has been asking and asking for you.'

'I'm here now.' He sounded weary. As though he was only here because it was something he was required to do. An extra duty to tick off for the working day.

'He's asleep,' Sarah informed him icily. 'Probably for the night.'

'Oh…' Rick's gaze slid away. 'I'll come back in the morning, then.'

'Sure…' Sarah watched him turn away. She harnessed her anger and let it escape in a sarcastic tone. 'If it's convenient, of course.'

He turned back. He pushed stiff fingers through his hair. 'I've had a busy day,' he said quietly. 'I've got a thirteen-year-old boy in Intensive Care who's in trouble. He started having seizures and—'

'You've got a nine-year-old *son* who's in trouble,' Sarah snapped. 'And you haven't been anywhere near him.'

Rick sighed. 'I'm here now.'

'Too little,' Sarah snarled. 'And too late. He's had a horrible day and the one thing that could have made it better might have been having a visit from his dad, and it didn't happen. What's going on here, Rick? You've been avoiding him for days. Has the novelty worn off or something?'

Rick gave an incredulous huff. 'I've been in to see him every single day.'

'Only once. You used to come two or three times,

remember? Set a precedent with kids and they have this funny trust that it's going to carry on. They're a bit like dogs that way.'

He seemed to wince at the comparison. He opened his mouth to say something but Sarah didn't give him the chance.

'You said you'd give being a dad your best shot.' Sarah tried to sound accusing but the telltale wobble in her voice was a sure sign tears weren't far away. She needed to wrap this up fast. 'If this is your best shot, it's not good enough. It would have been better not to get involved with Josh at all than to let him think you cared and then—' she had to swallow to get rid of the sudden lump in her throat '—avoid him like this. It's not fair, Rick…' Her voice had lost all its power now. It was hardly more than a whisper. 'It's not even nice.'

'I'm not avoiding Josh.'

'You *are*.' For once, Sarah managed to catch and hold Rick's gaze. 'You might not think so but that's what it's like on this side of the equation. You hardly come and when you do you don't stay very long. You're avoiding him.'

'I'm not.'

It felt like Rick's gaze was holding hers now, instead of the other way round. His features softened. His eyes were dark and intense but one corner of his mouth lifted in a wry, lopsided smile.

'I'm not avoiding Josh,' Rick said. 'I'm avoiding *you*.'

'Why? What have I done?'

'It's more what I've done. Or maybe what I want to do.'

Sarah swallowed hard. Here it was, out in the open. They had the chance to talk about this and get it sorted. For Josh's sake. She took a quick breath as she screwed up her courage.

'Tell me,' she whispered.

But Rick jerked his head in a sharp, negative gesture and made a rough sound that could have been a strangled groan. He was about to turn away but Sarah grabbed his arm and tugged so that he had to face her again and somehow it had brought them even closer together.

'Rick...*please*... We have to talk about this. I need to understand.'

The movement of his throat suggested he was finding it difficult to swallow. When he spoke, she hardly recognised the deep drawl.

'*This* is what I'm talking about...'

She knew what was coming the moment Rick began to pull her into his arms. She also knew that this was going be nothing like the brief, almost impersonal kisses they'd already given each other. He was moving in for the real thing.

She could have pulled free. She knew quite well that if she'd made any protest, Rick would have let her go instantly, but if he did, he'd probably walk out and they would never have the chance to talk. She'd be left still angry and confused and miserable and would have to stay that way...maybe for ever.

She might spend the rest of her life wondering what it would have been like to be properly kissed by Rick Wilson.

And...she deserved just a moment for herself, didn't

she? Time out from being mother to a suffering child. A respite from remembering all the misery of today's procedures and problems and imagining what was still to come. A bit of nostalgia, even, for a time when she had had no one to be responsible for other than herself and men had made her feel desirable.

Was it so wrong to want to feel wanted?

Even if it was, she was powerless to resist the pull. The pull into Rick's arms and into the delicious heat of desire. Tiny flames that ignited at the mere touch of his hands and exploded into a blinding white heat as his mouth shaped itself to cover hers.

No chance of pulling free now. The possibility didn't even occur to Sarah as she closed her eyes and lifted her arms to wrap them around Rick's neck.

No. There was no way out of this.

She was completely lost.

CHAPTER EIGHT

THIS was the most astonishing kiss of his life.

The feel of Sarah's mouth under his. So soft, so sweet, so…responsive. The way her whole body seemed to soften in his arms so that merely the desire to mould her closer to his own body seemed to be enough to make it happen.

He'd known it would be this perfect that first moment he'd set eyes on her. What he hadn't realised was that it would feel so…*right*.

He could let his hands roam and shape her breasts. Or cup her bottom and pull her against the urgent need pulsing in his core. He could peel away her clothing and then his own and he *knew* there would be none of that first-time awkwardness. They would just morph from a first kiss into being lovers and it would be like they'd always been together, only better. Much better, because it would still have all the excitement of being totally new.

Of course, he couldn't do any of that. Not here. He might be so involved in this kiss that he wouldn't care if half of Queen Mary's medical staff had gathered to watch in this reception area but he wasn't insane. Some things…OK, a great many things that he intended to do to Sarah Prescott needed complete privacy.

For a moment he let himself revel in the anticipation of those things but when it threatened to become too powerful to resist, he eased himself away from her. Reluctantly. Just his lips to start with.

'Come with me,' he murmured. 'I know a much better place for this.'

He felt the way her body tensed. It was slow process, like the development of one of those Polaroid pictures he took for Josh. Was she having that much trouble focusing because of that kiss? He liked that idea. Enough to make him close that tiny distance between them. He wanted to scramble her brain all over again and make her aware of only him and what he could do to her senses.

But Sarah resisted this time. Her hands slid over his shoulders to rest on his chest. She even pushed at him faintly. And she shook her head. She seemed ready to say something but no words emerged from her parted lips. Rick could sense a growing distress. Capturing her hand, he led her to one of the armchairs. He needed to reassure her somehow. Good grief, this wasn't *that* big a deal. He was talking about sex here. Potentially mind-blowingly good sex. But it wasn't as if he was planning to disrupt her entire life. Or his, of course.

Sarah's legs buckled without hesitation and she sat down. He perched on the edge of the adjacent chair, still keeping her hand firmly clasped in his.

He raised an eyebrow as he smiled gently. 'Problem?'

Sarah shook her head but then she nodded. 'I can't… *we* can't…'

'Why not?' It seemed such a no-brainer to him now that he knew she was as interested as he was. They'd be seeing quite a lot of each other from now on so why not make it a whole heap more enjoyable?

The tiny huff of breath from Sarah told him that the answer should be obvious.

'Because of Josh.'

Rick considered that. He might have expected her to say *because of Lucy*. Or because she knew he was a rat or because she wasn't really interested. No, he knew that one wasn't true. He had to hide the way his lips wanted to curl again. Nobody could kiss like that if they weren't interested. Very, very interested.

'This is about us, Sarah,' he said slowly. 'It has nothing to do with Josh.'

'How can you say that? You're his father.'

'True.' Amazing how he didn't have the slightest hesitation in agreeing to that statement now. He couldn't imagine denying it, in fact.

'You're going to be part of his life, for a long time. I hope,' she added after the tiniest hesitation.

This wasn't the time to be talking about prognoses. 'I will,' Rick said confidently.

A faint warning bell was sounding somewhere in the back of his mind. Heralding concern about that 'part of his life'. That more could well be expected of him than he felt willing or capable of giving.

'And I'm a part of his life, too. It's all connected.'

The bell got louder. Connections. Expectations… Rick could almost feel a mental door closing, shutting off the sound. Listening instead to the husky note in Sarah's voice that advertised her arousal. This was about now. About *them*. The strength of his desire for what the next hour or two could hold was more than enough to make any further thought into the future irrelevant.

He nodded, more an acceptance of the direction of his own thoughts than anything Sarah had just said. He had loosened his hold on her hand now and was stroking her palm with his thumb. Feeling the shape of all the tiny bones in there. When he moved his fingers as well, he could feel the way her fingers and knuckles moved. Whether she was aware of it or not, her hand was responding to his touch. A discreet, intimate little dance.

'And that's a bad thing?' he queried softly.

He heard another small huff. Or maybe it was a sigh at his lack of comprehension.

'My relationship with Josh is one thing,' he said. 'My relationship with you is something else. We could be—'

'Friends,' Sarah interrupted. That huskiness in her voice had increased. She sounded almost hoarse now. 'Friends would be good.'

'Absolutely.' Rick closed his hand around hers to increase the pressure of his touch. 'Good friends.' He waited until she looked up. '*Very* good friends.'

He smiled at her with the most winning expression he could muster. It wasn't a hard call. He had a lot to lose.

Sarah's hair rippled with the subtle shake she gave her head. It was enough to catch the light over the reception desk and send a shower of golden sparks over her head. 'And if it didn't work? If we stopped being such good *friends*?' There was another play of light through her hair. 'It would be Josh who'd catch the fallout, Rick. I can't let that happen. You're important to him. I don't think you have any idea how important you've already become to Josh.'

Rick stifled the urge to catch a handful of her hair and move it so he could see more of those glints. She was worried that whatever was happening between them was going to fizzle out in no time flat. Maybe she thought all he wanted was a one-night stand like he'd had with her sister.

It wasn't true. This was a very different proposition. *He* was a very different person. He didn't want a one-night stand. Good grief, no. He wanted…he wanted…

The answer wasn't there but it didn't matter because Rick at least knew what he didn't want and that was to lose the opportunity to get to know Sarah a lot better. To just *be* with her. The future would take care of itself. It always had, hadn't it?

'Josh is important to me, too,' he said sincerely. 'So are you, Sarah. I'm attracted to you.' He grinned. 'Just in case that wasn't already clear.'

Sarah ducked her head with an endearingly shy movement. 'It was,' she murmured.

Rick grinned. 'Well, you did say you needed to understand what was bothering me.'

He let his breath out in a sigh. 'I want to be with you,' he continued in a much more serious tone. 'So much that it *has* been interfering with how often I've been coming to see Josh. I'm sorry about that. I was

trying to avoid torturing myself and it was selfish and...
immature.' He tried to smile again but it was a crooked
effort. 'I am trying to grow up. Honest.'

The huff was laughter this time but he could also see
a shine in Sarah's eyes that had nothing to do the light
over the reception desk so it had to be from tears.

'I'm sorry I ever said that you needed to grow up,
Rick. You're perfect just the way you are.'

The words gave him a very odd sensation inside.
As though something was melting. No...more like expanding. A bubble of something shiny that would pop
and send a glow right through him. She thought he was
perfect? Oh...*man*...

He had to concentrate on finding the right words.
'Josh is my son,' he managed. 'And I'll start being better
at letting him know how important that is. Nothing's
going to change that, including whatever might happen
between us...if we let it.'

'But...' He watched the way Sarah caught her bottom
lip between her teeth and felt a stab of renewed desire
deep in his belly. 'What if it's just...physical?'

Rick raised an eyebrow. 'Are you going to avoid
any kind of relationship because you've become Josh's
mum?'

'I...um...haven't given it any thought. It's...' Sarah
sighed heavily, clearly releasing something she hadn't
intended to admit. 'OK, I haven't met anyone who's
made me think about it. The fact that you're Josh's dad
makes it...complicated.'

'But mightn't it be even more complicated with
someone who wasn't Josh's dad? Given what happened
in your last relationship?'

That seemed to score a point, judging by the way Sarah frowned at the reminder.

'I don't—'

'Sarah…' Rick put both his hands over hers. 'If you think about worst-case scenarios you'd never do anything in life. And if you live in the past or in the future, you risk missing what's happening in the present and that's…well, that's your life.'

She didn't say anything but her gaze was locked on his. She was certainly listening.

'We're in the present. The person I used to be—that Lucy met—is long gone. This is now. My attraction to you is now and it's real. We're both grown-ups.' He paused just long enough for a quick smile. 'I'm getting there, anyway. None of us know what the future holds. If this thing—whatever it is—between us doesn't go anywhere, we can handle it. Look at all the divorced people out there who manage to co-parent their kids just fine.'

'That's true…I guess.'

'And it's not as if we're planning something heavy like marriage.' Rick did his best to make that sound like the only really big deal there could be. 'Think of it as stress relief if you like. You deserve it.'

Once more, he lowered his tone and slowed his speech so that when the words came out they sounded more solemn than anything he'd ever heard himself utter.

'I promise I won't let it hurt Josh.'

A silence fell. They were still connected by their eye contact and the way their hands were tangled together. He could *feel* her. Body and soul.

'Let's just think about the present,' he said softly. 'You and me. What we want. I know what *I* want.' He paused again, holding her gaze and her hands. Trying to draw her closer to him by sheer willpower. 'What do *you* want?'

'*You.*' The word was a whisper.

Rick leaned close enough to brush her lips with his. 'Come with me, then.'

'I can't go home with you, Rick. It's too far. Today's been—'

'I'm not taking you that far. There's an on-call room that's got my name on it for the night. It's private. It's got a bed.'

She caught her breath in a tiny gasp. He watched the way her pupils dilated, making her eyes dark with desire.

'You might get called.'

'I'm not actually on call. I just didn't want to be too far away in case something goes wrong for Simon again.'

'Simon?'

'The boy in ICU. The one I've been struggling to get stable again today. He's looking good at the moment. Better than he has been, in fact. It's highly unlikely that I'll get called.'

He stood up, still holding her hand, but he didn't pull her to her feet. This had to be her choice.

He saw the way she took a deep breath as she made that choice. Time stopped for a moment, kind of like the way it had when he'd first seen her. This decision was as important as her arrival in his life. Right now, it felt as if his life depended on it.

Sarah got to her feet. He felt her hold on his hand tighten. Her answer was in the slightly tremulous smile she gave him. Rick didn't feel the need to say anything more either.

Hand in hand, they went through the double doors into the main block.

Sarah was grateful for the strength she could feel in Rick's hand and the way he was gently guiding her.

Her brain felt as confused as it had been for some time now but it was as though a coin had been flipped. Instead of that endless circuit of denial and frustration and worry and guilt, this was a jumble of the promise of ultimate pleasure laced with good reasons for permission to experience it.

She knew there were plenty of flaws in Rick's point of view. Like the way some children could be used as pawns in the games played by parents whose divorce was less than amicable. And that while it was true her last boyfriend had dumped her because of Josh, he'd been presented with the unexpected addition of a child in the equation well after the relationship had started. It would be different if she met someone now.

Counter-arguments that could have undermined Rick's persuasive efforts were locked away, however, and if Sarah tried to access that part of her brain, she became aware of a flood of irresistible sensation instead. The way Rick looked at her in the lift. The way he locked the door of the tiny room upstairs and pinned her against it to kiss her. Not on her lips but on the side of her neck, exactly where she could feel her pulse stumbling with unbearable anticipation. The feel of his lips and the touch of his tongue went straight into her bloodstream and coursed through her body, igniting fierce desire in her belly and making her legs weak.

He undressed her with the kind of expertise that should have reminded her of his past and rung alarm bells, but they'd been silenced along with the counter arguments. Worry about Josh needing her was tucked away as well. She had her mobile phone. The nurses could contact her if she was needed.

Sarah gave herself up to what she wanted most and she wanted to believe everything Rick had said. And it was easy because she recognised the truth of it. Angsting over the past—including Rick's playboy antics and her sister's part in them—or worrying about the future that encompassed how she could deal with the fallout this might produce could totally override what was happening right now and *this* was the moment she was living.

As herself. Not as an aunt or mother or sister. Or a guardian or nurse.

This was about what was at the centre of her being. What she loved and wanted. And it tapped into long-neglected hopes and dreams. It was…

Heaven.

Rick's hands and lips roamed her body and brought so many nerve endings to life her skin was on fire. Her own hands and lips were further conduits of the incredible heat as they made contact with Rick's skin. The firmness of his chest, the silky skin interrupted by whorls of soft hair. The softness of his lips and the delicious scrape of a rough jaw. The fresh taste of his mouth and the heady musk of far more intimate parts of his body.

This was urgent, this first time. Pent-up desire claimed precedence and Sarah heard herself begging for Rick to take her. She wanted him inside her. She wanted to wrap her legs and arms around him and hang on for dear life as they rode this unbelievable wave of sensation.

They were both gasping for breath by the time reality had a chance to intrude. A tangle of limbs in a bed that should have been too narrow for what they had just accomplished. This was the moment when things could have become awkward. When any doubts in her head were released to roam free and potential complications could bring a vanguard of regret.

Sarah was afraid to open her mouth in case words were the key so she stayed silent, trying to hold on to the astonishing feeling of being exactly where she was supposed to be. The place she'd been searching for her whole life without realising it. Rick was also silent.

Verbally, anyway. His hands were speaking for him. Touching her body with what felt like reverence. Smoothing long strands of her tumbled hair from where it had stuck to perspiration-dampened skin on her breasts and face.

And then he kissed her lips. Slowly. With a tenderness that washed away the possibility of allowing any doubts significant head space. She couldn't let this go. It was worth keeping, no matter what. It was worth fighting for with everything she had.

'Next time,' Rick murmured against her lips, 'we'll go slow. OK?'

Sarah simply smiled. He felt it and let his breath out in a satisfied sigh.

Next time wouldn't be tonight. They both knew that. This uninterrupted privacy had been a gift. Too precious to risk by taking advantage of it. But Rick seemed as happy as Sarah was to linger just a little longer. She was loving the latent strength she could feel in the arms holding her so gently. She wanted to soak in the rise and fall of his chest against hers. The strong, steady beat of his heart and the soft tickle of his breath on her face.

She would remember all these things with such clarity. She would be able to pull them around her like the softest blanket when she needed comfort as she went to sleep alone in the corner of Josh's room.

The need to be back there returned so gradually it seemed a mutual agreement when they untangled themselves and got dressed again. The process was interrupted more than once as they brushed against each other in the small space and had to pause and touch properly. To hold and kiss each other.

But finally they were back at the double doors leading to the bone-marrow unit.

'Shall I come in? In case Josh wakes up?'

'I'll tell him you'll be coming tomorrow. In the morning?'

'First thing,' Rick promised. 'I'm going to go and check on Simon now and then I might go home for a bit. There's something I should check on. It might need feeding.'

Sarah blinked up at him. 'Feeding? It's alive?'

'If it hasn't been caught.' Rick was smiling. 'That

dog Josh saw that day? It followed me home last night and it was still sitting in my driveway this morning.'

'Oh…' Josh would be *so* happy to hear that. So excited. He would be pulled into his dream of a perfect future. Transported.

Kind of like the way she'd felt in Rick's arms such a short time ago?

'Should I tell him, do you think?'

Rick understood instantly. The concern that darkened his eyes to ink showed how fast his thoughts meshed with hers. He knew how much it would mean to Josh. What the repercussions might be further down the track.

'Leave it with me,' he said. 'I might have an idea.'

With another soft kiss, he was gone. Sarah was left watching the space he had vanished into beyond the doors.

She wrapped her arms around herself. He had understood. He cared enough to take a share of the burden with the intention of making it lighter somehow.

For her? For Josh?

It didn't matter. She loved him for it.

Or maybe she'd already been loving him and the combination of tonight's revelations had simply allowed her to recognise the truth of it.

There was no going back. It was frightening but it was wonderful and it was happening now.

'One day at a time,' she whispered. Only now the mantra held the promise of a dream. Something to hang on to, not endure.

CHAPTER NINE

THIS day just kept getting better and better.

Rick had had a very early start. He'd been dreaming about Sarah and he was still thinking about her as he watched the sun come up over the harbour and bring the world back to life. He didn't bother with breakfast because he had too much to do but when he finally got close to arriving at work, he stopped in at a fast-food restaurant and bought bacon-and-egg muffins and French fries. A supremely unhealthy meal but Josh seemed to be through the bad spell of the last couple of days and it might tempt him to eat something.

It did. He took several bites of the muffin and slowly nibbled his way through half the little paper bag of salty fries. Sarah looked so happy it was hard not to grin like an idiot every time he looked at her.

Which he found himself doing at rather frequent intervals. Ever since the dramatic change in their relationship the night before last, the atmosphere in Josh's room had been like being on a different planet. So much of the tension was gone it had become a happy place. Positive. Filled with an intense anticipation of good things to come. Not that he and Sarah had made it back to the on-call room or anywhere else that private but they knew they would. Soon.

They'd managed a quick coffee together a couple of times and lunch in the cafeteria yesterday, which had been great because when he was away from Josh's room Rick didn't have to be careful of how often he looked at her. He could even touch her discreetly. Fingertip to fingertip as their hands lay on the table. A hand on her back that could slide down to that delicious curve of her rump as he ushered her through a doorway. A stolen kiss between floors on an elevator.

By tacit consent, they were keeping this new development secret because this was between them and neither wanted it to impinge on their relationships with Josh. The reminder of the small boy who had brought them together but was making this new relationship more complicated was always there. Conversations always included him. How he was feeling. What the latest results of tests might mean. What plans they could come up with that might entertain him.

'What happened about the dog?' Sarah had asked at lunch yesterday. 'Was he still there in your driveway?'

Rick had shaken his head sadly. 'No sign of it. Sorry.'

He'd seen the sparkle in her eyes fade to disappointment but he hadn't said anything else. Today he would. Later. He had some work to do first and even that was adding to the satisfaction of this particular day.

Up in the ICU, Simon was showing a dramatic improvement in his condition.

'He opened his eyes,' his mother told Rick. 'He squeezed my hand and—'

'And he said "Mum",' his father added, when his wife was too overcome to continue. 'He recognised her and he can *talk*. He's coming out of his coma, isn't he, Doc?'

'Sure looks like it.' Rick was only too happy to share the joy. He spent longer than necessary checking his young patient. Simon was deeply asleep again but this was a turning point. It wasn't going to be easy or quick but they all had reason for genuine hope now that he might recover.

Rick floated through the rest of his rounds and an outpatient clinic, knowing that the best of this day was still to come. Late that afternoon, he went back to Josh's room. His son's eyes widened when he saw what Rick had brought into the room with him.

'What's that for?'

'You.' Rick gave the wheelchair a bit of a twirl. 'Thought you might like to see something other than these four walls.'

Sarah looked horrified. 'He can't go out of here.'

'He's allowed to,' Rick assured her. 'He'll have to wear a gown and mask and some gloves and we won't go anywhere there's a lot of people. He's been in strict isolation for a while now and something a bit more exciting could be very good. That is, if he feels up to a wee adventure.' He turned back to Josh. 'How 'bout it, buddy?'

Josh was already starting to climb out of his bed. 'Where are we going?'

'It's a surprise.'

Sarah was looking almost as undecided as the moment before Rick had persuaded her to go to bed with him. He smiled at her, holding her gaze, sending her a message he hoped she would read and accept.

Trust me.

She didn't smile back but she did release the breath she'd been holding and nod faintly. She helped Josh into the wheelchair and found the protective clothing he would need. Rick carefully transferred the bag of IV fluid to the pole attached to the side of the basket on the back of the wheelchair. He also picked up the Polaroid camera and put it into the basket.

He took them out of the bone-marrow unit, along the corridor and into an elevator that was only for staff use. On the basement floor he propelled the chair along deserted corridors past places like the medical records department and a prosthetic limb workshop.

'Where are we going?' Josh piped insistently more than once.

'There's something I want you to see,' was all Rick said.

There was an isolated parking area down here that gave access to delivery trucks and vehicles that needed to arrive discreetly. Rick was keeping his fingers crossed that a hearse wasn't due to make a collection. There were windows that looked out onto the bare concrete at the bottom of a ramp that led to ground level. There was a vehicle there but it was the one Rick was expecting. A grunty four-wheel drive. Max was in the driver's seat and gave him a thumbs-up before jumping out and going round to the back.

'What on earth…?' Sarah murmured.

Max opened the back door of his vehicle and a large shape emerged.

'Oh...' Josh tried to stand up in the wheelchair and Rick had to steady him with a hand on one of his shoulders. The frailty of the bones he could feel made something twist, deep inside. So did the way Josh's scalp showed more and more through the little that remained of his hair.

'You said he wasn't there any more!' Sarah exclaimed.

'He wasn't. The dog catcher had taken him to the pound.'

Josh managed to drag his eyes away from the window and look up at Rick. Sarah was staring at him, too.

'The council knew him well. There'd been complaints about him for weeks, ever since he'd escaped from the pound when they first caught him. Nobody had claimed him then. He's not registered or microchipped or anything and they were only too happy to let him go to a good home.'

'But...' There was a flash of alarm in Sarah's face. 'How are you going to keep a dog at your place?'

'I'm not. That's where Max and Ellie come in. They're happy to look after him for the moment.' Rick was trying to give Sarah a very reassuring look. He had taken care of every possibility here. But she still looked worried. As if he was presenting her with a major problem of having to find somewhere new to live the moment Josh was released from hospital.

'Max and Ellie think he's wonderful,' he added quietly. 'If things don't pan out, they're more than happy to adopt him permanently. Josh could visit any time he wanted.'

'*No*.' Josh was staring fiercely out of the window again. Max had come closer and they were only a short distance on the other side of the glass. The dog was sitting, staring back at Josh, his ears flattened and his tail waving madly. 'He's *my* dog.'

A heartbeat of eye contact between Rick and Sarah said it all. This kind of joy could speed his recovery. And if the worst happened and Josh didn't make it through this, the dog wasn't simply being used and discarded. He had a back-up family. Sarah's smile wobbled and Rick had to look away.

'He hasn't got a name yet.' Rick crouched beside the wheelchair, focusing on Josh to give Sarah a moment. 'Max and I thought you should do the honours.'

Josh had a dreamy look on his face now. 'Can I go outside and pat him?'

'Not today, mate. Sorry.' Rick was busy with the camera now. He took a photo that got Josh and the dog locked in joyous communion through the sheet of glass. 'He can come and visit again when you've got a few good blood cells ready to fight off bugs.'

'I'm getting better,' Josh said, still fierce. 'It won't be long, will it?'

'No.' Sarah sounded like she was still trying not to cry. She cleared her throat. 'He looks cleaner than he did last time we saw him.'

'He's had a bath. Been de-wormed and de-fleaed. He's a new dog.'

'He's really hairy.'

'That's what I'm going to call him,' Josh said.

'What? Hairy?'

'No. Harry. Like Harry Potter.'

'Hairy Harry.' Rick grinned. 'Cool.'

Max waved apologetically. A laundry truck was at the top of the ramp. He walked back to his car and pointed to the rear hatch. Harry obediently leapt inside.

'He's really smart, isn't he?' Josh said happily.

'Sure is. Time for him to go home, though, and time for you to get back to bed. It's almost your dinner-time.'

But Josh was way too excited to want to eat. He was clutching the photograph and grinning from ear to ear. Sarah eyed the tray of food and looked worried.

'Tell you what.' Rick was brimming over with inspiration today. 'I'll stay with Josh and read him a story or talk dogs or something. He'll settle down and I'll get his dinner reheated. Why don't you go and pamper yourself for an hour or two?'

'What?'

'Must be a while since you've got out of here properly.' Rick let his gaze remind her of the most recent, memorable break she'd had and he enjoyed watching the colour rise in her cheeks. 'You could go shopping maybe?'

'I could pop back to the apartment, I guess. I could do with some different clothes and a soak in a bath.'

'Mmm. Sounds…nice.' Rick's drawl was only intended to sound encouraging but it obviously occurred to both of them at the same time that sharing a bath needed to go on the list of future activities.

Sarah's colour went up a notch. 'Well…if it's OK with Josh.'

'It's cool.' Josh sounded offhand. He didn't look up

from the photo. 'See you later. And can you bring a new battery for my Gameboy?'

'Sure.'

With Sarah gone, Rick settled down to talk dogs and whatever else took Josh's fancy. He was happy. More than happy. Today had gone even better than he'd planned. This being a part-time dad thing wasn't so bad. In fact, how lucky was he? How many guys could get presented with such a great kid who was so easy to make happy? And how many would get the incredible bonus thrown in of a gorgeous woman who also seemed very easy to make happy?

Josh went from being wide awake and excited to sound asleep within the first pages of the story he'd chosen but Rick was more than content to stay in the armchair and contemplate how good he was feeling. And how much better he would be when he got the chance to make Sarah very happy again.

Maybe later tonight? He might just make an enquiry as to whether there was a free on-call room. It wasn't as if they had to worry about getting a babysitter at the last minute. Things might be more complicated once Josh was home again but they'd manage. Of course, it would be nice to whisk Sarah away for a weekend some time but that wasn't really a goer. They'd have to take Josh with them, which wouldn't be so bad, but how could they continue where they'd left off with a kid in the next room? That was way too far out of his realm of experience to seem acceptable.

A sense of urgency sneaked up on him. How much longer would Josh be in here, all going well? Two or three weeks? He released his breath in a sigh. It was a bridge that didn't need crossing yet. He would just have to make the most of every opportunity he had until then.

The apartment had a musty, damp, unused feel to it.

Sarah opened a window or two while she put a load of washing on and sifted through accumulated mail, most of which appeared to be bills. She started a bath running and went to her bedroom to find some fresh clothes to take back to the hospital. Dumping them onto her bed, she went and tipped the remnants of a jar of bath salts into the steaming water and then started to take her clothes off.

Oh…Lord. Why did this simple action take her straight back to when Rick had been doing it for her? The caress of warm, fragrant water as she sank into the bath was equally sensuous. Sarah gave up fighting it and allowed her mind to float in the same kind of pleasurable space her limbs were currently experiencing. She hadn't felt this good in… Heavens…she'd *never* felt this good. Josh was doing well and there was real hope for the future. And there was Rick… The possibilities of what that future might hold had expanded exponentially.

Did he feel anything like as strongly about her as she did about him? Would he fall in love with her? Imagine if he did…if they ended up being a family. A healthy Josh with maybe some younger siblings. With them all living in a house with a garden for Harry to roam in.

That would be…perfect.

By the time Sarah climbed out of the bath she was totally relaxed and buzzing with the joy her fantasies had lured her into. She dried herself, found the prettiest underwear she possessed and then went to pull on the clean jeans from the pile on the bed. She paused with one leg inside them. When had Rick seen her wearing anything other than jeans? That long dress at the wedding didn't count because that was ancient history now. Before she could even have imagined feeling so… happy.

She went back to her wardrobe and searched. She found an old knit dress. Long-sleeved, with a deep scoop neckline. It clung to her body until the hips where it flared into soft folds that swirled around her knees when she did a twirl. It was just right. Nothing over the top but it was different and the deep colour made her eyes an astonishing blue.

Instead of pulling her hair back into the loose braid she usually favoured to keep it under control, Sarah brushed it until it was a sleek, golden river. She made two tiny braids at the front and fastened them at the nape of her neck with a small, diamanté clip. Feeling a little silly, she even put some make-up on.

'Anyone would think you were getting ready for a hot date,' she admonished her reflection. The secret little smile came from nowhere.

Maybe she was.

The effect of the dress was certainly gratifying. Rick's eyes popped when she arrived back at the hospital and stood by the window, waiting a moment before putting on her gown and mask. Josh was propped up on his pillows, picking at a plate of food. He also stared at Sarah.

'You looked really pretty,' he said generously, when she went into the room. He eyed Rick. 'Didn't she?'

'Yeah…' Rick's voice had a gravelly edge that Sarah could feel deep in her belly, like the sparks from the scrape of a match.

'Did you remember the battery?'

'Oh, no! Sorry, Josh, I completely forgot about that. I wonder if the hospital shop is still open?'

Rick checked his watch. 'It's seven-thirty but they do stay open for evening visiting hours. I could go and have a look.'

Katie came into the room. 'You finished that dinner yet?' she asked Josh. She looked at the plate. 'Hmm. At least you've had something. Anyone else hungry?'

'Starving.' Rick and Sarah spoke at the same time. They looked at each other and smiled.

Josh was watching them. 'You could take Sarah somewhere,' he suggested to Rick. 'Cos she's all dressed up.'

Rick's gaze slid away from Sarah instantly. He shrugged. 'You think?'

Josh nodded.

'But I've already been gone for ages,' Sarah said. 'Don't you want some company?'

'I was asleep while you were gone so I didn't notice.' Josh smiled winningly at his nurse. 'You could keep me company, couldn't you, Katie?'

His smile had been so similar to one of Rick's that Sarah's heart gave an odd little lurch. Would he grow up to be like his dad? She'd love to watch that happen.

'Sure,' Katie said with a grin. 'Go on, you two. Go

and have some dinner and let me have some time with my boyfriend here.'

Rick was still being careful not to catch Sarah's gaze and give anything away but her heart was thumping erratically. Josh *wanted* her to date Rick?

That fantasy future she'd conjured up in the bath lost some of its fuzzy edges to take on a more believable shape.

'No worries,' Rick said to Josh. 'We'll see if we can find you a battery along the way.'

'See you later, then, short stuff,' Sarah hoped he couldn't hear the tiny tremor in her voice. 'If you're still awake, that is.'

Josh *was* awake when they finally returned.

Katie gave them an unmistakably knowing smile as she excused herself but Josh seemed too sleepy to notice anything that might have given them away, like Sarah's dress being somewhat crumpled and her eyes glowing like stars. Her hair could do with a brush, too. Rick's fingers itched to bury themselves in its soft length and comb it into less of a tumble.

He was feeling a bit rumpled himself. Maybe next time they should make the effort to hang their clothes up instead of leaving them in a pile on the floor of the on-call room where they'd got trampled in their haste to get horizontal.

Worth it, though. Way better than the first time. Slow and sweet and so good, they'd both forgotten they were hungry for food. The less-than-adequate dinner of sandwiches from a vending machine on the way back downstairs had also been worth it.

Rick was standing close to Sarah. Close enough to be aware of her warmth and the scent he could quite easily become addicted to. She'd said he didn't need to come in and say goodnight to Josh because he'd probably be sound asleep but Rick said he wanted to rescue that photo and put it on the corkboard. If Josh slept with it clutched in his hand, it might get wrecked and it could be a while before he could arrange to get another one.

Josh blinked sleepily at them. He'd obviously made an effort to stay awake till they returned. He smiled.

'Hi, Dad.'

It was the first time he'd called him that. Rick couldn't analyse the odd squeeze in his chest. Didn't want to, anyway.

'Hi, buddy.'

It was Sarah's turn next.

'Can I call you Mum?' Josh asked.

Sarah's smile was poignant. 'Sure, hon. If you want to.'

'I do.' Josh let his eyes drift shut. 'I want to have a mum and a dad cos it's cool. And when I get out of hospital we can all live together.'

Rick felt his blood draining away from anywhere particularly useful. He felt suddenly chilled. He couldn't think even.

There was a moment's loaded silence and then Josh's eyes snapped open.

'With Harry,' he added firmly.

And that was that. Within seconds, he was asleep. Sarah fussed with his pillows and blankets. She didn't seem to know what to say and no wonder. Rick sure as hell couldn't think of anything. His mouth felt dry.

'I…um…guess I'll see you tomorrow.'

'Sure.'

Sarah glanced up and Rick knew she would be smiling but his gaze involuntarily averted itself so fast he couldn't be sure. He knew he should say something. Make sure that he and Sarah were on the same page and that they would be able to come up with some explanation for Josh as to why the happy-family thing wouldn't be happening. Laugh it off maybe and everything would feel right again.

But the words just didn't seem to be available. Or rather there were too many of them. Loud words, crowding his head. Making him feel trapped.

He had to escape.

'Chill? How can I, Max? Josh thinks we're all going to live together. That I'm going to sell my place and find something with a picket fence and be there every day to help him throw sticks for his dog.'

'He's a little boy, Rick. He's got a wish list with what every kid wants at the top of it. A family.'

'I'm *not* a family man. You know that.'

'Do I?' The voice on the other end of the line sounded thoughtful. 'I know you didn't think you were but things change, you know? It's not as bad as you think, mate. In fact, I have to say, it's got its advantages.'

Rick closed his eyes, shutting out the lights of the wharf. He hadn't been home for that long but the sanctuary of his bachelor's pad didn't hold any of its customary magic. He let his head sink onto the back of the couch and used his free hand to rub his forehead. Max was being no help at all here. He should have expected that. His friend was newly married, with a family home and a baby. There might not be a picket fence around that hillside property on the other side of the harbour but he was happily hemmed in by what it represented.

'Rick? You still there?'

'Yeah...'

'Don't get freaked out. He's just a kid. They say stuff.'

'Sarah could have said something. *Hell*, maybe she *did* say something. Maybe that's why he's thinking like that.'

'I'm sure she didn't but it makes no difference anyway.' Max sounded serious. 'The pace is your choice. You've had some big stuff to get used to in a very short space of time.' His voice lightened. 'It might not have been the best idea to jump Sarah so soon but, hey, I can totally see why it happened. You guys are perfect for each other.'

'We're just seeing each other, that's *all*. Having fun. Nobody's supposed to get hurt, including Josh. *Especially* Josh.' Rick groaned. 'I put my hand up to help. I was happy to be a donor. I even quite like being a part-time dad but if I'd seen this coming, I could have stayed a million miles away.'

There was a moment's silence before Max spoke quietly.

'Would you?'

Rick said nothing. That confusing mix of guilt and desire he'd felt before this thing had started between himself and Sarah had nothing on how he was feeling right now. His life was a mess. He couldn't even think where to start trying to unravel it all.

Into this silence came the bleep of his mobile phone.

'Got to go, mate,' he told Max. 'I texted Jet to call me when he had a moment and that's probably him.'

'No worries. Talk to you later. Just…hang in there, OK? It'll sort itself.'

'Yeah…sure.' Rick ended the call on his landline and picked up his mobile. 'Jet…Hey!'

'Hey, man. I've got precisely two minutes. There's a pilot about to start tapping his foot out on the runway. What's up?'

No pressure here. Any hope of finding a starting point evaporated. It would sound silly to say that his son had acquired a dog but wasn't that what had started this? He wanted a place to live with Harry. Parents to go along with the house. A twenty-four-seven family. The spiral of thoughts was getting faster. Too quick to catch. Much easier to shove it all into that 'too hard' basket.

'What's up with you? Where are you flying off to?'

'Haven't you heard? There's an island exploding. What planet have you been on for the last few hours, man?'

One that he'd really, really like to get off. 'Tell me.'

'Major earthquake on this island north of New Zealand somewhere. There's a team of people from the Department of Conservation there and there's been major injuries from the 'quake. It's kind of urgent to evacuate them because this island happens to be an active volcano and the 'quake seems to be a pre-eruption warning.' Jet was talking very fast. This was clearly an exciting mission. 'There's nowhere to land a plane and any ships are too far away to be helpful. We've got choppers deployed in other places so they're calling in a civilian Medevac bird. I'm flying into Auckland to collect it. Should be first on the scene.'

'Wow.' This certainly wasn't the time to be asking Jet for advice on how to manage the insignificant problem of how to deal with an exploding relationship. He knew what he'd say anyway.

Cut loose, man. Plenty more fish in the sea.

And maybe he didn't actually want to hear that despite having rung for precisely that advice. There weren't plenty more like Sarah out there.

Or Josh, for that matter.

This wasn't helping any more than talking to Max. His mates were at opposite ends of the spectrum and Rick didn't want to climb onto that seesaw to find himself sliding up and down, completely out of control. His head was quite messed up enough already, thanks very much.

'Good luck,' was all he said. 'Enjoy.'

'I intend to.' Jet's chuckle was carefree. 'Talk soon.'

The beeping on his phone told him that Jet had hung up. Rick dropped it onto the couch beside him and closed his eyes again. Silence settled around him, as heavy as his heart.

Happiness and misery.

Two sides of a coin that could get flipped. Just like that.

Sarah had seen the expression on Rick's face when Josh had been dreaming out loud in an uncanny echo of her own fantasy.

Nobody could have missed the way his face had gone pale. How he couldn't get away fast enough.

From Josh.

From her.

From any notion of a shared future.

And then, as if things weren't bad enough already, Josh had woken an hour or two later. Sarah had scrubbed the tears from her face to find him running a temperature. Another few hours and he was coughing. His oxygen saturation levels started dropping and his breathing had an ominous sound.

By morning it became alarmingly obvious that Josh had somehow picked up an infection that was serious enough to be a match for any of the antibiotics he was already on. His consultant, Mike, had been here for some time, along with his registrar. A technician with a portable X-ray machine had come and gone. Blood and other samples had been despatched and results were expected soon. Katie had just been sent to chase up the labs.

So many people in and out of this small room but one person was still conspicuously absent. Was Rick going to deal with some new emotional obstacles by doing a repeat of his avoidance tactics? Now? When Sarah needed him there so desperately? Josh needed him here, too, even if his level of consciousness was so low he might not realise it.

Mike was listening to Josh's chest with a stethoscope. The disc looked too large against small ribs that were so prominent due to how hard it was getting for him to breathe.

'We might have to intubate him and get him onto a ventilator,' Mike said as he straightened. 'I'm sorry, Sarah.'

She couldn't say anything. The lump in her throat was too painful to try and shift it by swallowing.

'Could you go and get Katie for me? We'll need some extra hands.'

It was good to have something to do when you felt so incredibly helpless. It wasn't far to the nurses' station where Katie was probably still on the phone, talking to lab staff.

Josh's nurse *was* talking but not on the phone. Rick was leaning against the other side of the counter and they were both smiling at whatever was being said. Sarah's steps slowed. She was shocked by how relaxed they looked. Didn't they know the world was falling apart?

She was also shocked by Rick's smile and his body language. It took her right back to when she'd seen him that very first time at the wedding. The way he'd looked at her. She'd known he'd fancied her and she'd seen that he was used to getting what he wanted from women.

Was he looking at Katie like that?

A knee-jerk reaction to the awful prospect he'd been presented with last night of having to spend the rest of his life with only one woman?

She was closer to the desk now. Katie and Rick both looked up and any lightness seemed to drain rapidly from their expressions to the point where they both looked…worried. Guilty, even?

Oh...*Lord*...

'You're needed, Katie,' Sarah managed to say. 'Mike said—'

She didn't get a chance to pass on the consultant's message. An alarm began to sound behind the counter and a red light on the wall was flashing.

'*Cardiac arrest*,' Katie gasped.

'Where's the crash cart?' Rick snapped.

'Here.' Katie was already pulling it from the corner of the station area.

'What room?'

But Katie was running. Sarah had to step aside to let her pass and Rick was following. They were running over the same route she'd just taken to get to them.

She watched them skid to a halt and her silent prayer became pointless.

The door to Josh's room was flung open.

CHAPTER TEN

SARAH could only see the backs of the doctors bent over Josh's bed when she rushed into the room.

Were they doing CPR?

'Suction.' That was Mike's voice. 'Katie, grab a bag mask, would you, please?'

The nurse was standing beside the crash cart, holding a package that Sarah knew contained paediatric patches for defibrillation. The package was dropped, unopened, as Katie pulled open a drawer beneath where the lifepack was positioned on top of the trolley.

Were the patches not needed? Was it too late or were they just going to give some respirations first, the way you had to with children?

Oh...*God*...

Sarah wrapped her arms around herself, pressing closer to the wall to stay out of everybody's way. This couldn't be the end, surely? Not like this. If she'd ever let herself think of such a dark moment, she had imagined she would be lying on the bed with Josh. Holding him in her arms.

Was it only yesterday she'd been feeling so hopeful? So damn *happy*?

Her dreams were nothing but a cloud of dust right now. If only she'd been there with him last night. How could she live with knowing that in their last hours together she'd gone away to lie in a bath, dreaming about a man? Even worse, that she'd left him with his nurse so that she could go and spend hours in bed with her lover. A man who only wanted to have fun. What had he called it?

Stress relief.

The thoughts flashed as fast as bolts of lightning in her head. Blinding and painful.

Sarah hated herself.

No. She hated Rick.

She had to move as the door opened behind her and more people tried to come into the room.

'Crash crew,' someone announced.

'Stand down.'

Mike stepped back and Sarah's breath caught as she saw Josh. Propped up on his pillows, an oxygen mask covering his face. His eyes were open. Moving. He looked terrified, until his roving gaze found Sarah. And then she could see his relief. His *need*.

With a sob, she pushed past Rick to get to the bed. Close enough to touch Josh. To make that close eye contact that had helped them both through countless, frightening incidents since this nightmare had begun.

'I'm here, hon,' she whispered fiercely. 'I'm here with you.'

The expression in his eyes was heartbreaking. She wouldn't leave his side again. Not for anything. Or anyone.

Dimly, she became aware of Mike, talking to the new arrivals who were still hovering at the door.

'Respiratory arrest…suction…cleared the obstruction.' His words became more authoritative. 'Everybody out, please. This is an isolation area.'

Rick's voice was much closer. 'He's OK, Sarah. His breathing's improved and the saturation levels have gone up with the oxygen.'

Josh was still breathing too fast, though. And his skin was hot and dry. Sarah smoothed back his hair, resting her palm on his forehead, knowing that it would feel cool for him. She looked past Rick to find Katie.

'I need a cloth,' she said. 'And a bowl of tepid water.'

Mike also had instructions for Katie. Different drugs that he wanted to add to the IV fluids. A monitoring schedule and a list of the tests that would need to be repeated. A plan had been made and was being put into action.

Josh slipped in an out of consciousness for the rest of that interminable day. People came and went, gowned and masked so that they almost blurred into one entity. Even Rick failed to stand out from the rest.

She knew he had a right to be in there, as Josh's father, but it still didn't feel right. He had only ever wanted involvement on *his* terms. Part time. Nothing that would really disrupt his life too much.

Sarah would do anything it took to get Josh through this but she had nothing to offer except her love and the desperate, silent pleas that he would survive. She sat beside his bed and held his hand. Things happened around them but she was so focused on Josh she just let them happen. Josh was hanging on and she was there with him. Helping him.

Giving him all the strength she had in her heart.

'Did you sleep here last night?'

'Yeah…' Rick patted the arm of the reception area chair and managed a smile. 'Bit hard on the neck but it's not so bad. Katie gave me a couple of blankets.'

At least he'd had a few hours' rest. He could be pretty sure that Sarah hadn't slept a wink, even though this crisis had been going for thirty-six hours now.

Max and Ellie exchanged a glance.

'Have you persuaded her to take any kind of a break yet?'

Rick shook his head wearily. There was no point whining about Sarah not listening to anything he said. Or caring about how he might be feeling. He could understand her preoccupation with Josh, of course, but she didn't seem to understand that he was a part of all this. Or maybe she didn't want him to be now that crunch time had arrived.

Whatever. He had been shut out. Sarah was so silent. Sitting there, almost ghostlike, by that bedside. Even when she did look at him, Rick had the feeling she couldn't see *him*. He was just another staff member orbiting the unit that she and Josh had been welded into.

'I've brought her some fresh clothes and a few things she might like to eat and drink.' Ellie looked down at the bags she was holding. 'I'll go and tap on the window or something. Max?'

'I'll sit here with Rick for a bit.'

Ellie's face creased into a sympathetic smile as she

looked back at Rick. 'She knows you're here,' she said quietly. 'What you're doing is important, too.'

Rick gave a single nod. Both he and Max watched her walk into the business end of the bone-marrow unit. Then he cleared his throat.

'Any news?' he queried. 'About Jet?'

Max nodded. 'Helicopter did go down. They both survived. They're trapped on the island now, though, thanks to the ash from the eruption. It'll be a day or two until a ship can get there.'

Rick smiled wryly. 'He'll be all right. He's a survivor.'

Max grinned. 'He's probably thriving on the adventure of it all. He's never happier than when his adrenaline levels are sky high, eh?'

'Yeah. He does seem to attract it, doesn't he?'

'What, adventure? Danger?'

'Excitement, anyway. Bikes, planes, dramatic emergency medicine.' Rick snorted softly. 'Women.'

Max shook his head. 'He'll get tired of bouncing around like a human ping-pong ball ones of these days.'

'When he grows up?'

'Yeah…'

Rick lapsed into silence. Was that what had done it for him? Had he grown up enough, thanks to recent events, to feel tired even thinking about a lifestyle like Jet's?

Like his used to be?

What had been so great about the freedom of being a bachelor anyway? That he could do whatever pleased him? Jump on his bike and roar off up the motorway without anyone telling him how dangerous it was? Maybe he wanted someone to care about him that much. Or was it the fact that his sexual playground would be fenced off for ever? The thrill of the chase and conquest gone?

Rick felt his lips curl in distaste. A future, even with an endless array of beautiful women to play with, was just so unappealing right now. Relationships that were so shallow because they never got past a single dimension.

He only wanted one woman.

Sarah.

And why had he been so afraid of taking a step towards being a real father and having a family of his own? Because his had been an unhappy example? Well, he wasn't his father, was he? Knowing what *not* to do should give him a great springboard into creating something good. Something so powerful it would keep him safe for the rest of his life.

Yes. He'd grown up all right. He had wisdom. He knew exactly what he wanted. What he *needed*.

Ellie came back, looking very sombre. 'Poor Josh,' she said, her voice choked. 'And poor Sarah.'

Her gaze, as she blinked hard, included Rick amongst those needing sympathy. She hugged him. And then Max hugged Ellie. They all sat together in silence for a while. One long minute dragged into another but it seemed that it was all they *could* do.

Wait.

Everything possible that could be done for Josh was being done. The raft of drugs, support for his breathing, intense monitoring of all his vital physical functions.

The invisible battle being fought was in full cry and they were simply spectators.

'Can we get you anything, Rick?' Ellie whispered.

He shook his head. There was only one thing he wanted right now and, sadly, even his best friends couldn't give it to him.

He wanted Josh to pull through this. To get better. So that he didn't lose him.

He wanted to throw that ball for Harry, dammit, and see the grin on his son's face. He wanted to take them both to that beach with the sand dunes and watch them run and play until they'd both had enough and then to go…somewhere. *Home*. With a soggy, sandy dog and a slightly sunburned small boy and have Sarah waiting for them with that look that women only had for the menfolk in their lives they loved. That tolerant 'boys will be boys' kind of look.

'You guys should go home,' he said a little while later. 'Look after Mouse. And Harry. I'll call if…if anything happens.'

Which could be tonight. How long could a small, frail body hang on under the onslaught of infection?

And why was he sitting out here, for God's sake?

'I'm going in,' Rick said, standing up. 'I need to be with my…family.'

The word had come from nowhere, the hesitation barely perceptible.

Max and Ellie understood.

Would Sarah?

Sarah couldn't feel her body.

An odd kind of numbness had crept in, due to

exhaustion and sitting so still for so long. Her eyes could move normally, though, and she'd seen Rick come in and position a chair on the other side of Josh's bed. She'd seen him take hold of Josh's other hand and then he'd looked up and she'd met his gaze properly for the first time in what felt like for ever.

She found her head could still move, too, as she nodded slowly. Even her lips curled and it felt strange to be smiling, even this tiniest bit.

But this felt right. So right she overcame the numbness and stretched out her other hand over the top of the bed, towards Rick. He did the same and their hands touched, their fingers interlacing.

They became a small circle of humanity. Each adult touching Josh and connected to each other.

Sarah could feel Josh's small hand enclosed within hers and her hand within Rick's. It was so much more than simply physical awareness. Time—place, even—ceased to be relevant. The world was holding its breath, maybe pushing just a little, as something new was born.

Something that held all three of them. Sarah could almost hear the echoes of laughter and tears around them. She could feel the warmth of ultimate comfort and a bottomless well of strength.

Love.

In its purest form. Flowing from hand to hand in this precious circle. And when Sarah raised her gaze to meet Rick's it seemed to flow faster. To make everything brighter. Clearer.

Part of it hurt. Maybe it was the truth she could see

in the dark gaze cradling hers. She'd wanted Rick to be more than just involved by being the donor in this journey she'd been on with Josh. She'd pushed him into getting to know his son and having an emotional investment in the outcome. Well, she'd got what she wanted, hadn't she? The love Rick had for his son and the pain he was experiencing himself was as solid as his presence in this room. And his pain was her pain.

'I'm sorry,' she whispered.

'What for?'

'I've put you through so much and it might be…' The next words died on her lips.

Don't say it, Rick's gaze commanded. *Don't even think it.*

'I'm not sorry,' his voice said. 'Never think that.'

His gentle smile nearly undid her. He really meant that. Oh…dear Lord. Sarah had to look away. To focus on Josh again. She couldn't fall apart now. She had to concentrate.

To hang on.

Rick could see exactly what Sarah was doing as she took what remaining strength she had and gave it to Josh.

It was in that precise moment that he realised how much he loved this woman.

Not that he could tell Sarah that. This wasn't the place and it certainly wasn't the time.

All he could do was try and show her that he was there for the long haul. For better or worse. By being here now. By holding her hand and trying to infuse her with some of *his* strength.

He had enough for both of them.

For *all* of them.

When Katie came in to check on Josh she worked quietly around his parents. The first few times they were sitting up and were aware of her taking Josh's temperature and making notes of everything the bedside monitors were recording.

On her visit when a new day was almost breaking, she caught her breath on entering the room. Josh lay pale and still. Sarah had her head down on one arm, her face covered, and so did Rick. When she came closer, she breathed a sigh of relief and then found herself smiling. They were all sound asleep but they were all still holding hands.

She smiled again a minute or two later. Josh's fever had broken. His breathing was a lot closer to being normal.

The crisis appeared to be over.

Everybody was exhausted.

Josh continued to improve steadily physically but he was miserable. Too weak to do anything remotely interesting. Even concentrating on watching a DVD was too much, days later.

'I hate being sick.'

'I know, hon, but you're getting better every day.'

'I'll just get sick again.'

'Maybe not.' Sarah's smile was full of genuine hope. 'Your blood count's getting heaps better. Dr Mike was pretty happy this morning, wasn't he? He says the new bone marrow is starting to work and that's why you're getting better.'

But Josh wasn't listening. He had his hands on his head and tears welled in his eyes. 'I've got no hair. I'm a freak.'

'It'll grow back.'

'No, it won't,' Josh sobbed. 'I want…I want my mum.'

Sarah's heart squeezed painfully. '*I'm* here, short stuff.'

'You're only pretending to be my mum.' Josh was in a darker place than Sarah had ever seen him. It terrified her.

'And Rick's not really my dad.'

'Yes, he is.' At least Sarah could sound completely sincere about that. He was there for Josh, a hundred per cent. The joy she had seen in his face when they had woken to find Josh was winning the battle had told her that. He loved his son.

'He just didn't get the chance to be your dad before this,' she told Josh. 'He really does love you.'

And out of all the reasons she loved Rick, this was one of the most important. It was enough for now. They had a bond through Josh that meant that his father would always be in her life. Maybe, when all this was really over, there would be a chance to be close to him again for herself, but it was Josh who needed him most for the moment so Sarah was content to have him focused only on this brave little boy.

He'd been a constant visitor these last few days. Quietly supportive. Positive. Doing everything he could think of to try and cheer Josh up. Yesterday it had been a photograph of Harry, wearing a brand-new collar. He'd brought a matching lead in and hung it over the end of Josh's bed.

'Waiting for you, buddy,' he'd said. 'For when you're ready to take Harry on his first walk.'

But Josh had barely looked at the photograph, which was now pinned beside the first picture of the dog on the corkboard. The contrast between this pristine print and the first one with its curled edges from being held too much was horribly poignant.

Josh noticed what Sarah was looking at.

'He doesn't want to live with us,' he said sadly. 'Or with Harry.' He was crying again. 'I'm too sick and... and I've got no *hair*.'

Rick turned away from the door.

They hadn't heard him open it or seen him—stopped in his tracks by the sound of his son crying. He'd been shocked enough to wait, trying desperately to think of what he could possibly do to make things better.

He needed to find the right thing this time but he couldn't think straight. He needed to be somewhere he couldn't see the bowed shoulders of the woman he loved or feel himself being torn apart by the sound of a small boy's sobs.

The shower was the best place to cry.

Even though she was only a few feet away from Josh in the *en suite* bathroom, Sarah could let herself go and Josh wouldn't know how miserable she was. She could have a good cry and then patch herself up and carry on being strong and cheerful.

She'd done it before, many times, so why did today feel so much harder? Maybe she was just too tired. Or perhaps letting go of that dream she'd had about her future was taking away too much joy. Sarah gave herself a stern talking to as she dried herself and got dressed again. She'd only postponed the dream, hadn't she? Not given up on it completely. She should be over the moon that Josh was really getting well this time. That the bone-marrow transplant had been pronounced a success. There was every chance that Josh was now on the road to complete recovery.

His hair would grow back and he'd be able to go to school and be with his friends and she'd find somewhere they could live and keep Harry. And Rick would visit them and they'd be almost—but not quite—a family.

And that was almost—but not quite—enough.

The murmur of voices came through the door of the *en suite*. Sarah turned the handle carefully and opened it quietly. Josh didn't notice because he was staring, open-mouthed, at the visitor who sat with one hip perched on the end of his bed.

Who was it?

The adult figure in the gown had a completely bald head.

Confused, Sarah stayed where she was.

'So...what do you reckon?'

'No.' Josh shook his head firmly but he was smiling.

Smiling.

And Sarah had recognised the visitor's voice. How could she not, when that deep rumble was so familiar now? So beloved she could feel it in every cell of her body? The knowledge that Rick had shaved off his gorgeous hair, presumably to convince Josh that he wasn't a freak, undid any resolutions she'd made to present a cheerful face. Tears were streaming down her cheeks and Sarah had to hang on to the door handle and struggle for composure.

'He wouldn't mind,' Rick was saying. 'Dog's hair grows back too, you know.'

'He'd look silly.'

'But we'd know he was still the same Harry. It wouldn't matter what other people thought. Do I look silly?'

'No-o-o.'

'He'd get a bit cold, though, so maybe you're right. We'd better not shave Harry. How 'bout Sarah?'

Josh actually giggled.

'No.' It was Rick who dismissed this new suggestion. 'I love Sarah's hair just the way it is.'

'Me too.' Josh was still staring at Rick. 'Do you love Sarah?'

There was a hesitation. A silence in which Sarah stopped crying. Stopped breathing even.

'I do.'

It was a wonder they didn't hear the ragged breath Sarah took then. Maybe they did and turned to look at her but she had closed her eyes and was hanging on to the door handle for dear life, letting a wave of pure joy course through her, body and soul.

'She's pretty special,' Rick continued. 'You're very lucky to have her for a mum, Josh.'

'She's not really my mum.'

'Isn't she? What do mums do that Sarah doesn't do?'

Josh thought about that for a few seconds. 'Nothing, I guess.'

'And she loves you to bits, doesn't she?'

Josh nodded.

'So you're lucky. If Sarah loved *me*, I'd feel like the luckiest man on earth.'

She couldn't stand here and eavesdrop a moment longer. Sarah opened her eyes to find that Rick had known she was there all along. He was watching her.

Her breath caught again, somewhere in her throat. Without his hair, he looked so different. His eyes looked bigger. Darker. He looked vulnerable.

Heroic.

Two sets of dark eyes were fixed on her and the room was so quiet. They were waiting for her to say something and there was only one thing she needed to say.

'I *do* love you, Rick.'

'He's got no hair,' Josh said happily.

'I can see that.' Which wasn't entirely true because right now Sarah could see nothing but Rick's eyes and what they were telling her.

She could see *so* much love in them. They drew her closer. She had to touch him.

'It'll grow, you know.' Josh sounded supremely confident.

It would. Like the love. Sarah was very close to Rick now but they weren't touching yet. They didn't need to.

The connection in the smile and gaze they were sharing was strong enough to feel physical.

'Are you going to get married, then?' Josh asked. 'And be like a real mum and dad?'

'I hope so,' Rick said softly.

'So do I,' Sarah whispered.

'When?'

'Maybe when you're completely better,' Sarah said.

'When our hair's grown back,' Rick added.

'Can Harry come?'

'Of course. He's part of the family too.' But Rick's attention was elsewhere now. He was leaning closer, intent on kissing Sarah.

Josh made a disgusted sound. 'You can't do that in front of me,' he said. 'It's gross and I'm just a kid.'

Rick had Sarah in his arms now. She knew she was still standing on the floor but she had the oddest feeling that she was flying.

'You're *our* kid,' Rick said firmly. 'So you'll just have to get used to it, buddy.'

And then he kissed her.

THE TORTURED REBEL

BY
ALISON ROBERTS

CHAPTER ONE

A FIGURE clad completely in black emerged from the passenger seat of the vehicle.

Tall. Solid. Reaching for what had to be a heavy pack from the back seat and hefting it effortlessly onto one shoulder.

And then he turned and Rebecca could see his face under spikes of hair as black as his uniform. She could see the uncompromising features of a man she hated enough for the shockwave to steal the breath from her lungs and make her heart thump hard enough to be a painful tattoo against her ribs.

'No *way*.'

'What?' A grey-haired man, whose uniform bore the insignia of the largest rescue helicopter service New Zealand had to offer, moved away from the small cluster of people in front of a huge map that covered an interior wall of this upstairs office. 'Did you say something, Bec?'

The words had seemed like an agonised, internal groan, but apparently she had spoken them aloud. Maybe they'd had even more carrying power than reaching the ears of her boss, Richard. That might explain why the

man outside had turned his head so swiftly to look up.
Why his gaze had flown so unerringly to her face.

She could feel the way he stilled as he recognised her.
Did it require an effort to shift the weight of so much
guilt?

She hoped so.

'Ah…' The voice was now right behind her shoulder.

'Yeah…' She was testing her voice. Checking to make
sure that it did not betray her. 'The medic's arrived.'

'Bit more than a medic.' There was a note of awe in
her boss's voice as he raised a hand to acknowledge the
new arrival. 'James Munroe is the best the army has to
offer. Emergency specialist. Been with the SAS on and
off for the past six years and he can handle anything.
Perfect choice for a mission like this. Stroke of luck they
already had a jet coming up here that he could catch a
ride on.'

The incredulous huff escaped from Rebecca's tight
chest all by itself. A sharp punctuation mark. Rather like
the way James Munroe slammed the door of the vehicle
behind him, adding a flat-handed thump that dismissed
the driver.

'Problem?' Richard's tone was dumbfounded.

You have no idea, she wanted to say. Wisely, she
pressed her lips firmly together and kept her eyes fixed
on the flashing beacons of the airport security vehicle as
it sped off, flanked by bright runway lights that stretched
into the distance.

Lights that had looked as festive as Christmas decora-
tions only minutes ago as she'd watched and waited for
this arrival with all the excitement of a child expecting
a special gift.

Dismay could feel rather like anger, couldn't it?

This was…unthinkable, that was what it was. After so many years of earning the reputation of being as tough as they came, unflinching in the face of danger and ready to deal with any emergency in a heartbeat, Rebecca Harding had a horrible feeling she might have hit the wall.

So she said nothing as she tried to deal with it.

The perfect choice for the mission had vanished from sight now, which was helping. He'd be going into the small side door of the hangar. Climbing the stairs to this office—the operational hub of this rescue service. She could get a grip on whatever was making it so hard to breathe. Think, even. Deal with this overwhelmingly unpleasant sensation that had to be…fear? No. She didn't do fear.

Creases in her bright orange flight suit vanished as she straightened to her full height of five feet four inches. Never mind that at least one of those inches came from the heels of her steel-capped boots. Her fingers tightened around the strap of the helmet dangling from her hand.

'Not having second thoughts, are you?'

'Are you kidding?' Rebecca actually found a smile. 'I've been waiting for a mission like this for my whole life.'

She had. This was *it*. A night flight to a destination outside any normal flight zone that would push fuel capabilities. A volcanic Pacific island that had been rocked by an earthquake and could erupt for real at any time. A group of frightened conservationists that were trapped and injured and in desperate need of evacuation.

Oh, yes. Even in a career that had had more than

its share of excitement, this mission promised to be a highlight.

'Hmm.' Richard didn't sound entirely convinced. He stared at his top pilot for a long second and then a spark of comprehension dawned on his face. 'Don't tell me you and this James Munroe have some kind of history?'

History.

That was a good word for it. The past. An event momentous enough to wipe out your world. Or rather to blot out the sun so that life became so bleak that merely surviving seemed an impossible challenge.

Oh, yes. She and Jet had history, all right.

But Rebecca shook her head. She had made a choice a very long time ago not to let the past rob her of a future. It would be easy enough to find another pilot who would be more than willing to take on this mission. Finding another medic with the kind of skills this one had would be impossible. The past few hours had been tense enough as search and rescue commanders put this plan together. They were hardly likely to tolerate a hiccup that was purely personal. Not when lives were depending on its success.

So her past had come back to haunt her?

So what?

She had been chosen and she was up for the challenge.

The real question was whether the willingness to deal with the situation would be reciprocated, and she was about to find out because the door of the office opened and her past walked in.

* * *

I hate you.

I hope I never have to set eyes on you ever, ever again.

Words that had been spoken more than ten years ago and yet they were as clear in his head right now as if they'd just been uttered.

What on earth was Matt's sister doing in this room full of the men who were in charge of organising this urgent rescue mission that he'd just been flown in from his army base down south to be a part of? And why was she wearing a flight suit? Had she given up nursing to become a paramedic? Not that he was going to allow her to occupy more than his peripheral vision or thoughts at the moment. His attention was on the most senior-looking person in the group. The one who was coming towards him with an extended hand.

'James. Great that you could get here so fast.'

'Jet,' he corrected, his smile taut. 'Haven't answered to James in longer than I care to remember.'

Longer than the ten years since he'd last breathed the same air as the woman still standing by the window. He didn't need to look at her directly to be aware of how her shape had changed. He could even sense more than the physical maturity those curves under the overalls advertised. A curious mix of femininity and determination emanated from that side of the room like a scent but it wasn't quite powerful enough to wipe out the image of the girl he remembered.

A distraught teenager who'd pummelled his chest with her fists when he'd tried to hold her. Who'd told him that it was *his* fault.

That she would hate him for ever.

And that had been fair enough. He'd hated himself back then. Complying with the request never to be seen again had been no hardship. It hadn't been simply the guilt. It had been the gut-wrenching similarity she had to her brother.

The same wildly curly hair. The same dark eyes and cheeky grin. Not that any hint of a smile, let alone anything more joyous, could be detected from her direction. And even a grazing glance had shown that her hair was very different. Cropped so short the curls had gone but, if anything, that accentuated her eyes and they had always been a mirror of her brother's, with that darkness softened by a touch of vulnerability that drew an urge to protect like the most powerful magnet.

He may not have shared Matt's blood the way Becca did but they'd been brothers to the bone and the last thing he'd expected right now was the soul-piercing awareness of how much he still missed his best mate.

He was barely listening to the introductions being made to the other men. Senior representatives from search and rescue, civil defence and the navy.

'I understood I was the only medic being sent,' he growled, flicking his gaze sideways.

'You are. The auxiliary fuel tanks needed to go the distance which means there's no room for any other personnel.' Richard had seen the direction of his glance. 'This is your pilot, Rebecca Harding. She's just waiting for the mechanics to finish fitting the auxiliary fuel tanks.'

Pilot?

'What's the flight time expected to be?'

'Approximately four hours. Have you been briefed properly?'

'I'd appreciate an update.'

He was directed towards the wall map. 'Tokolamu's the largest island in this group here. Roughly eight hundred and fifty kilometres north-west of New Zealand. It's been a Department of Conservation nature reserve for some years now and is the hub of an important kiwi breeding programme.'

Jet nodded. He was listening. Or trying to. The projected flight time was echoing in his brain, however. He was going to be cocooned in a flying bubble with Becca as his only companion for *four* hours?

She had to be as unhappy about that prospect as he was.

'Island's area's approximately twenty-six square kilometres and the buildings are located here, in this southern bay.'

Surely there was someone else who could step in and fly the bird?

'Currently there's a group of eighteen people on the island for weed control, checking predator traps and tracking and monitoring the kiwis. All but four of them were in the hostel when the island got rocked by an earthquake, measuring 8.3 on the Richter scale, three hours ago.'

'Where were the other four?'

'Night tracking mission. Common practice, with kiwis being nocturnal feeders.'

'Are they accounted for?'

'No.'

'Any update on the injured people we know about?'

'The hostel got flattened. Three people are still trapped in the debris. Of the rest, there's one with a head injury who's unconscious and another with a compound leg fracture. Radio contact is patchy, however, and we haven't had an update for a while.'

So there were potentially major casualties and the number was still unknown. A lot for a single medic to stabilise and monitor until backup arrived but that was fine. Jet thrived on exactly these kinds of challenges and it wasn't as though he would have to worry about enemy fire this time.

Or would he?

He couldn't help glancing over his shoulder again. Until he arrived on scene, his life would be in the hands of the pilot and in this instance he wasn't at all sure he was comfortable about that. But he'd be even more un-comfortable if he was unprofessional enough to suggest a replacement. Personal issues were simply put aside in his line of work. They were irrelevant.

But this was…different.

He was looking directly at Becca for the first time since he'd entered this room. Making eye contact, and it was doing something very odd to his gut. So many questions were coming out of nowhere.

How are you?

What on earth made you become a pilot?

Do you still miss Matt as much as I do?

Questions he had no right to ask and would probably not get answered.

She was his pilot, dammit. A glorified taxi driver given that her only role was to get him to the island. Transporting patients would have to wait until the navy vessel got to the area and the men around him were discussing just how long that would be. Two days at the earliest. Three, probably, given the weather and sea conditions at the moment.

She wouldn't be there on the island with him so why did this feel personal enough to threaten his performance? She must have wanted this mission. Had she volunteered for it or been chosen and happy to accept? Either way, it sure didn't look as though she was having second thoughts in the wake of learning the identity of her passenger.

Or was she?

There was something about the tilt of her chin and the guarded expression in her eyes as she stared back at him that was…what, a warning?

The idea that it might be a plea seemed weird. Or maybe not. *He* was the person they wanted on this island, after all, and any pilot on this team would be skilled enough to make sure he got there safely. If he demanded a change, it might cause a few waves but it could probably be achieved. How long would it take to put those extra tanks in and connect up the manual fuel lines? Long enough to brief another pilot?

Was that what Becca wanted from him? The opportunity for something rather different and potentially more dangerous than usual?

He'd once been a part of having something desperately important taken away from her. The notion that he could give her anything at all was touching something very deep inside Jet.

It didn't matter that she hated him. She was Matt's sister and whatever she needed or wanted that was within his capability to provide, it was hers, without question.

What *he* needed and wanted was to break that eye contact. To get this mission kicked off and get firmly onto professional territory where he wouldn't have to be

aware of this odd stirring in his gut. The one that was
making it so hard to look away and was still firing off
questions he felt compelled to ask that had absolutely
nothing to do with what he was here for.

As luck would have it, he got assistance. A new
arrival in the room got everyone's attention instantly.
Dressed in the oil-spattered overalls of a mechanic, he
gave Becca a thumbs-up sign.

'Tanks are in. You're good to go.'

The interruption was a godsend.

Becca could have sworn she'd been drowning under
Jet's gaze. He'd known he had the power to get her
bumped off this mission and he'd seen that she wanted
it.

And he was prepared to give her what she wanted
despite any personal cost involved.

The weird prickling sensation at the backs of her eyes
couldn't possibly be tears. Becca didn't cry. Her lifetime
supply of tears had been used up ten years ago. It was
relief, that was all, and her eyes were more than dry as
she took her leave while Jet was to be given the last of
his briefing.

They were sparkling, in fact. She had a pre-flight
check to get on with so that she'd have the rotors turning
and be ready for lift-off as soon as her passenger left the
building. A green light to adventure. A take-off with so
much extra fuel on board it would be like handling a
bomb. A vast amount of unforgiving ocean to fly over.
The longest continuous time in the air she'd ever had in
a chopper.

Time with Jet Munroe as the only other living creature for hundreds and hundreds of miles.

OK. That was a bit harder to get her head around, so Becca focussed on her checklist instead.

Master power switch on normal.

Inverter switches both on.

Fuel prime pumps both on and lights extinguished.

The checks were automatic but precise. Fast but thorough. She got as far as checking that the pedestal circuit breakers were all in before something broke out of that mental cage she'd pushed Jet into.

She hated him, yes, but it hadn't always been like that, had it?

Hate was the flip side of love.

And a hate this vehement had to be the flip side of adoration.

A teenage crush.

A desperate desire to be noticed as more than just the kid sister of a member of that elite tribe. The four 'bad boys' of Greystones Grammar school. She'd only been eight years old when she'd first met him, when he'd come home with Matt for a holiday from boarding school. That had been the start of it.

Matt's death had finished it, of course. She'd never wanted to set eyes on Jet again.

Becca armed the emergency light in the helicopter and checked the voltmeter. She fired up the engines and finally watched the rotors start to move and pick up speed and height. It was then that the black-clad figure emerged from the hangar door, stooping a little as he came under the rotors to climb into the side door.

Her sigh was unheard, but heartfelt.

Maybe it was true that you should never say never.

CHAPTER TWO

THE ocean was never far away in this island country and the lights of New Zealand's largest city swiftly became a backdrop to the airborne helicopter.

The only communication on board had been between Becca and the mainland. The traffic controller supervised her clearance, confirmed her flight plan and provided a detailed report on weather conditions. For some time after that, the conversation was between others on the ground. Patchy conversations came through about the precise position of the closest ship to the island, the direction it was taking and how long it might be before they reached the island. Confirmation was sought and gained that Becca would be able to refuel using Department of Conservation stores on the island. A worrying update on the condition of the injured people was received and relayed and if it had been possible to fly faster, it would be happening.

With plans in place and the sense of urgency increased, it seemed that any further conversation between anybody was pointless for the time being and, nearly an hour into the flight, the only sound in the cockpit was the roar of powerful engines and the chop of the spinning rotors.

Jet was wearing a helmet with built-in earphones so he could hear whatever was going on. There were open channels to flight control, the helicopter rescue base and the army command in charge of this mission and he'd been taking notice of everything said. Becca could also flip channels so that they could talk to each other without being overheard by anyone else but so far Jet hadn't bothered to pull his microphone attachment down from the rim of his helmet.

He'd been content to listen and simply watch, in no small way amazed that Matt's little sister was doing this at all. Doing it well, too. He had plenty of experience in helicopters. He could fly one himself if he had to, so he could appreciate her skill and the calm control she had over this machine. Just as well, he thought wryly, given that they were carrying enough extra fuel to blow them both to smithereens if something had gone wrong on take-off.

Yep. However unlikely it seemed, Becca Harding had grown up to become a helicopter pilot. Maybe it shouldn't seem so odd. Matt had loved nothing more than getting out with the rest of them and pushing his body and a big bike to the limits. Or was that one of the things that had created the bond between them? The knowledge that Matt didn't have quite the same bravado and that his courage was tested every time? Part of Jet had been impressed. Another part had wanted to watch over him like a big brother and make sure that nothing bad happened.

But something bad had happened, hadn't it?

Jet pushed the accusation back where it had come from with a ruthless mental shove but that only seemed to send other things bubbling to the surface. An image of the small girl he'd met, way back when he'd gone home with Matt for a school holiday. A lonely child being raised by very wealthy and largely absentee parents. Another from years later when they had all stopped in for a day or two at the country mansion on a road trip. More specifically, the memory was the absolute admiration and adoration on a teenage girl's face as she saw her much older brother after too long apart. And the memory that had been captured unwillingly the next day when she had joined them in the swimming pool in her bikini and more than just his brain had taken note that she was no longer a child.

Holy cow! That particular memory had been buried with enough shame to ensure it never escaped. What was happening to him? Jet's scowl deepened as he slumped into his harness, letting minute after minute tick past. Given the roar of engine noise, it was amazing how the atmosphere in this cockpit was starting to feel like a brooding silence. How the tension was ratcheting upwards.

It was ten years ago! It hadn't been his fault, any more than it had been Max's or Rick's. They'd blamed themselves, of course. Especially him, because he'd been the one to have the hunch that Matt's headache wasn't just a hangover hanging on too long. He'd been the one to earn an ED consultant's wrath, arguing that a CT was justified despite the lack of any real symptoms. They had been such junior doctors then—already branded as being brilliant but maverick. None of them had been able to juggle rosters to keep an eye on Matt when he'd decided he'd go to an on-call room and sleep it off.

And it had been Jet who'd gone to try and rouse him, hours later. Nobody had argued about the CT being needed after that. The horror of finding him and learning that a brain aneurysm had ruptured as he slept would never go away completely. Or the pain of being shut out for the next few days as Matt's parents tried to cope with his grief-stricken sister and make agonising decisions about organ donation and turning off the life support.

They'd gone over and over it so many times. They'd made peace with it. He shouldn't have to go through it all again. Shouldn't have to be even thinking about it. It was Becca's fault. For being here. For still hating him.

How much longer was this ride going to last? Jet reached to touch the GPS screen and get an update on what distance had been covered.

'Hands off,' Becca growled. 'I'm the only person who touches the controls in here.'

'Whoa…' Jet drawled, his hand now in a 'stop' signal of mock surrender.

Another minute of an even more tense atmosphere. He sighed inwardly and then flipped his microphone into place as he slid a sideways glance at Becca.

'What if you pass out or something? You expect me to hurtle to my doom even when I'm perfectly capable of handling a BK117?'

Becca was staring straight ahead, as though she was driving a car and needed to keep her eyes on the road. A jerk of her head said that the notion was too farfetched to be worth commenting on.

'You want information, you ask,' she said. 'My bird. My rules.'

Man, she sounded tough. Jet would normally find that worthy of respect but this was *Becca* and the image she was presenting jarred with what he remembered of her. Especially the last time he'd seen her, a few weeks before her brother's death, at a party hosted by the four of them in the old house they'd rented together. Becca had just arrived in the city to start her nursing degree.

An eighteen-year-old, glowing with the excitement of launching herself into the adult world. She'd been all dressed up and ready to party with rings on her fingers and killer heels on her toes. Her hair had been a wild cascade of curls that bounced on her bare shoulders and she had even smelled...*amazing*.

The effect of witnessing this butterfly girl emerging into womanhood had been absolutely riveting. Matt hadn't missed the way Jet's jaw had dropped.

'Don't even go there in your *head*,' his mate had growled. 'You're the prime example of the kind of guy I intend to keep my kid sister well away from.'

The warning had been tempered with a good-natured grin and a friendly punch on the shoulder but it had been serious enough to cause a flash of fear later that night. When Matt had almost walked in on what had happened in the kitchen...

Oh...man. Did *that* memory have to surface again now, as well?

Of course it did. It had never been buried all that well, had it?

Jet had to break this train of thought. He sent a sideways glare at the cause of this mental turbulence. Becca was still staring resolutely straight ahead, seemingly confident of being in control. He couldn't even see that much of her head with that helmet on and it was helpful to remember that she was nothing like the way she was in that memory of that party night.

Now her hair was as short as a boy's and, as far as

he could tell, she was wearing neither jewellery nor make-up. And what had her boss called her?

Bec.

The shortest, sharpest diminutive of her name possible.

What was wrong with her old nickname? Was Becca too feminine now? Too soft?

What had happened to that girl?

Jet had to swallow hard. As if he didn't know.

And he didn't want to remember, anyway, did he? He hadn't seen this woman in a decade. They were strangers now. Besides, maybe it wasn't so out of character, now that he came to think of it. Jet felt a corner of his mouth lifting. He couldn't help it. He actually snorted with amusement.

'What?' Becca turned towards him. The helmet seemed too big for her and it made her look younger. Her eyes were narrowed and her lips almost pursed with annoyance. 'You have a problem with something? Like the fact that I'm in charge here?'

'Not at all.'

'What's so damn funny, then?'

'It just reminded me of something.'

'What?'

'You. Cheating at Snakes and Ladders.'

'I didn't cheat.'

'No. You just made up your own rules. What was it? Throw an odd number and you got to go up the snakes instead of down?'

'I was eight years old. A lifetime ago.' Her tone was a warning. 'Keep your memories to yourself, OK?'

'My game, my rules,' Jet murmured.

It was probably coincidence that they happened

to hit some turbulence at that precise moment but he glared suspiciously at his pilot anyway. He might have no choice about her being in charge right now but he didn't have to like it, did he?

Damn it!

She'd just begun to think that this wasn't going to be so bad after all.

Jet had always been the brooding type. An intrinsic part of the group but inclined to listen more than speak. To be there. Often leading the action, in fact, but fully informed and able to watch everyone else's back at the same time.

Powerful. With an edge of darkness that had intrigued her from the word go. She'd been scared of him on that first meeting, as any eight-year-old kid would have been, but then she'd finally seen him smile and chasing down that rare occurrence had become her mission. Learning that she could tease and coax him, as easily as her big brother, into doing exactly what she wanted—like playing Snakes and Ladders *her* way—had been a bonus.

Becca was checking every single dial and switch on her control panel. Altitude and power. Fuel supply and speed. RPMs of the main and tail rotors. Checks that were only necessary right now due to her desperate attempt to focus on nothing more than the job in hand.

Yeah… It had been going fine while her passenger had been sitting there quietly. She'd been a bit too aware of him, of course. His size and the sheer…maleness he had always emanated. The tension had been noticeable but manageable, as well. Becca was only too happy to put up with a silent, sulky passenger in this particular instance.

But then he'd tried to mess with her controls! He'd almost *smiled*. Made fun of the fact that she was in charge here. He'd even brought up a somewhat embarrassing reminder of her past and taken her back a little too clearly. Good grief, she'd actually *felt* eight years old again for a heartbeat or two.

She hadn't liked it, either. Not one little bit.

Because she didn't want to remember or was it because she didn't want him thinking of her as someone's kid sister any more?

The tight feeling in her chest increased until it was painful to suck in a breath. She wasn't anyone's kid sister any more, was she? And it was *his* fault.

And she really, really didn't want to spend the next couple of hours or so thinking about what life had been like back then and how much she still missed her big brother. It would have been bad enough simply seeing Jet from a distance. Being this close to him and *only* him, miles from anywhere, was almost unbearable. It was opening an old wound that had been too huge to ever heal over completely and the opening process was a threat. There were soft things underneath that scar that had to be protected at all costs.

Memories.

Feelings.

Hopes and dreams.

Her heart.

Maybe he was right to make fun of her being in charge and trying to sound tough.

Maybe it was all a sham.

The patch of turbulence was great. Becca could feel every tiny nuance of the buffeting and hear the changes in engine noise as though her chopper was talking to her.

She became absorbed in her flying and found the thrill creeping back. Being so connected that she became a part of the machine. Or maybe it was an extension of her body. Whatever. They were aloft. She could see the patchy moonlight catching the whitecaps on the ocean below and they were speeding into the night. The turbulence added just enough to the adrenaline rush of it all and by the time they were back into calm air, Becca had found an inner equilibrium, as well.

It didn't matter what Jet remembered or what he thought of her now. She *was* in charge. Of this chopper and who touched its controls. Of what communication, if any, took place between the people involved in this mission.

Flipping channels, Becca checked in with flight control and with her base. Richard was close to the radio.

'Any update on patient status?' she queried.

'No further communication,' Richard responded. 'The link was patchy and we think we might have lost it.'

'Roger that. Any update from the met office?'

'Aftershocks being recorded. Nothing major.'

'Roger. I'll get back to you when we're closer to target.'

Closing off her outward channel to the mainland, Becca left the internal link open. Just in case she felt like talking to Jet.

Which she didn't.

They had nothing in common other than this mission. If it had been anyone else with her, she'd be practically grilling him about what it was like to be part of an elite group like the SAS. What kind of training they got and where they'd been. She would have soaked up every story she could extract and revelled in vicarious dangers. But to ask anything would be opening a Pandora's box with Jet. She'd end up getting filled in on what he'd been doing for the past ten years. She'd probably hear about Max and Rick, as well, and she had to stay away from those connections to the past.

She didn't want to hear about how close they would still be with each other. That whole 'bad boy' vibe that had been a secret pact and bond that she'd been so in awe of. Good grief, she'd actually taken up nursing simply to stay in their orbit. All of them had been special but Matt and Jet had stood out, of course. So different from each other but way too much alike in the power they'd had over her.

The power to be the centre of the universe. Trustworthy and indestructible.

Yes. She had to stay away from it to protect herself. Because she knew now that it wasn't true. That it was just an illusion.

She had to focus on the present. That fact that she and Jet had nothing in common but this mission. She would take him to the island, drop him off and then fly out of his life and probably never see him again.

Her salvation lay in that, she realised. Or was it a bad idea to break the silence that had filled in such a good chunk of time now? She could be professional but distant. Discussing the mission might be vastly preferable to sitting in a verbal desert for hours and fighting the pull into the past.

'How much do you know about Tokolamu island?' The question came out abruptly, almost an accusation of ignorance. No wonder Jet's eyebrow rose.

'As much as I need to know.' The tone was laid back

enough to be a drawl. 'It's the tip of a volcano that could erupt at any time. There are people on top of it who need to get off.'

His voice was right in her ears. As dark and deep as everything else about this man. That mix of being offhand and supremely confident was him all over, too. A lot of people would find that insufferable rather than attractive.

Maybe she was one of them.

'Some of those people are hurt,' Jet continued. 'It's my job to look after them. Your job is to get me there.'

Yep. She was one of them. Arrogance, that's what it boiled down to.

'Tokolamu's more than just the tip of a volcano,' she informed him. 'It's a significant nature reserve. It's got about seventy species of birds on or around it and that includes a successful breeding programme for endangered kiwi.'

The grunting sound indicated minimal interest but the conversation was working for Becca. Impersonal. Safe.

'There's weka there, too. And even kakapo. Did you know they're the world's heaviest parrot?'

'Can't say I did.'

'They're also the only flightless and nocturnal parrot in existence.'

'Flightless, huh?'

'Yep.'

'They'd be mates with the kiwis, then?'

It was Becca's turn to make a vaguely disparaging sound. Was he putting her down again?

'Well, I reckon the other sixty-eight or so species of

bird must think they're a bit inferior.' There was something more alive in Jet's tone now. 'When did you decide you wanted to fly, Becca?'

Becca. Nobody called her that these days. She was Rebecca to people who didn't know her well and Bec to her closer associates. A short, firm kind of name. No frills. Just the way she liked it.

So why did he make it sound like that was her *real* name? As though everyone else, including herself, had been using the wrong one all these years? She shook the disturbing notion away and latched on to his query with relief.

'Ages ago. When I left nursing I went into the ambulance service. They needed an extra crew member on a chopper one night and I got picked. I'd only been up in the air for ten minutes when I realised I didn't want to be sitting in the back. I wanted the driver's seat.'

Oh…help. This was exactly what she hadn't wanted to be doing. Raking over the past. Divulging far more about herself than she'd intended to. Opening doors that had to remain shut or they would both be sucked into the worst space of all.

Jet's chuckle was so unexpected, her head swung to face him. The sound was more than one of amusement. It signalled sympathy. It said he understood. That he would have felt exactly the same way.

And that was when Becca remembered how he'd got his nickname. Not because his hair was jet black but because he'd had a passion for fast things. Motorbikes and cars. Aircraft. Even his women had to be sleek and ready to speed into his bed.

Hadn't part of his attraction been that he'd had the aura of the kind of things associated with flying? Things

like turbulence and danger. The thrill of feeling weight-
less and able to move with a freedom that could be pure
bliss. Maybe the rush she got from flying was the best
substitute she had ever been able to discover for how
she'd once felt being close to Jet. Being the focus of his
attention. Being close enough to accidentally touch.

Not that such a ridiculous notion had ever occurred to
her during the process of falling in love with flying and
chasing the dream of becoming a pilot. Why would it?
She'd never seen Jet again. She'd never been reminded
of what it felt like to be this close.

Her sigh was an admission of defeat. She couldn't
fight this. She might have lasted amazingly so far, given
the distance they had already covered, but she couldn't
continue to keep this time together totally impersonal
and safe. She had no choice but to face up to whatever
emotional fallout eventuated. She had to deal with it and
survive. She could do that. She'd done it before, hadn't
she?

'So, when did you get your pilot's licence, Jet?'

It was the first time she'd used his name. It curled off
her tongue and hung between them like a white flag of
surrender.

'I didn't.'

'I thought you said you could handle a BK.'

'I can. Through osmosis, to start with. Then I got to
be mates with some army pilots. They were happy to
bend the rules sometimes. And I learn fast.'

That was true enough. Of all the 'bad boys', Jet had
undoubtedly been the smartest. That was why he'd won
the scholarship to attend an elite, private school in the
first place.

'The formal endorsement of the ability was a bit out of my price range,' Jet added dryly.

Yeah…not only the smartest. Despite all those boys being sent to boarding school for reasons they'd had every right to resent, Jet had had the biggest chip on his shoulder about his background. The others, including Matt, had been there because they had parents who could afford to offload the responsibility of children they weren't particularly interested in. It had been years before Becca had learned of Jet's multiple foster-family background. That he'd thought of himself as a charity case. She'd never heard more than hints, however. It wasn't a topic ever up for discussion, any more than the blatant disparity in financial advantages.

Was that why he'd thrown it at her now? As some kind of barrier?

It was ancient history, surely. He'd proved how well he could do relying entirely on his own resources. Becca had a lack of patience for people who blamed life's disappointments on their backgrounds. If you let either the pain of the past or fear of the future dictate your life, you were just shooting yourself in the foot as far as ever being happy. When it came down to it, everybody had to be able to draw on personal strength, no matter what their childhood had been like. Maybe Jet needed to get over himself.

'Med school's not cheap,' she fired back. 'You managed that, no problem.'

'Unless you count the past ten years I've spent paying the loan off.' Jet was scowling but then he shrugged. His next words were barely more than a mutter, as though he was talking to himself rather than Becca. 'Maybe I will get my licence now. It's not as if I want to save up for a house or anything.'

'Gypsy lifestyle, huh?'

Becca regretted her choice of words as soon as she'd uttered them. It was supposed to be a light-hearted comment, to finish the discussion without adding more substance to that ghostly barrier coming into view. To make his life choices seem desirable, even. But the idea of a gypsy was a little too apt. A man going his own way in life, according to his own rules. A bit dark and dangerous. Yes, she could picture Jet Munroe as a gypsy all right. Or a pirate. Or... This had to stop.

'I know what you mean about the osmosis,' she said hurriedly. 'I reckon I could get an IV line in, if push came to shove.'

'I should hope so. Didn't you say you'd been with the ambulance service?'

'I didn't get quite that far with my training.' Becca knew she sounded defensive but did he have to make her sound inadequate? Was he determined to make her feel younger and far less experienced than she was? 'I work with a lot of intensive care paramedics who are brilliant at what they do,' she added crisply. 'My job is just to get them there.'

That seemed to score a point. Conversation ceased and they flew on with the engine noise filling the space. Like it had done a while back but this time it was different. It was like they were both unwillingly forced to be taking part in some kind of dance, Becca decided. They'd drawn closer. Touched on some level. And now they were wheeling apart. Circling. Knowing that they would be drawn in again and next time it would be even closer. Acceptance of the inevitability didn't lessen the dread so Becca said nothing. She was hanging on. Trying to delay the inevitable.

Jet seemed to be in tacit agreement with the tactic. It became a challenge. Who was going to break first? The time stretched and the challenge grew. A distraction all on its own. In the end, it wasn't either of them who broke it. The radio crackled and buzzed inside their helmets. Someone was trying to contact them but reception was bad. Becca switched frequencies and tested them.

'Flight zero three three. Are you receiving me, over?'

On her third attempt, Richard's voice was cracked but audible. They were clearly far enough away from base to be pushing the boundaries for communication and static was wiping out chunks of the speech they could hear.

'…return to base…'

'Please repeat,' Becca said. 'Message broken.'

'…in seismic activity…'

Good grief, had the volcano erupted? No. Becca looked up from the radio controls to stare into the darkness ahead. They were easily close enough by now to see the glow from such an event in the night sky. A sky that was lightening perceptibly with a faint line defining the horizon. Dawn was not that far off and that was good. It would make landing on the island a lot safer.

'…wind shear in the event of eruption,' came the end of Richard's latest broadcast.

So it hadn't erupted, then. Even better.

'…ash…' The single word was another warning.

'Message broken,' Becca said again.

'…pager…' The word was a command now. '…mo-bile…'

'Roger. Over and out.'

They flew in silence again for a minute. And then another. Becca was reluctant to follow the instruction. Even as broken as the communication had been, it was clear the mission was in danger of being aborted. And they were almost there, dammit. With no obvious cause for alarm.

'You going to check your pager, then?' Jet queried. 'And your phone?'

'Yep.'

Another minute passed. The sky was definitely getting lighter. Becca peered ahead. Was it too soon to expect to make visual contact with Tokolamu?

'Any time soon?' Jet murmured.

With a sigh, Becca unclipped the pager from her belt and handed it to her passenger. He activated the device and started scrolling through messages.

'These seem to be old messages. When did you go to Cathedral Cove?'

'Yesterday. About eleven hundred hours. Idiot teenagers diving off the cliff into some big waves. One of them mistimed it and got banged up on the rocks. Winch job.'

'And south of the Bombay Hills?'

'That was the job before Cathedral Cove. Motorway pile-up.'

'Nothing new on here, then.'

'I'm not surprised. Range for the radio should be better than the pager.'

'Give me your phone.'

The reluctance to let Jet read any text message she might have was surprisingly strong but Becca shrugged it off. It wasn't as if there would be anything too personal in there. Like a message from a boyfriend. She almost wished there was. She could be sure that Jet's love life wasn't a desert and her single status would probably be enough to count as another putdown. Or was some of this feeling of inadequacy coming from something she'd considered long since buried? She wasn't old enough. Or special enough. She was just Matt's kid sister and Jet was...

'Here it is. It says "Cancel, cancel. Seismic activity increasing. Eruption considered imminent. Risk unacceptable. Return to base."'

'No.'

'*What?*' But there was something more than astonishment in Jet's tone. It sounded like admiration. Respect, even.

'Look.' Becca pointed, and Jet peered into the grey sky of early dawn. 'Two o'clock,' she added.

Lumpy shapes that weren't waves. Getting larger by the second. The chain of islands of which Tokolamu was the largest. Becca could see it clearly now. Could see the tip of the volcano and it was as dark as the rest of the rocky land mass.

'We haven't got the fuel to get back,' she said calmly. 'Personally, I'd rather take my chances after a safe landing on an island than ditching in the ocean somewhere.'

There was a moment's silence as Jet absorbed the implications. Becca finally turned to look at him and, to her amazement, he grinned at her.

'Your bird,' he said. 'Your rules.'

His face was really alive now. Dark eyes gleamed beneath the visor of the helmet. They were breaking the rules and hurling themselves towards danger and he

was loving it. And…oh, Lord…that smile could probably persuade her to do anything, however dangerous
it obviously was.

Maybe she should turn back. There was a life raft on
board. They would know their coordinates and another
chopper could possibly already be on the way to meet
them.

But the islands were so close now. She could think
about spotting the buildings and then locating the nearby
landing site. People desperately needed the assistance
she was bringing. If she got stuck on the island because
an ash cloud prevented take-off then so be it. It wasn't
as though—

The oath Jet breathed cut off any thought of potential
safety.

Had she really thought the sky was so light now?
Against the glow of an erupting volcano, it had gone
pitch black again.

Ash would kill the engines. How long before it enveloped them? Becca began dropping altitude. Heading for
the closest island. Except that was Tokolamu, wasn't it?
And maybe it wasn't ash she had to worry about first.
The force of the eruption was about to hit them. Wind
shear would drop them like a rock…

It *was* dropping them. Becca was fighting with the
controls of her machine and she knew it was pointless. So pointless she didn't say a thing when she found
Jet leaning in to try and take over. She couldn't hear a
thing he was shouting because the noise outside was
overwhelming everything. The sky was on fire and the
island and its surrounding sea was rushing towards them
so fast she could barely process the information.

She was about to die and Jet Munroe was trying to save her.

The irony of the situation barely registered before the cacophony of sound and light around her vanished and everything became black.

CHAPTER THREE

HE WAS fighting for his life.

For Becca's life, too. Man, that look on her face was pure determination without a hint of fear. She was so small and fierce and seemed to believe that she could wrestle the force of Mother Nature and an out-of-control aircraft into submission.

The impression would have been laughable if it hadn't been so incredibly fleeting. Shoved aside with a million other, irrelevant thoughts as Jet let an automatic part of his brain loose. The part that stored emergency procedures backed up by remarkably honed survival skills.

Even so, in that mental maelstrom he recognised another motive to win this challenge. Maybe he had to do this for Matt. It was too late to save his best mate but he could save the person who'd been so important to him. The small, lonely girl that he'd tried so hard to be a substitute parent to. As well as a big brother and best friend all at the same time. Matt would have given his life in a heartbeat to save his sister.

Jet could do no less.

Except…they weren't going to die, dammit. Not if he could do anything about it. He added his weight to Becca's to fight the controls and, for a split second the sickening downward spiral lessened and he could see straight ahead. Towards the foam of waves breaking on unforgiving black rocks. And past the rocks to a tiny area of shingle beach. Would solid land be a better option than an icy ocean and the pull of its current?

Not that he really had much choice in the matter but the instantaneous, clinical evaluation of potential options filled those last few seconds before speed, gravity and the total failure of this machine to respond well enough combined and they hit…*something*. Hard.

Hard enough to knock him out?

He couldn't be sure. His head was spinning, filled with a roaring sound and bright flashes of light. He could be regaining consciousness after God knew how long or…this could be moments after the crash and the window in which he could escape.

And survive.

Something overrode that pure survival instinct, however. The knowledge that he hadn't been alone.

'Becca… *Becca*…'

He couldn't see anything. Couldn't open his eyes. Something was digging painfully into his face and it took a moment to realise that the pain was caused by broken pieces of his flight helmet visor. He wrenched them clear and pulled his helmet off, ignoring the warm, sticky sensation of bleeding.

Now he could see surprisingly well. Red light, like a fiery dawn, surrounded them. The Perspex of the helicopter was cracked and a horribly bent rotor blade was directly in front, framed by a large hole. A spray of water suddenly came through the hole and soaked him, cold enough to wake him up completely. Were they in the sea? No. He could feel something solid beneath them and the crumpled chassis of the chopper was rocking. Grinding on something hard.

The rocks. They must be caught on rocks, probably close to dry land. A wave could lift the wreckage and put it at the mercy of the ocean at any moment and that wouldn't be a good thing. The spray had barely stopped but Jet had released his harness and his attention was focussed on the crumpled body of his pilot.

'*Becca*. Can you hear me?'

The groan that came in response was the best sound Jet had ever heard.

She was alive.

Stripping off the gloves he'd been wearing, Jet moved to wedge himself between what was left of the Perspex bubble and a flight control panel that was bent and broken. A couple of faint, flickering lights caught his attention as he moved. Hopefully, one of them might be the emergency locator beacon activating. The other one was on the radio and, on the off chance it was still operational, Jet pulled on the curly microphone cord to wrench it clear of the central controls it had fallen into.

'Mayday, mayday,' he sent. 'Flight zero zero three down.'

Even if they got the message, they wouldn't be sending another rescue chopper. Flying into volcanic ash was impossible. The only hope of assistance would come from the ship already diverted towards Tokolamu and, what had they said about its ETA?

Thirty-six hours. A day and a half.

They were on their own.

Apart from another group of survivors on this island

who still needed help, of course. Jet depressed the button on the side of the microphone again.

'Abandoning aircraft,' he said decisively. If this transmission was getting through, at least nobody would waste time trying to search the crash site later. 'We'll head for the settlement.'

A faint crackle emanated from the radio then another spray of salt water came through the windscreen and the electronic equipment fizzed and died. He had wasted no more than about thirty seconds on what was probably a useless attempt to communicate with the outside world but it still felt like way too long.

Becca needed him.

Dropping the microphone, Jet used his hands and eyes to try and examine her. These weren't the worst conditions under which he'd done a primary survey on an injured person but they were nudging the top spot. He could feel the wash of the waves around the helicopter chassis and getting sucked out to sea and then smashed onto rocks again would be pretty much as dangerous as being under enemy fire.

Airway. Breathing. Circulation.

Becca groaned more loudly and mumbled some incomprehensible words but the attempt to speak was a good indication that her airway was clear. Breathing? Jet put his hands around her ribs, oblivious of the fact that he was cupping her breasts as he concentrated on what was happening below her ribs. Were her lungs filling well? The same amount on each side? Was her breathing too fast or too slow? God, she was so small.

Fragile.

Her breathing seemed OK. Jet ran his hands over the rest of her body. Feeling her abdomen to see if it elicited a pained response. Checking her legs for the deformity of a broken bone or the wetness of major bleeding. Amazingly, he found nothing. Until he checked her arms, anyway. When he felt her left arm below the elbow, Becca cried out and opened her eyes.

'It's OK,' he told her. 'You've hurt your arm.'

Broken it, quite likely, because of how hard she'd been gripping the controls at the point of impact. Her flight suit was ripped and she was bleeding badly. Jet ripped the sleeve farther and tied the strips tightly over the wound. There was no time to do more right now. This first check might have only taken sixty seconds but it was past time to get out of there.

'Becca? Can you hear me?'

Her eyes opened but she said nothing.

'Does your neck hurt?'

Her head rolled from side to side but she still made no sound.

'Can you move your feet?'

He felt rather than saw the attempt at movement because he was busy easing her helmet off and unclipping her harness. The queries had been automatic, anyway. Even if she did have serious neck or spinal injuries, he had to get her out.

The door on the pilot's side was crunched against solid rock. They were tilted slightly nose down and another huge rock was blocking the door on the passenger side. That left the side door in the cabin and the back hatch under the tail. One of those was bound to provide an escape route but it would take precious seconds to get there. A wave rolled them enough to lift the tail and knock him off balance even as he considered the options.

Becca's eyes were wide open and well illuminated by the eerie, red glow from the outside. Could she hear the frightening roar of the volcanic eruption that was almost enough to cover the horrible grinding of metal on rock? She was clearly putting the pieces together and starting to realise what had happened and where they were.

He saw the moment that fear kicked in.

A new surge of adrenaline came with the renewed urge to protect Becca. Turning and bracing himself on the back of the seat, Jet used his heavy, steel-capped boots to smash the edges of the hole in the Perspex to make it bigger. Big enough to climb out of with a small woman in his arms.

The world had turned itself inside out. It was threatening to crush her and there was nothing Becca could do about it.

She hadn't felt this afraid since…

Since the moment she had known Matt was going to die.

Nobody had taken her into his arms back then and held her as though he was capable of keeping the chaos and pain away.

Maybe this was simply an illusion now but if she was going to die, Becca would far rather be cradled in a pair of powerful arms that made it feel like her life was of the utmost importance to someone else than curled up alone in the pilot's seat of a crashed helicopter.

She'd obviously been knocked out on impact and the memories of her last moments of consciousness were patchy and strange. So was what she could remember about waking up.

Jet's hands on her breasts. Pressing on her abdomen. Tracing the shape of her whole body.

She'd known they were *his* hands. She'd always known what it would feel like to have them touching her because it had happened in so many, many dreams. It was muted in reality, however, because in those dreams her skin had always been bare.

The pain of having her arm moved had chased any pleasure away. It had woken her up too much, as well. Enough to make sense of where she was and what was happening. To realise that the weird red light was a re-flection that had to be coming from molten lava spewing from a very nearby volcano. To feel how unstable the remains of this helicopter were and that it was seawater splashing inside at regular intervals to pool around her feet.

Fear overrode any pain at that point and only in-creased as she watched Jet kick the remnants of Perspex from in front of them. He was going to escape, wasn't he? The way he had when Matt had been lying there dying in the intensive care unit. She would have to cope alone again and she was so horribly, horribly afraid.

But then he bent over and gathered her into his arms. She was rocked wildly as he completed the enormously difficult manoeuvre of climbing through a hole with jagged edges, holding such a large burden, trying not to get them caught or injured. Then there were sharp, slippery rocks to negotiate and Jet had to use one hand to steady himself every few seconds. Somehow, he still managed to hold Becca with one arm. She could feel it across her back and tucked under her thighs like the sturdy branch of a tree. Maybe it was helping that she'd wound her arms around his neck and had her face buried against his shoulder.

A roaring noise surrounded them that was far more than the sound the sea could make against rocks. The ground shook beneath them at intervals, as well. How on earth did Jet manage to keep them moving? Upright enough to avoid a nasty fall on this alien landscape of ancient, volcanic rock. Becca clung to him as tightly as she could. She fought hard when something threatened to prise her arms loose.

'Let go.' Jet's voice was a command. 'It's all right. It's safe now.'

Reluctantly, Becca let him unwind her arms. He was kneeling, she realised with surprise, and she was sitting on a flat area of shingle, having been deposited so carefully she hadn't noticed.

She looked around cautiously. Good grief...they could be on Mars. A lurid red sky and barren dark rocks were the only things she could see until she lifted her line of sight. And there, well out on the rocks, cradled in a wash of sea foam, she could see the sad wreckage of her beautiful chopper.

'Oh, my God,' she breathed, wrapping her arms around herself for comfort as the enormity of the situation became suddenly very real.

'Give me your arm.'

'What?' Becca stared at Jet in confusion. He'd just removed her arms from where she'd been clinging to him like a frightened child.

An eight-year-old, maybe? How did he do it? Strip away all her skills and hard-won strength to make her feel so incredibly vulnerable. And lost now. She couldn't pretend to be in control any more. She hadn't protected herself very well, had she?

She hadn't protected either of them. This was *her* fault. She could have turned back. She'd risked her life, which was bad enough, but she'd also risked Jet's life and that was…appalling. And he was hurt. There was blood on his face. Without thinking, Becca reached up to touch. The urge to find out how bad it was…to make it better somehow…was too powerful to resist.

'No.' Jet pushed her away. 'Your left arm.' He was leaning closer. Frowning. 'Where are you?' he demanded.

He didn't want her to touch him. Weird how much that hurt. 'H-here,' Becca stammered, confused again. 'With you.'

'Fair enough.' There was a curl happening to one corner of his mouth. Almost a smile. 'You got knocked out, Becca,' he said with a curiously gentle note in his voice. 'I'm trying to assess your GCS. Can you tell me where "here" is?'

'The island. Tokolamu.'

'Good. And what's my name?'

'Jet.' Becca said it slowly because it felt good. Like permission to go somewhere she had been denied access to for so long.

'My real name?'

'James Frederick Munroe.'

'*Ouch!* How on earth did you remember my middle name?'

Becca felt herself grin. 'I remember lots of things.'

What an understatement, a part of her brain chided. Did you really think you'd locked all that stuff away? It's still there. Every detail. The way he could scowl so fiercely whenever anything remotely emotional was happening. The astonishing intensity of his dark eyes when he was interested in something. The way his hair looked when sleekly wet coming up from a dive into a swimming pool, or damp and tousled by a towel after a shower. The way he'd sat with a small child and played Snakes and Ladders when he could have been doing far more exciting teenage stuff like playing video games or raiding her parents' well-stocked liquor cabinet. The dreams that had started a long, long time before any sexual content had crept in.

Dreams that had only gained momentum the night of the party.

The excitement of dressing up like an adult. Of finally being grown up enough to...

To have no hesitation at all in grabbing that opportunity when she'd been alone in the kitchen with Jet when they'd both gone to find a drink at the same time. When they'd been side by side in the narrow space between the open fridge door and the wall.

When she had turned and kissed him.

She could still remember that moment when their lips had actually touched. The sheer *bliss* of it...

And then there'd been the sound of her brother coming down the hallway. Calling out to Jet to see why the beer was taking so long to arrive. And Jet had let her go and turned so fast he had practically been on a fridge shelf by the time Matt came into the room seconds later.

And he hadn't even looked at her once for the rest of that night.

Her grin was fading as rapidly as Jet had dismissed her way back then. Pandora's box had been split wide open. During the crash? No. The cracks had been apparent the moment she'd seen Jet step out of that vehicle at the base. It had only been a matter of time before the contents began to spill out. There was so much of it, how could it all be appearing with such speed? Maybe it would be helpful to hang on to the devastation that had come in the wake of being ignored after taking the risk of that kiss.

Jet was just registering the mischievous grin that had already vanished. He gave an impatient huff. 'Your retrograde memory is too good. OK, remember these things coz I'm going to ask you again in five minutes. A brown dog, the number six and the name Reginald. Which is marginally better than Frederick,' he added wryly. 'Now, let me see your arm. It was bleeding.'

He'd tied a makeshift kind of tourniquet around it, she noticed. No wonder he was checking her level of consciousness. She had no memory of him ripping the sleeve of her flight suit to make the wide bands.

The wound began bleeding heavily as soon as the bands were loosened.

'Needs stitching,' Jet muttered.

Becca saw her own blood covering his hands as he examined her arm. She was horrified.

'You're not wearing any gloves.'

His raised eyebrows that framed a very intent look. 'Something you want to tell me?' He made a tutting sound. 'What *have* you been up to, Rebecca Harding?'

He was teasing her. Just the way he had when she'd been a kid and had come inside with grazed knees or muddy clothes. Only this was about a very adult subject.

Becca had been shivering with the cold but could feel heat suffusing her face right now.

'N-nothing.' Unfortunately true but did he really have to know how sad her love life had been for so long? Did she need current humiliation to add to a long-ago memory? Definitely not.

'Not recently, anyway,' she added in what she hoped was an offhand tone. 'Don't worry. You're not going to catch any blood-borne nasty. It's just not good practice, is it?'

Jet probably saw right through her small attempt to get a grip on things.

'Least of our worries right now, I would've thought.' He had retied the strips of the dense, waterproof fabric. 'Wriggle your fingers for me.'

The attempt wasn't impressive.

'Hurts, doesn't it?'

Becca shrugged. 'A bit. I'll be fine. What's happened to *your* head? You're bleeding, too.'

He wasn't going to be distracted from his careful examination of her wrist and arm. He bent her hand carefully.

'Ouch,' Becca muttered.

'Could be broken,' he pronounced. 'Could just be a bad sprain. I'll put a compression bandage on when I've sorted that bleeding. Anything else hurting?'

'No.'

'Really?' His gaze narrowed. 'No headache?'

'A bit, I guess.'

'What were the three things I told you to remember?'

'A brown dog…number six and the name…' The urge to tease was childish. Or maybe she couldn't resist seeking the same kind of rapport he might have been trying to tap into when he'd been chiding her about her possible sex life. '...Frederick,' she said decisively.

She held his gaze. Jet sighed heavily but she was sure she'd seen a gleam of appreciation there at her feeble attempt to lighten the atmosphere.

'Don't move. I'm going to get my kit.'

'What? Where is it?'

'In the chopper. Along with a lot of other useful medical gear I should try and retrieve. We've still got an appointment with some injured people who can't be too far away.'

'But...' Becca looked past him. The light was stronger now. A little less red maybe but no less strange. The air looked thick. With ash? She didn't know much about volcanoes but surely they'd need to find some kind of masks to breathe through?

The helicopter wreckage was clearly visible, a bent rotor sticking up in the air like a distressed swimmer's arm. The other rotor seemed to be wedged in the rocks but it wasn't enough of an anchor for stability. The mortally wounded aircraft was rolling with each wave. Tipping and sliding on the rocks.

'You can't go back inside,' she told Jet. 'It's far too dangerous.'

But Jet was standing up.

What if something happened to him? If he got trapped inside and the wreckage got sucked off the rocks by an extra-big wave? He'd drown and...and it would be worse than sitting here alone, waiting for a wall of molten lava to swallow her up.

'Don't go... *Please*...'

The words were a whisper but he seemed to have

heard them. He crouched swiftly, putting his hands on her shoulders.

'I have to,' he said quietly. 'We need the medical supplies. It won't take long.'

His gaze was holding hers. Was he trying to reassure her? Give her strength?

It wasn't working.

'I'll be right back,' Jet said with absolute confidence. 'I'll look after you, OK?'

Becca nodded but bit her lip at the same time. She shouldn't need looking after. She was a grown-up. A highly trained helicopter pilot. A woman in complete control of her life and her future. At least, she had been, until a very short time ago.

At this precise moment, she was only too grateful to be given that promise. To pull it around her like a comforting hug.

Jet was standing up again. He looked down. His face was half-covered in blood and his expression could only be described as grim but those dark eyes were so alive. Gleaming, in fact.

'We're on land now,' he told her. 'My game. *My* rules.'

And with that, he was gone. A shape so dark and lithe it was only seconds before he virtually vanished against the rocks.

Leaving Becca, huddled alone on that tiny, stony beach, was one of those 'lesser of two evils' decisions.

Jet's head told him that it was what had to be done. He needed his medical gear to help her as well as the other people on this island. What use were his skills if he had no pain relief or fluids or any of the dozens of other things compressed into his specialist backpack? There were items in the helicopter he'd been counting on, as well, but they would have to be left behind. Things like portable oxygen and traction splints and the life pack. There was no point in retrieving anything he wouldn't be able to carry himself.

Part of his brain was pointing out that Becca still had one good arm so she'd be able to carry something but Jet was arguing the notion as he scrambled back over the rocks. He could feel the pain in his hands, despite how cold they were, as he tried to grip the sharp surfaces and he made a mental note to keep an eye out for the leather gloves he'd stripped off in order to feel what he was doing in that first check on Becca's condition.

He'd felt it all right. No amount of mental discipline could shove it all into a doctor-patient box. The relief of finding she wasn't badly injured had warned him of an unprofessional involvement. The wrench of putting her down on the beach had been another warning and even that had paled in comparison to having to leave her behind moments ago, with that look in her eyes.

She had wanted him to stay with her.

She *needed* him.

Jet didn't try and climb directly into the cockpit. Eyeing the hole they had escaped through gave him a moment of satisfaction at the achievement. Would he have even attempted that without the incentive of getting Becca out as fast as possible?

Probably not.

This time, he went around to the back of the aircraft. Cautiously. Allowing a wave to break high on his legs and then ebb before going for the tail hatch. Another wave broke before he managed to get it open and the whole chassis rocked so that he barely kept his grip on the handle. He'd have to be quick about this but that was a good thing. It left no room for fear. Or the distraction of that image of Becca on the beach, looking to him to keep her safe.

His pack was easy enough to find and drag out from where it had wedged itself under the stretcher. He shoved it through the hole in the front with enough force to get it far enough up on the rocks to stay dry. The action made the hole even bigger, which would be good if he had to dive for safety but it was letting a lot more water in at the same time. He was sloshing around almost up to his knees as it was but he took the time to do a swift search in the dim light of the cabin. He grabbed a drug kit and an IV roll and bags of fluids, unzipping the jacket of his suit to tuck them against his body. A whole box of masks. He was adding a handful of extra bandages when the slide of the wreckage on rock tipped him off balance and he barely got himself upright before it moved again.

Without thinking, he snapped the clip holding the life pack in place and clutched it in his arms as he stepped forward and then turned to roll backwards through the same hole through which he'd lifted Becca to safety. His ankle caught and he felt a nasty wrench that wasn't coming simply from his own momentum. The chopper was really moving this time. Far and fast enough to break the rotor blade that had been caught between rocks.

Jet sucked in a breath as he realised that that relatively tiny piece of metal had been all that had kept the chopper where it was. It rolled away now, giving itself up to the sea.

He still had the life pack in his arms and lumpy supplies tucked into his jacket. His pack was safe. Carefully, Jet got to his feet, testing his ankle. It hurt like hell but it could take his weight, thank goodness. He could see that Becca was standing, as well. Staring in his direction. He couldn't see her expression but he could imagine what it was, having just watched her helicopter slide into the sea and probably not aware that he'd rolled to safety. He raised his hand, thumb up, to signal her.

Mission accomplished.

This time, the deep breath he sucked in was a satisfied one. He'd done what he'd set out to do. Showing Becca how capable he was, even in a dangerous situation, felt damn good.

He'd said it wouldn't take long and that he would be back. She would know she could trust him to honour his word.

He would do what he'd promised her he would.

He would look after her.

CHAPTER FOUR

THE sea was the same colour as the sky.

The colour of blood.

The dark silhouette of the man was only recognisable because it moved and the surrounding rocks didn't. When he stood still, having risen and raised his hand in a triumphant fist, he looked like another shape carved in stone.

A human rock.

Becca didn't bother reminding herself that she never cried. That her tears had all been spent on Matt. A choked sob escaped as she realised that, in no small part, this was still about Matt.

Her brother had been her human rock in a fluid, lonely world and Jet had been there beside him for as far back as she could remember clearly. Too real and too powerful to be considered a shadow but he'd still been in the background. Like a guardian angel. A flesh-and-blood angel with a loyalty that was so absolute it was impossible to think of Matt without thinking of Jet, and vice versa.

So it was like part of her brother was here with her now. Promising to look after her. Expecting her to trust him, but how could she when she knew that that trust could be broken? Unintentionally, maybe, but the effect would be the same and she'd be alone again. In the end, Becca knew she had only herself to rely on with that kind of certainty.

But the pull towards leaning on Jet and giving him that trust was so strong it was a physical pain and that was why Becca was crying now. Maybe, if she hadn't just watched in horror as the wreckage of her aircraft had slipped into that blood-red sea when she had been sure Jet was still inside it, she might have been power-less to resist that pull on her heart. But for just a few of its beats there she'd known how unwise it would be to give Jet any part of her heart, and trusting him would do precisely that.

For those few, ghastly seconds she'd known she was on her own again and she'd known that she *could* survive. She'd done it before and she knew how. She knew that a big part of being able to survive was about dodging emotional as well as physical damage. For however long it would take to get off this island, the man coming towards her now, weighed down by the bulky gear he was carrying, was just as dangerous as the exploding volcano high above them.

'Sorry, this is going to sting like mad.'

'You could just stitch it up. You don't need to waste the local.'

Jet snorted. 'I don't happen to have a bullet handy for you to bite on. Hold still… Damn, this light is still awful.'

'I'm sure you can do this with your eyes shut. Your reputation precedes you with the speed of light. Hey, well done! You're wearing gloves this time.'

Was she mocking him? Jet sent her a suspicious glower but Becca's head was bent. Good grief, she actually wanted to watch him cobbling up this nasty gash on her arm? And she was prepared to have it done without the benefit of local anaesthetic?

She had a mask on now. They both did. It was the first thing Jet had sorted, having arrived back on the beach and emptied the extra supplies from inside his jacket, just in case they suddenly got enveloped by an ash cloud. He was perfectly used to being around people wearing surgical masks. He was even used to being in environments where the light was weird due to explosions and smoke and so forth, but Becca had never been in a war zone, as far as he knew. This had to be an extraordinary experience for her, sitting hunched and injured on a beach in the middle of nowhere, bathed in the glow of molten lava and shivering with the cold and probably fear and yet, here she was, managing to keep her arm steady on his knee ready for him to do some minor surgery.

He grunted softly. A sound of respect. 'Pretty tough, aren't you?'

Becca shrugged. 'When I need to be.'

It had to hurt, sliding the needle in deeply enough to numb the edges of this wound. He saw the way she flinched and he could feel it himself. It wasn't that he was ever without sympathy for any patient he was inflicting a painful procedure on but this felt different. Unpleasant enough to make this an ordeal for both of them so it was best he got it done as efficiently as possible.

And he was wearing the damn gloves for her protection, not his.

Waiting only a minute or two for the local to take effect, Jet busied himself sorting the dressing and bandages he'd need. He located his suture materials and some small pouches of saline. Ripping the corner of the first pouch, he tipped the sterile liquid onto the wound. Becca sucked in her breath and Jet winced inwardly.

'Not quite numb, huh?'

'I'm fine,' she said through obviously gritted teeth. 'Just get on with it. We need to get out of here.' She was silent for a moment and when she spoke again, her tone was far less sure. 'Do you think we'll be able to get to the conservation base?'

'May as well give it a go,' Jet said cheerfully. 'Not too much else to do, is there? How much do you know about this volcano?' He was onto the second pouch of saline now, trickling it into the centre of the wound and tipping her arm carefully so that it drained towards the edges.

'What do you mean?'

'I'm wondering how many craters there are, for instance. And whether any of them had lakes.' Having made the wound as clean as possible, Jet swabbed it dry with clean gauze and then ripped open the packet containing the curved suture needle and attached thread. He had to swab fresh bleeding away then and decided it needed a couple of deep stitches before he closed the surface.

Becca looked away as the needle advanced. 'Does it make a difference? Having lakes?'

'Could do. Lakes mean you can get lahars. Rivers of mud and stuff that can do a lot of damage. They can move a lot faster than anyone can run and they set like concrete. They've been known to wipe out entire villages.'

'So we might get to the base camp and find it's too late,' Becca said quietly.

Jet made no response. What was the point? They might not even get there at all but they had to try.

'Lava's not so bad,' he said a short time later, now working swiftly to insert, knot and clip the neat sutures closing the wound. 'Generally moves slowly enough so you can keep out of the way. The problem will be if it's cut access off completely.'

'What about the gases volcanoes give off? Aren't they poisonous?'

'Some of them,' Jet admitted. 'But there's no point worrying about it given that we're a bit limited in what we can do. Staying upright is a good idea because a lot of those gases are heavier than air and will accumulate close to ground level. Respirators would be ideal but I guess we're lucky we've got these good quality antiviral-type masks. If we moisten them, they'll be more effective against gases as well as ash.'

He clipped the final suture and put a sticky, clear dressing over the wound.

'I'll bandage it for now. If it gets any more painful we'll splint it properly. Try not to put too much weight on it.'

'Thanks, Doc. I'll keep that in mind.'

Definitely mocking him now and he probably deserved it. Heaven only knew how rough the journey they were about to undertake might be. Becca might well need to climb up steep cliffs or get down rough gullies. Not using an arm was hardly going to be on a priority list if you were trying to save yourself from further injury.

'I should have kept our helmets on,' he muttered. 'Stupid.'

'I've got sunglasses.' Becca patted a top pocket of her flight suit. 'Have you?'

'Yeah….somewhere, I think.'

'Should help keep ash out of our eyes at least. Mine are starting to sting a bit.'

'Yeah…mine, too.' Jet tore the end of the bandage with his teeth and made strips to tie it in place around Becca's arm. 'There you go. That should hold together a bit better than crocodile clips.' He turned to begin putting unused supplies back into the pack.

'Leave some saline,' Becca ordered. 'And a sticky dressing. And have you got some Steri-strips?'

'What for?' He swung his head back towards her sharply. Was she hurt somewhere else, as well?

'Because you've got a dirty big gash on your forehead, that's why.'

'It can wait.'

'Have you not even noticed how often you're wiping blood off before it can get in your eyes? Quite apart from the risk of infection if it's not covered up, it might be helpful not to get your vision obstructed at some critical point.'

Jet grimaced but had to concede the point. He dampened another gauze dressing and swabbed at his forehead. The fluid stung enough to let him know the gash was not small.

'Give that to me,' Becca ordered. 'You're probably making it worse, scrubbing at it like that.'

With a frustrated growl, Jet sat down and handed

the swab over. Becca knelt beside him and peered at his forehead. She was concentrating on the task at hand but she was so close to him that Jet had to drag his gaze away from her face. Not before he noticed how amazingly thick and dark her eyelashes were even without the benefit of mascara, however. Or that her nose was small enough to barely dent the mask. And he hadn't needed X-ray vision to imagine what her lips were like beneath the stiff fabric. Did she still trap the tip of her tongue between them when she was totally focussed, the way she always had as a child?

He could actually sense her body heat in this proximity. Along with the light but confident touch of her fingers, it was disturbing.

'Get on with it,' he muttered. 'We need to get going. Get to higher ground, at least, so we won't be sitting ducks for a lahar.'

'Fine.' Becca used a fresh dressing to dry the wound. 'This could do with stitching, I expect, but Steri-strips will have to do until you get to an expert. You up to date with a tetanus shot?'

'Yep. Are you?'

'I think so.' Becca was trying to open the vacuum-sealed package containing the small, super-sticky strips. The corner of the plastic side was eluding her because her hands were shaking.

With the cold? Or was she finding this as disturbing as he was?

'Here. Let me.' Closing his hands over hers to take the packet without dropping it, Jet was startled by a blast of heat. How could Becca be shivering with cold when her skin could scorch his with such a brief touch? He had to suck in a deep breath.

He found himself sucking in a flashback at the same time.

That moment behind the fridge door at that party. The kiss.

It had just been a combination of teenage excitement and alcohol. Hadn't it?

She must have known as well as he had how Matt would have reacted. How impossible it would have been. And she'd been barely old enough for anything other than him being a 'big brother' figure to be remotely acceptable.

Hadn't stopped him thinking about it, though, had it?

Considering the amazing possibility that might be there if Matt ever came around to the idea one day. Thinking about how...*right* it would seem.

But Matt had never guessed his errant thoughts in those last few weeks he'd had to live and if it had been an embryonic dream, it had been buried along with his best mate. He hadn't even thought about it since.

Until now, that was. Jet cleared his throat, hoping to clear the memory, as well.

'You're not wearing gloves,' he managed to say casually as he handed her back the opened packet. 'Tch, tch.'

'Hmm.' Becca pressed an end of a strip to his forehead and then he could feel her squeezing the edges of the wound together to bring the other side close enough to capture. 'And I've probably got more to worry about in that direction than you have.'

Was he imagining an odd note in her voice? Disapproval?

Unless...

Unless there *had* been more to that kiss than too much champagne and being unexpectedly in such close proximity.

Maybe the attraction had been there on both sides.

But, even if it had been, it was ancient history. So long ago it was ridiculous to think it had any relevance now.

She hated him. She had told him that with a vehemence that had been absolute and he had known it would be there for ever. They might have been forced into being this close now but this was about survival. She needed him whether she liked it or not. And he needed her, too. This could potentially be the biggest challenge he'd ever faced and who knew? If it came down to the wire, the extra incentive of his determination to get Matt's little sister to safety might be enough to tip the balance from giving up to being successful.

'I think not,' he said aloud, in as cool a tone as he could manage. 'Thanks to a career in front-line emergency medicine, I get regular checks for any blood-borne nasties, as you call them. I'm as clean as a whistle.'

'Good for you.' The pressure of her fingers was even firmer this time. Enough to hurt. Not that he was going to let her know that. 'And now you'll have a sexy little scar on your head like a pirate. I'm sure it'll add considerably to your pulling power with women.'

The sound of her ripping the backing off a sticky dressing was rather similar to the edge that had definitely been in her tone that time.

Jet couldn't help teasing her. 'Cool,' he murmured. 'I'll be sure to remember to send you a thank-you card.'

She snorted. 'You'll need to get to a post office first.' She stuffed supplies back into a plastic compartment of the pack and zipped it shut. Then she fished her sunglasses from her pocket and put them on, foiling the attempt to read her expression that Jet had been unaware of making. She stood up, her very effectively disguised face pointed down at him. 'Well? What are you still sitting around for? Which way shall we go?'

Jet got to his feet. He opened a side pocket of the pack to extract a heavy-duty 'hazardous waste' plastic bag, which he handed to Becca.

'Make yourself useful,' he ordered. 'Put the extra stuff in there. Those bandages and masks and things.'

He hefted the pack onto his back as she complied. Then he lifted the life pack with one hand and held out his other hand for the bag she had filled.

'I'll take this. I can carry the life pack, as well.'

'What with? Your potentially fractured arm? I don't think so.' Jet was scanning the area, his gaze narrowed and focussed.

The red glow had diminished enough to bleach a lot of the colour from the sea and sky and the daylight was strengthening by the minute, but he could see the glow well enough to pinpoint the location of the eruption. He turned in a three-hundred-and-sixty-degree circle, trying to feel whether there was any wind. Even a small breeze would help keep them safe from the effects of ash or gas if they could move into it. They needed high ground, too. Not just to keep out of the way of a mud flow. The island wasn't that big. If they could get to more than one ridge, they would surely see the remains of the housing in the settlement area. Buildings that would be sheltering the injured people they had come here in order to help.

'This way,' he said decisively, moments later. 'Follow me.'

The going was rough.

Steep and densely forested, trying to navigate across this craggy, subtropical island was a daunting mission. It might only be twenty or so square kilometres in area, Becca thought, but if you added the distances from rock-strewn gullies to surprisingly high ridges it was probably ten times as big.

Her legs were nowhere near as long as Jet's and the steps he seemed to take with ease were a difficult scramble for her, especially with the lumpy bag of supplies she had under her uninjured arm. And trying to suck in enough oxygen through a now sweat-soaked surgical mask.

It seemed crazy to be still wearing the masks. Totally incongruous that the sun was out, filtering down through the lush forest of palm trees they were currently climbing through. A breeze from the sea, now well behind them, was ruffling the palm fronds high above their heads but, unfortunately, it wasn't getting down to ground level. Becca was getting hotter and hotter, toiling behind Jet up the side of what felt like a sizeable mountain.

Her head ached, her arm hurt and she was extremely thirsty. How long had they been walking? An hour? Two, maybe. Jet was showing no sign of slackening his pace and Becca certainly wasn't going to be the first to suggest a break. She'd keep going, dammit. She'd show him that she could keep up. That she was as tough as she needed to be, like she'd claimed.

He wasn't talking to her and, for that, Becca was grateful. Not just because talking would have made it even harder to keep her oxygen level up. Did Jet share the weird feeling that they weren't alone on this journey?

That Matt's ghost was walking between them?

Oh…help… Becca needed to change the direction of her thoughts. Desperately.

'Hey…Jet?'

The response took several steps to come.

'Yep?' He didn't turn his head and he sounded vaguely surprised, as though he'd forgotten he wasn't alone. Was this the soldier in Jet? Totally focussed on the mission and nothing else? If so, it was a new side to this man. He'd always been very aware of those around him. Too aware, in some ways, able to pick up on things that people might have otherwise left unsaid. Becca didn't think he'd changed that much and that awareness was a more likely scenario. He was deliberately trying to blot out her presence because he would prefer her not to be here with him.

Well…tough.

'Do you think we really need to keep these masks on?'

Another short silence fell as Jet appeared to consider her query.

'The air looks fine.' Becca almost stumbled as she took her eyes off the ground to look up at the bright green canopy of palm fronds. The bright flash of a bird she didn't recognise flicked past and she could hear the calls of countless others around them. Patches of vivid blue could be seen and Becca couldn't help giving an incredulous huff of sound. 'It looks like such a gorgeous day.'

'Yeah…' Jet's tone was wry. 'We're lucky. The eruption's obviously over, for the moment at least, and we've got a good breeze behind us. Any volcanic ash is being blown towards the other side of the island. I'm hoping the settlement's on this side, as well.' He tugged at his mask. 'You're right. Let's ditch them. We've got more if we need them later.'

'Later' was like a piece of string. It could be any length at all. At least it felt slightly easier to breathe without the covering of fabric on her face.

'It's a shame the coast was too rough to get around.'

'Seemed like a good idea to get to higher ground and a bit farther away from the volcano.'

'How long do you reckon it'll take us to get to the others?'

'We're nearly at the top of this ridge. I'll tell you then.' He glanced over his shoulder. 'You OK to keep going for a bit?'

She wasn't, but something in his tone suggested he'd stop if she needed to, despite the urgency of his next goal. It made her want to ignore the aches that were getting bone deep and carry on. For his sake.

'I'm good' was all she said.

On they went. And up. Until, finally, the ground became less steep. The trees thinned and the landscape was changing. Becca recognised splashes of red amongst dark green grey foliage.

'Good grief. Pohutukawa trees. I feel almost at home.'

Jet didn't seem to be interested in the botanical features of this island. He did seem to be listening to something, however.

'Hear that?'

'What…the birds?'

'No…sounds like water.'

Suddenly Becca was thirstier than she'd ever been in her life. And hotter. A mirage-like image swam into her head. A mountain stream. A waterfall and a deep, still pool in front of it. She'd rip her clothes off and dive right in. Oh…she could almost feel the deliciously icy embrace of that water on her naked body.

And Jet would peel off his clothes and dive in right after her. He'd be submerged and she'd wonder where he was until she felt a tug on her ankle and squeaked in fright. He'd come up then, laughing…and then he'd pull her into his arms and…

Laughing? Jet?

What an absurd flight of fancy. A real smile had always been at the top end of his happiest expressions. Laughing was far too joyous a sound to associate with Jet Munroe.

Had that always been part of the attraction? A recognition of an intensity that was part of her own soul? If so, they'd be the worst possible combination of personalities, wouldn't they? They'd probably fight like demons.

Or make love with a passion other people only dreamed of finding.

'Here.' Jet's voice broke into her wild fantasy ride like a bomb exploding. 'Let's stop.'

How had she not registered the increase in that sound? There *was* a waterfall. A fairly small one and there was no pool to dive into but at this moment it was almost a relief. The water bounced and splashed over rocks before disappearing downwards.

'Where's it coming from? Aren't we on the top of this ridge?'

'There's a higher ridge. See? It's like a stairway and we're on a bit of tread here.'

Peering through the trees, Becca realised she could see more greenery instead of sky in the direction Jet was pointing. It wasn't a matter of a flattish hike and then heading upwards again, however. The disappearance of the stream revealed that a gully lay between this ridge and the next slope. How deep was it? Would they have to scramble right back to sea level and start climbing again?

It was enough of a setback to feel almost like defeat.

It could take them days to reach their goal. They might get there and find the other occupants of the island had already been rescued by ship. Would they think to send a search party for herself and Jet or assume they had gone down with the helicopter into the sea?

Becca sank down, still clutching her bag of supplies. Jet had put the life pack down. He eased the straps of the pack off his shoulders, arched his back to stretch it and then strode towards the stream.

The fact that he didn't even look tired made Becca feel even worse. The only muscles she had the strength to use right now were attached to her eyes and they didn't have to move much to watch what Jet was doing.

He scooped up handfuls of water and splashed them onto his face. He raked his fingers through his hair and used another handful to rub the back of his neck.

'That feels better,' he said in a satisfied tone. He turned his head, eyebrows raised in unmistakeable invitation. 'You should try it.'

'Mmm.' Her legs felt like putty as she tried to get up again.

Could she blame her weakness purely on exhaustion or did it have something to do with the image of Jet like that, with his hair in tousled spikes as though he'd just stepped out of a shower? With an invitation glimmering in his eyes...

He was in front of her now. Extending a hand to help her to her feet.

'I wouldn't drink it yet,' he said. 'I've got some sterilising tablets it might be prudent to use.'

The hand was irresistible despite the insistent voice in Becca's head that told her ignore it and show him she was more than capable of leaping to her feet unaided. The grip was firm and warm and the upward tug made it so easy to stand up. Some of that heavy disappointment that they were still so far from their goal ebbed away. The touch of Jet's hand was like being plugged into a current of strength. A power source.

The cold water felt wonderful, even when it trickled down her neck and into her flight suit. She splashed again and again as Jet filled a specially designed bag with water and added a tablet. He set it on a rock to process and Becca sat beside it to rest.

'I've never broached the survival kit in this pack before,' he told her. 'It's got a lot of useful-looking bits in it.'

She leaned forward to look. 'Like what?'

'These water-purification pills. A good multi-tool. A lighter for getting a fire going. And...let's see what's in here...' He unzipped another waterproof pouch.

'We won't need a fire.'

Jet made a noncommittal sound. 'We'll have to see

how far we get by nightfall. Don't think we want to be climbing near cliffs in the dark.'

So he was also thinking it could take them a long time to reach the settlement. He wasn't at all defeated by the prospect, though. He was simply thinking in terms of coping with it. Dealing with whatever obstacles presented themselves.

Becca could do that, too.

'Don't suppose there's any chocolate in there?'

'Something even better. Muesli bars.' Jet held up a foil-wrapped bar. 'Might be a bit stale.'

'It'll be great. Thanks.' Becca took the bar but didn't open it. 'I need a drink first, I think. Right now I'm so dry I wouldn't have enough spit to swallow anything.'

Jet held the bag up to the light and examined the contents. 'Should be done. There's a valve at the bottom. Pull it out and suck on it. Like a drink bottle.'

It was the most delicious liquid Becca had ever tasted.

'Take it slowly,' Jet advised. 'Don't skull.'

With the intention of giving him a scathing glance to let him know she knew what she was doing, Becca let her gaze drift sideways as she kept drinking. She was startled to find him staring at her intently, his expression unreadable. Her thirst suddenly slaked, she lowered her arm and handed the bag over to him.

'I'll fill it up again before we head off,' Jet said, accepting the bag. 'There'll be more later.'

She found herself watching him drink just as intently as he'd watched her. The way the muscles in his throat rippled as he swallowed. The way his lips were closed around the valve that her own lips had been touching only moments ago.

She should be getting used to this odd, unsettling sensation deep in her gut but it was getting stronger. What had Jet been thinking as he'd watched *her* drink?

And why did she have to be remembering that kiss yet again?

He'd been astonished. She'd read that in the tension in his lips instantly. Had relived it too many times in the weeks that had followed. But she'd also relived the sure knowledge that the surprise hadn't been unpleasant. His lips had softened. Shaped themselves to hers and moved with what felt like the same kind of wonder she'd been feeling in every cell. The sheer magic that sparkled into existence and had been just about to explode when they'd both heard the sound of Matt's voice in the hallway.

Becca ducked her head as she felt the heat in her cheeks. She busied herself unwrapping the muesli bar.

'I hope you've got dinner tucked away in there,' she said lightly. 'Just in case we do end up stuck out here for the night.'

Spending a night with Jet. Who would have thought? Becca didn't dare look up to meet his gaze because she knew he was watching her.

'Does that worry you?' he asked, a long moment later.

Was he kidding?

'No,' she lied. 'Not really.'

The silence hung between them like an unexploded bomb. Becca searched swiftly for something that she could use to defuse it.

'I did a survival course as part of my pilot training,' she offered. 'I can build a pretty good snow cave.'

'Useful.'

'I can make a brush shelter, too.'

'How 'bout a tree hut?'

That earned a glare. She was being at least partially serious here. Did he have to try and make her feel like a child again? That teasing note in his voice. Talking about things like Snakes and Ladders…tree huts…

'In case you hadn't noticed,' she snapped, 'I'm all grown up now, Jet.'

He still had a hint of a smile playing with his mouth but his eyes darkened perceptibly and became very serious.

'Oh…I've noticed all right.'

It was just as well Becca had finished her muesli bar because her throat tightened to the point where it would have been impossible to swallow anything without choking. It was hard to breathe, even.

It took her back to that kiss again. To the tiniest moment when they'd peeled their lips from each other's. A graze of eye contact that had lasted less than a heartbeat but she'd known the attraction had been mutual.

He might have denied it and ignored her. It might have been apparently destroyed by what had happened later, but it had been there.

It was there again now.

She couldn't look away. This was far more than an acknowledgment that she was an adult. A woman.

He was letting her know that she was a desirable woman.

That *he* desired her.

It was a moment she'd once dreamed of but now it was here and there was no way she could go there. It was way too complicated. Too painful. It *wasn't* going to happen…

Forcing herself to look away from Jet finally, Becca

stared over his shoulder. Eyes narrowed but focussing on nothing. Simply trying to breathe evenly. Trying to gather up what felt like fragments of herself and put them back into some semblance of order.

Jet's voice seemed to come with the breeze that was making her skin prickle.

'Yeah…he's here,' Jet murmured softly. 'He always is.'

CHAPTER FIVE

THE second time she stumbled, Jet was close enough to turn and catch her.

'You want to stop again?'

'No. Not yet.'

It had taken them at least two hours to go as far as they could along the top of that first ridge. Now they were heading down into a gully and Jet reckoned that when they reached the next ridge they should be able to see the other side of the island and pinpoint their destination.

'Ditch the bag. You'll be able to keep your balance better without it.'

Becca shook her head. She'd carried it this far. She wasn't about to give up now despite how badly her arm was aching. 'You'll need the supplies.'

'They've probably got all that stuff in the first-aid kit at the station.'

'If it's not buried under rubble or mud or something.'

Something like molten lava? Their journey was bringing them closer to the volcano with every hour that passed. The blue sky had been left behind and it was a dense grey above the tree canopy and mountaintops now. Cloud or ash? The air still felt clear enough that they hadn't put masks back on yet.

Jet merely grunted in response, turning and moving on again. He had the harder job by far, choosing the path they were taking and pushing through any undergrowth. He got to test the footing, as well, and more than once a rock or rotten branch had proved unstable. Becca was sure she'd seen him limping for a while after one such incident and he seemed slightly more cautious now.

'Watch your feet,' he instructed.

That was precisely what she did need to do. She had to keep her mind on the job instead of letting it endlessly circle back to that gobsmacking comment Jet had made so casually.

He's here. He always is.

So he *was* just as aware of Matt's ghost as she was. And not just because she was here. The matter-of-fact delivery of the statement had been spine-tingling. It had been more than ten years ago but Jet made it sound as if it was still as much a part of his everyday life as… breathing or something.

The really piercing effect of the words, however, had been the whisper of sadness behind them. For the first time, it occurred to Becca that maybe she hadn't been the one who'd been most affected by Matt's death. The assumption had seemed justified. He was her brother, for heaven's sake. He'd been the most important person in her life since she'd been old enough to realise that he'd cared more about her than her parents had.

But they'd both been sent to boarding school at the earliest possible age and holidays had seemed few and far between. By high school, Matt had been in Jet's company day and night for months at a time. Well before the end of their schooling, they had been spending holidays as well as term time together. They had been inseparable so for the past ten years of Matt's life Jet had spent far more time with Matt than she had. And they had chosen their friendship, not had it there automatically because of family ties.

It was—astonishingly—conceivable that Jet had loved Matt just as much as she had.

That he'd been just as devastated by losing him.

She'd never allowed him that, had she? It hadn't even occurred to her when she'd blamed him for Matt's death. When she'd told him she hated him and never wanted to see him again.

She'd been wrong.

Just those few words and the eddies of emotion well below their surface had told her that. So convincingly it was impossible to stop thinking about them. Or to stop tears welling occasionally that were more than enough to blur her vision and make her miss her footing.

No one else in the world would have that connection. Even Max and Rick, while welded into the unit the four of them had made, had been a step removed. It was she and Jet who had been the closest to Matt and this new insight told Becca that Jet would understand how much the tragedy had affected her life. Still affected it.

How much else did they share as a legacy? The addiction to an adrenaline rush, perhaps, because it felt so good to still be alive when it was over?

Or maybe, like her, Jet's heart was walled off from loving someone enough to make them a life partner because it was safer than risking having them ripped away from you.

Talking to Jet about such intimate things was not

going to happen. Even if she was prepared to expose her own soul, she knew that he never would. Not to anyone, probably, and certainly not to her.

Maybe he found it just as painful to be in her company as she had in his because of the memories it picked open.

Had. She'd put that thought into the past tense. Had something changed that much because she felt guilty about how she'd treated Jet back then?

Oh…yes.

'I'm sorry.'

'What?'

Dear Lord, had she actually made that apology aloud? No wonder Jet was scowling back at her over his shoulder. She couldn't tell him what she was really apologising for. Not yet, when she still needed time to get her own head around this shift in perspective.

'I'm…not keeping up very well. Slowing you down.'

'You're doing great.'

'You could leave me somewhere, you know…and send a search party after the ship arrives.' Becca could hear her voice trailing off. The thought of being left alone and watching Jet walking out of her life again made her feel astonishingly desolate.

His huff of sound was reassuringly dismissive. 'Not going to happen, babe. Even if I have to carry you.'

The thought of being carried in his arms to safety was the flip side of the coin with desolation on it. Happiness. Bliss, even? Becca didn't want to try and analyse that reaction.

'We'd better get there before the ship arrives or they might leave without us.'

'Why would they do that?'

'They might think we crashed into the sea and drowned.'

'If the emergency locator beacon was functioning, they'd see that we reached the island coastline. Plus I sent a message.'

'Really? When? How?'

'You were unconscious. There was a light flickering on the radio panel before it got too swamped with seawater. I sent a mayday. I also relayed that we were going to head for the settlement.'

'Oh…that's great.' Becca half crouched to slide down a steep bank between trees. Jet had paused at the bottom and was holding out a hand in case she needed help. She didn't, but when she stood up straight again she was very close to him and she looked up.

'Well done, you, on trying the radio. That makes me feel much better.' Her lips curled into a smile. 'Thank you.'

'Hey…no worries.' He was smiling back at her. 'I was looking out for my own skin, as well, you know. I'm not here purely as your guardian angel.'

It felt like he was. He had pulled her from the wreckage. Tended to her wounds. Was prepared to carry her through the jungle and across mountains if she couldn't make it alone.

She owed him a lot more than simply an apology for assumptions and accusations made so long ago.

Her head bent, as though weighed down with the heaviness of obligation, Becca trudged in Jet's wake and did her utmost to keep up with him and not slow him down too much.

* * *

Something had changed.

Somewhere in the gruelling trek they had been on for so many hours, the atmosphere had changed between them. It had been a gradual thing, a bit like the way the forest species changed from the palm trees to the pohutukawas or the way the sky had clouded over and the air temperature had dropped. Imperceptible while it was happening but suddenly you could see the difference.

Jet had become aware of the change in the moment Becca had smiled and thanked him because that smile had reached right into her eyes and made them glow with a warmth he'd never thought he'd see in her face again.

He could feel that smile touch places inside him that he'd forgotten existed but there was a poignancy in the sensation that made it almost physically painful. The pain was welcome in a way. It spurred him on as he led the way down the gully. Pushing on and ignoring the edges of exhaustion and the real physical pain in his ankle that was getting steadily worse. Thinking about Becca and that smile was an excellent distraction.

A window back in time. To a place where life had been as good as it got. The future had promised everything and more because, for the first time in his life, Jet had felt secure in a family unit.

And Becca had been a big part of that unit. A bright, feisty kid who was becoming an extraordinarily beautiful woman who thought he was the second most wonderful person on earth.

Man, he'd loved that. Right from the start, when he'd seen how lonely she was, there'd been a huge gap in her life that he'd fitted into perfectly. That very first holiday.

when Matt had taken him home to the Harding estate, the parents had been absent the whole time. Off on some conference in Egypt, apparently, that had included a cruise down the Nile and had been too good an opportunity to pass up despite the fact that it had covered the entire school holiday period.

Becca and Matt had clearly been used to being under the care of paid staff like the housekeeper, cook and groundsmen. The vast house had an equally grand setting with stables where Becca's pony had been kept, both an indoor and outdoor swimming pool, a home theatre and full-sized pool table in the games room. There had been trail bikes for the boys to play on in the surrounding countryside that had sparked the passion for motorbikes that had been the catalyst that had brought the 'bad boys' together.

Paradise for a teenage boy, in fact, as well as a chance to sample all the good things in life that Jet had only envied from a distance until then but, even as a confused and probably sullen adolescent, Jet had sensed the real gift he was being given.

Friendship and family.

The sense of belonging.

Of being looked up to as someone who mattered. Someone that people really cared about.

It had never been a hardship, giving up hours that could have been spent on the bikes or perfecting a game of snooker to entertain that small girl. Being teased had been a whole new experience for Jet. Being manipulated in a very unsubtle manner because someone was so determined to spend time in his company had been a pleasure all in itself. He'd learned to tease Becca back as he'd followed Matt's lead. They would spin the process out until nudging the boundaries of causing an upset but they would always capitulate. And she had always known they would.

At school, the bond had been with the three other boys and Jet had always watched their backs. Prepared to fight anything or anyone that threatened what was important to them.

Away from school that bond had been between him, Matt and Becca.

Fierce loyalty and an utter contentment when they'd been together.

He wouldn't have called it love. Maybe he wouldn't now, even. It certainly wasn't the soppy, warm-fuzzy stuff that most people associated with the emotion. It was more like a life force. Like…sunlight and rain. You could survive without them but when they were there, things grew and blossomed and life was an oasis instead of a barren wasteland.

The downward slope of the gully was levelling out. Soon they would start climbing again and Jet's instincts told him they were getting much closer to their target. Whether they could reach it before dark was another matter. They'd need to stop soon and drink something. Put their masks back on, too, because he could feel a change in the air they were breathing. Soon. But not quite yet because he wasn't ready to concentrate on the present. He needed to gather up the random shreds of memory and reaction and file them safely away.

It wasn't as though he didn't still have a measure of that life force in his life. He got it from Max and Rick and now there were others contributing. Ellie and Sarah and the kids. Baby Mattie and Sarah's boy, Josh. Jet wouldn't have admitted it in a million years but the addition of those kids to his inner circle of people was magic. The same kind of window back in time that Becca's smile represented. But now that he'd seen it again, he realised they were just a pale imitation of the real thing.

And that was why it was causing this peculiar pain. Because you couldn't go back in time. You couldn't change something as fundamental as the destruction of hero status and being sacked from the position of being the most important person to someone. As he had been by being blamed for Matt's death.

Becca had spent more than ten years blaming him. Hating him.

Why on earth would he think that one smile might mean that had changed? It wasn't the memory that was painful at all, was it? It was hope that her opinion of him had changed and that he could find his way back to that feeling of family. Hope that he knew would get crushed if he gave it any credibility.

He didn't even stop when the level ground was being left behind and a new and even tougher climb presented itself. It wasn't that he was trying to punish Becca.

He was punishing himself. For hoping.

Daylight was beginning to fade but Becca barely noticed.

She was numb to everything but the need to keep putting one foot in front of the other and breathe often enough to keep the burning sensation in her chest to a minimum. Taking her sunglasses off would help but the air felt gritty now and her eyes stung. Jet had produced fresh masks for them both when they'd stopped to drink the last of the bag of treated water a while back.

For ever ago. Becca had long since given up trying to keep any track of time. Her brain was as numb as her body but she kept going because if she didn't, Jet would pick her up and carry her and he had to be already hurting as much as she was. He was definitely limping and she'd seen the way he'd frozen for a moment to shut his eyes and deal with pain when he'd taken too much weight on that foot climbing over a rock not so long ago.

She'd have to see if she could help by strapping it up or something when they finally stopped.

If they ever stopped. Surely they were close to the top of this ridge by now. They might see the settlement building then and it would be stupid to waste hours waiting for daylight if they were within visual range of the people who needed them. The need wasn't one-sided, either. She and Jet badly needed the closest thing to civilisation on this island. They needed water and food and rest.

A place they could be rescued from along with everyone else.

Staying upright and continuing to move was more than an extreme challenge now. Becca slipped on something loose. Or maybe her legs just gave way. She had to grab at a scrubby bush for a handhold but that was loose, too, and it came away in her hand.

The whole bank seemed to be shivering. Moving. Becca was on her hands and knees. She lost her grip on the bag of supplies and items were spilling out and bouncing away down the slope. Clean, white bandages in their plastic wrappings seemed to glow in the gathering dusk. A loud, roaring sound increased and Becca was sure it was inside her head. She was about to faint, having gone past the physical limits she could push herself to.

Being gripped by her upper arms and hauled to her feet was unbearable.

'No! Just leave me, Jet. *You* go.'

Jet made no verbal response that she could hear. He was dragging Becca, having abandoned the life pack.

Incredibly, the roaring sound got even louder and the night became a living thing—moving and breathing around them. And then the light changed, flooded with an unearthly, red glow.

Something crashed into the trees nearby.

Jet's oath was spine-chilling. He was moving faster and Becca was struggling not to fall again.

'Jet...'

'Move, Becca. We've got to find shelter. That was a rock.'

Another crashing sound came. The crunch of rock on rock. A burst of sparks and the strong smell of scorching.

Much later, Becca would marvel how much difference a burst of adrenaline could make. Muscles she'd thought were useless suddenly came back to life. Her thinking snapped into coherency.

The volcano was erupting again. Hurling missiles into the sky that were landing around them. Lethal weapons, some of which were probably the size of a small car.

Because they were close to the top of this ridge, any cover they might have had from dense forest was gone. Trees were sparse here and bare, rocky formations offered no kind of shelter.

Or did they?

'There.' Becca tugged on Jet's hand, only now realis-

ing that they were joined by a determined grip on each other. 'Under the rocks.'

This bank of rock had an overhang. Not enough to call itself a cave but more than enough to shelter two people from airborne missiles. Maybe.

They were there within seconds and only just in time to save themselves from a shower of small rocks landing within metres of them. Some seemed to explode on hitting the rocks well above them and the sound and light show from the sparks made it all seem like some grotesque fireworks display.

Or how you would imagine the end of the world to look.

Another earthquake shook the ground beneath their feet with a vicious jolt and Becca cried out in fear. They were about to die. Both of them.

I'm sorry.

Jet gathered the terrified bundle that was Becca into his arms and his only conscious thought was the awareness of a deep shame.

Not that it was a shame his life was going to end like this, in the shadow of an exploding volcano. It wasn't a bad way to go for someone who'd lived on the edge for so long. He might have chosen it, in fact. A sudden death in the midst of a dangerous adventure. Mind you, if he'd chosen it, he would have timed it a bit better.

Like when he was in his nineties, maybe.

No. The shame came from a sense of failure that he wasn't able to protect Becca and keep her safe.

He was failing Matt.

He was failing Becca.

Most of all, he was failing himself.

He wrapped his arms tightly around her and turned so that it would be his back that got any impact first. He used one hand to cradle her head against his shoulder, letting her bury her face so she wouldn't see what was happening. He even curled over her protectively, resting his temple on the top of her head. Both their masks had been ripped off somehow in the past minute or two and when he turned ever so slightly, he could press his lips against her hair.

He told himself he was comforting her but he knew he needed the comfort himself just as badly. He didn't want to die, dammit. Life was too precious and he still had too much he needed to do. And learn. New things to discover that he might not even know existed yet.

Like this…this incredible sensation of holding Becca that was unlike anything he'd ever experienced with a woman in his arms. This was so astonishingly…tender. No wonder he'd never gone looking for it. The sensation seeped into every cell of his body and made him feel curiously…raw.

Vulnerable?

No. He might have an excuse for letting the volcano do that to him but Jet Munroe didn't do vulnerable. He'd learned not to at a very early age. Probably when he'd been a grubby kid with scabby knees and strangers had been telling him that his mother was gone but that they'd find some nice people to look after him instead.

If he thought of the shape he was holding as simply a frightened woman and not Becca, he might be able to lose that unpleasant sensation that was almost fear. It was OK to be afraid of the natural disaster occurring in the physical world but, if he was going to really protect himself, he had to back away from whatever explosions were happening somewhere in his mind. Or was it his heart?

She was a woman. A virtual stranger now, thanks to the years apart they'd had. But part of her was still the girl he remembered. The bond was still there and that made it impossible to simply let go.

And then Becca's arms stole around his waist and she squeezed him back, pressing her body tightly against his. She twisted her head to look up at him and because he was so close, with his lips on her hair, he ended up with his mouth only centimetres from hers.

She was looking straight into his eyes and whatever rational thoughts he was trying desperately to cling to shattered and vanished.

This was *Becca*.

And she was beautiful.

And he wanted her. He *needed* her.

Kissing her wasn't any kind of conscious action. It was the result of proximity. Of senses stretched to breaking point by what could very well be the last minutes of life.

Most of all, by sheer inevitability.

This had always been meant to happen.

Reality faded the instant his lips touched hers.

The nightmare became a dream. The culmination of many, many dreams, in fact. All the longing, the desire, the *love* that had been buried for so long came rushing back with the same kind of force that was still sending fiery missiles to land far too close to this precarious shelter.

It was a dream but it was real, too. The scratch of Jet's unshaven face. The incredible softness of his lips.

The way his hands cradled her head as though she was the most precious thing on earth.

They were both filthy. Battered and bruised and sweaty and so exhausted it felt like being drunk, but none of that mattered at all. This was about...*life*.

Not just surviving. It went deeper than that. It was beginnings instead of endings. Wiping out a barrier that should never have been there. One that had walled off what was probably the most important part of being alive.

There had only ever been one man for Rebecca Harding and she was holding him at last. Touching him. Able to offer herself without the slightest hesitation or doubt.

The kiss was hungry. As though they were both tasting something they had wanted but been denied for ever. As soon as the pressure eased even a fraction, the contact was snatched back and deepened. Becca clutched at Jet's head, torn between gasping for air and being unable to tear her mouth from his.

And it wasn't enough. She pressed her body against his, wanting...what? To slip inside his skin? To be *inside* him?

No. She wanted him to be inside *her*. As physically close as it was possible for two people to become. It had to happen. This wanting was so powerful, she would shatter if it didn't happen. Dragging her hands from his head, totally unaware of any pain in her arm or anywhere else in her body, Becca fumbled for the fastenings of his jacket. Pulling it open so that she could find and touch bare skin.

He caught both her hands and held them hard. Stopping her progress. Did he not want this? Shocked, Becca looked up only to find the heat in the dark eyes so close to hers was just as wild as the fire inside herself. He did want this. As much as she did. He was just checking. Seeking permission to kick away any traces of a barrier.

In answer, Becca reached up to touch his face, running her fingers softly over his lips. She closed her eyes and tilted her head back. Offering him her throat. Sending her desire though her fingertips.

His lips were on her neck in a heartbeat. His hands unzipping her flight suit and peeling it back. They slipped underneath the T-shirt she had on and pushed her bra up so they could cup her breasts, his thumbs soft against nipples that felt as hard as metal.

The cry that carried over the roar of sound around them was unrecognisable and yet Becca knew it had come from herself. She was lost in pleasure so sharp it hurt. Desperate for more. To give as well as receive.

A low growl of sound that blended with the roar of the volcano came from Jet as her hands found their way beneath his clothing and touched what they were seeking. Maybe the sounds and the heat came from beyond this shelter but it seemed unlikely and Becca didn't care.

She gave herself up to ecstasy and the world outside simply stopped turning.

One day, he might look back and joke about the most explosive sexual encounter he'd ever had but laughter had no place in the aftermath of the unleashed passion that had just occurred.

Mother Nature seemed to be in tune with them. When

Jet realised that the edges of paradise were blurring and eased himself gently from inside Becca, the night was very dark. Any glow from burning lava was gone. The eruption seemed to be over.

The roar of sound was gone, too, and it was suddenly so quiet he could hear Becca swallow. He could hear the rasp of the material her suit was made of as she unwrapped her legs and arms from around his body and moved to straighten her clothing.

The sense of loss was surprisingly sharp. Jet moved, too, to lessen its impact. He followed her example and tidied his clothing. Not that he had to do much. How on earth had they managed to have sex like that when they had been virtually still fully clothed?

The silence seemed to grow. He should say something. But what? He knew Becca was watching him but he avoided her gaze while he tried to think of something he could say. Anything. Unfortunately, the words pounding in his head right now were not any he could release.

He had just made love to his best mate's little sister. *What would Matt think?*

Maybe Becca would know what to say. She was grown up. Tough. She could handle anything, couldn't she?

Apparently not this. She was fully dressed again, sitting with her knees drawn up and her arms wrapped around them.

'Do you think it's over?'

'The eruption?'

He wasn't quick enough to avoid direct eye contact this time. The message couldn't have been plainer. He was an idiot. Of course she was talking about the eruption.

They both knew that what had just happened between them wasn't over.

Not by a long shot.

CHAPTER SIX

MOVING on was the right thing to do.

Jet would have been compelled to do *something*, in any case, given that the alternative was to stay there in the silence. With Becca.

With the knowledge that he'd opened the most enormous can of worms and he had no idea what he wanted to do about that.

The warning in that look on her face had been redundant. They had so much unfinished business between them, it would probably never be over. They'd made no attempt to discuss any of the issues of the past and now they had complicated it all to the nth degree by…having sex.

Was that all it had been? A wild coupling in the face of unbearable stress? A safety valve that had gone off because of too much pressure?

He was too tired and too shaken to be able to think about any of it. He could see the worms. Impossibly tangled threads. Memories of events and their associated emotions, some of which he'd never dared try to analyse. The sex had been like a giant, emotional can opener and now it was threatening to do his head in completely.

Jet knew how to deal with such an overwhelming

threat. He switched it off. Simple. It could all go into the 'too hard' basket for now. There would be time enough to debrief at some later, more appropriate time. If Becca would even concede having a conversation that involved the past, of course. What had she said?

Keep your memories to yourself.

The past was a no-go area. Whether they had a future at all was still in the lap of the gods. So the present was it for the moment, and Jet could deal with that.

'I've got a torch in my pack. I'm going to get to the top of the ridge and have a look around. Stay here and I'll come back for you.'

But Becca shook her head. 'I'll come, too.'

Any appreciation of how tough she was had been switched off, as well. Jet was in soldier mode. On a mission.

'Fine.'

Becca gave a terse nod. 'Can I use the torch for a minute? I'll go and see if I can retrieve some of that stuff I dropped when the eruption started.'

He went with her but they could only find the life pack and about half of what the bag had originally contained.

'We're wasting time,' Jet decided. 'It doesn't matter.'

There was a strong smell of sulphur in the air so they dampened masks with saline and put them on. Jet sacrificed a crêpe bandage and they wrapped a layer over the masks for extra protection. The sunglasses weren't going to be enough for their eyes but there wasn't much he could do about that.

'I'll keep some saline in my pocket. We can flush our eyes every so often. It might help.'

'Getting out of here would help,' Becca muttered. 'A lot.'

Once they were moving, it was easier to leave what had just happened between them behind. When they reached the ridge and could see the flames of a camp-fire that had to have been built by people, it was all but forgotten. They had an achievable goal and it was the destination they had been struggling to get to for far too many hours already.

'We'll go slowly,' Jet said. 'We should be able to keep away from any lava if it's got this far.'

There were trickles of fire to be seen well above them, trailing down from the glow that was the centre of the volcano. The air was thick and Jet couldn't decide whether his pounding headache and the vague fogginess in his head were due to his injury, his exhaustion or toxic fumes.

'How are *you* feeling?' he asked Becca a few minutes later. 'Physically, I mean,' he added in a silence that felt awkward.

'I've been better.' Her voice was muffled by the covering of mask and bandage but, even so, the tone was wry. 'Don't worry about me, Jet. I'll cope.'

She would, too.

Whose game was it now? Jet wondered as he led her downhill for the last time. Whose rules would have to be followed? If he wanted to continue playing at all, that was. It was a moot point. For the foreseeable future, he had no choice.

They reached what remained of the conservation work-ers' settlement within a couple of hours.

The small group of people sitting around the fire

watched their approach in stunned silence. Becca stared back. She tried to smile but realised it didn't matter that she couldn't because her face was hidden anyway. It was completely overwhelming. Seeing these people. Smelling hot food. Knowing that—maybe within hours—a ship would be arriving at this location to rescue them all.

Knowing that survival was a real possibility now. If she hadn't been so convinced that her world was coming to an end, would she have given in to that passionate desire for Jet? Would it have been unleashed at all?

The time since then had been surreal. She'd been in a strange, trance-like state where she'd still been able to feel exactly what it had been like when Jet had touched her. She could still taste his kisses. Feel him inside her. Hear his breath and the thump of his heartbeat. She could stay in that incredible moment when she'd felt... *whole* for the first time in her life.

It had kept her going. It had made the difficulties of the downward climb seem insignificant. It had made her forget about the parts of her body that cried out for rest. To begin with, at least, she'd been happy not to break the trance by talking. She'd wanted to keep it untarnished by any cliché or regret. But then the lack of communication had started to bite and the longer it went on, the more it strengthened the notion that, as far as Jet was concerned, it seemed like it had never happened. Had it just been a way to pass the time until they could get moving again? What on earth was he thinking about what had happened? About her?

In those few seconds of standing there, staring at the group of people that represented their return to the real world, Becca was snapped well out of any remnants of that trance. The thought that she and Jet might have to talk about what they'd done was both terrifying and inevitable. How could they not talk about it? But how could they talk about it without talking about everything else from the past?

Maybe the opportunity had already gone, anyway. They weren't alone any more.

Becca tried to say something in greeting to these people but that failed as much as the smile had. Her throat was too tight. She'd be able to blame the quality of the air for that. Or sheer exhaustion. If tears escaped, she could use the same excuses.

Jet didn't seem to be anything like as affected as she was, which only added weight to the fear that none of it had meant that much to him.

'Sorry we're a bit late, folks.' He was easing the pack off his back to put it down beside the life pack. 'Had a bit of a hiccup with the landing.'

'Oh, my God...' A woman stood up and came towards them. 'We knew you were due to arrive when the eruption happened this morning. We were sure there'd been an accident and that...you wouldn't have survived.' She was peering at them more closely. Taking in the wound on Jet's forehead and Becca's bandaged arm. '*Are* you OK?'

'A drink of water would be very welcome,' Jet responded. 'And then fill me in on what's needed here.'

Becca saw other people starting to move. Someone was bringing them water bottles.

'You must be hungry,' someone else said. 'We've been cooking sausages on the fire. It's nothing flash but there's plenty of bread and tomato sauce.'

Jet lowered his bottle and wiped a trickle of water

from his chin. 'Sounds awesome but save me some for later. I'm here for the patients.'

'Jack's the worst,' a young woman said, her voice hitching. 'He's…got a bad head injury. And Roger… his leg looks awful.'

'Jack's conscious,' the first woman put in. 'But he's not making much sense and he just wants to sleep.'

'Where is he?'

'Over there.'

Becca was beginning to realise why it was only a small group close to the fire. A tent-type shelter was off to one side and she could see people lying on the ground with others crouched over them. More people were over by the shadowy outline of a half-collapsed wooden building and sounds of hammering could be heard.

Jet was also scanning the area. He frowned at the sound of the hammering. 'You had people trapped, yes?'

'We got three of them out with only minor injuries, thank goodness. Adam's still stuck. His leg's caught badly. A couple of the guys are trying to shore things up to make it stable enough to saw through the beam that he's caught under.'

Jet's frown deepened. 'Do they know what they're doing?'

'Bruce is a qualified urban search and rescue technician. He's in charge.'

Jet nodded, clearly satisfied with the credentials. What would he have done if he wasn't? Becca wondered. Taken on an extrication task as well as patient management? Quite likely.

'Is Adam conscious?'

'Yes. He's in a lot of pain. We've got some pretty heavy-duty painkiller tablets here but they don't seem to have helped much.'

'I'll be able to deal with that.' Jet had his pack dangling by one hand. 'Jack and Roger had better be first on the list, though.' He waved his free hand at the life pack. 'Can someone bring that, please?' He was already heading towards the tent.

Becca had had a good drink of water. She shook her head at the sausage wrapped in bread that someone was offering her. It could wait. Picking up the life pack and following Jet might have been a kind of apology for losing most of that bag of extra supplies. Or maybe she simply wanted to be the one who helped him.

There were three people lying under the canvas awning. The area was well lit by kerosene lamps and the patients had blankets both underneath and on top of them. They even had pillows. Only one appeared to be unconscious and that had to be Jack. He had a bloodstained bandage around his head and a woman was sitting beside him, holding his hand.

'I'm Erica,' she introduced herself. 'I'm a nurse.'

'Excellent.' Jet unzipped his pack and started opening pockets. 'You can get me up to speed, Erica. I'm Jet Munroe, by the way. ED doctor and army medic. And this is Becca.'

Becca could see the way Erica drew in a deep breath, smiled and then released the breath in an audible sigh of relief. She nodded at Becca but the respect on her face increased noticeably as her gaze returned to Jet. If anyone could help Jack and the others, he could.

She put down the life pack, feeling a little out of place. Jet was a doctor. He had a nurse to assist him.

A young and rather attractive one at that. It had been many years since she had worked as either a nurse or an ambulance officer and her skills as a pilot were hardly going to be helpful here. There wasn't that much room in the tent so maybe she should go back to the fire and leave them to it. She could have something to eat except, strangely, she didn't feel at all hungry.

Nobody seemed to notice her taking a step back. And then another, until she found herself in a corner, where she sank down to sit, wrapping her arms around her knees. Exhaustion, and probably very low blood sugar, were making her feel spaced out. Oddly detached. As though she wasn't actually here at all. She was invisible. Floating above the scene and simply taking it in. She wasn't consciously watching or thinking about any of it, she was just there. Absorbing what she saw and how it made her feel.

Jet remembered to pull some gloves out from his pack and put them on. She saw him pause and look up as he pulled the second one in place. Looking for her? Because wearing gloves was a kind of personal joke now—a thread of new connection that had contributed to the resurrection of a much older and much stronger one? Or maybe he was just getting his head around where he needed to start work. The glance was brief, anyway, and didn't take in the direction that included where she was sitting so quietly. If he had thought of her at all, he'd probably assumed she'd done the sensible thing and gone to find some food and rest.

Which was exactly what she should be doing but she wasn't connected enough to her own body at the moment to make it happen. She watched Jet become the professional medic he was as he turned his attention to the injured people who needed him. The man with the bandaged head. Another with an injured leg. An older man who looked grey but had no obvious injuries to be seen. Jet talked to them. He laid his hands on them to examine their injuries. He pulled out gear and supplies to begin treating them.

He stuck electrodes on the first patient's chest and Becca could hear him quizzing Erica.

'How long was he unconscious for to begin with?

'Does he have any other injuries you've noticed?'

He cut away the remains of clothing around another young man's broken leg. Erica drew up the drugs he requested for pain relief and they talked about needing to straighten the limb. That would have to wait until he'd assessed the final patient here, the older man.

Utterly focussed, he managed to move with speed but it was obvious how thorough he was being. Becca had no idea how much time was passing as she sat there unnoticed. Maybe she even dozed for a while and some of her thoughts and impressions were a dream. About a doctor who was also a soldier. A real-life hero.

If these people were in any danger, Jet was the man to save them. They had known that back at headquarters, of course, and that was why they'd gone to the lengths of having him rushed to the rescue base by private plane.

But if he was so damn brilliant, why hadn't he saved Matt's life? Had he had the same abilities and skills as a newly qualified doctor? He must have had some of them. Maybe he just hadn't bothered using them on his best friend. Her brother.

The old anger was still there, wasn't it? Simmering not far beneath the surface. It made her feel more awake again and in a way it was almost comforting. Easier to accept than the wildly confusing feelings that had been aroused when Jet had been making love to her.

So Becca found herself nursing that old anger. Watching Jet with her eyes narrowed now, feeling even more detached from what was happening around her.

The nurse, Erica, was helping him. They were taking the blood pressure of the older man. Jet was putting in an IV line and Erica was hanging up a bag of fluids. Becca could hear the way they were talking to each other. Like trusted colleagues.

'What's his blood pressure now?'

'Gone up a bit. One-oh-five on sixty. I think we could give him a bit of morphine. Could you draw it up for me, please?'

'Sure.'

Her eagerness to help was almost palpable. So was how impressed she was by the man she was working with. Becca saw the way she was watching Jet's face as he injected the drug, rather than the patient or even the procedure.

What woman wouldn't be impressed?

Attracted?

What would Erica say if Becca told her that she'd had the best sex of her life with Jet during that last volcanic eruption? She might not believe her. Becca wasn't sure she believed it herself right now. Maybe she'd fallen down that slope and been knocked out again and it had all been wishful thinking.

She really needed to let go of that nebulous hope that Jet might have felt the same way she did. That them being together was written in the stars or something stupid like that. Watching Erica had just reminded her that Jet had always had, and probably always would have, women lining up wanting him. What on earth made her think she might stand out from the crowd? For old times' sake? Hardly, given that the 'old times' were too painful for them to even talk about.

Her exhaustion hit her full force now. Along with a wave of nausea. She had to get out of here and find some food and water. And some rest. Her vision was blurry. Perhaps that was why she didn't see Jet moving in her direction until he was crouched in front of her. Touching her hands.

'What are you doing in here?'

'Watching.'

'Oh…' Jet was frowning. He didn't understand. Becca wasn't sure she understood herself. Part of her had simply wanted to be near him. Another part was busy fanning the sparks of the old anger. It was all so confusing and she was too tired to think about it any more.

Jet's nod seemed to agree with her. He was too tired to pursue the matter.

He rubbed a hand wearily over his face. 'We've got things reasonably under control for the moment,' he said. 'Erica can keep watch. I'm going to go and check on Adam but it's time we both got some food and rest before we fall over.'

He helped Becca to her feet and led her outside. He disappeared into the half-demolished building for some time and she sat and waited anxiously, unable to eat until she saw him emerge safely.

'How is he?'

'Still trapped, but they've figured out a way of getting him out without collapsing the timbers around him. I've given him some pain relief and have some fluids running and I've told them to come and get me before they shift any of the weight. With a crush injury, he'll need careful management when he gets free. It won't be for a while yet, though.' Jet hunkered down beside Becca and nodded at a woman who was bringing them food. 'I've got time to take a break.'

They sat near the warmth of the fire and ate cold sausages wrapped in bread. They drank water. Someone even made them a hot cup of tea but then they were left alone. The people that weren't occupied with looking after the injured or helping with Adam's extrication had given in to exhaustion and were trying to get some sleep.

It felt like Becca and Jet were alone. Sitting in front of an open fire in the middle of nowhere and in the middle of the night. The driftwood flames flickered and hissed softly, sending out tendrils of comforting heat.

'Mmm,' Becca murmured. 'I love fires.'

Jet made a soft sound, half chuckle, half sigh. Poignant enough to make Becca turn her head to look at him directly. And then, of course, it was impossible to look away. Shadows played on his face, making the lines sharper and his eyes far too dark to read, but he was looking back at her and his lips had a shape that Becca knew all too well. An almost-smile. It sucked her in every time and brought her way too close. Into dangerous territory.

'What?' Her voice came out in a whisper.

Jet shrugged. 'I know how much you like fires, that's all. I lit your first one, didn't I?'

Oh…he was so right. In more ways than he would ever know. She'd told him to keep his memories to himself but this was different somehow. The memory of a happy time didn't seem so painful. Like the warmth and light of the fire they were sitting beside, it was oddly comforting.

Not that she was going to encourage it but she couldn't help thinking about it so she turned her head and stared into the flames to disguise her thoughts.

She'd been, what…nine or ten? It hadn't been the first time Jet had come home with Matt for a holiday. The boys had decided to camp out in the hills on a far boundary of the property and Becca had demanded to be allowed to accompany them.

The pup tent had been put up for her. Matt and Jet were going to sleep rough under the stars, like real outback men. They'd made a cairn of rocks and she'd helped to gather deadwood from the bush and there they'd been—just the three of them. Miles from anywhere, on a night so dark the stars had come alive, blazing like diamonds on black velvet. So cold that Becca had been shivering and so *big* that she'd been scared enough to think that maybe she'd bitten off more than she wanted to chew after all and she should have stayed home in her own bed. But then she'd experienced the thrill of those first flames leaping into the night.

'Do you still wish you were a boy?' Jet asked softly.

Oh…God. She had said that, hadn't she? Shouted it, actually, as she'd danced around the fire with a long stick, ready to poke the embers back into life if it was needed.

'I wish I was a boy.'

'Why?'

'Coz then I could light my own fires whenever I wanted to.'

The boys had rolled around laughing. It had seemed an eternity until they'd sobered enough to be serious.

'You'll be able to light as many fires as you want when you grow up.'

'Why do I have to wait that long?'

'Because you have to know how to control them. How to put them out if you need to. And you have to know the right places to light them or you can get into really big trouble.'

Becca could even remember the rider Jet had added when Matt had finished his brotherly advice.

'Fire's dangerous. Doing dangerous things can be exciting but it can also be wrong.'

She had her hand pressed to her mouth now, as the past somehow morphed into the present.

There'd been a kind of fire between them up on the mountain. More exciting than any she'd ever known.

Dangerous? Oh...yes. Why? Because it put her back into the place where she wanted to trust Jet. To offer him her heart. And that would make herself utterly vulnerable.

Wrong?

No. How could it have been wrong when it had felt so...right?

But maybe Jet felt otherwise. Becca slanted him a direct look.

'No,' she said quietly. 'I'm glad I'm not a boy.'

His face was very still and he waited a heartbeat before responding. 'Me, too.'

They were still staring at each other. He was telling her he didn't regret their lovemaking. Maybe even that he wanted more? The moment stretched and grew. A turning point. A suddenly terrifying one.

Becca's heart was pounding. She felt dizzy. The whole world was spinning. She had to look away from Jet. To try and catch something solid.

Hang on! The warning came from nowhere. A wordless fear. The same one she'd had in that moment on the beach when she'd thought Jet had been sucked into the sea along with the wreckage of the helicopter.

Don't fall. You'll crash and burn.

'I get to light my own fires anyway.' Her voice sounded odd. 'If I want to.'

Jet grunted. 'Of course you do. You're all grown up now.'

Becca was holding her breath. What would he say now? That they had a new connection that was all about being grown up? Being a man and a woman? That it was too powerful to ignore?

But Jet stretched and looked away from her. His breath came out in a sigh. 'Me, I just get to help put out the fires other people can't control.'

The moment had passed. They were back on safer ground now. Away from the past. Away from talking about what had happened between them or any connection they might have with each other. So he didn't want to talk about it. Or maybe the real truth was that he didn't even feel it.

That was more likely, given the way he'd been able to dismiss it and carry on as though nothing important had happened. At least it made it easier to hang on. Becca wasn't about to make herself look like a fool along with putting her heart at such risk. A fool who'd never got past a teenage crush.

She snorted softly at her own stupidity but managed to make it relevant to the conversation. 'Don't give me that, Jet Munroe. You light your own fires by choosing to go there. You love living dangerously.'

'Pot calling the kettle black, isn't it? Flying choppers for a living isn't exactly a quiet life.'

'So we're both adrenaline junkies. Nothing wrong with that, is there?'

'Hell, no.' Jet was smiling. 'Nothing like nearly getting killed to make you feel really alive, is there?'

It was Becca's turn to sigh. 'I'm not sure how alive I feel right now.'

Being able to relax for the first time since this day had gone so terribly wrong was making Becca aware of every ache in her body. She held up her left arm, flexing her fingers and then making a fist.

Jet grasping her hand was unexpected. Becca tried to pull free but the movement hurt and she sucked in her breath.

'It's got worse, hasn't it?'

'No.'

'Squeeze my fingers.'

Becca complied. This was a medical evaluation, wasn't it? Except…she made the mistake of looking up as she returned Jet's grip and suddenly the skin-to-skin contact was anything but professional.

Oh…Lord…

The depth in his eyes was disturbing. Had she really thought he was unaffected by the emotional side of what was happening here? That making love to her had simply been a way of passing the time? She was seeing something that she just knew no one else would be allowed to see. The turmoil of a man who didn't know quite what to do. Someone who was teetering on an emotional precipice and was feeling very, very unsafe. Like he was about to fall.

She hung on to his hand. Held his gaze.

It's all right, she wanted to say. *You're safe. We're safe, as long as we stay together. We wouldn't fall. We'd...fly.*

She took a deep breath.

'Jet...'

'Oh, my God!' The shout came from somewhere on the other side of the fire. *'Mandy... Steve...'*

Figures were emerging from the darkness. Coming from a different direction from which she and Jet had reached the settlement.

Other people came running. Amongst the cries of joy and hugging going on, it became apparent that Mandy and Steve and two others had been the people who'd gone on a night tracking mission for the kiwi breeding programme. They'd been missing ever since the first earthquake and here they were, having achieved an almost impossible feat of climbing around the coastline to get back. They were bruised and scraped but otherwise uninjured.

Had Jet been aware that he'd still been holding Becca's hand as they watched and listened to the joyous reunion? He certainly noticed as a man Becca hadn't yet met approached them.

'Jet? We're ready to get Adam free now.'

He let go of her hand instantly. 'Let me get my gear. You haven't lifted the beam yet?'

'No.'

'I'll be there in a minute.'

The man nodded. He looked totally exhausted but then he noticed what was happening around him.

'Good grief… *Steve*?' He moved away to greet the new-comers.

Jet was moving away too and all Becca could do was watch him go. She was too tired to offer to help and he hadn't asked. The opportunity to say anything had been snatched away from her and now she was wondering whether he would have wanted to hear it anyway.

He'd been eager to leave and get on with possibly the last medical challenge this rescue might present.

Relieved, maybe, to get away from her before she said anything that might have pushed him over the precipice?

She was on the same emotional ledge. Terrified of falling. Unsure of what to grasp that might allow her to pull herself back to safety.

Maybe they were both kidding themselves if they thought they could return to the safe place they'd been for the past ten years.

They'd started falling the moment they'd touched each other.

CHAPTER SEVEN

WHAT had Becca been about to say to him?

That she forgave him?

That she had missed him?

That look in her eyes… He could almost imagine that she'd been about to say, *I love you*.

And, for that split second, they were the words he had been waiting his whole life to hear.

Reality had snapped in, though, hadn't it, when those new people had arrived? The moment had gone so fast he wasn't sure he'd even read it correctly.

Even if he had, what was he thinking? Hearing those words would be about as terrifying as the seconds before crash-landing that helicopter, and at least then he'd had some idea of what he needed to do to attempt to regain control.

He wouldn't have known what to say to any of those possibilities, especially the last one. It would be like those awkward minutes after the sex. Knowing that something important had just happened. That something needed to be said. And feeling completely…lost.

Just as well he had the default mode that allowed him to simply move into the next moment and do what had to be done rather than what should be done.

He went to supervise Adam's release. He gave the young conservation worker additional pain relief and made sure fluids were running freely into his veins to help dilute any toxins that might be released when the weight was lifted from his lower leg. He attached the life pack leads and monitored what was happening to his heart, breathing and blood pressure.

And then he saw what he had to deal with and any thoughts of Becca and the past were easily put aside. The arterial bleed from a partially amputated foot had been controlled by the weight of the beam and it proved impossible to control once they got Adam out. Jet fought for a long time with direct pressure and then a tourniquet and even an attempt to find the artery and tie it off.

Adam lost a lot of blood. He lost consciousness. In the end, Jet had to put in a nerve block and complete the amputation. The young man would have lost his foot anyway. He was not going to let him lose his life, dammit. By the time he was confident he'd won the battle and Adam was in the tent with the others, sleeping peacefully rather than exhibiting a dangerous drop in his level of consciousness, the new day had well and truly broken.

It was now more than forty-eight hours since Jet had slept and he had to catch an hour or two or he'd be no use to anyone. Erica was exhausted, too, but sure she could stay on top of monitoring the condition of the injured people until Jet had had some rest. For the moment all the patients seemed stable, though the oldest amongst them, Jim, was a worry. He had an internal injury that probably involved his spleen.

Jet raked his fingers through his hair, which felt thick with grime. Backup was desperately needed but it couldn't be too far away now, surely. It was a new day. Someone could spot the big navy vessel on the horizon any time. There would be medical personnel and supplies on board. A mini-theatre, even, in case they needed to do an emergency splenectomy on their oldest patient.

Someone found him a blanket and a pillow and advised going close enough to the fire to stay warm. Jet was drawn back there anyway, because that was the last place he had seen Becca.

She'd offered to come and help with Adam but she'd stumbled in her exhaustion just trying to stand up as he'd gone past with all the gear he'd needed. He'd ordered her, in no uncertain terms, to stay put and rest. He'd told her that Erica had already been briefed to assist him.

He hadn't stopped moving on his way to the half-demolished building but he'd seen the flash of something like defeat on her face.

Loss, almost.

He remembered that look now, as he saw her again. Still in the same place. She had also been provided with a blanket and pillow and she was curled up, sound asleep, with her head cradled on her arm.

Her face was unguarded. A dark tangle of lashes on a pale cheek. A mouth that almost smiled in repose. She looked astonishingly young. Defenceless.

Jet lay down beside her. He closed his eyes but moments later he opened them again. He propped himself up on one elbow and gazed at Becca again. The pull had been simply too powerful to resist.

He was quite close enough to reach out and touch her face. To run a gentle stroke from her forehead to her chin.

Becca's eyes fluttered open, full of confusion, and then they focussed and her lips parted. She turned her head on a sigh. Just enough that her chin and cheek pressed into the palm that was cupping her face.

A gesture of gratitude?

It felt more like an acknowledgment of a connection too deep to put into words.

Without thinking, Jet leaned closer. He kissed her, very softly, on her lips.

'Go back to sleep,' he whispered. 'It's going to be OK, I promise.'

It took several seconds to come awake properly. The first thing Becca was aware of was how incredibly hard the ground beneath her was. And then she noticed how much her body was aching and how thirsty she was.

As she opened her eyes to bright sunlight, she was reaching out with her arm at the same time. Jet had been there, hadn't he?

Right beside her.

He had kissed her with such tenderness that Becca had allowed sleep to claim her again, feeling completely safe.

Or had it been a dream?

Jet wasn't there beside her now.

Becca sat up with some difficulty. She'd never felt so stiff and sore in her life. Her eyes felt gritty and the sunlight hurt.

Sunlight?

Squinting, Becca looked around. The sea was very close and blue. Tiny whitecaps were visible on the swells and seagulls circled overhead. There was no beach here. The waves broke directly onto black rocks but she could see that a jetty had been built and a dinghy with an outboard motor was tied down on the end of the structure. Presumably, ships anchored some way off the island and small boats were used to transfer supplies or people.

Stretching her back and wriggling her feet to try and warm up her muscles, Becca turned her head from one side to the other. Lush, green forest blanketed the craggy slopes inland and there, at the highest point, she could see a plume of smoke from the volcano.

Quiescent now, but she would never forget the sound of its wrath. Or the fiery glow in the sky and fountains of sparks. The deadly missiles that had sent her in panic to share that meagre shelter with Jet.

And she would certainly never, ever forget what had happened in that shelter. Even now, Becca could feel a sensation of pure pleasure melting the pain of overused muscles and joints. An exquisite liquid that was generated deep in her belly and trickled deliciously into her limbs, making her heart rate pick up and her lungs stretch to take in more of the surprisingly fresh air.

'Hey…you're awake. Want a cup of coffee?'

'Sure.' Becca blinked at the young woman near the fire.

'I'm Mandy. I wasn't here when you arrived. We were out tracking kiwi and got cut off by some lava. Took for ever to try and scramble back round the coast. You guys came overland, I hear?'

'Mmm.' Becca was getting cautiously to her feet. 'What time is it, do you know?'

'My watch got wet. I think it's late morning. 'Bout eleven?'

'Good grief, I've been asleep for hours.'

'You needed it. You're probably feeling a lot worse

than I am and I feel bad enough.' Mandy smiled. 'Here you go. Sugar?'

'Please.' Becca stirred two heaped spoons into the mug. She needed a good energy boost.

'Want something to eat? I can do a honey or peanut-butter sandwich.'

She should eat but Becca shook her head. The hot drink was enough for now and there was an urgency about drinking it.

'Maybe later,' she said. 'I need to…'

Find Jet. To catch his gaze and then she'd know if it had been a dream when he'd kissed her like that. As though…as though he *loved* her?

'To see what's happening,' she trailed off, handing the mug back. 'Thank you so much. That was the best coffee ever.'

'I'll come with you,' Mandy said. 'Hang on a tick and I'll just make a coffee for Jet. He'll need another one by now. Black, no sugar, right?'

She clearly knew more than Becca did about Jet's coffee habits and was only too keen to be doing something to help him. How did he get women on side so fast when he went around scowling so hard and looking unapproachable?

As if she didn't know. She'd been more than prepared to push herself past any known physical limits to keep up with him. And she'd been the one to grab that heavy life pack he needed before anyone else got a chance to. You'd think that never smiling and being so focussed on your job you could come across as surly would make others wary but, with Jet, it just seemed to make them make more of an effort to get noticed.

How had he got on with Erica during Adam's rescue

in the night? Becca found out soon enough as she went into the tent that now looked like a mini-hospital. Jet was there, on the far side, crouched beside a young, bearded man who had a heavily bandaged leg raised on pillows.

Erica came into the tent behind her, carrying bottled water. She paused and smiled at Becca.

'I hope you got some real sleep.'

Becca nodded, feeling a bit ashamed of herself, but Erica's nod was pleased. 'You needed it. You missed the excitement, though.' The nurse's gaze shifted. 'Your man's a bit of a hero all right.'

Her man.

In her dreams.

He had been, though, hadn't he? Just for a blink of time, up there on the side of a mountain.

There was no way she could prevent her own gaze shifting to Jet. Soaking in the picture he made. He was taking Adam's blood pressure with a hand holding the disc of a stethoscope in place on Adam's elbow and using his other hand to release the valve of the bulb. His face was intent as he watched the dial clipped to the cuff around his patient's upper arm.

And, yes…he was scowling.

Absurdly, it brought the sting of tears to Becca's eyes and curled the corners of her mouth into a smile at the same time.

She loved everything about him. Even the surliness.

She could make him smile. How many others could claim that distinction?

'We had an operating theatre going,' Erica was telling

her. 'Adam's foot was such a mess, he was bleeding to death.'

'Really?' Becca was still watching the doctor with his patient. She saw Jet's satisfied nod and he was saying something to Adam, who gave him a smile in return and a thumbs-up sign. The blood pressure was obviously at an acceptable level. How had Jet managed to get a patient in danger of bleeding to death into such a stable condition given the relatively primitive surroundings and limited medical supplies?

'He had to amputate the foot,' Erica said quietly.

'Oh, no… That's awful.'

But Erica shook her head. 'He would have died otherwise and *that* would have been awful. Adam's the nicest guy you could ever meet and we're all over the moon that he's still with us. I think he's pretty happy about it, too, and he knows he owes his life to Jet.'

Jet's status around here had clearly reached new heights.

'How are the others?'

Erica's smile was back. 'Jack's got a headache that he says is worse than any hangover he's ever had, and that's saying something for Jack. Jet reckons he's got a severe concussion but there's nothing too dangerous going on. He'll need scans and stuff when he gets to hospital.'

Jet was beside Jack now, shining a small torch in his eyes and then holding a hand up in front of him.

'How many fingers?' Becca heard him ask.

'One. Trick question, right?'

'Keep your eyes on it for as long as you can.' Jet moved his finger up and down and then from side to side, watching closely to see how Jack was tracking it visually.

Erica still hadn't moved to take water to those who needed it. The two women stood side by side, watching Jet.

Everybody was, Becca realised, scanning the interior of this makeshift medical centre. There were several onlookers. Like Mandy and some others Becca had yet to meet. And why wouldn't they all be watching? Jet was their hero. He was using his astonishing stamina and praiseworthy skills to care for them all. To save the lives of the people they cared about.

He was brilliant and she felt proud of him. She loved him, as much as it was possible to love anyone. So why did she have this gnawing sense of unease? A kind of tension pressing in on her and making her feel restless?

The answer came when her gaze returned to Jet to find he'd finished assessing Jack and was looking directly at her. How long had he been watching her soak in the results of all his hard work? The hero-worship he had earned from all these people?

He looked…uncomfortable. Embarrassed.

And then it hit her. That moment of eye contact had ignited a connection that went further back than what had happened on this island. It came with a wave of pain. He had saved the life of at least one complete stranger here.

Why hadn't he been able to do that for his best friend?

There was nothing for Becca to do in here. Plenty of people were available for the routine nursing and companionship these patients needed, and Jet and Erica were there for anything clinical. Becca went back outside and somebody made her another cup of coffee and then presented her with a doorstop sandwich thickly spread with both honey and peanut butter.

It was hard to swallow, however.

A heavy knot seemed to have lodged in her stomach. A weight that told her she still hadn't forgiven Jet.

Sure, she could understand that he'd been just as devastated by Matt's death as she had been. She could feel bad that she'd made him feel worse with her accusations. Knowing that might have changed how she felt about Jet was enough to erase the hatred but, however much she wished it wasn't, the core of that ill feeling was still there.

The idea that he could and *should* have done more. That by doing even the tiniest bit more, he could have prevented the tragedy.

Did she still believe that?

Yes. Somewhere, deep inside, that belief was still alive. A spotlight had revealed it lurking in a recess and that light had come from the evidence all around her here. In Jet's abilities to beat the odds. To negotiate inhospitable landscape. To save someone's life when they were bleeding to death.

Was part of why he'd been so affected by Matt's death due to feeling guilty that he hadn't done that little bit more? Maybe the answer to that had been telegraphed in the discomfort she'd witnessed when he'd seen her taking in what he'd managed to do on Tokolamu.

The knot inside her was a kind of grief.

She loved Jet but if she was incapable of forgiving him completely there could never be any kind of future with him even if he felt the same way. And that kiss had suggested he might.

Forgiveness implied trust.

Trust made you vulnerable.

Was she, in fact, prepared to make herself vulnerable? She had worked hard for a very long time to protect herself from the pain you could risk by being vulnerable. To prevent herself ever falling over that precipice.

Maybe she should just leave well enough alone. She had always wanted to be with Jet and have him touch her intimately. Now she knew the reality of it and perhaps a perfect memory was the best outcome for both of them. Why ruin it by digging up things that could only push them apart and make them regret what had happened here?

The navy vessel was sighted early that afternoon and even after it had anchored safely away from the rocks surrounding the island, there was still enough daylight to embark on the treacherous task of evacuating everybody safely.

The injured went first because it needed a huge team to carry stretchers over the rocks and down to the jetty. Despite the willing team of volunteers, it was a slow process. Getting from the jetty into the inflatable craft was tricky and then they needed to be winched up a daunting height to get on board the ship at the other end of the short journey.

Jet made the trip with every one of the injured. First Adam and then Jim and then Jack. He handed them over to the ship's surgeon and made sure his patients were settled and stable before returning to the island. The others could be taken off in small groups but the sun was almost setting by the time the last group had a boat available.

Becca was in that last group. Jet and Steve, who was

manning the outboard engine because he knew every rock to watch out for, were a tight team by now. Jet hung on to ropes on the jetty, trying to keep the boat reasonably stable in an increasing swell. With his free arm, he offered support to each person making the controlled jump from the edge of the wooden jetty into the boat.

He made sure he caught Becca's uninjured arm and he gripped it firmly. No way was he going to let her slip and go into the sea between the dinghy and the jetty. A wave rolled past as she stepped out and the boat tilted sharply. Jet let go of the rope, caught Becca in his arms and rolled onto the bottom of the dinghy, ensuring that he landed on his back to provide a cushion for her. A whoop of approval came from Steve and the others on board clapped and cheered.

'Score!' Someone shouted.

The relief of being rescued, combined with exhaustion and the aftermath of adrenaline release, was beginning to make them all feel somewhat euphoric. Even Becca was grinning as Jet helped her up and onto the shelf seat along the side of the boat where she could get a grip on a loop of rope. Another two people to get on board and then they were off, skimming over the top of the waves, leaving the island of Tokolamu and its angry heart behind.

For the next hour or so happy chaos ensued as the rescued were assigned cabins and given access to hot showers and fresh clothes. Jet took advantage of all the facilities himself but only after checking again on all the patients. Jim was creating the most concern.

'BP's dropped,' the ship's surgeon told Jet. 'I've got some fresh, frozen plasma running but I'm not happy.

We'll arrange a helicopter transfer as soon as we're within range but that's not going to be until morning.'

'Are you set up for surgery if it's needed?'

'Yes. Most we've ever done at sea is an emergency appendectomy, though.'

'Splenectomy's in the same ballpark.'

'You're experienced?'

'I've done a few.'

'Good.' The older doctor nodded with approval. 'Here, take this pager. I'll beep you if anything changes. Or would you like me to look at that cut on your head now?'

'It can wait. I'll clean up first.'

So Jet had a shower and put on some grey track pants and the white T-shirt he'd been provided with. He picked up the pager and clipped it to the waistband of the pants. Seeing the last glow of the sunset on the horizon through the porthole of his cabin as he got dressed, he made his way up on deck and to the stern of the now slowly moving ship. He wanted a final glimpse of the island that he knew would loom large in his memory for as long as he lived.

When he got to the railing at the stern, just over the churning wake, he found he wasn't alone.

Dressed identically, in the soft grey pants and a white T-shirt that was way too large for her, was Becca.

With the backdrop of an island that was already look-ing small and a dying sunset that stretched as far as the eye could see across a vast ocean, Becca looked tiny. The urge to gather her into his arms and protect her was strong enough to immobilise Jet for a heartbeat as he joined her at the rail.

Protect her from what?

They were safe now. Heading away from the danger of this unexpected adventure and back towards their normal lives. So why this overwhelming feeling that there was something she still needed protection from? What was it?

A job she had chosen and clearly loved that was actually a lot less dangerous than what he chose to do with his own life at regular intervals?

The past? Would trying to sort out that tangle of unhappy memories somehow protect Becca from renewed pain in the future?

And why did that matter so much? Did he see himself as part of that future?

Yes.

No.

Confusion held him in utter silence. They stood there, side by side, staring at the shape of the island that was now being swallowed by the night.

Jet didn't do involvement with women. Not long term. He couldn't invite Becca into his life and then walk away from her, though, could he?

If he took that step, it would be for life.

And it would irrevocably change *his* life.

Could he even give her what she'd want? Or need? What she deserved?

Highly unlikely, given that he'd never been able to give it to any other woman in his life. He had long since accepted that he was a lone wolf. He had his pack, with Max and Rick, but he needed too much freedom.

He'd end up hurting her.

She'd end up hating him. The way she had for the past decade. Nothing fundamental had really changed, had it? How could it when they hadn't even talked about any of it?

With no conscious awareness, Jet had somehow moved closer to Becca. Their hands were touching where they rested, side by side, on the railing. He became aware of it because it was like an electric current. Stealing up his arm and into every cell of his body. When Jet looked up from his hand in a kind of wonder at the speed of that current, he found Becca looking up at him.

The night was closing around them. The tropical breeze caressing them was making Becca's newly washed, short hair do its utmost to curl. Her eyes were shining with an emotion he couldn't identify. Relief, perhaps, that they were leaving the trauma of the island experience behind?

Her lips were parted and he saw the tip of her tongue emerge to dampen them. Perhaps she was planning to be the first to say something but Jet didn't give her the chance. Maybe he didn't want to hear anything that might break the spell that had been suddenly cast.

So he bent his head swiftly and kissed her.

It was only intended to be a gentle gesture. An acknowledgment of something that was far more profound than mere sexual attraction. But how on earth could he have forgotten that explosion of heat that came from touching Becca like this?

It melted self-control, that heat. It spread like the volcanic eruption they had witnessed last night until it felt like his whole body was glowing with it. It radiated from his fingertips and yet he could feel even more heat coming from the skin they were touching. On Becca's face. On her neck. Under that T-shirt where they encountered the smoothest, most delicious curve of her belly and the tiny ridges of her ribs and then the soft swell of a perfect breast.

He heard her gasp as he cupped that breast, letting his thumb caress her nipple. He heard the tiny groan of surrender as she pressed herself into his hand and reached for *his* skin.

He also heard the insistent beeping that was coming from the device clipped to his track pants. The pager summoning him because someone was in trouble. Probably Jim.

Letting go of Becca was the hardest thing Jet had had to do in his life.

And that, in itself, was as strident a warning as the sound coming from the pager.

His voice felt raw. 'I have to go.'

Becca simply nodded. She stepped back and turned towards the railing again, gripping it with both hands. Jet heard the way she sucked in a new breath as he moved away and it sounded oddly like a sob.

And that was when he understood.

She did still need protection from something.

Him.

CHAPTER EIGHT

THE helicopter made a perfect landing on the designated expanse of deck at the stern of the ship.

'Nice.' Becca nodded.

With the loud whine of rotors about to slow to an idle, her admiring comment couldn't possibly have been overheard by the group of people standing around the stretcher but one of them looked up and mirrored her nod.

Maybe Jet was the only one of them who could appreciate the skill needed to bring a chopper down so neatly on a moving target.

It was what Becca had come on deck to watch so there was no reason to stay any longer.

Every reason not to, in fact.

Did she really want to watch the stretcher being loaded and the aircraft taking off again?

Jet was here with his patient. The man he'd been with for most of the night, according to the ship's grapevine. Emergency surgery had been needed and then careful monitoring afterwards. Becca, like most of the others rescued from the island, had stayed up until they'd heard the news that the surgery had been successfully completed. With that crisis dealt with she had suddenly had as much sparkle as a deflated balloon and had gone off to the cabin she was sharing with Mandy to curl up in her bunk and escape into blessed unconsciousness.

Of course, it had been successful. Another life had been saved. She had expected nothing less. Just like she expected that Jet would climb into that military helicopter to accompany his patient to the nearest large land-based hospital.

Yes. He was about to exit her life with just as much drama as he'd stepped back into it. But did she really want to watch?

She might never see him again.

Becca swallowed hard. She tried to tell herself that it was a good thing. In the past two days, ever since the moment she'd set eyes on Jet again, her life had been tipped upside down and shaken violently. The physical trauma and danger were things she could easily deal with but the emotional roller-coaster was something else entirely. Nobody could survive this kind of turmoil unscathed and the problem was generated by Jet's presence. When he vanished, life as she knew it would at least have a chance of resuming.

It had to. Despite hours of sleep, gently rocking in that narrow bunk, Becca simply didn't have any reserve of energy or strength left. Not even enough to make her legs work and take her away from watching Jet leave so she stayed where she was and watched the stretcher being loaded and secured in the belly of the helicopter. Jet was talking to the army medics in their flight suits and helmets but then she saw him step back and the rear hatch of the chopper was closed and locked.

The rotors picked up speed and Jet was in a half-crouch as he got well out of the way. Becca saw the thumbs-up signal of the pilot and watched the skids lift smoothly from the deck. The chopper hovered for a moment, moved sideways and then banked as it gained height rapidly and left the ship behind. In no time at all it was a dot, disappearing into the horizon.

Still she didn't move. She watched the small crowd disperse. All the conservation workers who'd come to wish their colleague a speedy recovery and see him taken away filed through the narrow door to go back inside. The ship's surgeon and the crew members who'd been involved in the transfer went off to their work.

Everybody had gone. Except Jet. He came towards her and Becca's mouth felt dry. It was curiously hard to say something.

'How come you didn't go with them?'

'He's stable and he's in good hands. They'll be back later to transfer the others, anyway.'

'So you'll catch a ride then?'

Jet shrugged. 'Maybe I fancy an overnight cruise.'

Becca couldn't read his expression but he seemed to be watching her carefully. Gauging her reaction. Why? Was he choosing to stay with the ship because of her?

Because he wanted to be with her?

Oh…help. She had to look away and the vast expanse of the ocean was soothing after the focus she'd seen in Jet's eyes.

The deck was shifting under her feet far more than the roll of the sea could account for. She'd steeled herself to witness his departure. She'd been ready to deal with it and get on with her own life but the rules of this game were changing.

Or were they? This had something of the intensity of that moment by the fire the night before. If he was choosing to stay because of her, that meant he was acknowledging what hung between them. And, again, he was sidestepping. Changing the subject. Making a joke about being on a cruise ship.

Now it was her turn. If she said the wrong thing, did she get to slide down some kind of emotional snake? Instinctively, she knew this wasn't the time to get serious. She was being given a clear direction of what her move should be and that was to make some light comment along the same lines. About the failure of the last port of call to live up to the promise of the brochure perhaps? Or to wonder what the activities officer had in store for the passengers today? If she did that, would she find herself with a ladder to get to the next level of the game?

But, if this was a game, the stakes were too high. The implications of winning or losing would be with her for the rest of her life.

This was as huge as the volcano on Tokolamu.

And just as terrifying.

She hadn't expected him to stay.

But how could he have left like that, with the last image of Becca being her hands clutching the railing of the ship and her choked sob as she struggled for composure?

As hard as it would be, somehow they had to talk or they might be left with more than Matt's ghost haunting their lives.

He wasn't going to promise anything he couldn't deliver but, at the very least, he had to let Becca know that he would never forget her. That she had a friend for life and if she was ever in any kind of trouble, he would move heaven and earth if he had to in order to help.

The prospect of parting on good terms had seemed entirely plausible in the early hours of this morning, when Jet had been sitting in the ship's infirmary amongst quietly beeping monitors and patients who were all sleeping peacefully.

Standing here now, close enough to touch Becca, Jet realised he might have been kidding himself. Maybe he'd just been dreaming up an excuse to stay a little longer because he couldn't face the notion of never seeing her again.

'It's just one night,' he said, aiming to keep it casual. 'We'll be pretty busy sorting out the other Medevac transfers for the rest of today but…hey, I've been invited to eat at the captain's table. Would have been rude to say no.'

He heard a tiny snort of amusement. They both knew that high-ranking officials in military service would not appreciate being called a captain.

'Lucky you,' she said.

'The invitation apparently includes a partner.'

'Oh…'

He wished she'd stop staring out to sea like that and would look at him so he might have some idea of what she was thinking. She'd folded her arms around herself as though she needed comfort.

He could provide that, if she'd let him. But she wasn't the girl he remembered. She was grown up and she could look after herself. She might not want anything more from him. She might have *wanted* him to disappear along with that helicopter.

She didn't look so grown up right now, though. Holding herself like that made her look tiny and...alone. Even her voice was small when she spoke.

'Got someone in mind?'

'Yeah...you.'

Her head swivelled and her gaze flew up to meet his and she looked...scared.

Jet groaned inwardly as he reached out and took her into his arms. Her body felt stiff but she wasn't trying to pull away. Jet held on, closing his eyes.

'I didn't want to leave just yet, Becca. Not before we've had a chance to talk. We might never have another opportunity and if that's the case, we might regret it. I know I would, anyway.'

It took more than a heartbeat but he felt the tension in her body ease. Then he could feel the movement of her head on his chest. A subtle movement but definitely up and down. Agreement.

He pulled back far enough to smile at her. 'So it's a date?'

'For dinner?'

'More like after dinner, I think. When we can get some time to ourselves. Somewhere private.'

'I'm...sharing a cabin.'

'I'm not.' Jet gave her an encouraging squeeze and then let go. 'I think I've been given an officer's suite. Lots of room.' It seemed important not to mention the bed. Or even think about it. 'It's got armchairs, even.'

'Lucky you.' A tentative smile shaped Becca's lips but it didn't quite meet her eyes. 'I'll see you at dinner, then. Can't promise I'll be dressed appropriately, though.'

'Can't see anything wrong with how you look right now,' Jet murmured.

ALISON ROBERTS 133

But Becca was already halfway to the door leading off the deck. She didn't hear him.

It should have been relaxing.

A day on the high seas with nothing to do but rest and eat. There were books available and satellite television and even a movie put on for the extra passengers, but Becca couldn't concentrate on anything well enough to enjoy it.

Jet might have been absent physically, helping the ship's surgeon give everyone from the island a check-up between helicopter transfers of the others who needed hospital care, but he might as well have been right by her side as far as her awareness of him was concerned. Holding her hand perhaps, so that she could think of nothing more than the extraordinary feeling of how connected they were.

Kissing her, even, because she knew that she would never experience lovemaking like his from anyone else. Ever.

When it came time for dinner, Becca felt ridiculous being seated with the commanding officers of the ship in their immaculate uniforms, while she was wearing track pants and a T-shirt. Her apology was charmingly dismissed.

'Elegant clothing is a disguise that some people have no need of.'

The men waited until she sat down before taking their places at the table.

'Besides,' another added, 'we like to dress our guests the same. That way we won't mistake them for crew and put them to work.'

Becca smiled and nodded. And allowed her gaze to

rest on Jet, who was seated opposite her and wearing an identical outfit. They were a matching pair.

And it was true. Becca could imagine him sitting there in a tuxedo, looking breathtakingly elegant and gorgeous, but it wouldn't change the way his body owned the space it was in. Or the way he held his head with that curious stillness that disguised how alert he was. It was pure Jet. So was that look in his eyes that told her they were more than a matching pair for clothing.

They were two sides of the same coin.

Desire warred with grief. They might never see each other again. She had to look away and try to focus on something else or she might do something incredibly embarrassing, like burst into tears.

It was a three-course dinner. The food and accompanying wine were delicious but Becca had no real appetite and she struggled to pretend she was enjoying her meal and not counting every second until she could be alone with Jet. With a supreme effort she did her best to seem just as engaged with the conversation going on around her.

By the time she excused herself and Jet followed her from the dining table, she was having difficulty remembering anything that had been discussed. Only two things had made enough of an impact to stay in her head. One was that the ship would reach dock at some point during the night so they would be able to disembark as soon as they woke. Transport had been arranged to take them to where they needed to go.

The other was that Jet needed to get back to his army base. He would probably be deployed on a new mission within forty-eight hours. Afghanistan was the most likely destination.

And, yes…he was looking forward to it.

So this was it.

An hour or two in his cabin to talk about things Becca had never wanted to talk about to anyone. And in the morning they would say goodbye and go their separate ways. Back to their own lives.

Jet could get killed in the next dangerous mission that would start within days, but even if he survived a dozen such missions it was unlikely they would ever spend time alone together again.

How could she say goodbye to this man?

How could she not?

By shipboard standards, Jet's cabin was luxurious. A wider than normal single bed, a small table and two comfortable chairs beside a smaller door that must lead to an en suite bathroom. The brass edging of the porthole gleamed in soft light that came from a bedside lamp. Maybe the same person who had turned on the lamp had also turned the bed covers back so invitingly.

It was still a small room. Just a few steps from the door to the chairs. An even smaller distance from the chairs to the bed. Jet's presence in this space with Becca seemed overpowering. Her legs refused to take her to a chair. Did she really want to be here?

Tilting her head, she found Jet looking down at her. There was a question in his eyes.

A plea?

She could see the same kind of turmoil she'd seen by the campfire two nights ago. The vulnerability that let her know that Jet had a patch of his soul that matched the one she worked so hard to hide. The lost and lonely part.

Yes. Of course she wanted to be here.

She wanted to reassure him. To let him know that, if he ever wanted to, it was safe to fall. As long as he was with her, because she'd keep him safe, no matter what it might take.

He wasn't saying anything and the tension in this small space lurched upwards. Becca could actually feel the pull Jet was exerting on her. She could feel herself tilting ever so slightly. Leaning towards him.

She could see the way Jet's Adam's apple moved up and caught as he seemed to swallow with some difficulty.

'So…' His voice was hoarse but he didn't try to clear his throat. 'You want to talk?'

'I want…'

You, her body screamed. Or was it her heart? Somehow, her head stopped the word emerging from her mouth.

Maybe it escaped through her eyes.

That might explain why Jet's pupils flared and swallowed his already dark-as-sin irises, making his eyes completely black. Why the atmosphere around them suddenly smouldered and crackled with suppressed fire. Was he trying to stop himself touching her?

Why?

This was only one night and they'd probably never see each other again.

The prospect was oddly similar to that belief they were both about to be killed by debris being expelled from an erupting volcano. Only this time they were safe. They had soft light and…and a bed.

They had all night. There would be plenty of time to talk. How could they possibly talk now when she, at least, felt like she was suffocating with her need to be touched? To touch in return.

Communication *could* be telepathic. Or maybe she'd made some kind of audible sound. Either way, the heat surrounding her was suddenly alive with tiny flames that licked at her skin. Jet gave a stifled groan and his head dipped until his lips covered hers.

What was he doing? He'd brought Becca back here with the intention of having an adult conversation. To tell her that he would always be there for her, for ever, but he couldn't give her what she might need or want in a life partner.

And she'd looked at him like *that*. As though he was the only thing she wanted.

Of course he could give her his body. For tonight, at least. It wasn't as if they'd be able to have any kind of conversation other than physical right now. Not when he couldn't string two coherent thoughts together, let alone words.

It might have been an adrenaline rush of danger and desire on the mountain but this was a whole different planet.

One that Jet had never been on.

Oh, he'd been with women often enough. He knew about soft lights and beckoning beds and how to take his time and wring the most out of every sensual second for both participants.

But it had never been like this.

Maybe the astonishing tenderness he felt came from having known Becca for years. The sheer wonder came from the miracle of how perfect a woman she'd grown into. And the mind-numbing excitement from an old whisper that this was illicit. It would be disapproved of.

Not by him, that was for sure.

And not by Becca, if her amazing responsiveness was anything to go by. The way her skin seemed to shiver when he touched it. Breathed on it, even. The way her nipples hardened instantly into tiny berries when he finally allowed himself the joy of putting his mouth to those small, perfectly formed breasts.

Her moist centre that would have told him she was more than ready for him even if she hadn't arched her body against his and cried out his name.

The sensation of totally losing his mind as he entered paradise at the same moment he entered Becca. The feeling that *this was it*.

He'd found it.

At last.

The tears came from nowhere.

Silently and softly, they trickled down Becca's cheeks as she lay cradled in Jet's arms, slowly coming back to the real world.

The sex up there on the mountain had been astonishing. As good as she'd always known it would be with Jet, but *this*…this had taken her into a different dimension. Just as exciting but…different.

Heartbreaking.

The *tenderness* with which he'd touched her. The way he'd made her believe that she was special.

Loved.

That was where the tears were coming from. To truly

love—and be loved—was a place Becca hadn't been in since her brother had been ripped away from her.

It was a place where life took on a whole new meaning. It *gave* life the meaning it should always have.

She didn't want to leave. Ever.

'You're crying.' Jet's thumb stroked moisture from her cheek.

'No, I'm not.' Becca pushed his hand away as she scrubbed at her face. 'I never cry.'

The careful silence told her that Jet was remembering the last time he had seen her really crying. That equally silent, personal anguish she had suffered on hearing that there was no point in keeping Matt's life support going. The black, black time just before she'd turned her despair into anger and directed it at Jet.

That devastating time when she'd learned that you couldn't trust that loving place. That the only real meaning that life had was what you could squeeze out of individual moments.

This was one of those moments. She wasn't going to ruin it by thinking of the past. She propped herself up on one elbow so that she could reach Jet's face. She kissed him.

'I'm happy, OK? That was…' She couldn't think of a word to encompass the magic of what they'd just shared. She knew she'd never find it again. Damn…those tears were still far too close for comfort.

'Yeah…' Jet's arms tightened around her. 'It sure was.'

Becca found herself smiling. A wobbly smile, tinged with heartbreak but a smile nonetheless. 'Who would've thought?'

'Not me.' But then Jet sighed. 'That's not entirely true, actually. I *did* think. Once.'

'When?'

'At that party. Remember? When I kissed you in the kitchen.'

'I seem to remember it being the other way round. *I* kissed *you*.'

'Did you?' She could hear a smile in his voice. 'Guess it was so good I wanted to take all the credit.'

Becca snorted. 'So good that you proceeded to ignore me for the rest of the night so that I felt like a complete idiot.'

'I couldn't not ignore you. I had your brother giving me the evil eye. He'd already told me that I was exactly the kind of guy he intended to keep you well away from.'

'Oh...' That changed the memory significantly. Jet had been attracted to her and he'd been hiding it? If only she'd known...

'And he was right. I'm not a good bet.'

'Oh?' Becca was still busy rearranging her memories of that night. Thinking of how different things could have been.

'I don't stay in one place for long. Or with one person. I'm a loner, I guess. Maybe you weren't so far off base calling me a gypsy.'

Becca was silent for a long minute. Aware of the warmth of Jet's body beside her. The rise and fall of his chest as he breathed. The steady thump of his heart against her ribs. Aware of how much she loved him. Of how different he was from anyone else she'd ever had in her life. He was a lot of things, this man, and all of them made him special. A gypsy. A pirate. A hero. A maverick. But a lone wolf?

No. His pack had been everything to him once. Maybe he didn't want to be loved but he *was* capable of loving.

'It's hard, isn't it?' she whispered into the silence. 'To trust someone enough to love them? Even harder to let them love you.'

She could feel the subtle tension gather in his body. He didn't want to talk about anything so personal. He was pulling away from her. Sadness crept back into the mix of emotions bathing her.

'Sometimes,' she added, almost inaudibly, 'it's lonely.'

That did it. Jet made a sound she couldn't interpret and rolled away from her. He sat up and then leaned over the bed to pick up his track pants.

'Want something to drink? There's a little fridge tucked in under the table.'

'No. I'm good.' Becca sat up but didn't reach for her clothes. She pulled the sheet up, bent her knees and wrapped her arms around them, watching as Jet fished out a can of beer and popped the top.

Finally, he sent a glance in her direction. 'I'm not lonely,' he said quietly. 'I have my life exactly the way I want it. And I have friends. Good friends.'

'Max?' Becca wanted him to keep talking, even though it was hard to delve into the past. 'And Rick?'

'Yeah.'

'Do they do what you do? Never stay in one place or with one person?'

Jet grunted. 'They used to. Things have changed.' He took a long pull at his can of beer.

'Are they still practising medicine?'

'Oh, yeah.'

'Specialists?'

'Yep. We all decided early on where we were heading. Max is an emergency specialist, like me. Rick went into neurosurgery.'

Becca blinked. There were so many specialities they could have gone into as young doctors but they'd all chosen the fields that had been of the most significance when Matt had become so ill. Was there a connection?

'And they've got families now.'

'Really?' If the rest of his pack had changed, maybe Jet would one day, too. The bubble of hope couldn't be dismissed.

'Yeah…' Jet seemed happy to be talking about other people rather than himself. He sat down in one of the armchairs and stared at the can of beer in his hand. 'Rick's with Sarah. She's got a little boy who's really sick with leukaemia and it turned out that Josh was Rick's son so he became the donor for bone marrow. I talked to him earlier today. There's been a bit of a crisis but it looks like Josh is going to be OK.'

'That must be a huge relief.'

'More than that, I'd say. I got the impression Rick's got no intention of letting Sarah out of his life. Maybe I'll get to be the best man this time.'

'This time?'

'Rick was the best man when Max got married.'

'Who did Max marry?'

'Ellie.' Jet chuckled. 'She's about as feisty as you are. She turned up on his doorstep and had a baby.'

'What? On the doorstep?'

'Pretty much. We'd just been out for our anniversary

bike ride and there she was, banging on the door. Rick and I took off because we had a shift to get to and there I am in ED and Max turns up with Ellie in labour and trying to bleed to death.'

'Was it Max's baby?'

'It is now. You should have seen him when the baby was born. It needed kangaroo care and he sat up there in PICU doing skin-to-skin stuff with this tiny kid. I reckon he fell in love with Mattie before Ellie was even in the picture.'

Something cold and nasty washed over Becca. The kind of shock you'd get if you were lying in the sun and someone threw a bucket of iced water over you.

'*Who?*'

'Ellie.' Jet's tone was guarded now. He was frowning at Becca, clearly puzzled by her vehemence.

She sat up straighter. 'No...what did you say the baby's name was?'

She saw the way Jet closed his eyes, shutting her out. She saw his chest heave even though she couldn't hear the resigned sigh.

'Mattie. Short for Matilda.'

Or short for Matthew.

'How could he do that?' Becca's head was spinning, her tone one of puzzlement. 'What made him think he had the right to name a baby after Matt?'

'It's a special name for all of us, Becca.' Jet sounded weary. 'You don't have the monopoly on missing him, you know.'

'I don't believe this. How *could* he?' Becca was moving now. Finding her track pants and the damn T-shirt. 'He had *no* right.' She had to get out of here. 'None of you do.'

Even as the words burst out in that horrified tone, Becca knew she was being unreasonable. They had every right. As much as she did. And they had the opportunity, which was something she would probably never have. And maybe that was what was causing this pain.

'We weren't to blame for Matt's death.' Jet was standing up, watching her nearly frantic movements as she dressed herself. 'We did everything we could. *Everything*. If I could have done anything else…if I could have made it me instead of Matt that it was happening to, I would have jumped at the chance.' He swore softly. 'But you're never going to accept that, are you?'

Becca's could hear the bitter tone of his voice but his words were sliding past with no real meaning. She was still reeling from what felt like a physical blow. There was a child in the world who had been named after her brother. A sense that the 'bad boys' had more of Matt in their lives than she did.

Good grief…could this jealousy rather than anger be in any way justified?

She couldn't think straight. There were too many thoughts crowding her head. So many feelings jostling inside that she couldn't begin to know what she really thought. Anger was the easiest to recognise. To hang on to.

She looked at Jet, standing there, scowling defensively, and she could think of nothing at all to say to him. How could she begin to explain how she felt to someone who would be prepared to defend his pack—and any decisions they'd made—to the death?

However much she had once wanted to, she had

never become part of that pack. And now it was too
late. They'd all moved on, without her.

And they'd taken Matt with them.

She was going to cry but no way was she going to cry
in front of Jet and say things that would make her seem
pathetic and needy. She was still clinging to the anger
anyway and if she opened her mouth she'd probably say
something that would only make things worse.

So she turned away.

And left.

CHAPTER NINE

NOTHING was the same any more.

Even his beloved superbike wouldn't start on its first kick. Hardly surprising given that it had been under a tarp for weeks in the basement of the converted warehouse he shared with Rick, but nevertheless it was yet another unsettling factor to add to the many others he had suddenly accumulated in his life.

Jet put more force into his leg action and the powerful bike coughed and then growled into action. He revved it into a throaty roar but his smile was grim rather than satisfied.

This was all wrong.

Here he was, about to embark on the longest road trip he'd ever made, from one of the southernmost cities in the south island of New Zealand to the very tip of the north island and...he was doing it solo.

It would have been unthinkable even a year ago. He would have had no trouble persuading Max and Rick to come along for the ride back then if they'd been able to juggle their rosters. They would have gone from Dunedin to Picton in a day, chilled out with a few beers on the ferry crossing between the islands and then had a great night out in Wellington. Another day on the road and a night exploring old haunts in Auckland and then a final blast up as far as you go north. He would have stood beside his mates by the lighthouse at Cape Reinga and pointed out to sea in the direction of Tokolamu island.

'Bet you're sorry you missed all that action,' he would have said.

And a year ago, six months ago even, they would have been sorry.

But nothing was the same.

He shouldn't even be back here in Dunedin.

Having left the ship early enough to make sure he wouldn't have to face Becca, Jet had got himself back to the army base to find they had nothing for him.

Correction. They had something he wasn't at all sure he wanted. A full-time career, training elite army medics. A commitment to military life that would probably have seen him excluded from active deployment. The army wanted him but someone up high had decided it was going to be on their terms from now on, not his.

He didn't like that. He'd stood his ground. Ultimatums had been delivered. They'd given him a week's leave to think about it.

So he'd come back to the closest thing to home that he had but they'd had nothing for him here, either. Locum positions in the emergency department were all currently filled. Of course, if he wanted a permanent position as an emergency consultant, that might be a different story. There was just such a position being advertised but they wouldn't take on someone who wanted to disappear for months at a time at short notice. You couldn't staff a hospital like that. Applications weren't closing for the job for a week or two yet. He had time to think about it.

Had someone on the hospital board of trustees been

having a conversation with some influential acquaintance in the armed forces perhaps?

Had they decided it was time for Jet Munroe to settle down?

Jet rammed his helmet into place and pulled on his leather gloves. He coasted down the driveway and glanced both ways to check for traffic.

He was the only person who would decide when, if ever, he was going to commit to one career, thanks very much.

The road was clear. Leaving a faint rubber mark on the driveway, Jet took off into the dawn.

Everything had changed.

Oh, her apartment was still the same. So was her job when she returned after being forced to take a few days off to recover from the Tokolamu mission. She was wearing the same uniform, eating the same kind of food and seeing the same people she had known for years.

But nothing felt quite right.

Everything seemed flat. Almost pointless, in fact.

'You're very quiet, Bec,' her boss, Richard, commented. 'You sure you're ready to be back at work?'

'I'm sure. And I'd go stir-crazy if I had to spend any more time staring at my apartment walls.'

Not that the relative blankness of her walls was the problem, exactly. It was more like their ability to act as a movie screen for what was in her head. What was really threatening to drive her crazy was her inability to stop thinking about Jet Munroe.

'Hmm.' Richard sounded unconvinced. 'A crash is not a small thing to get through, you know. We've got some good people available if you want to change your mind about some counselling.'

Becca's headshake was definite. 'Don't need it.' She summoned a grin. 'You really think you could keep me away when that shiny new helicopter's just been delivered?' Her grin faded but she kept her tone light. 'What doesn't kill you makes you stronger.'

'There is such a thing as post-traumatic stress.'

'I know.' Becca had no trouble looking serious now. 'And don't get me wrong. It *was* a big deal. But I can handle it. Physically, I'm fine. See?' She held up her arm and flapped her hand. 'It was only a good sprain and maybe a mild concussion. I'm good.'

Her boss raised an eyebrow. 'It wasn't the physical repercussions I was referring to.'

Becca shrugged. 'I'm tough. I've been through worse.'

Which was true. Picking up her life and forcing herself to carry on after Matt's death had felt like wading through a mental swamp of sadness, with sinkholes of real depression to avoid.

Richard accepted her statement with a thoughtful stare and then a nod. He turned back to his paperwork with a sigh. Becca pushed her hair back from where it was tickling her forehead. She needed a haircut. She also needed to move, to try and clear the strength-sapping lethargy that was stealing through her body.

If only a job would come through. She'd been here since 6:00 a.m. this morning and it was now early afternoon and there hadn't been a single callout. Not even a transfer from a rural hospital into the city. She'd played with the new chopper, admiring everything more than once. She'd even warmed it up and given it a bit of a

hover to make sure she was happy with the way it responded.

She'd hung out with her paramedic crew as they'd
checked and rechecked all the gear, putting up with
their ribbing about the extremes she'd gone to in order
to get them new toys.

In desperation, she'd come up here to the office to
try and find a distraction. Enough motivation to make
her feel...*normal* again.

She stood up from the armchair she'd flopped into
on arrival and paced across the office.

No death had been involved in this latest chapter of
her life so why did she have this slowed-down, caught-
in-a-swamp sensation again?

Because it *was* a kind of death, wasn't it?

She was standing beside the window now. Looking
down at the patch of tarmac outside headquarters.

Had she really believed that her feelings for Jet had
been buried and long forgotten? Effectively destroyed
by nurturing anger and blame?

Her mind was only too eager to pull up the image
of Jet stepping from that vehicle that night and it didn't
seem to matter how often that scene was replayed. She
could still feel an echo of the shockwave that recognition
had generated.

And she only had to sit in the cockpit of a helicopter,
as she'd already done that morning, going through the
pre-flight check routine to remember the way the old
feelings had started to creep back thanks to Jet's reap-
pearance in her life.

To know that, deep, deep down she had been glad to
see him. To spend time with him.

To know that what had really caused that first, overwhelming shockwave was the recognition of far more than the identity of a person. She had been looking at the missing piece of the jigsaw puzzle that made up the picture of who *she* really was.

So it was a kind of death she was having to deal with now.

The end of the possibility of ever feeling truly whole.

And, in a way, it was worse than losing Matt because the finality wasn't there. Things could have been so different.

If Jet wasn't so afraid to let love into his life.

If he wasn't such an adrenaline junkie who chased danger to make him feel alive. To give his life meaning. Becca knew that's what it was because she'd done exactly the same thing herself, all those years ago.

That first helicopter ride, when her passion had been born, had been what had pulled her back into living her life properly. The final escape from the edges of that horrible swamp. The buzz of the danger. Or was it, in fact, the buzz of feeling safe again? Knowing that you were alive simply because you could have been dead?

Her brain tried to catch that notion and explore it more. There was something in there. Something important, but she couldn't quite catch it. Like a fragment of a dream that evaporated when you woke up. Instead, her mind whirled on, fast-forwarding to give her something else to angst about. Another reason why things had gone so wrong in the end of that precious time she'd had with Jet.

If only she hadn't reacted the way she had to the idea of a baby being named after her brother.

It was still a shocking revelation but that initial reaction had been so wrong.

Giving a new baby Matt's name was a lovely tribute. Maybe the only one they'd ever been able to make. The 'bad boys' had come to Matt's funeral. They'd stood right at the back, flanking the exit, wearing their leathers, with their helmets dangling from their hands, but they hadn't come to the graveside.

And Becca knew why.

It had been her decision to exclude them. To keep them from their rightful positions as pallbearers. Her anger had been so huge. She'd confronted her parents and shouted at them. Told them that Matt would still be alive if his so-called friends had done a better job of looking after him.

That, if they were chosen as pallbearers, she wouldn't be attending her brother's funeral. She wouldn't speak to her parents again for as long as they lived. They would lose both their children if that happened.

Oh…it was still shocking. More so, perhaps, because the truth of it all was so clear. She'd done so much harm to everybody involved.

Most of all to herself.

She had pushed the 'bad boys' out of her life and by doing so she had excluded herself from what was the most tangible link she could have kept to her brother.

A place where his memory was so strong and important it would always be alive. Joy could be found in memories like that. In giving a new life a name that was so special.

She could have been a part of it.

She wanted to be—with all her heart.

But there was nothing she could do about it.

Jet was probably back in a war zone by now, doing hero stuff and saving lives. And, if she was going to survive, she needed to hang on to what she had and just keep going.

Becca pushed that wayward lock of hair that was almost a curl back from her temple again. She *really* needed a haircut.

The sleek black machine, with the figure hunched down to cut wind resistance, ate up mile after mile of the highway.

Jet bypassed the large metropolitan area of Christchurch, stopped briefly to refuel with the impressive backdrop of the Southern Alps on one side and the sea on the other in Kaikoura, and then kept going until he reached Picton and wheeled the bike into place on the lower deck of the inter-island ferry.

It was late afternoon on what had been a gloriously sunny day. The scenery, as they moved through the Marlborough Sounds, was stunning. Countless green islands in deep blue water so calm and glassy, the only disruption coming from a school of playful dolphins that was racing the ferry on its journey.

A journey that felt far too slow. Jet couldn't sit still. He didn't like someone else being in control of how fast he was moving. He didn't like being on a ship again because it reminded him way too clearly of being with Becca. Seeing her standing against the rail at the stern of the navy ship.

He stalked the decks, scowling harder at the cries of ecstasy from tourists who had spotted the dolphins. The cold beer he had purchased from the bar inside wasn't relaxing him nearly as much as he'd anticipated. Maybe it was the sight of so many damned islands out there and the reminder of Tokolamu and…inevitably, of course… of Becca.

Why couldn't he shut her out of his mind?

God knew, he was trying hard enough.

He'd been angry enough to be glad to leave her behind on that ship. The way she'd reacted to hearing Mattie's name. If he'd needed any proof that she was never going to put the past behind her and forgive him for his part in it, that had been it.

He'd told the others about it last night, when he'd gone to visit Max and Ellie. Rick had even been persuaded to leave Sarah and Josh at the hospital for a couple of hours and go with him, but if Jet had been hoping for an evening anything like the 'bad boys' would have had in the past, he'd been disappointed.

Disturbed, in fact. Almost as disturbed as he'd been when he'd first seen Rick again.

'There's no way I'm going to get used to that,' he'd decreed. 'I can't believe you went and shaved off all your hair.'

Rick had just grinned. 'Hair grows,' he'd said. 'It's no big deal.'

Ellie had shaken her head vigorously. 'It's a *huge* deal.'

Jet's nod had been approving. At least someone agreed with him. But Ellie's eyes were suspiciously moist and her smile was one of utter admiration.

'He did it because of Josh,' she told Jet. 'His hair's all gone from the chemo and he felt like a freak and so Rick shaved his off to make him feel better. He even offered to shave Harry.'

'Who the hell is Harry?'

Turned out Harry was the disreputable-looking dog currently living with Max and Ellie but due to move in with Sarah and Rick and Josh in the near future. When Rick had sold the warehouse and found a more suitable family home, that was.

Jet drained his bottle of lager and debated going back into the crowded bar to queue for another one. He changed his mind when he saw that the ship was nearly at the entrance to the sounds. There were whitecaps on the open sea ahead. Maybe Cook Strait was going to live up to its rough reputation and provide a bit of excitement. A stiff breeze and a decent swell would send most of the tourists inside and Jet could enjoy the distraction of a decent bit of sailing in peace.

He needed…*something* that might make him feel less at odds with his own life. Nothing was the same all right. His whole world was in chaos.

The only home base he had was going to be up for sale in the near future because Rick was moving on with his life and the perfect bachelor pad was no longer suitable. Jet could buy the warehouse himself, of course. It wasn't as if *he* was going to need a family-type home.

But if he did that, there would be no good reason not to end up committing to a full-time job in the ED in Dunedin.

He'd be trapped.

His mates had partners now.

He'd be alone.

They hadn't even understood what it had been like having to see Becca again.

'She's a helicopter pilot?' Max had said. 'Wow. Matt would be proud of her.'

She wasn't just a skilled pilot. She was tough and courageous and feisty. Good grief….he was proud of her himself.

'She still blames us, you know. *Me*, anyway.'

'Nah…' Rick had shaken his bald head in disagreement. 'I don't believe that. She knows we did everything we could. Did you tell her how much we still miss him? That we go on our anniversary ride every year to honour his memory?'

'I told her that there was a baby named after him and she hit the roof. Said none of us had the right to have done that.'

The silence had been uncomfortable. Ellie had cuddled her baby and Jet had intercepted the look she'd exchanged with Max. They weren't about to let Becca's opinion undermine something so special to them. No one and nothing could diminish the bond they had.

The love in that glance had been the last straw.

The glue of absolute loyalty to the exclusion of anyone else that had held the 'bad boys' together as a unit for so many years had come unstuck. Rick had been unable to resist the pull back to the bone-marrow unit in the hospital, where Sarah and Josh were, a short time later, and it was then that Jet knew that he and Sarah would be sharing a similar kind of look.

He couldn't shake the chill of feeling excluded. A tug back to a time when he'd been an outsider. When he'd first arrived at Greystones Grammar school. An angry teenage boy who'd had nothing he could count on in his life. To those days before the 'bad boys' had come into existence.

It was then he knew he had to get out of Dunedin. To leave with the breaking of a new day and see if enough speed and distance might let him ride out the turbulence he had unexpectedly plunged into.

The heavy swell in the strait was great. Jet decided to leave his next beer until he got to his hotel in Wellington. It could be more than one, then. Maybe enough to let him get to sleep and not have his dreams filled with the taste and touch of a small, feisty helicopter pilot.

Finally. A job.

Becca was out the door and onto the helipad almost by the time her pager had finished buzzing. She was halfway through her pre-flight checks by the time her paramedic crew came running to climb on board.

She hadn't even waited to get all the details of the mission. 'Where are we going?'

'Coromandel peninsula.' Tom, the senior medic, was in the passenger seat beside her. 'A lookout on a hill near Cathedral Cove.'

'Cool. One of my favourite places in the world.' Becca programmed the GPS with a few, deft movements.

Her glance sideways was brief. It was a good thing that Tom was wearing the bright, red flight suit of the rescue service. If he'd been sitting there dressed in black from head to toe, it might have been a lot harder to focus.

'What are we going to?'

'Status-one patient. Under CPR.' Ben, the second crew member, was in the back, buckling himself into the seat. 'Sudden collapse. Thirty-nine-year-old woman.'

'Good grief!' Becca had the rotors turning now, picking up speed nicely. She reached to flick a switch on the communication panel. 'Flight zero three three, bound for the east coast of the Coromandel peninsula. Request clearance for take-off.'

The control tower responded immediately. 'Zero three three, you have clearance. Vector two.'

'Roger.' Becca lifted the chopper and used the designated air corridor to clear airport space. This wasn't going to be a long job but it was a beautiful day for flying and they were, hopefully, off to save the life of a person who was far too young to be having a cardiac arrest.

That she would get to test this new machine over her favourite country was a bonus. She loved the forests and beaches of this peninsula and the jagged mountain range often provided a bit of fun with weather and wind conditions.

Things were looking up. This was exactly what she needed to be doing instead of sitting around thinking far too much about things she couldn't do anything to change.

'I like it,' she announced, with a grin, a minute or two later.

'What? Being back at work?'

'That, too, but I was talking about this baby. He handles like a dream.'

'*She,*' Tom corrected, rolling his eyes. 'There are some rules that can't be broken, Bec.'

'Just as well you've never played Snakes and Ladders with me,' Becca muttered.

'What?'

'Nothing.'

'And just while we're on the subject of rules, Ben and I have made a new one.'

'And that is?'

'No uncontrolled landings while we're on board. Particularly when seawater might be involved. We don't want to get wet, OK?'

'No worries, mate. Been there, done that. Once was enough.'

More than enough. Not that Becca was about to admit it to anyone but her heart had skipped a beat or two on take-off that couldn't be attributed to the excitement or satisfaction of finally being given an urgent job to do.

Yes. There was a new thread of tension to be found in her career now. An awareness of just what it was like when things went terribly wrong.

It wasn't a bad thing. It might make her a much better pilot because she would be a little more cautious and make sure she was keeping everybody safe. She would certainly think at least twice before she ignored instructions from her boss or anyone else who might have a better handle on the level of danger she was in.

That crash might never have happened in the first place if she hadn't had Jet beside her. Encouraging her to court danger because he was on exactly the same wavelength as she was. Becca sucked in a breath as she remembered those dark eyes gleaming with approval at her decision to flout authority and keep going.

They were way too alike. Bad for each other.

So, along with her new caution, it wasn't a bad thing that they were so apart now.

So why did it feel so...*wrong*?

Becca swallowed hard. Dipped her head as she turned to find distraction. 'Look at that...'

They were over the craggy landscape of the Coromandel Ranges already. The radio message that came through was an update for the paramedics.

'Ambulance on scene. Patient in asystole. CPR has now been in progress for sixty-five minutes and may be about to be terminated. There's a doctor on scene, as well.'

'Roger that.' Tom's tone was terse. Sixty-five minutes of CPR was unsurvivable. Especially if a doctor was present. Anything that could have been done in the way of drug therapy and defibrillation and intubation would have already been attempted. Was the mission about to be called off?

There was a slight hesitation on the other end of the transmission, as though the comms officer wasn't sure the next information would be welcome.

'The doctor is the husband of the patient.'

'Roger that,' Tom repeated.

Becca saw the glance he exchanged with Ben. There was no reason for them to continue when there was nothing they would be able to do. But there was a doctor there. A husband of a young woman who wasn't going to make it. If nothing else, their presence would be a courtesy for someone in the same profession.

'What's your ETA?'

'Less than five minutes.'

That clinched it. They were not ordered to return to base.

The location appeared deserted as they hovered over it a few minutes later. They could see the ambulance but its back doors were closed and there were no people to be seen. There wasn't even another vehicle in this small car park that was positioned to enjoy one of the most spectacular views you would find anywhere on earth.

There was just enough room to bring the helicopter down beside the ambulance. Becca landed, pointing forward, aware of how little space there was between the machine and a fence that kept people from going too close to the sheer cliff in front of them. Far below was the extraordinary blue of the sea and the irregular, green lumps of many islands. Turning her head to the side, she got a glimpse of the beach that was only accessible by boat or a long trek. Cathedral Cove was really two beaches, joined by rock that had an amazing, arched hole that allowed access to the second beach.

No. Actually, that wasn't all she could see.

Beyond the fence, crouched right on the edge of the cliff, was the figure of a man.

Becca turned to alert Tom but he and Ben were already clear of the chopper, stooping as they ran, carrying gear towards the ambulance.

Who was he? And what on earth was he doing?

Becca had been planning to let the chopper idle, ready for a quick getaway because there was nothing her crew would be able to do other than confirm death and offer sympathy, but she couldn't just sit here and potentially watch someone jump off a cliff. She shut the engines down and unbuckled her seat belt.

Less than a minute later she was climbing—cautiously—over the fence. She stopped a few metres away from the hunched figure. Frozen to the spot, she realised that she'd probably done the wrong thing here. She should have gone to get Tom and Ben. Or radioed HQ and got advice from Richard. There were bound to be protocols for dealing with this kind of situation but they hadn't been covered in her pilot's training.

She was doing exactly what she thought she was over doing. Breaking rules. Doing what *she* wanted to do without stopping to think about how it might affect

other people. What if this guy looked up and saw her
and that was the final straw and he hurled himself over
that cliff?

He *did* look up.

Becca had never seen such desolation on anyone's
face.

No, that wasn't true. She *had* seen just such a look
once. In the mirror.

'I know,' she heard herself say softly. Her eyes filled
with tears. 'I know how you feel.'

The man stared back at her. A puzzled line creased
between his eyes. 'How?'

'I've been there.'

'You haven't. No one has.'

Behind her, Becca was aware that the ambulance
doors were open. That there was someone lying on a
stretcher in there but nothing more was being done for
the patient. The ambulance officers, along with Ben and
Tom, were all standing, staring in horror. At her.

It wasn't hard to put two and two together. Any further attempt to resuscitate the female patient wasn't a
goer. The man close to her had to be the doctor. Her
husband. The attempt at resuscitation had been stopped,
probably only moments before their arrival. Why?

The man seemed to follow her thoughts as she looked
over her shoulder and back again.

'There was no point in really starting,' he said bro-
kenly. 'I knew that. But I had to try, didn't I?'

'Of course you did.' Becca sank down to a crouch.
Somehow, she knew it wouldn't be a good idea to try
and get too close. Because she knew how tender that
space was? How unbearable the intrusion of a stranger
might be?

'I lost someone once,' she told him. She had to sniff hard and swipe at the moisture on her face. She didn't need to tell him that she'd thought her world had ended. He would know.

'It wasn't your fault, though, was it?'

Becca's breath caught and she held it. Carefully. As though breathing out would do something terrible.

'She told me that she had a headache. I could have done something. I'm a *doctor*, for God's sake…'

No-o-o. Becca couldn't let her breath go. Couldn't take another one.

'She wanted to come for a walk at lunch time. Thought it might get rid of her headache. We got here and she said it was worse…she gave this awful cry and then collapsed in my arms…'

He was crying now. Racking, painful sobs.

'I didn't even have my damn phone. I knew she was dead but I had to start CPR… Had to keep going until a car stopped and I could send them to call an ambulance… Had to wait until someone else could tell me…'

'It had to have been a subarachnoid haemorrhage.' The doctor was talking so quietly he seemed to be talking to himself. 'If I'd known, I could have taken her to Auckland. Got a CT scan or an MRI. They could have operated…' His cry was heart-wrenching. 'I let her take aspirin…'

Which would have made the bleeding worse but it was highly unlikely it would have made the difference between survival and death. His poor wife would have had an aneurysm. A defect in a major blood vessel in her brain. It had begun to get worse for some reason and then it had burst.

Just like Matt's had.

Jet and the others had known he'd had a headache. They'd been doctors, too. Matt hadn't wanted to go for a walk, though, had he? He'd wanted to sleep it off.

Had Jet ever felt this bad? So destroyed that ending his life might have been an option?

'It wasn't your fault,' Becca said fiercely. 'Don't ever think that.'

'How can I not?' The man shook his head. 'It's what everyone else will think. What am I going to tell the children?'

Becca's jaw dropped. There were children involved?

The doctor saw her face. As impossible as it seemed, his face grew even paler.

'Oh, my God…the kids…' He edged himself back from the cliff face. 'I have to get to the school…'

'Of course you do.' It was Tom talking, from close behind Becca. He stepped past her to offer a hand to the man and help him back over the fence. He glanced at Becca and she saw approval in his face, as though he thought she'd done something to help avoid further tragedy here.

But she hadn't done anything.

Except to relive a particular part of her life. From someone else's point of view.

To see just how much damage she had really done.

And she'd done it to the one person she truly loved.

It was unbearable.

CHAPTER TEN

THE plan had turned to custard.

He was supposed to have stopped in Auckland for the night. There were colleagues from his early days at Auckland General who would have been glad enough to see him. An impromptu barbecue might well have been organised by one of them and a reunion party would have gained momentum.

And maybe that was why Jet hadn't stopped to find a motel and make some calls, even though he'd already been on the road for too many hours today and was bone weary.

He would have been welcomed, he knew that. He was a minor celebrity amongst the dozens of people from med school and the wide variety of departments he'd cycled through as a junior doctor.

His identity had never been unique, though, had it? He was known as one of the 'bad boys' and it was the group as a whole that people had been drawn to. Even if he'd been the star attraction at a party, everyone would have been remembering the 'bad boy' who wasn't there any more and probably carefully avoiding the subject. They would enquire about Max and Rick instead, eager to know what they were up to these days.

Had he ever had a real identity that was all his own? His early childhood was a fuzzy blur of memories he'd rather not explore. 'Jet' Munroe had been born, in a way, when he'd arrived at Greystones Grammar and found that connection with Matt that had led to the others. They were the ones that had come up with the nickname and James Munroe had ceased to exist in any meaningful way.

There was only one person who might really see him as an individual. Might even understand and accept him, warts and all.

Becca.

Jet slowed his bike as he reached unsealed roads and gravel spat in warning when he slewed sideways. He was in a semi-rural area well north of Auckland city. The rich farmland had been sliced into small 'lifestyle' blocks and their proximity to New Zealand's largest city made them some of the priciest real estate in the country.

The old Harding estate wasn't far from here. The place that had given the underprivileged James Munroe a taste of what it was like to have extreme wealth.

That wasn't what had subconsciously drawn him back, though. It was the taste of family he'd also been given.

That bond with Matt.

And Becca.

Not that he had any intention of going near the property. He didn't want to see the outdoor pool complex and remember the time he'd noticed that Becca was becoming such a beautiful young woman.

He didn't want to scan the hills because he knew he'd be trying to spot the gully they'd camped out in that night. When Becca had danced around the flames of that bonfire, yearning for the kind of adventures she'd thought only boys were entitled to.

Yes. She would understand him all right.

The memories would be waiting for him even if the property was no longer owned by the Harding family. Or was it? Jet knew that Becca's parents had died a few years ago. It had hit the news when they'd been amongst the unfortunate tourists that had been killed by that tsunami in Thailand.

Had Becca kept her inheritance? Funny that he'd never thought to ask, or even offer sympathy for the loss of her remaining family. The loss they'd really needed to talk about had taken precedence and even that had been engulfed by the tension of their situation and the form of release they'd indulged in.

He had to stop. He needed a break or he'd be putting himself, and possibly others on the road, in danger. Not just from his physical weariness but from the sabotage of thinking processes that any thoughts of Becca were capable of. Especially any that involved what had happened between them physically.

The old stone church up ahead on this road was an entirely logical place to pull over. Totally deserted on a weekday and heavily somnolent on a late, sunny afternoon. Ancient trees offered enticing shade and the scent of old roses hung heavy on the air. When Jet parked his bike round the back of the church and pulled off his helmet, the only sounds were the buzzing of bees and the clear notes of native bellbirds.

His whole body felt stiff after so many hours hunched over his bike. Hanging his helmet over the handlebars, he set off to walk a little and stretch. It was only when he turned the corner and saw the heavy wooden door set into the stone arch beneath the steeple that he realised exactly where it was he'd chosen to stop.

Custard was far too soft a word for what had happened to his plans. This was more like some kind of implosion. How could he not have recognised this place? OK, it had been ten years since he'd been here and the visit had been brief and awful, but this had to be the only church within a huge radius of the Harding property.

At some level, he'd known, of course. He'd simply ignored it and allowed himself to be drawn in. He must have wanted this.

Why?

A form of protest, maybe? Claiming the right he'd been denied all those years ago?

None of them had been welcome at the funeral as far as Matt's immediate family was concerned and everybody else there had been embarrassed by their exclusion. They all knew that these three young doctors should have been amongst the pallbearers. To be allowed to be with one of their own at the very end. To honour and respect a friend who was as close as any brother could have been.

Neither had they been allowed to be with him when they'd turned off the life support and let Matt die. They'd been out on the road together. Three 'bad boys' exceeding a speed limit on a back road not a million miles from here. They reckoned Matt had been riding pillion with them that day—the exit his spirit would have wanted.

But the funeral? They'd come late and stood in a silent row beside the door, holding their helmets. Jet had been holding two. His own, and Matt's. They'd left before the graveside ceremony. Before Becca could publicly shame them for not having done what they should have done, and saved her brother.

He'd never come back.

There would be a memorial to Matt somewhere in this churchyard and he'd never even seen it.

That was why he was here.

Maybe he'd known all along when he'd taken off on this lonely journey that this was where he'd end up. His life was in chaos. He would pick up the pieces and move on but a whole chapter of it was closing and he had to accept that first. Total closure couldn't happen until he completed what he should have done a long, long time ago.

It wasn't hard to find the headstone in the small country graveyard. A simple memorial that had only the name Matthew Samuel Harding and two dates, the year of his birth and that of his death. Jet didn't have to do any kind of calculation to know the difference was only twenty six.

The last of the day's sun pressed down on him as he stood, staring down at the headstone. It made him far too hot in his leathers but he didn't want to leave just yet.

'I'm here, mate,' he muttered aloud, 'but it's flippin' hot, isn't it? I'm going to go and sit under that tree for a bit.'

The oak tree was well over a hundred years old and the branches so heavy with acorns they drooped almost to ground level. Jet sat down, propping his back against the gnarled trunk. He was here, and it felt right. He would stay and soak in the peace and somehow something would fall into place and he'd be able to move on.

A tension he hadn't realised had been such a huge knot inside him began to ease.

Jet closed his eyes and simply let it happen.

Going home wasn't an option.

No way could Becca be in her apartment by herself the way she was feeling by the end of her shift. The tragedy of the young doctor's wife had been the only topic of conversation as she'd flown her crew back to base.

'Poor guy,' Tom had said, not for the first time. 'He's going to blame himself for the rest of his life.'

'As if there was anything he could have done, anyway. Man, they're scary things, aneurysms. Who's to know we don't have a time bomb like that ticking away in our own heads?'

'Some people survive, don't they?' What was she trying to do? Becca asked herself. Find some kind of exoneration for blaming Jet? A plausible reason to have never totally forgiven him?

'Depends on the size of the bleed,' Tom told her. 'If it's small enough and you're close enough to a first-class neurosurgical unit, you've got a reasonable chance. A big bleed, especially if the brain stem's affected, the best you could hope for is to get someone on life support for long enough to make organs available for donation.'

'She would have had to have been in hospital already for that,' Ben observed. 'Respiratory and cardiac function got knocked out almost immediately, by the sound of it.'

'Poor guy.' It was Becca saying it now. 'I hope he'll be OK.'

She'd told him it wasn't his fault and she'd been a hundred per cent sincere.

She could have been saying it to Jet with just as much sincerity and maybe, in her heart, that was exactly what she *was* doing.

Would she ever be able to tell him that face to face? It wasn't a question of forgiving him at all because there was nothing to forgive.

No. That wasn't true.

There was plenty that needed forgiveness but not from her. She was the one who needed to *be* forgiven.

The misery that had been circling for days was drawing closer and threatening to pull her under but Becca knew just how to deal with that. As soon as she got home, she stripped off her red flight suit and donned a very different set of clothes. An old, soft T-shirt. Tight black leather pants. Heavy boots that were very like her workboots apart from the silver studs that decorated them. A leather jacket with well-padded elbows went on last and she zipped it up and then fastened the studs on the flap that covered the zipper.

She collected her helmet from the table near the door and went out to her garage.

Her latest motorbike was only a couple of months old. She'd waited for its delivery with bated breath since she'd seen the advertisement and knew she had to upgrade.

'Light enough for a woman,' it had read, *'with power made for a man.'*

She'd been riding bikes for years but this was, indeed, something special. The speed and adrenaline rush of a good blast would be even better than the turbulence she'd unsuccessfully wished for on the way back from the Coromandel peninsula that afternoon.

Becca didn't give any particular destination any head room. She simply got out of the city and went for it. Only logical, really, that she found she'd taken a route so embedded in her memory it was automatic. Not that there was any point going near her property. She'd had it land banked and leased out ever since inheriting the acreage. She wasn't sure she ever wanted to set foot on it again.

There was somewhere else out here she hadn't been in a while, though.

The only place she could still feel close to her brother and talk to him without feeling like a complete head case. She sure needed someone to talk to today and Matt would have understood. Sorting her thoughts into words and just imagining what he might have said would help.

It had helped on more than one occasion in the past.

It was the throaty roar of a Ducati engine that woke Jet from a deep slumber in the long grass under the oak tree.

Someone was stealing his bike, dammit!

Leaping to his feet, he raced past the gravestones and around the back of the church. He could just see the sleek lines of his beloved black bike heading out of the churchyard. It took off with a burst of speed that sprayed gravel and raised a cloud of dust.

He skidded to a halt then, utterly confused.

His bike was exactly where he'd left it.

But it had definitely been a similar engine he'd heard and the bike had been black.

Who else would be riding a classy sports bike like that out here? Who would have wanted to come into an isolated place like this on a sleepy afternoon?

The answer came as he recaptured the image of the departing bike. He could only just hear it way up the road now but even from this distance he could detect something about the sound that wasn't quite what he would have expected. Less…grunty. He'd thought it was his bike, but what if it just looked that big because the figure on it was small?

Who else would come here?

He didn't need three guesses. How many women were gutsy enough to be riding a superbike, come to that?

But where the hell was she going now? She'd taken off in the opposite direction from getting back to town.

Kicking his bike into life, Jet took off.

He had no idea where this gravel road was heading. Fortunately it had straight stretches so he could catch frequent glimpses of the dust cloud ahead but it was proving hard to catch up.

Riding this fast on an unsealed road was crazy. Jet could feel his face settle into lines that got progressively grimmer as each minute passed. Not only was the surface of this road unstable, they were getting into hilly country and there were tight bends. He felt his own back wheel slip and he started muttering oaths that matched his expression.

This kind of behaviour was so reckless it was downright stupid. He could use his bike like it was an extension of his own body but he was struggling to stay in control here. He would have slowed down. Turned around and gone home, in fact, if it had been anybody else in the world ahead of him. Instead, his fury mounted and his speed increased.

Until he was right behind her. And still she didn't see him, so intent was she on pushing herself and her bike to the absolute limit. A dramatic spurt of speed on a straight stretch that actually lifted the front wheel of her bike into the air like some trick rider at a bike show. A sideways skid that had him catching his breath in horror but somehow she threw her weight and righted the bike from its dangerous slant. A bend that was so tight he could see her boot making a furrow in the chips of stone. A bend that went on and on.

And right at the end of that bend she lost it. The bike tipped just that fraction farther and then shot sideways with sparks coming from its metal. It seemed to increase speed as it hit the side of the road and became airborne. The rider came off at that point and, as Jet came to a slewing halt on the road, he could see the small, leather-clad body curl itself into a ball as it hit the ground and roll away downhill until it got caught in clumps of dense tussock.

The bike hit an outcrop of rocks much farther down-hill. The petrol tank must have been punctured because there was a flash of flames, an explosion and then a thick cloud of black smoke spiralling into the sky.

The body of the rider was absolutely still.

Jet reached it in about three strides and didn't even feel his boots hitting the ground. He wasn't breathing as he dropped to his knees and rolled the body gently towards him. He had never been this afraid.

Ever.

Becca's eyes were open. Staring at him with disbelief.

'Am I dead?'

'Not for lack of trying.' Jet made no effort to hide his fury. 'You *idiot*. What the hell did you think you were *doing*?'

Where had he come from?

And why was he so angry?

Had she bumped her head with that spill? Nothing hurt. So she'd been going a bit fast, so what? Winning the battle of control over an adversary like an unsealed road was the kind of rush that made life worth living. As if Jet didn't know that as well as she did.

Carefully, Becca sat up. She eased her helmet off and tilted her neck to one side and then the other. Nothing hurt so that was good. She took a deep breath. Her ribs felt OK, too.

Jet was still crouched right beside her. Waiting for an answer.

Glaring at her.

'You know perfectly well what I was doing. You've done it often enough yourself.'

'I do not.'

'How fast were you going on *your* bike, Jet? To catch up with me? I *know* this road—the camber of every twist. I've done it a hundred times.'

'Hey…I wasn't doing it for *fun*.'

'Neither was I, dammit.' Becca glared back at him.

The frown lines on Jet's forehead seemed to move. To become puzzled instead of angry. Some of the tension left his body and he sank lower until he was sitting beside her with the tussock making a surprisingly comfortable cushion. He fiddled with the catch on his helmet to take it off. It was still hot, even though the sun was well into its descent now. They had an hour or two of dusk and then it would start getting dark. It was very, very quiet. Apart from the occasional bird call, there was obviously no one else for miles around.

It was Jet who broke the silence.

'Then...*why*, Becca?'

She couldn't look directly at him. She needed to try and find the words. She also needed to find the courage to utter them.

'*You* know,' she said finally. 'When you cheat death and you're safe again, you can feel alive. Really alive. Like you're making the most of every second and...and you *have* to do that because...'

'Because you don't know how many seconds you might have,' Jet finished for her.

Becca nodded. Whatever rush her ride had given her was wearing off. Things *did* hurt. Her shoulder was aching and there was an odd pain in her chest that made it hard to take a deep breath.

'And it's the same when you challenge yourself at work,' Jet continued. 'The bigger and scarier the challenge the better, because you feel safe when it's over and you feel like you've done something worthwhile.' His voice was so soft it was virtually a whisper. 'Like *you* are worthwhile.'

Becca rolled her shoulder with caution. It still worked. 'Doesn't last, though, does it?' she asked sadly. 'The thrill. That safe feeling.'

'No.' Jet's breath escaped in a weary sigh. 'I guess that's why people like us go hunting for it all over again. Why we keep doing dangerous, *stupid* things.'

'Like crashing helicopters.'

'And bikes.'

They both looked farther downhill at the smouldering remains of her motorbike. Becca shivered.

'I could have killed myself,' she said quietly. 'You're right. I am an idiot.'

Jet put his arm around her. 'Yeah…don't do it again, OK?'

Becca said nothing. She snuggled closer to the warmth of Jet's body, loving the feeling of his arm holding her so securely.

It took her back to those precious minutes of lying in his arms, in his bed, on the ship. Feeling like there was nowhere else in the world she ever wanted to be. Nowhere that could feel that safe.

And, suddenly, she could see the truth and it was so simple.

The rush you got by putting your body in danger and surviving was purely a physical thing. If you were brave enough to put your heart and soul into danger, the rush of surviving would be a safety that would never have to fade. You'd never have to keep hunting because if you found it and looked after it, it would just get stronger and stronger.

But you couldn't do it on your own. For the first time in her adult life Becca had to admit she couldn't rely only on herself. She needed someone else. Jet.

'You know why we keep doing it?' she ventured. 'And why that thrill gets harder to find so you have to keep doing bigger and more dangerous stuff?'

'Because we get good at it.'

'No. It's because we know what we're really scared

of. We're happy to risk our bodies but we're too afraid to risk our hearts.'

The deep rumble of his voice could be felt as easily as heard. 'I'm not afraid.'

The way his arm tightened around her gave Becca a rather different answer, however. One that gave her the courage she really needed.

'I love you, Jet,' she said.

He made another rumbling sound. A kind of growl that was totally incomprehensible but it made Becca's heart skip and then soar as it chased away the last of that fear.

'You love *me*,' she said softly. 'That's why you came after me, wasn't it? Why you're so mad at me.'

'I'm mad because you've ruined a perfectly good bike.'

Becca said nothing. She just smiled.

After a long, long silence Jet bent his head to look down at her. 'Of course I love you,' he growled. 'You're—'

A final flash of fear came. Surely he wasn't going to say she was Matt's little sister?

'You're…*you*.' Jet's voice sounded curiously thick. 'I think I always loved you. But…'

'But you think there's no way we can ever be together.'

The silence was alive now. Tense. Terribly important.

'You think that loving someone and letting them love you is stupid because it's so dangerous. And that if you don't, you can protect yourself from ever getting really hurt.'

His arm tightened even more around her. Enough to

make her shoulder ache harder but there was no way Becca wanted him to loosen that possessive kind of grip. There was an edge of desperation in the hold that squeezed her heart to breaking point and made that odd pain more intense. She didn't have a chest injury. She just had a heart that needed healing.

She slipped her arms around this man she loved so much.

'Have you ever stopped to think how much we miss out on by thinking like that? That *that* is what's really stupid?'

'Maybe…' The admission was cautious. 'Once or twice…recently.'

'What if we got told, right now, that we both only had a day to live? How would you want to spend it?'

'In bed.' She could hear the smile in his voice. 'With you.'

'Mmm.' Becca tilted her face up and found her lips only an inch or two away from Jet's. 'Good answer.'

The kiss was perfect. Soft and slow. So tender it made her melt. It could easily have grown into something much more passionate but Becca pulled back. She needed to finish what she'd started. For both their sakes.

'What if it was a year, Jet?'

'I'd still want to spend it with you.'

Becca gave a soft chuckle. 'In bed?'

'Not *all* the time. We could do something else in the daytimes.'

'Like dodging landmines in Afghanistan?'

'No way. You're not going anywhere near anything that dangerous.'

'Maybe you could be a flying doctor and I could be your pilot.'

'Hmm.' Jet was actually giving this serious thought. 'If we only had a year, wouldn't you want to have a bit more of a challenge? Use your skills to do something a little bit dangerous but really worthwhile?'

'Like what?'

'Oh…join Médicins Sans Frontières, perhaps?'

'Not a bad idea.' Becca thought about it for a nano-second. 'No, it's a great idea. Let's do it.'

'OK.'

'But what then?'

'What do you mean? You said we only had a year to live.'

'What if we don't? It's far more likely that we'll be some of the lucky ones and have thirty or forty or fifty years left.'

She could actually hear Jet swallow. He was holding her with both arms now. As though he never wanted to let her go. As though he couldn't.

'I'd still want to spend them with you. I'd want a house for us to live in and…and kids. A little girl who looked just like you.'

'And a boy?'

She could lose herself in those dark eyes that were fixed on hers. She could read exactly what was going on behind them, too. A little boy might look like her, as well. Like Matt. And she could see something else. Something she'd never, ever seen before.

'You're…crying.'

'Am not. I haven't cried since I was about six years old.'

Becca stroked the moisture away from his cheeks as Jet squeezed his eyes shut.

'What happened to Matt…it wasn't your fault,' she said softly. 'I know that now. Can you ever forgive me?'

Jet cleared his throat. 'Don't need to.'

'Yes, you do.'

'No.' His eyes were open again, locked on hers. 'I forgave you a long time ago, Becca. About the same time I finally forgave myself.' He touched her lips with his. 'I love you. I can't spend another day away from you because…if you're not right, it might be the only chance I get to feel like this.'

Becca caught her lip between her teeth. 'Alive?'

He was watching her mouth but his gaze lifted to catch hers again. '*Really* alive,' he murmured. 'Like I've just been born or something.'

He kissed her again and this time it spiralled into much more than tenderness. Becca found herself pushed into the tussock but it put pressure on her shoulder and she winced. Jet drew back instantly.

'You *have* hurt yourself, haven't you?'

'Just a bruise or two. Nothing a soak in a bath and a good sleep won't fix. Don't suppose you could give me a ride back to town?'

Jet helped her up to her feet. 'Not a problem.' His grin was wicked. 'You don't really think you're going to get a good sleep, though, do you?'

Becca grinned right back. 'Not a problem. I can sleep when I'm dead.' She felt his hand tighten around hers and she squeezed back. 'That's a very long way off,' she assured Jet. 'I know I'm right. We're going to be amongst the lucky ones. We'll have the rest of our lives. For ever.'

'We're already the luckiest people on earth. We've got each other.' He started leading her up the slope towards where his bike was on the road but then he paused and smiled down at her. 'For ever is a nice long time, isn't it?'

Becca nodded happily. She dropped the helmet she was carrying and put both her hands around Jet's neck.

'But don't you go thinking that's a good excuse not to make the most of every second.'

She didn't need to exert any pressure to bring his face down to hers.

'I won't,' he murmured, as his lips covered hers. 'And that's a promise. I love you.'

Becca wanted to say it back but her lips and breath had been captured. She had to say it with her kiss instead.

And that was not a problem.

EPILOGUE

THE three men stood in close proximity.

Tall. Dark. Silent.

Clad in uniform black leather, motorbike helmets dangled from one hand. They each held an icy, uncapped bottle of lager in the other hand.

Moving as one, they raised the bottles and touched them together, the dull clink of glass a sombre note.

Speaking as one, their voices were equally sombre.

'To Matt,' was all they said.

'Yes,' a much softer voice chimed in. 'To Matt.'

The smaller figure making a circle with the three men had to stretch to touch her bottle to the others. She also had a motorbike helmet dangling from her hand and was dressed in black leather from head to toe, albeit with a few more decorative studs.

'Eleven years,' Jet said solemnly.

'And you've always managed to be together to make this tribute ride? Every single year?'

'Every year,' Max nodded.

'It's sacred,' Rick added. 'Always will be.'

'Sure will.' Max was smiling now. 'This marks another anniversary now, too. A really happy one.'

'The day you met Ellie.' Jet nodded. 'And Mattie was born.'

'I wish I'd known,' Becca said wistfully. 'About the rides. I used to go and put flowers on Matt's grave on the anniversary and sit there and talk to him for a while. I'll bet he was laughing at me coz he knew I was missing out on the fun you guys were having.'

'He comes with us,' Max said. 'Rides pillion.'

The others nodded. Jet's glance at Becca was a warning. 'That's all you're going to be doing from now on,' he said quietly enough not to be overheard. 'If that.'

Becca looked mutinous but Jet's smile had a smug edge to it.

'Let's join the girls,' Max suggested. 'The *other* girls,' he amended hastily as he caught Becca's glare.

Sarah and Ellie were in the kitchen as the small group came inside Max's house from where they'd been out on the terrace. They both exchanged glances with their husbands, understanding their absence but welcoming them back from a space they hadn't wanted to intrude on.

The 'bad boy' space.

Only now it was the 'bad boy and girl' space.

One girl, anyway. *His* girl. He could feel his chest having to expand to accommodate that warm, buzzy sensation. Pride? No. It was more than that. Way more.

Jet draped his arm across Becca's shoulders, loving the way her hair had grown long enough to tickle his hand. Loving even more the way she pressed in closer. As if it was exactly where she wanted to be—as close as possible to him.

'How was the ride?' Sarah asked.

'Awesome.'

A small boy with soft black curls was at the far end of the country-style kitchen. He was bent over, his hands firmly grasped by a baby, who was trying very hard to walk but had no balance. A large, shaggy dog was plodding beside them, watching the progress intently. The boy's face was tilted up, however, his gaze fixed on Rick.

'I'll be able to go along with you one day, won't I, Dad?'

'Sure.'

'Over my dead body,' Sarah said mildly.

Rick grinned and winked at Josh. 'I'm working on it,' he told the boy. 'We've still got plenty of time to convince your mum.'

Josh sighed theatrically. 'Becca got to go this time,' he grumbled.

'Of course she did. Matt was her big brother.' Max dropped to his haunches and held his arms out. With a squeal of glee, the baby let go of Josh's hands and hurled herself forward in a tottering run that could only end in collapse. Fortunately, Max had judged the distance perfectly and he swept the tiny girl into his arms and stood up.

'Did Mummy see that, do you think, Mattie?'

'She did,' Ellie smiled. She planted a kiss on the back of her daughter's head. 'Clever girl.'

'I'll have one of those,' Max said. 'I'm clever, too.'

Rick snorted. 'Who told you that?'

'Hey… I got us all together for the anniversary, didn't I? You said I'd never persuade Jet and Becca to come back from the wilds of South America.'

'Actually,' Jet said apologetically, 'we had to come back anyway.'

'Oh?'

They had everyone's attention all of a sudden.

'But didn't you plan on spending a full year with MSF?'

'They have rules, apparently.'

'About what?'

'About where you're allowed to be if you're pregnant.'

The silence was absolute for all of two heartbeats and then it erupted into cries of congratulations and everybody trying to be heard at once. Harry, the dog, let out a volley of excited barking and baby Mattie clapped her hands and shrieked joyfully. Rick and Max thumped Jet on the back and then hugged Becca a lot more gently.

Sarah and Ellie were both smiling through happy tears.

'How far along are you?'

'Twelve weeks.'

Sarah and Rick looked at each other and they both laughed.

'What's so funny?' Jet demanded.

'Well, we were kind of waiting for the right moment to tell you lot but—'

'I'm twelve weeks along, too,' Sarah told Becca.

'They'll be like twins,' Ellie said happily. 'Except... where are you going to live?'

'Haven't thought that far yet,' Jet said. 'We might hang around for a bit, though. We thought maybe it's about time we got, you know...'

'*Married?*' The squeal from Ellie could easily rival one of Mattie's.

'Your garden's had a bit of practice as a venue,' Becca said to Max. 'We were wondering if—'

'Yes,' Max interrupted, grinning from ear to ear. 'Of course. When?'

'Soon.' Jet and Becca spoke at the same time.

'It'll be the third wedding here,' Ellie observed. 'You guys are extra lucky, did you know that?'

Jet looked down at the woman he loved with all his heart and soul. She was looking right back at him and it was exactly the same look of love that was making her eyes glow like stars.

'Yeah…' His smile got caught. On that lump in his throat, maybe. 'I knew that.'

'I think we all are.' Max had one arm around Ellie now, with Mattie still tucked under the other arm. Rick was moving towards Sarah.

Josh eyed all the adults in the room. 'You're all going to do gross stuff like kissing, aren't you?' He sighed, even more heavily than he had last time. 'Come on, Harry. We're outta here.'

* * * * *